Acknowledgments

As always, thanks has to go to the unparalleled group of people behind the scenes who help make my books the best they can be. Thanks to Keren Reed, for your invaluable insight. To Hope and Jess at Flat Earth, I love how much you love these guys and how you give your everything to get it right. To Dianne at Lyrical Lines, thank you for your eagle eyes, especially catching that one horrible mistake that proves everyone, even a native New Yorker, can really mess up.

A special thank you to my cover artist and dear friend, Reese Dante who knows my vision for my characters better than I do and always gives me a cover that is head and shoulders above what I could have imagined.

And always to the readers, I couldn't do what I loved if you didn't give me all the encouragement. Thank you for making the dream possible.

The
GHOST
and
Charlie
MUIR

Felice Stevens

The Ghost and Charlie Muir
August 2020
Copyright (c) 2020 by Felice Stevens

Cover Art by Reese Dante
Edited by Keren Reed
Copyediting and Proofreading services by: Flat Earth Editing
Additional Proofreading by Lyrical Lines

Dedication

To those who have waited for their happily ever after, sometimes it's written in the stars or waiting at the end of the rainbow.

Chapter One

It all started with a letter he'd almost thrown away.

"We represent the estate of Miss Lucy Muir, and it has come to our attention that you may be one of her heirs. Please contact our office so that we may discuss this matter further."

Several confusing as hell legal meetings and one DNA test later, Charlie Muir sat in the Court Street law offices of Norse, Bynes, and Trumble, facing a man he didn't know, who'd changed his life with a simple sentence.

"Repeat that to me again, please?"

The lawyer, Roger Norse, a thin, gray-haired older man, peered over his reading glasses. His kindly smile set Charlie's heart beating faster. "You heard me right,

Mr. Muir. The DNA test was a match. You're the only surviving relative of Lucy Muir. She is your great-great-aunt, and the house on Willow Place is yours."

The top hat Charlie had worn for the formal occasion sat heavily on his head, and he removed it to wipe at the sweat that had gathered. For the occasion, he'd dressed formally, in an Edwardian frock coat, ruffled shirt and slim-fitting jeans tucked into high-polished boots, all perks of working in a vintage clothing store. His fifty percent discount was the best. That and having first crack at trying on all the clothes when they came in.

It was only early May, but, of course, the weather hadn't cooperated, and New York City was experiencing one of those freakishly hot days where the temperature hit over eighty degrees and humidity nearly suffocated him on his walk home from work. Charlie couldn't wait to get out of his clothes.

"How can that be? I didn't even know I had a great-great-aunt." *Or a mother, for that matter*, he thought to himself. He could've used one, instead of being shuffled back and forth from foster home to foster home while growing up.

"Our client, Miss Muir, was, to put it bluntly, very rich. She earmarked money in her estate for us to hire a private investigator. We've been searching for over two years, hoping to discover any living relatives. She was very clear in her instructions that we were to look for her brother's granddaughter—your mother—and if she could not be found, then we were to continue searching for the next in line, and the house was to be theirs. Not only that, but a trust is established to pay the taxes and expenses, so you don't have to worry about anything. We chased down a lot of leads, but all roads led to you, Mr. Muir. The DNA doesn't lie. You were the only match we found."

"Me." Having zero grasp of the legal system, except for ways to keep his nose clean, Charlie still found it difficult to believe that he, a twenty-seven-year-old guy working in a vintage clothing store during the day, while halfheartedly attempting to write the great American novel at night, was now the owner of a house. Half the time, he was lucky if he remembered where he put the keys to his roach-infested apartment. How was he going to take care of a house?

"Do you know what happened to my mother? I was put in foster care when I was young, and I only have a vague recollection." Perhaps it was his stubborn pride, but Charlie had never once tried to look for his mother. If she didn't want him, and would have rather had him be raised by strangers, he had no use for her.

But late at night sometimes, he'd swear he could smell the scent of a familiar perfume, or recall a husky laugh and the glow of a cigarette in the dark.

"She died in 2001. A car accident. I'm sorry." Norse made sympathetic noises and shuffled the papers in his hand.

Was his detachment at that news odd? His mother was nothing more than a stranger, so Charlie could feel sympathy for the loss of a human life but not much else. "Do you have any information on my father? I have a copy of my birth certificate, and it only has my mother's name. There's no entry for the father's."

"No, I'm sorry. We didn't seek to find him, as that wasn't what we were hired to do."

"I see." Not really, but Charlie didn't know what else to say. He truly was a nobody.

"There are some papers for you to sign, and then I'll register the deed for you tomorrow. All formalities, I can assure you. There's only one thing."

There it was. The catch. "What is it? What do I have to do?" Hopefully it wasn't to get married and have a kid.

"One stipulation. Miss Muir stated that her heir must agree to live in the house for a period of one year. If at any time you abandon the premises or put it up for sale, the ownership will be revoked, and the house sold by auction to the highest bidder."

This whole day was getting odder and odder. Charlie should've known something bizarre was about to happen when a black crow followed him from his apartment off Third Avenue to the store in Prospect Heights where he worked.

"Why would I do that? I don't know the condition of the house, but I intend to clean it up and live there. I'd have to be crazy not to."

"Wonderful," Norse exclaimed with a smile, obviously happy not to have to argue with him. "Here are the keys. Congratulations, Charlie." Norse extended his hand, two keys on a plain black metal key chain sitting in his palm.

"Thanks," Charlie said, reaching out, but before he could touch them, the keys turned a bright, glowing green. He snatched his hand away. "What the hell?"

Mr. Norse stared at him curiously. "What's wrong?"

"Didn't you see that?"

"See what?" Brows arched, Norse pursed his lips as he peered at Charlie. "Is everything all right?"

"Th-they glowed. Green."

"What did? The keys? Green?"

Charlie nodded, aware he sounded ridiculous.

Norse's expression remained impassive. "Maybe it was a trick of the light? I can assure you, I've had them in my possession for over two years, and I've never seen them glow any color."

Could it be possible? Unsure, Charlie chewed his lip. The sun was setting, so it might be a weird light-to-metal thing. What did he know? Whatever it might've been, at that moment, the non-glowing keys sat in the palm of Norse's hand, ready for him to take possession. He reached out again, picked them up, and heard them jingle. All perfectly normal.

"I hope you'll be very happy there, Charlie."

Charlie gave the lawyer an absent smile. "I'm sure I will."

* * *

Three days later, after work, Charlie and his friend Bryan Jaworski stood on the sidewalk in front of his house on Willow Place. His house. Beams of sunlight slanted on the brownstone, and Charlie spied rosebushes planted along the side, their plush blooms nodding in the spring breeze. A high, thick hedge ran between his home and the one next door, leading to the backyard.

A home with a yard. God, that sounded so weird to say or think, considering he'd never had either.

Like many others on the block, the town house stood tall but narrow, close to eighteen feet in width and three stories high. A large bay window faced the street, and wide curved steps led up to the front door, which was painted a glossy green with white trim. A brass knocker shaped like a pineapple gleamed in the sunlight.

"You're shitting me." Bryan flicked his lip ring, an annoying habit to Charlie, except when they were kissing. Then he kind of liked the little hard loop pressing into his mouth. He and Bryan had been friends with benefits for a few years. A bit silly but always agreeable, Bryan was someone Charlie could rely on to come over and hold him when the loneliness of living by himself in the city got to be too much.

"Nah, man. It's all mine. Some old relative died, and I'm her only next of kin. I got the papers and the key to prove it."

"Cool. The place must be worth a fortune. You could sell it and be set for life. Buy a place wherever you want."

True, but the moment he'd turned the corner to this hidden street, Charlie had felt a pull to this house. Which, of course, was silly because he'd never heard of Willow Place and had definitely never been on the one-block area, and yet it somehow seemed familiar. As if he were coming home.

Excitement built inside him as he mounted the steps, Bryan on his heels. Charlie turned the key in the lock, and the door swung open to an entrance close to eight feet wide. A staircase rose before him on the left, and all the rooms lay to his right, with a long hallway bisecting the home. He'd expected...well, he had no idea what to expect, frankly, but a quick peek revealed a fully furnished home, complete with pictures on the walls.

"Dude, this is the shit."

Bryan truly had a way with words.

"Yeah. It's pretty incredible." Charlie's gaze traveled up and down the walls, and as he walked, he touched them, still disbelieving this was all his. All so strange and yet so familiar. "I had no idea it was furnished. The lawyer didn't say anything about it. I thought it was an empty house." He'd planned on bringing a pillow and a blanket and sleeping on the floor. It was the first time he had someplace to call his own.

They wandered into a room with a fireplace and the kind of furniture Charlie remembered one of his foster mothers kept covered in plastic and beat his butt if she caught him sitting on it. Quickly pushing that ugly memory to the far corners of his mind, he walked across the room to the rear of the house. A large, wavy-glass window overlooking a backyard let in the sunlight, still bright in the spring evening. It spilled warm and golden over the polished wood of a dining table.

His table.

Charlie smoothed his hand over the shining surface, thinking back to when he was young and wished he could have Thanksgiving and Christmas dinners at a table like this. There would be plenty of food and heaps of desserts and laughter. A family to love and love him.

Blinking away his daydream, Charlie peered out the window to the surprisingly large garden. The kitchen door opened to a concrete deck with room for a grill and a lounge chair or two. Charlie counted five steps to a grassy area with wildly growing, colorful, flowering bushes. The lawn was overgrown but green and lush.

"Dude, you even got a dishwasher and everything."

Bryan had found the kitchen and was poking around in the cabinets. Charlie joined him in the center of the room and surveyed the stainless-steel appliances and white countertops. Pale-wood cabinets lined the wall, and above the deep sink, a window overlooked the yard. He opened a few cabinets, expecting them to be empty, but plain white plates and bowls sat stacked, and glassware and platters were set beside them. The vibe here felt almost as if he were expected.

"I feel like I'm in an episode of *House Hunters*, but I already own the place."

"And you didn't have to pay nothing for it either."

Bryan grinned at him. "That's the best part. Let's go upstairs and check out the rest of the place. Lookit." He pointed to a stairway tucked against the wall, which Charlie hadn't noticed. "You can sneak down in the middle of the night for a snack."

Charlie mounted the steps. "Who am I sneaking away from? I'll be here by myself."

They reached the top of the stairs, and Bryan put his hands on Charlie's waist. "I'm happy to stay with you." He kissed Charlie's neck. "You know, in case you get scared."

A floorboard creaked, and Charlie stiffened. "Did you hear that?"

Bryan, whose hands had moved from Charlie's hips to cup his crotch, mumbled, "No. Didn't hear nothing. Where's the bedroom?" He popped the button on Charlie's jeans and unzipped the fly.

Pleasure soaked through Charlie, and forgetting the noise, he stiffened under Bryan's probing fingers. "I don't know. Remember? I've never been here." He pointed to the door closest to them. "Try this door."

Bryan gave him one last squeeze before stepping away. He reached the door in two steps and put his hand on the knob. "*Ow*, shit. That's hot." The skin of his palm blazed an angry red, as if burned.

"What happened?" Charlie grabbed Bryan's wrist. "You got burned? How?"

"I don't know. I touched the doorknob, and it was like putting my hand over an open flame." He shook it and blew across the skin.

"That makes no sense." With trepidation, Charlie reached out a finger to the doorknob, prepared to jerk it away from the searing heat, but it was cool to the touch. "It's not hot."

"What the fuck?" Bryan continued to puff air across his palm.

"Maybe the sun was shining on it a long time and it got really hot? I have no idea." With a firm grip, Charlie turned the knob and opened the door, revealing a nice-sized room with a king-sized bed, matching nightstands with lamps flanking each side, and a dresser with a large, ornate gilt mirror hanging over it. A fancy chandelier hung over the bed, and the windows had curtains hanging from them. Charlie felt like he was living in one of those old movies he loved to watch.

"It doesn't hurt too bad. Not anymore." Bryan moved close to him, and Charlie looped his arms around his neck.

"No? So you don't want me to kiss it and make it better?" His lips met Bryan's, and they kissed while Bryan walked Charlie backward to the bed. He fell onto it, and Bryan remained standing, blue eyes already heavy-lidded and hazy.

"I got something else you can kiss." He cupped his crotch, and Charlie could see the outline of Bryan's full cock. His ass clenched. Bryan was big, the biggest he'd ever had, and there was nothing, Charlie had discovered when he'd started having sex regularly, that he liked more than getting plowed by a big fat one. Bryan might be kind of dopey, and they might not have much to talk about, but Charlie didn't care. Sometimes sex was enough.

"Hurry," he said, pulling Bryan's zipper down to release the rigid thrust of his erection.

"You like it? Wanna take me in your mouth?"

Breathing heavily and totally turned-on, Charlie licked his lips. "Yeah." He yanked Bryan's jeans to his knees and cupped his crotch.

Ready to go to town, Charlie startled as a crash

sounded behind him. "What the hell?"

Bryan howled. "Let go of me. You're pulling my dick off."

But Charlie didn't answer; he couldn't catch his breath. The mirror hanging over the dresser had fallen off its hook, but that wasn't what had him so freaked out. In the glass he saw the reflection of a lady in old-fashioned clothes—turn of the last century, he observed. She gazed at him with a disapproving face, mouthed the word *no*, then disappeared.

The lights from the nightstand lamps flickered on and off, and the shades tilted to crazy angles. The chandelier hanging above them began to sway, its crystals tinkling.

Bryan's face paled. "What the fuck is going on here?"

Charlie jumped up, his heart pounding. "I-I don't know. Maybe there's an earthquake, or something's going on with the electrical wiring."

The sheer curtains billowed out, but the windows in the room were firmly shut. Charlie could see the tall oak tree outside, its leaves and branches perfectly still. Goose bumps popped up on his arms, and hairs rose on the back of his neck.

Something weird was going on.

"It's fucking Brooklyn, not LA. We don't get earthquakes. Dude, I'm getting outta here. I'm getting a creepy vibe." With his hands on his now-soft dick, Bryan stuffed himself into his briefs and pulled up his jeans. "Are you coming?"

Before Charlie had a chance to answer, Bryan cried out, "*Oww, oww, shit.* Something's squeezing my balls. Help. *Oww.* Fuck." He danced on his toes, his face screwed up in agony. "*Owww*, Charlie, help *meeee…*"

Dumbfounded, Charlie watched as Bryan, hopping on

his feet, was manhandled out of the room by some invisible force. He teetered at the top of the stairs, his eyes huge.

"Help me, it's ripping my dick off. *Owww.*" Face red, he pawed at his crotch and stumbled down the stairs.

Charlie heard the front door slam and ran into the bedroom to catch a glimpse of Bryan out the window, racing across the street, legs pumping as fast as he could.

The house settled, and Charlie sat on the bed. The lamplights were now off, the tilted shades returned to their original, upright state. The previously swinging chandelier remained unmoving. Maybe he was hallucinating? But then he saw the fallen mirror lying on the dresser.

It's old. Maybe the hanging wire broke.

But when he went to check, the wire still stretched from end to end, and the hook remained bolted firmly to the wall. Charlie scratched his head. "What the heck is going on?" He picked up the mirror, grunted at its weight, and stood on his tiptoes to rehang it. When he stepped back to see if it was straight, he screamed and jumped.

"Shit. Who the hell are you?"

The same face as before, an older lady in a dark, high-necked gown, gazed at him. He spun around to see her by the bed. He rubbed his eyes and opened them wide, but she still stood there.

Stood being an exaggeration. More like hovered. He could see her feet, and she glowed...no, that wasn't right either. Charlie closed his eyes for a moment and reopened them, but she remained. Light from the outside shone through her. Silvery? *Hmm.* Not quite. She was... transparent. Sort of. He rubbed his face.

"What the hell. Who are you? Is this a joke or something?"

She pursed her lips and spoke in a disapproving tone.

"You should be ashamed of yourself, bringing that man into this house."

"What?"

She levitated several inches off the floor and peered down her nose as she floated closer. Charlie's heart pounded and he wanted to move, but his back pressed into the dresser. He had nowhere to go.

"Answer me. Am I dreaming? I must be dreaming. This can't be real."

Wake up. Now. Please.

Charlie blinked and rubbed his eyes, but she still hovered in front of him, looking like a cross between an angry Mary Poppins and Mrs. Doubtfire. He pinched his wrist and felt pain. *Shit.* He wasn't sleeping.

Was he talking to a ghost? No fucking way. There had to be an explanation. Maybe they were shooting a movie outside, and this was a reflection. He'd seen lots of movie trucks in Brooklyn over the past week. But even as he thought it, Charlie realized how crazy that sounded.

Crazier than seeing a ghost and having a conversation with her?

The figure floated away, then disappeared.

Whoa. What the hell?

He must be going fucking crazy.

Chapter Two

There was probably never a right time to break up with someone, but choosing the morning after a night where he'd had too much to drink was probably not the best decision Ian Gregg had ever made. But when Deena, the girl he'd been dating for the past three months, woke up and started talking about moving in together, buying new furniture for his apartment, and planning trips for the following year, Ian had to say something. And that something was: "I don't think we should keep seeing each other anymore. I'm sorry."

Wide-eyed with horror, Deena sat up in bed next to him. Her full lower lip trembled. "But I thought we were gonna be together." She sniffled, and Ian prayed she wouldn't start crying for real. Once a woman started crying, he was helpless. Early on, his three older sisters had discovered that secret weapon and used it to their advantage unmercifully.

"Deena, we've only been seeing each other three months. I just don't think we're looking for the same things." He ran a hand down her arm, meaning it as a soothing gesture, but she pulled away from him.

"Don't touch me." Naked, she climbed out of his bed and stood glaring at him. "Tell me the truth. Was I just another screw to you? Was I?"

"No, that's not true." His head throbbed from the multiple shots of tequila he'd done with the guys, but Ian tried to make it right with her. "I like you. We have fun together." Their sex life had been mediocre, but Ian didn't expect more. When his friends talked about having sex with their girlfriends and going to the moon and all that, he'd nod without understanding. Sex was sex. It felt good, but nothing off the charts. Even looking at Deena standing in front of him with her sexy, curvy body on full display didn't give him a hard-on.

"But you're not in love with me." She picked up her clothes and began to dress.

He hung his head. "No, I'm sorry. I don't want to lead you on. You're a nice person and you should be with someone who deserves you."

Deena zipped up her jeans. "I'm sorry too. But we had fun, right?"

His boxers lay on the floor by the bed, and he pulled them on before giving her a hug. "Yeah, of course we did. You're amazing. I know you'll find someone who'll love you to pieces." He hopped into his jeans and walked her to the front door. "It really is a case of it's not you, it's me."

"I guess I thought it might happen with us. I really

liked you. You're a nice guy." She gazed up at him. "Can I have a kiss good-bye?"

Why not? He dipped his head to touch his lips to hers, but she wrapped her arms around him and clung to his shoulders, pushing her tongue into his mouth. Caught off guard, he allowed it to last a little longer than he should've because he didn't want her to feel rejected. But no matter how hard she tried, there was no pleasure in it for him, and after a few seconds she got the message and pulled away.

"You're really not into me."

What was her first clue? If he didn't want her when she was naked in his bed, kissing him when they were dressed wasn't going to change his mind.

"Is there anyone else? Another girl?"

"What? No, of course not." He had to stop himself from repeatedly apologizing.

"Okay. Are you sure you don't want just a little break? I'm okay if you want to not see each other for a week."

"I don't think it's going to work out. You should be with someone who's crazy about you. You deserve that in a boyfriend."

There was nothing left to say, and he watched as she got into her Uber, the scent of her perfume on his skin and in his nose. He would miss having someone to hold at night, but it wasn't fair. Ian never wanted to be the one to hurt anyone.

Once he'd showered and dressed for an afternoon of puttering around in the garden, he slapped together a few peanut butter and jelly sandwiches and ate them while looking through his messages. He checked his Instagram and saw Deena had already taken him off her profile picture, and they were no longer an official couple. Hazard of modern dating—everyone had to know your business.

Ian was sure his friends would be messaging to find out the score, but he had little desire to talk to anyone.

Ian left his apartment and, coffee in hand, he walked through the main house out to the back deck. When his parents retired and moved to Florida, he'd jumped at their suggestion to live in the ground floor apartment and take care of the rest of the house for them, in lieu of rent. It wasn't one of those big brownstones so common in the neighborhood, but rather a smaller redbrick town house. Ian wasn't complaining. His sisters, all married, had settled in different parts of the country, but he'd stayed in the city. He'd thought about moving, but something inside him balked at the idea. Plus, his parents depended on him, and free rent was a big hell to the yeah.

"Ahh." He savored the first sip of coffee and stretched out his legs.

The new neighbor, a guy who looked to be his age, was already out on his deck, sunning himself on a lounge chair. He'd moved in about two weeks ago, and Ian had spotted him coming and going, probably to work, dressed in weird, old-fashioned clothes. Maybe he worked for a movie company. He gave the man a side-eye to see what he was wearing today, but his shirt was off and all he had on was a pair of thin black-and-white-striped shorts. A weird golden glow surrounded him, and Ian blinked a few times, wondering if the unusual spring heat was getting to him.

Maybe it was allergies. Or the remnants of his hangover. He rubbed his eyes.

Not wanting to be caught staring, Ian finished his coffee and grabbed the pruning shears he'd brought out from the house along with thick work gloves. When Miss Muir, the old lady next door, was alive, she'd hired him to keep her garden, but once she died and the house closed up, the gate had been locked and Ian had to stop. He guessed the new owner would work on it, but it was too bad. She had some beautiful trees and flowers.

He spent the first hour mowing the lawn, then dealt with weeds. He planted the tomatoes he'd bought and dug rows for zucchini seeds. Satisfied with his handiwork, he next tackled the many different rosebushes, and after cutting off the dead and dying branches, Ian pruned them back. He planted impatiens along the border, clipped the azaleas and the evergreens, and stopped for a minute to wipe the sweat dripping from his brow.

"Want a cold drink?"

Ian's shears fell into the grass as he spun around to see his new neighbor waving and peering at him from his deck. That same strange golden glow from earlier still enveloped him. Ian noticed the man's knee-length shorts had settled below his hip bones, coming dangerously close to slipping off completely. A thin line of hair disappeared past the waistband of his shorts, and it looked like he wasn't wearing underwear.

Ian blinked. Now why the hell had he noticed that?

"Oh, yeah, sure. Thanks. That'd be great."

"Come on over. I'll unlock the gate for you."

With a bright smile, he ambled down the stairs of his deck, while Ian stripped off the work gloves and set the shears on his steps, then walked through the house to get to the opposite side. His house and the neighbor's were connected by a shared wall, with a narrow path on Miss Muir's side leading to her backyard gate. The guy waited by it as Ian approached.

"Hi again," he said. "I'm Charlie Muir."

Big green eyes crinkled as he smiled, and a sprinkle of freckles dusted the bridge of his slightly sunburned nose.

They were familiar eyes, but how could that be? Ian had never seen or heard of Charlie Muir before this moment. Charlie held out his hand, and Ian grasped it.

An electric shock sizzled through Ian at the contact of their fingers, and the golden glow surrounding Charlie like a second skin pulsed brighter. Ian's breath caught, and prickles of awareness rose on his skin. Ian's gaze captured Charlie's, and those big eyes widened.

He dropped Charlie's hand but noticed Charlie's mouth forming an O of surprise.

So he felt it too.

"I'm Ian Gregg. You're related to the Miss Muir who used to live here?"

"Yeah, I guess. It's a weird story. Come on inside." He waved his hand. "Still want that ice water? Or would you rather have a beer?"

His body still dragging from the previous night, Ian shook his head. "I'm good with the water, thanks." Following behind Charlie, Ian noticed his slightly freckled skin as they walked inside the coolness of the house.

"You better put some lotion on. You look like you burn easily."

Charlie checked his arms, his long lashes fanning down on his cheeks. "Thanks. I have some, but I haven't spent much time in the sun this season. I work all week, and I never had a backyard." He took a pitcher of water from the fridge. "This homeownership stuff is all new to me."

Charlie poured two glasses, and they sat at the round wooden table. The room surprised Ian with its hominess. On the rare occasions Miss Muir made appearances outside, she seemed stiff and formal with people, but this kitchen with its lemon-painted walls and pale-wood cabinets gave off a comfortable country vibe.

"So," Ian said, once again feeling in control but still disconcerted by the brightness clinging to Charlie, "I'd seen lights on but wasn't sure if anyone had bought the house."

Charlie's long fingers encircled the glass. "I didn't buy it. I found out I inherited the house. Miss Muir was my great-great-aunt."

"Oh, wow. That's crazy. So you were close with the family?" Ian rubbed his jaw. "I've lived here all my life but don't remember ever seeing you."

"And you'd remember him," a voice whispered in his ear.

"What? Huh?" He spun around in his chair to look behind him, but all he saw was the empty kitchen.

"What's wrong?"

Facing forward, Ian found Charlie's watchful, big green eyes on him.

"Nothing. I've got a hangover from last night, and my head hurts."

"Here." Charlie jumped up and took a bottle from the cabinet. "Take some aspirin."

"Thanks." Ian shook out two and popped them into his mouth, washing the pills down with his water.

"Back to this house," Charlie said. "I grew up in foster care, so I didn't know I had any family and never bothered to try and find them."

"How come?"

" 'Cause I figured if they didn't want me, why waste my time looking for them? I didn't need them when I was grown up. I needed them when I was a little kid."

"That sucks. I'm sorry. I have three sisters and always joked when I was little that I wished I were an only child or lived by myself." But Ian could sympathize. Poor guy. Much as he bemoaned his sisters, he loved his big, noisy, nosy family.

"No, you don't. Trust me." Charlie's mouth drooped momentarily. "Anyway, about a month ago, I got a letter from this lawyer's office saying they traced me from hospital records, and we did a DNA test. My mother was Lucy Muir's great-niece, and so a blood relation, and I'm her only known living relative, which means the house is mine."

"Wow. That's crazy, but lucky you. The house is worth a ton."

"Yeah. The first time I came and brought my friend, he said I should sell it and get the money."

Those words sent a rush of panic through Ian. He didn't want that. Why? Damned if he knew, but it was imperative to him that Charlie stay in this house.

"Are you gonna?" he asked cautiously.

Charlie gnawed on his lip. "I don't wanna, but some crazy stuff happened."

"Crazy like what?" Did he see that golden glow surrounding him? Did he know?

Silent for a moment, Charlie cocked his head as if studying him; then he stood up and beckoned him. "Follow me."

Without even thinking to question Charlie, Ian took the side staircase behind him. Charlie stopped on the second floor, outside a room. Funny, though he'd never been inside, having only worked in the garden, from the moment he entered, Ian had a picture in his mind's eye of what the house would look like.

"Would you mind opening the door?"

Ian shrugged. "Sure, I guess." With Charlie watching intently, he grasped the doorknob and turned it, and the door swung open.

"Is your hand okay?" Charlie sounded anxious.

Ian showed his palm and flexed his fingers. "Yeah, why?"

But Charlie didn't answer, merely shook his head and muttered, "Weird." He brushed past Ian and entered the bedroom. When they made contact, Ian's body tingled to awareness as if fingers of fire lay over his skin.

"So what happened?" Ian remained in the doorway.

Charlie sat on the bed. "Well, I brought a friend to see the house, and we came upstairs. We were, uh, fooling around…" His face turned pink, and he couldn't meet Ian's eyes.

A shocking wellspring of fury ignited within Ian at the thought of Charlie having sex with someone, and he struggled to bank the anger and understand it. Why the hell would he care who Charlie banged?

"Go on," he said roughly, caught between wanting to hear what Charlie had to say and punching a hole in the wall.

"First the door handle almost burned his hand, then the mirror fell off the wall, the lights started flashing on and off, the chandelier swayed back and forth, and the curtains blew, even though the windows were closed."

"Hmm." Ian walked inside the bedroom. It all seemed normal. "Can I check the lamps?"

"Sure."

Ian tested the switches and unscrewed the bulbs. "Well, I'm an electrician and a contractor, and I don't see anything bizarre. The switches are tight, and the bulbs are pretty new."

"So what could cause that?"

"Can I see your circuit box? Sometimes there's a short, and that can cause lights to flicker."

"I know," Charlie said. "But what about the chandelier swinging and the mirror falling off the wall?" He pointed to it. "It's heavy, and the wire didn't break."

"Is it possible you bumped into the dresser or banged against the wall? That could've caused the mirror to fall."

Charlie's face reddened. "N-no. We'd, uh, stopped by that time."

Ian walked over to examine the mirror. Something flickered before his eyes. Was it a reflection? Couldn't be, as only he and Charlie were in the room. He scratched his head. "It looks pretty solid to me."

Charlie's face shone with relief. "Good. Lemme show you the fuse box. It's in the basement."

They took the stairs to the basement, and when Charlie continued to give off enough light for Ian to see in the murky darkness, Ian couldn't keep it to himself anymore. "Do you know you have this glow around you?"

Charlie stopped so abruptly, Ian banged into him and had to grab his arm to keep from falling forward. His fingers curled around Charlie's bicep. God, the man's skin was smooth under his fingers, and Ian ran his palm around the curve of muscle. Warmth flooded him, and Ian found himself helpless to prevent his hands from touching Charlie. It was as if his body had a will of its own, separate and apart from his brain. The light emanating from Charlie enveloped him in an almost sexual rush.

Charlie turned his head, and his shocked, open mouth hovered next to Ian's cheek. Damned if Ian couldn't feel the hot press of those lips on his. Charlie's breath hitched, and at the sound, Ian's dick stiffened to embarrassing hardness. Knowing Charlie must be able to feel him through those thin shorts he wore, Ian gulped. Maybe he was still drunk from the night before.

"Sorry. I don't know what's going on." He forced his hand off Charlie's arm and stepped back.

Charlie drew in several deep breaths. "It's okay."

That husky voice sizzled through Ian, and his gut clenched. "No," Ian muttered. "It's not. I'm not gay or anything."

" 'Or anything.' What does that mean?"

"I'm not into guys. I don't want you to think I was coming on to you. But…" Ian didn't know what to say without sounding like a dick, but he wanted to be straight with Charlie. "I don't know, man. When I first saw you outside, I noticed a light surrounding you." Ian motioned over Charlie's head and around his body. "Head to toe." Those big eyes grew larger, staring at him as if he'd spoken in a foreign tongue. Ian held his hands up in the air. "I know. It's weird. Maybe I should get my eyes checked."

Confusion settled in Charlie's eyes. "I don't understand it either. No one else has ever mentioned it." Carefully, he patted his head. "Up here too?"

Ian nodded. "Yeah. Your hand goes through it. Maybe it's the cheap tequila I drank."

"I hear tequila makes people do strange things." Charlie chuckled, and Ian felt better that the uneasy mood between them had disappeared.

"Can you check the circuits first, and then I'll tell you what I mean."

"Sure." Ian opened the circuit box. "Huh. There are a few tripped, so that might be the issue. I'll flip them for you, and that should do the trick." His smile to Charlie attempted to be reassuring even though he wasn't too certain himself. "All done. You know, a lot of these old houses have wacky lighting, even if they are brought up to code. Plus, the foundations settle and make strange noises all the time. I wouldn't take it too seriously."

"Okay, thanks. I don't know anything about houses, old or new." Relief filled Charlie's eyes. "Let's go up. This place gives me the creeps." They tramped up the stairs and wound up back in the kitchen. "You know, I think I definitely need a beer now." He took a bottle from the refrigerator. "Are you sure you don't want one?"

Ian wiggled his fingers. "Hell yeah, give it here. I've changed my mind."

After sipping the cold brew for a minute, Charlie said, "Tell me more about it. The light around me, I mean."

Feeling foolish, Ian took a gulp of the beer. "Well, like I said, it's like you're lit up from the inside and your whole body glows." Helpless, he lifted both hands up in the air. "I know you're gonna think I'm crazy, but—"

Charlie interrupted him. "I feel like someone's watching me. Inside the house."

"What? Like through your windows?" Ian peered over Charlie's shoulder as if expecting to see someone staring at them through the kitchen window.

"No. Like…" He shook his head and shrugged. "Never mind. It's dumb. I think it's because I'm not used to being by myself, so I pay attention to every little noise now, where before in an apartment building, it could always be someone else."

A troubled expression settled over his face, and Ian wondered who'd be watching him. Charlie must be smoking some crazy shit, Ian decided. It was the only explanation for the visions he was having. "Has anything else weird happened?"

"Well...Bryan...the guy I was with..." Here he stopped, and his entire face tinged red. Ian felt bad about what he'd said in the basement, yet he couldn't forget his inexplicable anger at Charlie being with someone, along with this curious pull toward him. A force beyond his control. As if to prove his words, the hairs stood up on the nape of his neck, and goose bumps rose on his arms.

"Go on," Ian spoke softly. Remembering the touch of Charlie's soft skin, he shivered. The light surrounding Charlie pulsed, and Ian's breath caught at the unearthly glow.

Charlie blinked. "Bryan told me it felt like someone was squeezing his balls and ripping his dick off. And when he reached the top of the stairs by the bedroom, something invisible seemed to kick him in the ass and push him down the steps."

"That's nuts. Were you guys smoking anything?"

"I don't do drugs," Charlie replied frostily. "I'll have a beer, but I don't like getting high or out of control."

"Everyone should lose control once in a while," Ian responded, then shut his mouth. He couldn't remember much from the night before except Deena bringing him home in an Uber while he concentrated on not throwing up. After she undressed him, he'd attempted to initiate sex but failed and passed out. With the clarity of a head no longer fuzzy from alcohol or a hangover, Ian regretted acting so uncouth and stupid, but he couldn't help wondering if he tended to drink so much when he went out on dates to mask his dissatisfaction. He tried so hard to enjoy sex, but it never measured up to what everyone else said. "But it's good to stay sober too. I might try it myself." He eyed his half-finished beer.

"You can start after you drink that, so you don't waste my beer," Charlie said, his infectious smile lighting him up while the glow around him thinned to a pure golden haze, gilding the tips of his reddish hair. Again, Ian felt drawn to this man, who with each passing moment, seemed less like a stranger and more like someone he'd known all his life.

"I guess so." Ian took one long swallow and set the now-empty bottle on the table. "If you ask me, I think you should find out what's going on. I have no idea why you look all golden to me." He rubbed his eyes. "I may've gotten hammered last night, but tequila or not, I'm sober now and still seeing it."

Without saying a word, Ian reached out toward Charlie's light. Warmth and an incredible sense of peace filled him when his fingers touched Charlie's hair. "So soft."

Charlie remained mute, his green eyes glittering as Ian continued to slide his fingers through the silky waves. Warmth turned to heat, and his hand rested on the back of Charlie's head, cupping the curve of his skull before sliding around the angle of his jaw. Bristles scratched his palm, and a pulse beat madly in Charlie's neck, pushing against Ian's thumb. Light gilded the smattering of freckles along the bridge of Charlie's straight, strong nose.

Okay, this was too fucking weird. Why was he touching Charlie again? He wasn't attracted to guys, yet Charlie wasn't like any other guy he'd ever met. Their eyes locked across the table.

What would it be like to kiss him?

A *thud* sounded from above, and they both jumped. The odd mood between them broken, Ian cast a wary glance to the ceiling.

"What was that?"

A bit frightened, Charlie gazed back at him. "I don't know."

Pretending more bravado than he possessed, Ian rose from his chair. "Let's go find out."

Chapter Three

Don't fall for him. Don't be an idiot.

That was the refrain running through Charlie's head as he followed Ian upstairs. When it came to the golden glow Ian mentioned, Charlie suspected from Ian's slightly red-rimmed eyes and pouchy, dark bags underneath that the supposed light was more the result of his gorgeous neighbor still suffering from the aftereffects of a hangover than any psychic occurrences. Staying up late on the weekend was the only time Charlie could find to work on his novel—a story about a young gay man who finds love when he least expects it—but more often than not, he ended up staring out the window. That was when he'd seen Ian's girlfriend helping him out of the car around one in the morning the night before.

If he had to confess, Charlie watched Ian quite a bit. In the two weeks he'd been living in the house, Charlie had caught sight of him working in the garden numerous times. The past Saturday had been freakishly hot, and Charlie, sitting on the deck, almost swooned when Ian pulled off the T-shirt he wore, baring all his luscious, tanned skin and rippling abs. A dark happy trail led down that tight six-pack to beneath the waistband of his pants, and when he bent to pull the weeds, his sweats slipped, revealing the top curve of an ass so beautiful, Charlie's mouth dropped and his heart almost stopped. To keep himself from passing out, Charlie had to walk away and hit the shower to get off.

He debated telling Ian about the ghostly old lady he'd seen in his bedroom, but he didn't want to come off as a freak. Plus, he wasn't sure how Ian felt living next to him now, especially after that comment about not being gay. One revelation per evening was enough.

"Where do you think it came from?" Ian asked, biting his lip.

Returning to the present, Charlie shifted on his feet. "I don't know. Let's look in my bedroom first." He opened the door, and they walked in. Too late, Charlie remembered he hadn't made his bed, but even worse was the white bottle of lube, labeled *Slick*, showing up clearly against the dark-blue fabric of the comforter. Charlie could only hope Ian wasn't paying attention.

They walked around the room, and Ian kneeled to peer under the bed. "Nothing there except dust." He wiped his hands on his jeans and stood, surveying the area. "Maybe it was a squirrel miscalculating the distance, and we jumped to conclusions. Those little fuckers are always running across my roof."

Another hard *thud* sounded. Ian's mouth fell open. Wide-eyed, he sidled closer to Charlie.

"What was that?" Ian's lips tickled Charlie's ear, sparking all sorts of dark thrills despite his nerves.

"I don't know, but it sounded like it came from the next floor up. I've only been to the third floor once."

They stared at each other, and Charlie watched as Ian's gaze traveled to the ceiling.

"You wanna go see?" Ian rubbed the back of his neck.

Not really, Charlie wanted to say, but he nodded, feeling more secure with Ian there. Hopefully the ghost lady wouldn't appear.

"This way." He waved his hand. "The staircase from the kitchen doesn't go to the third level. We'll have to use the main one." He exited the room with Ian right behind him and walked to the front of the house.

As if they'd arranged it, they marched slowly up the staircase with Charlie in the lead and Ian right on his heels. Three closed doors greeted them from the small landing— two on one side and one on the other.

"Let's do this one first." Charlie pointed to the closest room.

"Go ahead."

Gingerly, Charlie put his hand on the knob and turned it. The door opened to a small dim room smelling of musty drapes, dampness, and wood. A beam of sunlight shone through the lone narrow window, highlighting a fine sheen of dust over the wooden floors, untouched by any footprints.

"Nothing," he whispered over his shoulder to Ian. "Looks like no one's been here in years."

"You've only been up here once since you moved in, you said?" Ian murmured.

The atmosphere called for subdued voices and

slow movements. Charlie wondered what long-ago conversations and secrets the walls of this house held.

"Yep. Just a quick peek. It gets too hot and gives me the creeps."

They backed away from the door, and Charlie shut it behind him. Two other closed doors faced them, and inexplicably, his heart banged.

It's just a door, dummy. You've been through worse.

He turned the knob, pushed the door open, and again viewed an empty room, save for a single chair by the window, as if it waited for someone to take a seat and gaze out to the street. Dust motes danced in the air, and Charlie sneezed several times in succession.

"Looks like it's gotta be that squirrel, like I thought." Ian retreated to the center of the hallway, his gaze roaming over the walls and ceiling as if he could see through the thick plaster.

"Maybe. We still have one more door."

But like the first room they checked, the final one proved devoid of any furniture or presence. The air grew thicker, the musty smell heavier.

Ian stood in the center of the hall and sniffed. "You might have a problem with your roof. It smells like there could be a leak somewhere. I could take a look another day if you want, but earlier when there's lots of light."

Having Ian stretched out on his roof? Hell yeah, that was a sight Charlie wouldn't turn down. "That would be great. When do you think you could do it?"

"Tomorrow? I don't have any plans."

Damn, but he did. He'd made brunch plans with Morgan, a guy who'd been coming into the clothing store for several months. They'd flirted subtly at first, and then one day, Morgan took Charlie's hand in his, kissed it like an old-fashioned gentleman, and asked him out.

"I've been dying to go out with you for so long, but I've been tied up with a project. I'm so attracted to you, Charlie. I hope you like me too."

Who could resist that?

Until Ian stepped into the picture, Morgan had been the only man on Charlie's mind all day. He'd planned on a night of preparation with a facial, soaking in the tub, and a full-body scrub. He had no idea if Morgan would be seeing him naked, but hey, a guy needed to be prepared.

Now Charlie was torn, but on a fool's mission. Ian wasn't gay, and Charlie had a chance at something with a man he'd been thinking about for months. Someone with potential to be a real boyfriend. And yet…

"I have lunch plans, but maybe you could come by around four? That should be good, right?"

They descended the main staircase to the first level, and Charlie waited with Ian as they stood in the entranceway.

"Yeah. Works for me." Ian craned his neck. "This is a really nice place. My parents' house is a little smaller, but they have the apartment downstairs. What they don't have is that back staircase." His blue eyes twinkled. "I could've used that in high school."

"Sneaked out a lot?" Charlie could imagine Ian, good-looking and popular, had tons of girlfriends and parties.

"God, the stupid stuff I did." Ian snorted and shook his head. "Drinking, partying…you know." His wide and friendly smile hit a chord inside Charlie, releasing a pang of loneliness he hadn't admitted to himself in a long, long time.

"Not really. Living in foster care, I didn't really stay in one home long enough to make friendships like that. I changed schools a lot and stuff, so…" He shrugged. "I'd rather not get into it. Do you want to have a look around before you leave?"

Ian's easygoing smile faded. "Shit, I'm sorry. I didn't mean anything by it." He ran a hand through his hair, mussing up the thick dark strands.

Over the years Charlie had learned to keep the painful memories of his childhood locked away, so it was easy to brush it off. "Don't worry. It was a long time ago. Feel free to wander around. I haven't done much with the place because it came as is."

"Damn, that was lucky for you." Having already recovered from his embarrassment, Ian started roaming through the rooms. "Wow, nice inlay on the floors and plasterwork. Lookit the original windows. You know how you can tell?"

Charlie shook his head.

"C'mere and I'll show you." Ian waved him over, and Charlie stood at his side. Ian pointed, his arm brushing Charlie's. "See the waves in the glass?"

"Yeah," Charlie said, breathless from the contact.

"That's how you know it's really old glass."

Heat swelled through him with Ian at his side. What Ian said became less important to Charlie than the movement of his lips, the scent of his skin, and his hard body pressed up against Charlie's. He smelled good too, some Eau du Delicious scent that made Charlie's toes curl inside his sneakers.

He closed his eyes. Not only could he see the warning signs flashing, he could feel them pummeling his brain, beating a rapid tattoo: *Not again, not again.* He needed to remove himself from Ian's very disturbing, very sexy presence.

"Look around as much as you want," he mumbled and fled to the safety of the stairs. Once away from Ian, Charlie leaned against the newel post of the staircase and breathed deep to steady himself, waiting for Ian to finish his self-guided tour. Why was he so ready to jump Ian's bones? Charlie loved sex and didn't get it often, but he also didn't fall into bed with strangers. Especially not *straight* strangers.

"Have fun?" he asked as Ian approached.

"As much as I can with my clothes on." Ian winked, his grin so infectious, Charlie couldn't help but laugh. "Your jokes are terrible."

"Made you laugh."

"So I'll see you tomorrow?" He didn't want to let Ian go without the assurance he'd be coming back.

"Yeah. You got a date, or what?"

"Yeah." He ducked his head. "Nothing big. Someone who's been coming into the store where I work, and we clicked."

"Where do you work, by the way?"

"A Vintage Affair. It's a vintage clothing store in Prospect Heights."

Ian eyed him. "Gotcha. That explains the clothes. I thought you worked for a movie company." He stretched. "Where are you gonna go for lunch? Around here?"

"Yeah. French Louie, on Atlantic."

"Nice. I've never been, but I hear it's great."

"Me neither. Morgan picked it."

"Morgan's your date?" Ian's blue eyes met his, shimmering, and Charlie's stomach did a funny little flip. He didn't usually talk to people about his social life. Then again, he didn't have much of one, or many friends to hang out with. There was Mona, the girl who worked with him, and Bryan. That was it. And after their disastrous experience in his bedroom, Charlie hadn't heard from Bryan, even though he'd thought they were friends.

"Yeah. He's a graphic designer."

"Cool." Ian scratched his neck, and Charlie guessed he was bored. Ian probably went to trendy clubs in the city with all his friends. Ian said, "Well, I'd better be going. I need to shower and have dinner before meeting my friends."

"Where do you all hang out?" Might as well live vicariously.

"We go for the dives. Not gonna lie. I don't like shelling out fifteen bucks for some fancy-ass cocktail or ten bucks for a beer I can get for half the price at Montero's around the corner. And sometimes the guys wanna watch the dancers at Lucky 13." He gave an apologetic smile. "I didn't go 'cause I was dating Deena and it wasn't respectful, but maybe now…"

"Why not?" Charlie shrugged. "I go watch guys dance. It's not a big deal."

Ian's eyes grew wide. "Like Chippendales?"

Charlie snorted. "Not really. That's like a show. I'm talking about on a much smaller scale."

"I didn't even know they had that."

"Oh, you'd be surprised." Charlie's first job after he finished college was as an exotic dancer, where he could dress up in his vintage outfits and lose himself in dancing. It had only lasted six months, but in that time he'd had an affair with a client he danced for. The man insisted he was straight, but he couldn't keep his hands off Charlie. He even told Charlie he loved him, giving Charlie dreams of a future and a happily ever after. When Charlie told Lou

35

he loved him too and maybe they could move in together, Lou freaked out and said he was getting married. He never came back, and after two devastating months, Charlie left dancing and found his dream job, working in the Vintage Affair clothing store.

Charlie opened the door and watched Ian walk away, admiring the view. Shaking his head as he closed the door, a chill gust of air whispered across his face.

* * *

"I like this place. I've been meaning to try it but never had the chance." Charlie drank some of his Brooklyn Lager.

"I'm glad we're getting the chance together. And the food looks delicious. I can't wait for my mussels." Morgan sipped his mimosa and made a face. "The champagne is flat."

"Oh, no. Ask them for another drink. Everything looks so good."

"You do too. I love the striped bow tie." Morgan reached across the small table and traced the pointy edges.

"Thanks." Charlie's cheeks warmed. It had been so long since he'd been on a proper date—he half expected to creak, he was so rusty at it.

They buttered the *petit* croissants, and as they snacked on those, Charlie listened to Morgan talk about the big graphic-design project he was working on and how much responsibility he had. Stuff like that never meant much to Charlie. He would've rather heard more about Morgan the person than about his job.

"Here we are." The waiter plunked down his omelet,

potatoes, and toast, then Morgan's mussels with fries. "Enjoy."

Morgan's eyes widened. "Wow. This looks and smells amazing." He picked up the tiny fork they provided and pushed open a shell. "*Ow.*" He dropped the mussel on his plate and sucked his finger.

"What happened?" Charlie asked. He forked the delicate eggs into his mouth.

"It snapped back on my finger." Morgan picked up another mussel and cracked it in half. As he reached inside with the tine of the fork to take out the mussel, a long white tongue reached out and wrapped itself around his finger. "*Ahhh*, shit. Get it off me." Screaming, he shook his hand, but whatever it was clung to his finger with the black shell dangling. His cries brought the waiter over.

"Sir, is something wrong?"

"Is something wrong? Look!" He held up his hand, and the mussel fell onto his plate, having returned to its normal appearance.

"Um, I don't see anything. Would you like something else?"

"You can have some of my eggs," Charlie offered. "There's a lot here."

"Thanks. I'll eat the fries."

He poured the ketchup and dipped the fries. He bit into one, and even Charlie heard the loud crunch. "Dammit." Morgan held his hand to his mouth.

Charlie's heart sank. "What happened?" Was the whole date destined for disaster?

"I think I broke a tooth. Can you see?"

He bared his teeth in a grin, and Charlie could see that part of the side of a tooth had chipped off. "Yeah, it's a little chipped."

"Shit," Morgan said in disgust.

"Have my eggs and hash browns. They're soft."

He slid part of his food to Morgan's dish, and they finished in silence.

Morgan frowned. "I wanted this to be nice for us."

"It is. Don't worry. I'm having a great time," Charlie soothed him. "Why don't you come by my house? We can have dessert there and sit on the deck."

Eyes bright, Morgan nodded. "Let's get out of here and be alone." He raised his hand. "Check, please."

Hand in hand, they walked down Hicks Street toward Charlie's house. He knew they drew attention, not necessarily because they were a same-sex couple, but because of the way they were dressed. Charlie wore a typical Edwardian men's casual outfit: linen pants and a high-collared shirt with the bright bow tie. A straw boater with a black band sat at a jaunty angle on his head. Morgan, even in the warmth of the late spring day, wore all black, and with his black hair in a bun and pale eyes, looked like something otherworldly.

"Here's my house."

They climbed up the steps. Morgan's cheeks, already pink from the heat, deepened to crimson.

"You're so gorgeous." Morgan tipped Charlie's chin up. "Charlie, can I kiss you?"

For a moment Charlie grew impatient, wishing Morgan would take what he wanted and not ask, but that wasn't him. Morgan's previous kisses had been sweetly lingering and what Charlie had thought he desired. A man who'd seduce him with kind words and gentle touches.

Until he moved here and would see Ian with his now

ex-girlfriend pressed against the gate in front of his house, kissing so desperately, he wondered if once inside, they ever made it to a bed. Unashamed at playing voyeur, he'd watch them feed on each other's hunger, and how Deena would cup Ian's ass and rub up on him. Charlie got so caught up in their lovemaking, he'd remain restless and aching for hours after they'd gone inside the house.

Charlie now wanted that kind of hot and frantic greediness in a lover. He wanted that rip-your-clothes-off, can't-make-it-to-the-bed feeling.

"Yes."

Surprising himself with his initiative, Charlie wrapped his arms around Morgan and rose up on his toes. When he pressed his mouth to Morgan's, the man sighed and held him tight while their tongues played hide and seek.

"Oh, my God." Their kiss must've unleashed something in Morgan. He peppered kisses along Charlie's cheeks, jaw, and neck with increasing urgency. "You taste amazing."

Charlie whimpered when Morgan kissed him again, harder and deeper. For several minutes they stood on the stoop, their movements growing more frantic until Charlie couldn't take it anymore. "We should go inside."

"I was wondering if you were ever going to say that." Morgan's eyes burned with a fire Charlie hadn't yet seen in his mild-mannered date. "I want you."

"I want you too." Desire fired his blood, and Charlie's hands shook as he tried to unlock the door. "Dammit."

"What's wrong?" Morgan pressed his lips to Charlie's ear.

"I can't get the key to turn in the lock." Try as he might, it wouldn't budge.

"Let me do it." Morgan brushed him aside and grunted.

"Jesus. What's going on?"

"I don't know, but I guess I'll have to see about oiling the lock."

Hard as they both tried, they couldn't get the lock to open. Frustrated, Charlie took off his straw hat. "Okay. I leave the back door open. I'm going to hop the fence and go through the house. I'll open the front door from the inside."

"Okay." Morgan kissed him again. "Don't take long."

He flew down the steps and to the yard. He hadn't climbed a fence since high school, but he nimbly found his foothold and dropped to the other side. Once up the stairs of the deck, he breathed a sigh of relief to find the kitchen door open and raced to the front door, which opened with ease.

"Weird," he muttered to himself, then took Morgan by the hand. "This way. Upstairs." He tugged him along behind him, and Morgan grabbed his ass when they reached the top.

"I can't wait to be inside you."

An ache radiated upward through his belly, stiffening his cock. "Me too," he gasped, and they stumbled into his bedroom and fell onto the bed.

Morgan pinned Charlie underneath him, pressing kisses to his face while Charlie reached for his pants to pop open the button. A creaking noise from above distracted him, and when he glanced up, the chandelier began to sway. He stiffened, and Morgan, who'd buried his face in Charlie's neck, sucking and licking the tender skin, lifted his head.

"What's going on?" he rasped out, pale eyes glazed.

"N-nothing."

"Don't stop. You have no idea how long I've waited to have you under me." Morgan kissed him again, and Charlie closed his eyes, trying to fall into the moment, but it was hard when he had no clue what might happen next. He didn't want a repeat of the last time with Bryan. He tried to relax and enjoy Morgan's kisses.

He'd almost succeeded when a squeaking noise sounded above them, and Charlie opened his eyes again to see the chandelier swinging faster than before.

Shit, shit, shit. Again? What the hell was going on? Why couldn't this wait until after he got laid?

Charlie twisted away from Morgan. "Let's go into the other bedroom. Okay?"

A bit dazed, Morgan panted. "Huh? What? Why?"

Charlie heard the whine of frustration in his voice, and thinking fast, rolled off the bed. "I haven't changed the sheets." He opened the nightstand drawer and pulled out the lube and condoms. "Don't worry. Necessities are portable." He winked.

Morgan got up stiffly and followed Charlie across the hall to the other bedroom, where a queen-sized bed awaited them. With satisfaction, Charlie noted there was no chandelier in the room, nor a mirror. Only the bed, an armoire, and two nightstands with lamps. They should be safe. He looped his arms around Morgan's neck, hoping the fire hadn't died out.

"Should be better in here."

"I don't care where we are. You turn me on so much." Morgan hooked his fingers in the waistband of Charlie's pants to pull him even closer, then slid both hands down his thighs.

"Oh my God, that feels amazing."

"You're amazing." Morgan walked him backward

toward the bed, and they lay together. Morgan braced himself above Charlie. "I can't wait to be with you. I've thought about it nonstop since we planned today's date." He undid the bow tie and began to unbutton the high-collared, ruffled shirt Charlie wore, when the lamplights flashed on and off and the drawers of the armoire flew open.

Morgan's eyes grew wide, and he jumped up and off Charlie and rolled to the opposite side of the bed. "What was that?"

Charlie's heart sank. "Um, what?"

"Don't you see it? The lights, the slamming drawers?"

A chilly wind blew into the room, and like the time before with Bryan, despite the windows being tightly shut, the curtains fluttered. Morgan's eyes popped wide open, and he began to stammer. "Wh-what's g-goin' on?"

"I don't know." Charlie hopped off the bed. The room grew colder, and the tip of his nose hurt, as if frost had nipped at the exposed skin. Earlier in the afternoon, the temperature had reached seventy-five degrees, but now Charlie shivered and hugged his arms around his waist.

Morgan remained frozen in the bed, his terrified gaze fixed on the armoire's drawers slamming back and forth. "Is this a joke or something?" he stammered. "What're you doing?"

"Nothing. I'm not doing anything."

"What do you call th—*ahhhhh*." In the middle of his sentence, Morgan flew up and off the bed; then his long body sailed out of the bedroom. With a *thump*, he landed flat on his ass in the hallway. Charlie watched in shock and horror as a bowl filled with pasta—a bowl he knew came from his refrigerator because he'd put it there the other night—coasted through the air and dumped its contents over Morgan's head. The strands of spaghetti stuck to his face, and sauce dripped down his hair and cheeks.

Damn. He'd planned on eating that for dinner.

Charlie might be freaked out by what was happening, but he also had a right to be pissed off. That sauce was Rao's and cost seven bucks a jar. Shit was expensive.

Morgan, on the other hand, sat on the floor, screaming his head off. "Don't just sit there. Help me!"

Another bowl, this time with the rest of the salad he'd made, joined the pasta, and Morgan howled with outrage. Charlie scrambled out of the bedroom. He needed to do something before he lost the entire contents of his refrigerator. He knew he had a half gallon of Coffee Heath Bar Crunch ice cream he'd been saving, and he'd be damned if he'd lose it to Morgan's head.

"I guess dinner's on me?" He couldn't help laughing. "Or to be exact, on you."

"You think this is funny?" Morgan's pale eyes blazed. Gone was the sweet-tempered man who'd been afraid to kiss him. "You're fucking crazy. As crazy as this house. Get me the fuck out of here."

Charlie watched him trip down the steps and winced at the loud slam of the front door. He stood in the center of the hallway, waiting. He wasn't sure for what or if he wanted to know, but this was getting ridiculous and repetitive. Not only was he not getting laid, but this damn ghost was going to cost him a fortune in groceries.

"*Charlie,*" a reedy voice sighed by his ear, but when he whirled around, no one was there. The faint scent of lilacs teased his nose, and without thinking, he followed it into his bedroom. The lilac smell grew stronger as Charlie entered.

The door slammed shut behind him, and before he

could react, Charlie found himself sprawled on the bed, facing the same ghostly, disapproving woman he'd initially seen in the mirror.

Chapter Four

A normal lazy Sunday for Ian would be waking up around noon, sex with Deena, then lunch, followed by maybe more sex and then whatever game was on television. Not much to do and exactly how he liked it.

But now Deena was gone, and somehow, Ian had involved himself, doing work for his new neighbor, who had something funky going on in his house and in his life.

The noises were most likely from the house settling, or a squirrel or maybe even a raccoon scuttling around somewhere. Years ago his mother had once had to face down an opossum in the backyard, and Ian could still hear her shrill screams for help. Nasty fuckers looked like giant rats, with those long pink tails.

Since his refrigerator was empty and he was tired of

living on peanut-butter sandwiches, he decided to walk to Trader Joe's and stock up. After a quick shower, Ian walked to Atlantic Avenue. When he passed by the little restaurant where Charlie and his date were having brunch, he stopped and pretended to look at the menu while really peering inside the windows through the lacy curtains to see if he could spot Charlie and the guy. No such luck.

With the sun in his eyes, Ian strolled the few blocks over and entered the store. Pushing a wagon in front of him, he noticed several good-looking women shopping alone and recalled his sister Jessie telling him to be more aware of his surroundings. *"You never know when you're going to meet someone. There are plenty of other places to find a woman besides a bar or a club."*

Who knew the produce aisle would be one of them? Ian stood in front of the boxes of berries: juicy red strawberries, inky blackberries, and dusky blueberries.

"They all look good, don't they?" a husky voice spoke in his ear, and he glanced over to see a woman in her late twenties with big brown eyes and dark, glossy hair drawn back into a high ponytail. She was dressed in workout clothes, black leggings and a tight white T-shirt that showcased her curves.

"Everything does," he said with a slow smile that brought a blush to her cheeks. "Which are your favorites?" He picked up a plastic container of blueberries.

"I have to have a taste first." Even, white teeth gleamed in a flirty smile. "I never buy without sampling the merchandise." Crimson-tipped fingers plucked a blueberry from the container. "Mmm."

"Good?"

She licked her lips. "Very. Want to try?"

"Very much so," he replied, anticipation tingling in his

chest, already wondering if he could get her number. She reached inside and chose a berry for him.

"*Ahhhh!*" she screamed as the contents of the plastic tub flew into her face. "What'd you do that for?" Blueberries caught in the strands of her hair.

"I-I didn't do anything." His attempts to help her were met with slaps. It was as if an invisible hand had flung the blueberries at her.

"Jerk." She reached into her purse and pulled out a napkin to wipe her face.

He set the box of blueberries down. "I'm sorry. I don't know what happened. Let me take you out for coffee to apologize. I swear I'm not crazy." Still dabbing at her face, she remained dubious. "My name's Ian. What's yours?"

"Margo. I don't know."

"Come on, Margo." He gave her his most winning smile. "This could be a funny how-we-met-in-New-York-City story to tell everyone."

Finally she relented, even giggled. "I guess no harm was done. Okay. I'm finished here, so I can meet you outside when you're done?"

Her basket held some kale, a loaf of sprouted-grain bread, and dairy-free cheese. Ian shuddered. Maybe he should've checked that out prior to asking her on a date. But he could suck it up for a face and body like hers.

"I'm just going to get some strawberries." He picked up a plastic tub, but before he could set it in the wagon, the lid flew open, and one by one, the berries pelted Margo all over, staining her shirt.

She put up her hands as if she were warding off an attack of killer bees. "Get away from me," she screamed. "You should be arrested. Crazy asshole." She ran to the front of the store, and he stood with an empty container in his hand, a crowd of people gathered around him, whispering and pointing. A store employee came over and began to sweep up the strawberries and blueberries rolling around on the floor.

"I-I'll pay for the fruit. I really don't know what happened," he stammered to the skinny, bearded worker. "It's like it exploded out of my hand."

"Just take the empty containers to the register and tell them." The guy gave him a once-over, shook his head, then walked away.

Muttering to himself, Ian tossed them into his wagon and decided to leave. He'd had enough and lost the desire to be in the store any longer.

A day that had started out clear and bright had turned gloomy and oppressive while he'd shopped in the store. Matched his mood, for sure, and Ian grumped all the way home.

"Well, that sucked," he said out loud, entering his apartment and slamming the door behind him. "And not in a good way." Maybe he should stop trying to pick up women and be single for a while. Nothing wrong with that. His stomach growled, and he frowned.

He decided he'd better eat something, seeing how it was after two in the afternoon and he'd had nothing except coffee.

"That's what you get for picking up strange women. Shame on you."

The same voice he'd heard the night before when he sat in Charlie's kitchen echoed in his ear. Shame on him? What the hell was that about? Who was scolding him?

Ian stuck his face in his still-bare refrigerator, and seeing nothing worthwhile, slapped together the old faithful, peanut butter and jelly. He flopped into the chair near the front window and chewed the sandwich dispiritedly.

It had cooled off a bit, and Ian opened his window, hoping to catch a breeze. One nice thing about living on Willow Place was its location. Only a block long, not many people knew of its existence, so growing up, he and his friends could ride their bikes in the street without fear of cars zooming by. Ian sat for a while with his face turned up to the warmth of the sun, enjoying the cool air flowing past his cheeks. Oak trees lined the sidewalk, their branches forming a canopy over the street, and chickadees and sparrows flitted from branch to branch.

A door slammed outside, and footsteps pounded down the steps of Charlie's house. A tall figure sped past his window, and Ian spied a guy dressed in black, running in the middle of the street like a bat out of hell.

"What the hell?" Was that Charlie's date? Did something bad happen? Was Charlie hurt? What if this guy was a nutjob and beat Charlie up…or worse? Not bothering to think, Ian tore out of his apartment and ran up the steps to Charlie's house. He banged on the door with a closed fist.

"Charlie. Charlie!" Receiving no response, he banged again, then tried the door. It swung open, and a sense of foreboding overwhelmed him. "Charlie, where are you? Charlie?"

"Upstairs. He's upstairs in the bedroom."

Ian whirled around to see where that same weirdly echoing voice he'd heard earlier came from, but no one was there.

"What? Who are you?"

No response. The only sound that met his voice was his own labored breathing. Ian made his way upstairs, mounting the steps to the second floor two at a time as he rushed toward Charlie's bedroom. He heard Charlie speaking and stopped to listen, but something pushed him forward. He found himself standing in the doorway and saw Charlie sitting on his bed. The golden light around him flared brighter, and warmth spread through Ian even though over six feet separated them.

"Hey."

Blinking as if coming out of a fog, Charlie stared at him for a moment before answering. "H-hi. What're you doing here?"

"Who were you talking to?"

"Nobody," Charlie answered quickly.

"I heard voices."

"Myself," he said with a sheepish smile. "I was talking out loud to myself about what went wrong."

"What happened to your date?"

"He's…gone."

"I figured that, but why?"

A blush crept up Charlie's neck, reddening his cheeks. "We weren't really getting along."

"In what way?"

"Lots of different things. Guess we weren't as compatible as I thought." Charlie's full mouth turned down.

Ian's protective instinct kicked in. "Did he hurt you? Do anything to you? He looked like a fucking creep, if you ask me. Who dresses all in black in this heat, like a fucking vampire?" He strode into the room and stood over Charlie, who gazed up at him with a strange expression on his face.

"No, he didn't hurt me. We were having a good time

until weird stuff started happening again."

"Weird stuff? Like what?"

Was Charlie hearing voices too?

Uncertainty flickered in Charlie's eyes. "I-I don't know. Just funny noises. Anyway, I don't wanna talk about this anymore. I have to clean up the mess in the hallway."

"Mess? There's nothing in the hallway."

Charlie's brows knitted together. "Really? Are you sure?"

"I would think so. I was there a minute ago. There was nothing there."

Fixing him with a troubled, disbelieving look, Charlie pushed past him without responding and stood in the doorway. Ian heard him mutter to himself, "What the actual fuck."

"Charlie, are you okay?"

Ian might not know anything about the guy, but it had to be hard, growing up in foster care, not knowing who your family was. To discover after everyone was gone that you did have people and that they were rich...well, Ian knew if it were him, he'd be damn resentful that they not only gave him up but didn't even try and look for him. It would certainly fuck with his head. "It must be overwhelming to have all this happen to you so quickly. I wouldn't blame you if you needed to take a break from everything for a little while and give yourself a chance to regroup."

"You think I'm losing it?" Charlie's eyes narrowed. "That I'm crazy?" His jaw thrust out mulishly.

Ian put his hands up. "Whoa, no, of course not. I'm not saying I don't believe you," Ian soothed. "Don't take it the wrong way."

Charlie's shoulders slumped. "I-I don't know. I'm sorry for jumping down your throat. It's just, I'm disappointed. I thought Morgan and I were having a good time, and then…" He shrugged. "Whatever."

Dejection radiated from Charlie, and Ian hated seeing him upset. "Want to have dinner after I look at your roof?"

Charlie peered at him over his shoulder. "Are you sure?"

"Unless you have any other plans."

"I was just going to go through some stuff I found in boxes in the bedrooms."

"I can help you if you want. I've got nothing else to do."

Charlie gave him a hesitant smile, and the golden light surrounding him burned bright.

Chapter Five

After the clusterfuck of his date with Morgan, Charlie was almost reluctant to agree to have Ian hang out. What if those crazy things happened while he was on the roof? He could get hurt. And yet...

"I'd like that," he said quietly. "But, are you sure you want to go up on the roof?" He cast his gaze to the ceiling. "Isn't it kind of dangerous?"

Ian gave his boyish, disarming grin. "I like living on the edge. Keeps me ready."

Charlie wanted to ask, *Ready for what?* but was a bit chicken to find out the answer. "Well, okay. It's probably gonna be wet up there, since it rained pretty hard last night."

"Not a big deal. I've been through worse." Another flash of that cocky grin, and again Charlie ignored the kick of his heart. Ian flexed his shoulders. "Show me to your ladder, and I'll see what we're working with."

"Um, I don't know if I have one."

"Yeah you do. I used to use it to prune the tall bushes for Mrs. Muir."

Ian proved to be correct and he hoisted the ladder from the side to the rear of the house. Charlie had to force himself not to stare at Ian's biceps rippling under his T-shirt from the heavy weight.

Why was he obsessing about Ian? He refused to fall for a straight man. Again. That never ended well. At least it hadn't for him. Vowing to keep his libido under wraps Charlie stayed a safe distance, several yards from Ian. The man was too damn tempting.

"Take me to your rooftop," Ian said in a creepy voice, and Charlie choked back a laugh.

"Dude, that was...bad."

"So you're saying I should give up my dream of being a stand-up comedian?" Ian's blue eyes twinkled, and Charlie couldn't help an answering smile. "Now tell me, where do you think I should start?"

Charlie shrugged. "You're the expert."

Ian studied the roof for a moment, then pointed to the rear of the house. "That was where we smelled the wet, right?"

"Yeah."

"All right." He pulled out the extension to the ladder, laid it against the house, and with sure, nimble steps climbed to the top. Most of the homes built in the late 1800s had flat portions of rooftop, so Ian was able to stand at first, then bend over for a closer inspection. After about ten minutes, during which Charlie did his best not to stare at Ian's very fine butt in his faded jeans or the flash of bare skin where his T-shirt rode up, Ian climbed down.

"All clear. Looks like an almost a brand-new roof. Mind if we go upstairs again so I can look around in the rooms? See if there's any wetness on the walls or stuff?"

"Are you sure? You don't have to bother."

"Charlie, I said it's okay. I'm willing to help you. We're neighbors."

A dark cloud passed over the sun, blocking out the light. Was it his imagination that he saw a face in the cloud? What if she made it impossible for Ian to stay? At this rate, Charlie was fast running out of friends as well as food.

"I guess."

"I'll take that as a yes." Ian folded the ladder, laying it flat on the ground. "Let's go inside before it rains."

But as soon as he and Ian began climbing the stairs to the deck, the cloud faded and bright sunlight shone.

"This is the wackiest weather I've ever seen," Ian remarked as they entered the kitchen.

"Yeah." Charlie barked out a nervous laugh.

They trekked up the two flights and reached the third floor, where the stifling-hot air pressed against their faces. That same uneasy feeling followed Charlie up here, and his heart raced.

"Damn, it's stuffy." Ian sniffed. "But I don't smell anything now." He pointed at the farthest door. "Let's go in there."

Ian strode toward the room and opened the door. Charlie might not know Ian, but he could tell his take-charge, go-right-ahead personality was in full effect.

"I'm going into the closet to check the walls."

Not a question, but a statement of fact. Charlie always did like a man who knew what he wanted.

Stop. He's not your date.

Ian stepped inside the walk-in closet. "There's no bulb, so I can't see what the walls look like, but there's no smell of damp. Huh."

"Huh, what?"

"I found this knob on the wall."

"Yeah?"

"It's like a little doorknob. Can I try to open it? Or do you want to?"

Charlie shrugged. "Go for it. See what happens."

A creaking sound, and then Ian said, "Ooh, there's a lockbox inside." He left the closet, eyes sparkling with excitement, and they walked to the window to catch the light and see the box more clearly. Rust clung to the flaky metal surface and a coating of dust covered it, as if it had been forgotten and sitting inside that hidden closet for years. A lock dangled from the latch.

"Maybe it's filled with cash and you're rich."

"Ian—"

Ian shook it, and the contents rattled. "You always hear stories like this in the news."

"It's probably nothing."

Ignoring him, Ian sat on the floor in the middle of the dirty room. "Maybe it's an original copy of the Declaration of Independence."

"Ian—"

"Or," Ian continued, ignoring Charlie, plunging straight into fantasyland, "maybe it's instructions to where they buried gold in the backyard."

"Dude, you're losing it." Charlie lowered himself down to sit by Ian's side and nudged the man with his shoulder. "Let's open it."

But when he took the box from Ian, the lock wouldn't budge. "No key in there, huh?"

Ian ran into the closet to check. "No, dammit." Ian returned to his side and grabbed the lock, yanking on it. "Nothing. It's strong, but I think we can knock it open. Let's get a hammer, or do you not have that either?"

"Yes, I have a hammer. I'm not a complete homeowner fail." Charlie rose to his feet, holding the box under his arm. "Follow me."

Once they'd returned to the kitchen, Charlie rummaged in the junk drawer until he found the hammer. Ian had set the box on the floor, and though Charlie tried five or six smashes, nothing happened. Breathing heavily, he set the hammer down in disgust. "I can't do it."

"Lemme try." Ian snatched up the hammer. "We should take it outside on the deck," he said, and with the box under his arm, opened the back door. "I can see I need to really put some muscle into it, and I don't want to crack the floor here," he explained. He set the box on the ground, took aim, and gave the lock three good whacks. The lid popped open.

"Yes!" He fist-pumped, and Charlie couldn't help but share in his infectious grin. There was something about Ian that made you happy to be with him. "Let's see what's inside." He held the box out to Charlie. "Go ahead. You should be the one to see first."

"Well, if it wasn't for you, I'd never have gotten it

open, so you get to share with me. Let's go inside. It's getting breezy, and I don't want anything blowing away by accident."

"You're the boss." Ian held the door for him, and they reentered the house and sat at the kitchen table. Charlie's anticipation grew as he stared at the box for a moment, and then, holding his breath, flipped the lid open. Two envelopes and several photographs lay inside.

Charlie picked one up, and a sense of warmth and peace radiated up from his fingers through his arm to his heart.

"Shit." Ian drew in a sharp breath.

"What?" Charlie faced him.

"When you touched the letter, that light around you turned bright gold."

"What?"

Ian blinked, narrowing his eyes. "I already told you that I saw a golden light around you."

"I thought it was because you were hungover," Charlie whispered.

"Yeah, well, so did I, but I still see it, and I haven't had anything but a peanut butter and jelly sandwich today, soooo…" Ian's confused blue eyes met his, and in their depths Charlie glimpsed a hint of longing. As they stared at each other, the bright blue changed to silver, like moonbeams over water. Charlie blinked…and Ian's eyes were blue again. He rubbed his face hard. *Must be a trick of the light.*

Ian persisted. "I'm not hungover, and I still see the light around you. It flared up bright gold like a flame when you touched the letters." He glanced around the kitchen. "You're not filming some crazy show for television, are you? You don't have cameras and stuff hiding in here, do you?"

"No, of course not. Look, I'm really curious to see what's in here. Can we talk after?"

"It's your house, your stuff. So your decision."

Without speaking further, Charlie opened the first envelope, but when he scanned the document, disappointment flooded him. "Eh, it's nothing. Just the deed to the house."

"Oh." Ian sounded just as disappointed.

A grin ticked up the corners of Charlie's lips. "Did you really think we'd find long-lost secrets to buried treasure?"

"I dunno. Certainly something better than that."

"Let me see the other one. Maybe it's something better."

He opened the second envelope. It was a notice from the Army—a death certificate—with the name Edward Robinson. His vision blurred and Charlie stood so abruptly, the chair scraped against the wooden floor and almost tipped over.

"Thanks for your help. I appreciate your checking out the roof for me."

Anxious eyes met his. "Are you sure? I thought we could, uh, get a pizza or something."

"No, I can't." Charlie swayed, and Ian grabbed hold of him.

"What's wrong? Dude, you're pale as a ghost. Are you okay? You look like you're gonna pass out."

A buzzing sounded in his ears. Charlie could barely stand and a curious weakness permeated his body.

"I don't know," Charlie mumbled. "Gonna go lie down." He moved his leg to trudge up the steps, but even that effort proved too much, and he found himself pitching forward. He reached out and grabbed Ian's forearm to stop himself from face-planting on the floor.

"C'mon. I'll help you."

Wrapped in Ian's arms, Charlie allowed himself to be led upstairs and put to bed. Ian waited at his side until he stretched out.

"Thanks. I don't know what happened." His body felt pummeled, his skin raw to the touch.

Ian stood over him, still anxious. "Are you sure you don't want me to get a doctor or something?

Charlie pressed his palm on his aching chest, hoping he wasn't having a heart attack. "Hurts so bad," he whimpered.

"What?" Ian sat on the edge of the bed. "What hurts?"

"My chest," he gasped. "It's like someone is sticking a knife in me and twisting it."

Without asking, Ian placed a hand on Charlie's chest and remarkably, the excruciating pain dulled to an overall ache, then faded.

"Better?"

"Yeah. Thanks. I-I need to go to sleep. I think I stayed up too late last night, and with the beers, I guess I'm just really tired."

"Are you sure you feel okay? You don't want me to call anyone?"

"No." *So tired.* "I'm fine."

"Night, Charlie. Talk to you."

He listened to Ian's footsteps trek down the stairs and waited for the front door to close. The reflection in the mirror wavered, while a curious silvery mist ringed the heavy gilt frame.

The old lady he'd seen before met his eyes, her face no longer stern but surprisingly soft with concern. *"Listen to what I'm about to tell you, Charlie. Look and listen."*

She faded away, and in the mirror, a scene began to play out, bright and vivid as a movie. A roaring filled Charlie's ears, and he was no longer in his bedroom in Brooklyn....

He was in a muddy field. The sky hung overhead, an ominous yellowish-green, and thunderous booms pounded. Screams split the air.

The life he'd left behind seemed so far away now. He could barely remember his comfortable bed and fully stocked refrigerator. A longing welled up inside him for those lazy summer days spent in the garden, with the sun on his face, climbing trees to escape his younger sister, who loved to follow him around.

Discovering the smell of Robert's skin. The taste of his lips and tongue.

"Down, get down."

Dirt filled his mouth as he was shoved face forward into the dry, hard ground. His heart pounded, and tears trickled down his face. He missed his mother and father. He wanted to scold his little sister one more time for spying on him and tease her about the boys she liked. He was a soldier, but God, he was only twenty years old and so afraid. He didn't want to die.

"This way, this way."

Dutifully, as he'd been taught, he followed the voice of his colonel, and along with the rest of the men in his group, they stumbled behind a thick barrier of trees. Bullets spit into the trunks, and he watched people around him fall as they were hit.

"We're trapped. We're all gonna die." His friend Artie McCarren dry-heaved his fear into the dirt. Artie, fresh out of the cornfields of Oklahoma. He and Edward had been fast friends since boot camp.

"No, we're going to be okay. We're going to get out of here. You have Sally Holmes waiting, and I'm going to go home and work with my father." More than anything, though, Edward wanted to be in the backyard behind Robert's house, kissing him.

A barrage of shots pounded them, and when he looked down, he saw blood pouring out of his chest. Pain lanced through him as his body turned numb.

Robert...Robert...

Heart thundering, the metallic taste of blood rising in his mouth, Charlie blinked, and the battle scene disappeared and the old lady reappeared in the mirror.

"You have much work to do. You and Ian."

"What? Who are you? What's going on?"

He tried to climb out of bed, but his body refused to cooperate. Frightened, he watched her sail out of the mirror to float above him on the bed.

"Oh, Charlie. You have no idea how long I've waited. Everything you've been through was to prepare you for this time. Now your journey can begin. You'll have to take my word for it, but I promise you'll understand soon enough."

"What do you want from me? And what do you mean, Ian and I have work to do?"

"Soon enough. Soon. There's much to discuss. Now, get some sleep."

The only way to explain it was that she dematerialized, leaving Charlie blinking and confused.

He let sleep take him away, where his dreams were filled with a ghostly figure chasing him and Ian as they ran down a long, dark hallway.

Hours later he woke up, in the pitch black, and it was then that he recalled how in his dream, he and Ian were holding hands.

Chapter Six

"Yo, Ian, we thought you died."

His friend Mickey McAllister slid a beer across the table.

"You're a riot. And stupid. Some of us are busy, you know?" Ian drank the cold brew.

"There's busy, and then there's being a hermit." His other friend, Patrick D'Angelo, finished his bottle. "We ain't seen you in weeks." A dark brow arched. "You meet someone? Holding out on us? Who is she?"

"Nah. I haven't met anyone. It's only been a couple of weeks since Deena and I broke up. Been working on my garden and doing some odd jobs in the neighborhood for people. Making some extra money, ya know?"

"Yeah, I hear you." Patrick drank some of his beer.

They were at a club in Bushwick Ian would normally never find himself in, but Patrick's sister knew someone who knew someone, and they not only got to skip the line to get in, they even managed to score a table. It wasn't his scene, but Ian hadn't been feeling much of anything lately and figured it couldn't hurt to branch out from his usual stomping grounds.

"I saw Deena the other day. She's dating some fireman from the Bronx." Mickey eyed him to see his reaction, but Ian merely shrugged.

"Good for her. She's sweet and deserves a nice guy to make her happy. That isn't me." He spotted a pretty redhead sitting with her friends at the bar and smiled. She dipped her gaze for a moment, then met his eyes with an answering curve of her full lips.

"Ian, you dog. No grass growing under your feet. She's hot." Mickey kicked his foot under the table. "And I like her friend with the glasses. She's cute. Really cute."

Taking a final bite of his burger, Ian wiped his mouth and drained his beer. "She sure is, and I happen to need another beer." He stood and picked up his mug. "I'll be right back."

"Don't rush on our account." Patrick raised his mug. "I like to watch the master in action."

Ian strolled through the crowded bar area and joined the group of women the redhead sat with. She was dressed to kill, in stilettos and a tight dress with a plunging neckline. Liking her juicy curves, Ian leaned over and whispered, "Wanna dance?"

"Sure." She swung off the barstool and smoothed the clingy dress down. He slipped his arm around her waist, and she pressed up against him. "I'm Savannah."

"I'm Ian. Where are you from?"

They reached the dance floor and joined the rest of the couples. The music switched from a pounding beat to something smooth and sensual. He gathered her close, and they began to sway back and forth.

Savannah said, "I live around the corner."

"But you're not from Brooklyn, right?"

"No, I'm from South Carolina. How did you know?"

"Your sexy accent." He chuckled and touched the little cleft in her chin. "Plus, no one from New York City is named Savannah. It's a pretty name."

Her smile gleamed, and they danced a little while before Savannah began to kiss his neck. Normally Ian loved having his neck kissed, but Savannah's mouth left an itchy trail where it touched, and he wiggled away from her.

"What's wrong?"

"Nothing." The moment she'd stopped, the itching ceased.

"You smell amazing." Again her lips touched his cheek and kissed a path along his jaw, making her way to his mouth. He'd had a few beers and was feeling fine. Maybe she could break him out of the rut he was in. Her full breasts pushed up against him, and he tipped his head down to press his mouth to hers. She pushed her tongue into his mouth, and he sucked it.

"*Oww.*" He pulled away from Savannah, his lips, his tongue, his whole face numb and on fire, as if he'd taken a giant mouthful of hot sauce. "Water," he gasped, and leaving her standing dumbfounded on the dance floor, Ian raced to the bar and pushed his way through the throngs to wave wildly at the bartender. "Water, please. A pitcher."

The neon-haired bartender snickered as he filled a pitcher with the requested ice and water. "She too hot for you, man?"

Wishing he could punch the smiling idiot in his face, Ian grabbed it and didn't bother with a glass but drank directly from the pitcher. The water soothed his burning throat and tongue, but they still felt raw and tender.

"What the hell happened? Why did you leave me standing there?" Glaring at him, Savannah stood with her hands on her hips.

"Did you eat anything spicy earlier?" He wiggled his tongue, wincing at the soreness.

"What? No, of course not." She licked her lips. "I don't like spicy things."

"I-I don't know. It was like someone put a cup of Frank's RedHot sauce on my tongue." He touched it with his finger. "My whole face went numb."

"I didn't taste anything."

Her friends, who'd been watching their interaction, surrounded them, and Ian figured he might as well invite them to join him and his buddies.

"Want to come have a drink and meet my friends? They're all good guys." He pointed to the table where Patrick and Mickey sat. They both waved, and Savannah and her friends whispered among themselves.

"Sure, okay," Savannah said finally, and their little group trekked across the bar to his table. Patrick and Mickey grabbed some empty chairs, and Ian made the introductions. He learned Savannah's two other friends' names were Andi and Brianna, and they all worked together as sales associates at Macy's Herald Square.

"You must have interesting stories." Patrick directed his question to the three women, but his eyes were all over Andi, the petite, dark-eyed, dark-haired woman in a bright-red dress with lots of chunky jewelry.

"Ugh, nothing you'd want to hear." Andi's expressive hands moved as she spoke. "I work in the children's department, and when we have a sale it's brutal."

"What about you, Brianna?" Mickey smiled at the woman he'd eyed earlier. She sat quietly, but Ian could see her eyes were all over Mickey. "What department do you work in?"

"Handbags and accessories."

"My mother would love to meet you."

Ian smiled to himself at Mickey's attempt to draw out the quiet Brianna. It intrigued him to see Mickey so taken with her, as he normally went for the more outgoing, sexy-dressed women. Brianna wore a plain sleeveless top and skirt but nothing flashy.

A waitress stopped by. "Can I get you drinks?"

Ian picked up his glass. "I'll have another Brooklyn Lager. Ladies?"

The women each opted for a vodka soda, while his friends ordered their beers. When the drinks came, they all toasted, and Ian stretched his arm around the back of Savannah's chair. He leaned close to her, enjoying her light perfume and the silky feel of her long red hair. He'd never been with a redhead, and he wondered if the freckles dotting her creamy skin continued under her clothes.

"I'm sorry about what happened," he whispered, and a hum of pleasure rippled through Savannah. He watched her nipples harden beneath the clingy material of her dress.

"It's okay. You can make it up to me."

"I can?" His palm caressed her jaw, while his fingers teased along the shell of her ear. "How?"

A slow smile curved her mouth, and he almost groaned out loud as she ran her tongue along her red lips. "I'll think of something."

He shifted closer and shot a quick glance at his friends, who were busy chatting up the other two women. "How about this?" He placed a finger under Savannah's pert little chin and lifted her mouth to meet his.

"*Ow, ow, ow.*" She pushed him away. "What're you doing? You're hurting me. Get away. You're crazy."

Without saying another word, she picked up her purse and fled the table. Her friends ran after her, leaving Patrick and Mickey staring at him.

"Dude, what'd you do to her?"

"Nothing. I swear. I was trying to kiss her when she started saying I was hurting her." Ian ran a hand over his cheeks, nose, and mouth. "Do you see anything wrong?"

"Still that same ugly mug as usual." Patrick cackled and drained his beer.

A large man approached the table. "I'm afraid you're going to have to leave," he addressed Ian, who raised his brows.

"Why? We're just sitting here drinking. We paid our tab."

"Come on, buddy. You caused a scene on the dance floor, and now you tried to hurt that girl?"

"What?" Outraged, Ian jumped out of his chair. "I didn't do a thing to her 'cept try and kiss her, which she was okay with."

"Not from what I heard. Now you can leave nicely, or I can make you." The guy, a wrestler type with a thick neck and shoulders that looked like he could pull a freight train, folded his arms and glared. "Your choice."

"Whatever. I didn't want to come to this bougie-ass place anyway." He finished his beer and rose from the table. "You guys coming?"

Mickey's gaze found Brianna, who stood in the corner, comforting Savannah. "Man, I was hoping to hang out with Brianna. I really liked her. She was sweet."

Dismissing Mickey, Ian appealed to Patrick. "What about you?"

"I mean, same, dude. Andi's a cool girl. I was planning on asking for her number."

"Jeez, so much for friendship. Whatever. I'll catch you later."

Ian left the club and called for a car to go home. The beers he'd had made him a little woozy, and he had to fight to keep his eyes open as the car drove through the darkened streets. He still had no idea what happened between him and Savannah. One minute they were all cozied up, the next she was running from him like a bat out of hell. Damn, he was tired of the pickup scene. Maybe he should sit his ass home for a while.

"Hey, buddy, we're here."

Ian glanced around to see they were idling in front of his house. "Oh, yeah, sorry."

He stumbled out of the car and made it to his apartment, where he drank two glasses of water before lying on his couch. The room spun slightly, and he picked up the remote. He could still watch the replay of the ball game. Ian flicked on the set, and an old lady glared at him. He blinked. Damn, those beers hit him harder than he'd thought. He searched for another station, only to have her disapproving face show up on the screen every time he changed the channel.

"What the…?" He rubbed his face, certain now he

couldn't hold his liquor.

"*Ian. It's time you stopped running around and paid attention to what's right in front of you.*"

"Huh? What?" He leaned forward. "Are you talking to me?"

"*Is there another Ian with you?*"

He knew his cable provider was crap, but this was ridiculous. Maybe it was time to upgrade his Smart TV and only use a streaming service.

"*Ian, watch. Watch and remember. Don't make the same mistake twice.*"

"Same mis—what the hell is going on?" he yelled, but she faded from the screen, only to be replaced by a scene that reminded him of the shows his mother used to watch on public television. He picked up the remote to turn it off, but something slapped it out of his hand.

"*I told you to watch.*" Her voice cracked like a whip, and he found himself riveted to the television screen and incapable of standing.

The edge of his vision whitened, and the room faded. Ian saw himself on the couch in his living room, yet he watched the scene unfold in front of him. He was awake, but somehow dreaming.

Strains of music from the bedside radio played around him, and peering into the mirror, Robert removed his top hat and placed it on the dresser. He couldn't help how pale he looked; he hadn't slept well since the wedding plans had begun months earlier. And now they were married. If there was ever a chance of stopping it, that was gone now.

"*You're so handsome.*"

At the sound of Charlotte's voice, he spun around, his eyes growing wide at the sight of her in a sheer nightgown and flowing robe. Her hair, loose for the first time since he met her, tumbled down her back in shining blonde waves.

Eddie had hair like that, *he thought and almost gasped out loud from the pain of his loss.* No more. This is my life now.

"You're beautiful. And you made a lovely bride. So elegant. Everyone was talking about your dress."

Twin spots of color appeared on her cheeks, and her eyes lowered. "I wanted to look pretty for you."

"My dear, you were a picture."

He removed the studs and bow tie, along with his tuxedo jacket, cummerbund, and vest. With each piece of clothing, Charlotte's breathing accelerated, and she moved closer to him.

"Husband. I quite like the sound of that."

Her perfume, a light lavender scent, teased him. Dispassionately, he gazed down at her. A tiny thing with pale skin and huge blue eyes, Charlotte was his aunt's neighbor's daughter, and they'd been introduced at a dinner party, then met at several more. He knew his family wanted the match from the first, but all along, he'd held out hope that this day would never arrive.

"Wife sounds lovely as well."

In preparation for the night ahead, which he anticipated would be hard to deal with, before the wedding ceremony he'd poured a goodly amount of whiskey in a flask and finished half of it by the time the ceremony was done. Now he was tired and slightly hungover. Not the best recipe to push forward and consummate the marriage, but he had no choice.

There had never truly been a choice. From the beginning, Robert knew he'd never live a happy life, and with Eddie gone, he'd been living in a fog. Tonight, reality hit him. Hard.

Charlotte surprised him by reaching her hand up to touch his face. "I always thought you were hiding something from me. Are you, darling?"

He blinked, fear slicing through him. Did she suspect something?

"N-no, of course not." He licked his lips and slipped an arm around her narrow waist. "I'm an open book for you to read." He forced a smile.

"I don't think a husband and wife should have secrets from each other. You know you can tell me anything."

"Of course. And you should be free with me as well."

She stood on her toes and pressed her mouth to his, and he held her hips as they kissed. They'd kissed a lot during their engagement, but never anything further. And as much as he wanted to feel, he remained soft and unmoved.

Taking matters in her own hand, Charlotte slipped the robe off her shoulders, revealing smooth ivory skin and a deep cleft between her full, perfumed breasts. Never taking her eyes from his, she shrugged off the straps of her filmy nightgown until she stood naked in front of him, the ideal portrait of a woman who'd warm any man.

And yet he stood cold—a lifeless statue carved from marble.

"You're very beautiful."

"Katie told me there are many ways to please a husband. I want to try them all with you, Robert. If you're willing."

Katie was Charlotte's best friend and had married two years earlier. The two were thick as thieves, and along with his wife's mother, planned every aspect of Charlotte's wedding. Including, it seemed, the wedding night.

Her small hands fumbled at his waistband, and he barely breathed as she unbuttoned his trousers, and along with his drawers, let them fall until he stood naked from the waist down, still soft and unaffected.

"I know a man is supposed to be hard when he desires a woman. Robert, don't you want me?" Her small hand brushed him, then held tight and began to stroke. He imagined her hand to be Eddie's and groaned.

"Harder, dear," he whispered, and she followed his instructions.

Stunned to feel himself harden, he began to breathe heavily as she sank to her knees, placed her mouth on him, and began to suck. Her golden head bobbed as she moved up and down, and Robert closed his eyes and wished himself away, under the oak tree in the backyard, where his dreams were born and died.

The television went dark, and Ian sat up, relieved he could move. He had no idea why his eyes burned and his cheeks were wet. His head spun, and he stood, staggering briefly, and returned to the kitchen to drink another glass of water and take three aspirin. An oppressive heaviness sat on his shoulders.

Ian had thought he was awake, but now he wasn't certain. The whole night had turned out to be a disaster, so why not end it with a fucking weird dream? Maybe he was getting the flu. He heard stories of people getting delirious and seeing things when they were sick.

"Oh, foolish boy."

Ian jumped at the woman's voice, spoken as clearly as if she were in the room with him, but he was alone. His heart pounding, Ian glanced over at the television, half expecting to see the old lady's face appear or something even more bizarre pop up, but the screen remained dark.

"I don't know what the hell is going on, but I'm going to bed," he muttered to himself.

He stripped out of his clothes, and after brushing his teeth, climbed under the covers, but sleep eluded him, and he lay staring at the ceiling, unable to close his eyes.

* * *

"Shit." Ian squinted into the bright sunlight that hit him square in the eyes. For a moment he didn't know where he was, and sitting up brought no relief, but rather a nauseating lurch to his stomach.

The old lady in the television. That dream that wasn't a dream. There was no other way to describe what he saw other than he'd acted as a bystander...a witness to the history of people whose identity had yet to be revealed.

Whoa. Where did that come from? Thoughts like that were way too deep for him to process so early in the morning, especially before coffee. "Dude, you are so cutting back on drinking. You should be thinking about some cute girl, not a grandma."

After a good stretch, he went to the bathroom to take a shower. Feeling more human, the first order of business was coffee and lots of it. One cup later, Ian stretched out on his couch and stared at the television. Should he try turning it on?

Here he was, almost thirty years old and scared to turn on his TV because an old lady might pop up. Defiant, he pushed the Power button, and to his relief, ESPN came on.

He picked up his phone to check if he'd gotten any texts. Both Patrick and Mickey had messaged him.

Patrick: *Called you to make sure you were okay. Lemme know.*

Mickey was blunter: *Where the fuck are you? Call me.*

"Now you're worried?" He continued talking to himself as he refilled his coffee cup. "Last night you were both too busy trying to score to be concerned. You can wait." He finished his second cup, muted the set, then called Mickey.

"You okay?"

"Why wouldn't I be?" Irritated, he put Mickey on speaker and poured himself some Cheerios and milk. "How'd you do? Did you get her number?"

"Her number and a date for lunch later today," Mickey gloated. "Brianna's not like any girl I've ever met."

"You mean you didn't screw her right away? She was shy but hot. A nice butt from what I remember."

"Fuck you. Don't talk about her like that."

Stunned by the anger in his friend's voice, Ian sought to soothe him. "Hey, sorry. I didn't mean nothing by it. Just that I know you, and that's how you usually roll. So if you didn't this time, well, props to you."

"Yeah. She's a sweet girl. Kind of sheltered and quiet-like. She hasn't dated much. I like that, you know?"

No, he didn't. Not really. Mickey had always been footloose and eager to score with as many women as he could, so him falling for a shy, quiet woman surprised Ian, but he went along with his friend. After all, nothing in his life seemed to be normal at the moment. "Happy for you, man. I still don't know what happened with Savannah."

"I do." He chuckled. "I think your girl must've been on something. She kept saying that it hurt when you kissed her. Like bees were stinging her lips over and over."

"You're kidding. Damn. Looks like I dodged a bullet with her."

"Definitely. Patrick did well too. I think he's going out with Andi again tonight."

"I'm gonna call him now."

"Sorry it didn't work out for you, man."

" 'S'okay. Have fun on your date."

"I intend to."

Ian disconnected and called Patrick, who grunted at him. "I'm on my way out. You okay?"

"Yeah, I'm fine. Where you going?"

"Me 'n Andi are gonna go running in the park."

"You spent the night with her? *Daaamn.*" Patrick was the one who normally took things slowest among the three of them.

Patrick's voice dropped low. "She's incredible. I never met anyone like her." He sighed in his ear, and Ian couldn't help grinning. The romantic of the bunch, Patrick had never made it a secret that he wanted a girlfriend and to get married, but he'd yet to find someone he wanted to see more than a few times, claiming he got bored easily.

"What's so special about her?" She was cute, from what Ian remembered, but Patrick had always had cute, fun girlfriends.

"I don't know. I feel good around her. She listens to me, and she's interested beyond fooling around. We didn't even have sex last night. We just talked about all kinds of things and cuddled."

That sounded nice. His friends hung out with two cute girls, and what did he get? Yelled at by Grandma Goody Two-shoes and stuck watching some old-fashioned movie about a miserable guy at his own wedding. *What's wrong with this picture?*

"Cool. Well, have fun."

"Sorry it was a bust for you, man."

"No worries. I got lots to do around here to keep me busy. I'm not really looking for something permanent or long-term right now."

"Gotcha. All right. I gotta go. Talk later."

He flopped down on the couch and yawned. Nothing to get up for, so he might as well watch the game he missed yesterday. Obviously whatever happened the night before was a combination of too much to drink and the weed he inhaled outside the club. He'd been right—everything looked better in the daylight. Ian flipped on the television, ready for an afternoon of nothing but baseball.

"Oh, for fuck's sake."

The old lady glared at him from the set, and Ian, knowing he was wide-awake this time, rose to his feet to confront her.

"Is someone paying you to play a joke on me? Is it my sisters? Come on. You can tell me. Am I on a television show or something? I've seen this shit on one of those reality shows. Someone's going to come out of the closet with a camera, right?" Wildly, he scanned his apartment. "Are they under the bed or in my bathroom?" He ran around the room, throwing open doors and looking under the furniture, but found nothing. Breathing hard, he planted his feet wide and stood in front of the set, while Granny stared at him unperturbed and smiling.

"Such bad language. I'm only trying to help you."

"You know how you can help? Get out of my television. Go away. Leave me alone."

"Not until you watch this."

She disappeared, replaced again by the same two people as the previous night, only this time they were in bed. And now, like then, Ian found himself floating in a suspended state, unable to stop watching. His heart ached, the unknown man's pain as fresh as if it were his own—a wound on his bare skin.

They lay in bed together, Charlotte curled into him. His arm draped around her shoulders, and a soft breath tickled his chest.

"I hope I didn't disappoint you, dearest." Her lips moved, hot against his cool skin. "I know you're a man who's used to more experienced women."

He sighed. Charlotte need never know she was the first woman he'd ever been with. He could only hope to keep up the charade. She was a dear, sweet girl and didn't deserve not to be loved. The pain of losing Eddie would never leave him, but he'd made up his mind that as there was no hope of ever finding love again, he'd do his best to make her as happy as he could. He owed her that much.

"You were perfection, my love. I've never been happier."

Her smile beamed bright, and she hesitantly touched him. "Do you...are you able to...again? I heard sometimes we might make love more than once in a night. Did you like when I used my mouth on you?"

He closed his eyes and willed himself to feel. "I loved it. Do you mind, dearest?"

"Oh, no." She shifted down on the bed between his thighs. "I only want to make you happy."

"You do. You do." He tangled his fingers in her hair and stared at the wall.

The picture evaporated, and the screen turned to black. Ian jumped up, his gaze swinging wildly around the room. Without thinking, he ran to the set and yanked the television plug out of the wall. Maybe his cable needed a reboot.

Maybe his whole life did.

Chapter Seven

Charlie peered at himself in the mirror. "I think this looks good."

Mona, the other salesclerk at A Vintage Affair, reached across and straightened the bow tie. "Now it's perfect." She cocked her head and gave him the once-over. "You're looking sharp. Is that for a date?"

"No." He fingered the bow tie. "It's on sale, so I figured I might as well take advantage of it."

The bells tinkled over the door, and his eyes met Bryan's. They hadn't seen each other since that first time in his house. He figured Bryan had moved on.

"Hi."

"Hey." Bryan slouched inside, holding hands with

another man. Charlie's gaze focused on their entwined fingers. "How're you doing?"

"I'm good, thanks. But busy. Working." He didn't need to have Bryan shove a new relationship in his face.

"Can we talk a sec?"

Mona pretended she was oblivious to them as she started eating her lunch, unwrapping her sandwich and taking a big bite, but Charlie could see her gaze flickering to them.

"Sure." He shrugged and walked over to the set of windows on the opposite side of the store. Bryan came but also brought his friend.

"This is TJ."

"Hey," Charlie acknowledged him. "What's up?"

TJ gave him a bright smile, and to Charlie's surprise, interest kindled in his dark-brown eyes. "Hi."

Bryan leaned in to give Charlie a kiss, but Charlie pulled away. "Stop. What'd you do that for?"

"Last time we were together freaked me out. I don't know what happened."

"Me neither."

"But"—Bryan's gaze cut to TJ, who gave him a nod, and Bryan focused back on Charlie—"me 'n TJ started hooking up, and it's great, but I kind of miss you too. We always had a good time."

Bewildered didn't begin to explain Charlie's state of mind. "Okay, yeah, we had fun. But I get it. You found someone else. We weren't exclusive or boyfriends. I mean, I thought we were friends, but that doesn't mean you need to come here and shove your new boyfriend in my face."

"No, you don't understand. That's not it."

"So what are you trying to say?"

This time TJ did the talking. "Charlie, Bryan showed me a picture of you, and I thought you were cute." He licked his lips. "And really hot. So I suggested we all get together. The three of us." Without further ado, TJ grasped him around the neck and pulled him close, slamming their mouths together. With no time for Charlie to respond, TJ took advantage and slid his tongue inside Charlie's mouth, stroking and rubbing along Charlie's. For a hot second, Charlie allowed it, softening his lips to mold to TJ's. He'd missed the touch and feel of another person so much.

"Mmm. I knew it. So hot. Can't wait to be inside you," TJ mumbled, flexing his hips against Charlie's.

"N-no. Stop. What the fuck is going on?" Charlie tore himself away from TJ and stood in front of the two men, breathing heavily. "You want a threesome?" Thank God he remembered to keep his voice low. Mona was failing in her attempt to not gawk, and her mouth hung open.

TJ grinned with lazy confidence, and Bryan nodded, red spots rising on his cheeks. "Yeah. What do you say?"

About to snap back that it was ridiculous and outrageous, Charlie stopped and studied the two men in front of him. In the bars and clubs he'd heard plenty of guys talk about having one, with the consensus that they were wild and hot as fuck. And here were two guys who wanted him. Bryan had the size he craved, and TJ, with his glittering eyes, couldn't fake his desire.

What would be so wrong?

"Uh, maybe?" He rubbed his neck. "I mean, okay, sure."

Bryan's mouth fell open. "You're kidding. Yeah? Really?"

"Did you think I'd be against it?"

"Well, yeah, but I'm glad you said yes." He licked his lips. "Really glad." He kissed Charlie's cheek and leaned over to speak to TJ. "Wait until he blows you. He's got a mouth that'll suck you dry as the fucking desert."

"I can believe it."

Heat rose to Charlie's face, and he ducked his head. "Quiet, come on. I don't need everyone hearing about my private life."

"You're cute," TJ said. "How about we pick you up when you're finished here, and we go get some pizzas. Watch a movie, and then take it from there."

"I'm good with that." Bryan looked to Charlie. "How about it?"

"Yeah, sure. We can go to my place." He didn't normally hang out during the week, but he had nothing else to do. Not like his cute neighbor was going to come by after that crazy incident in his house when he got so sick. More importantly, Ian was straight.

Besides, Charlie hadn't gotten laid in forever.

Bryan's eyes widened. "Are you sure?"

Charlie glared at him. "Yeah, I'm sure. I have lots of room. Listen, I gotta get back to work. Mona is on lunch break, and I'm the only one on."

"All right, then. See you around six?"

He led them to the front of the store. "Sure."

They left, and Charlie stood, lost in thought, until he felt a poke at his side. He squeaked, jumping up. "What?"

"What's going on? I saw you kissing the other guy, not Bryan." Mona's big eyes blinked behind her rhinestone-studded, cat-eye reading glasses. "But weren't you with Bryan?"

"I'm not with anyone." His chest twinged, and he

rubbed it. Ever since he and Ian had explored his house, he'd had a curious tightness around his breastbone. "We're going to hang out tonight, that's all."

She eyed him doubtfully. "If you say so. But that kiss didn't look like a hangout kiss. It was more like a let's-get-naked kiss."

Heat washed through him. "*Shh.* Shut up." He darted a look at the customers walking in and meandering around the store. "You don't know what you're talking about."

Mona, nobody's fool, arched a brow. "Mmmhmm."

"I have customers I need to get to."

* * *

It had been a crazy rest of the afternoon, and Charlie hadn't even had time for lunch, so by closing time he was starving. On their way down Atlantic to his house, they stopped to pick up two pies and some beer. Proud to show off his house, Charlie pointed it out from the corner.

"That's it."

"Wow. You live there by yourself?" TJ held one pie, Bryan the other, and Charlie carried the beer.

"Yeah."

"Pretty cool. Now let's get inside and get naked."

A bit uneasy, Charlie led them across the street and set the two six-packs on the stoop while he reached for the key. Once he unlocked the door, Charlie pushed it open and turned around.

"Come on in."

As Bryan placed a foot on the top step, the pizza box flipped open, and slice after slice launched at his face.

Whoa. Charlie's heart sank.

"Get this shit off me," Bryan wailed, his voice smothered under a flapping slice.

"Dude, what the fuck?" TJ snorted with laughter, while Charlie watched in dismay as Bryan clawed at his face.

"This isn't funny. Help me." Each time Bryan picked a slice off his face, another would latch on and slap him like a fish flopping out of water.

"He's always been a klutz. Let's go in and put this stuff down, and then we'll come get him. Take this and I'll grab the beer. Charlie took TJ's pizza box, intending to set it on the table by the front door, but before he could, the box popped open and the pepperoni rounds flew off the slices and pelted TJ. "What the hell are you doing?" he screamed.

"Now you see what happened to me!" Bryan yelled from behind TJ.

A slice sailed through the air and landed on TJ's face with a *splat*.

"Get this shit offa me," TJ howled. Charlie struggled to pull the flopping pizza slice off TJ, and when he did, the look of pure outrage on TJ's face set Charlie off into peals of hysterical laughter. He couldn't help it.

"You're nuts, man. I don't care how good a fuck you are."

He was still laughing as Bryan and TJ sprinted away.

Deciding to take advantage of the beautiful twilight, Charlie changed course, and instead of going directly inside, he left the pizza boxes and beer in the front hall, tramped down the path along the side of the house, and entered his garden. A breeze rustled through the leaves, and birds began a noisy serenade in the huge oak tree in Ian's yard. He gazed at the branches, and a sense of peace filled him.

Speaking of Ian…his sexy neighbor was bending over his rose bushes, carefully checking the leaves and clipping off the dead blooms. Neither TJ nor Bryan generated the swell of desire inside him that simply watching Ian did.

"Hey." Ian straightened and waved.

He waved.

"You know, if you let me, I'm happy to take care of the roses in your garden. I'm dying to get my hands on them."

"Now?" A rush of pleasure filled Charlie at the prospect of unexpected time with Ian.

Ian picked up his pruning shears and made chopping motions with them. "No time like the present."

"Okay, sure. Come over and I'll let you in."

Five minutes later, Charlie stood beside Ian, watching as he carefully cut back the ivy choking several of his bushes. Ian handled flowers like everything else—firmly, confidently, and with humor. Even when the thorns caught on his skin and scratched him, he took it in stride, but with blood welling on his arms, Charlie sprang into action. Without thinking or asking, Charlie began to unhook the sharp barbs from Ian's skin. After each thorn was removed, Charlie smoothed his fingertip over the remaining abrasion.

The sound of birds chirping rose around them. Charlie, hyperaware of his close proximity to Ian, glanced up, only to find Ian's intense blue stare had turned that shocking silver. He took a step away, but Ian held on, his grip tightening around Charlie's wrist. Ian's breath came in short pants. Charlie had seen that look before.

Desire. Need.

But what the hell? Ian was straight.

Pretending a casualness he didn't feel, Charlie let out a nervous laugh. "You got to wash this, or it can get infected. Come inside with me. I've got something you can put on it."

"Okay."

The odd mood broken, Ian followed at his heels up the back staircase to his bedroom. Charlie took a tube of antibiotic cream from his medicine chest, and when he returned, Ian was sitting on his bed.

The stuff of fantasy to be sure, but Charlie steeled himself against the foolish banging of his heart and handed Ian the tube.

"Here you go."

"Do be careful, boys. You don't want to get hurt."

Both he and Ian scrambled across the bed at the sight of the ghostly lady speaking to them from the mirror.

Charlie hoped Ian wouldn't take off like Bryan, TJ, and Morgan had.

"Oh shit," Ian breathed. "You again?"

Charlie whipped around to gape at Ian. "You've seen her too?"

Wide-eyed, Ian nodded, and they huddled together on the bed.

"You didn't think I left, did you?" The ghostly old lady beamed at them from the mirror. *"I need you to see this."* And before they could answer, she faded away.

Charlie sat, riveted to the scene in the mirror. As it progressed, Ian's hand crept into his, holding on in a death grip.

"Hi, I'm Eddie," he called out and waved to the boy sitting in the backyard next door. *The boy looked around Eddie's age—fourteen years old—and he seemed to be*

88

drawing in the dirt with a stick. At Eddie's greeting, he startled and dropped it on the ground.

"Hello. I'm Robert." He gave Eddie a tentative smile.

"Do you want to meet out front and play stoop ball?"

The smile faded. "My mother doesn't like me to play that." His gaze flickered to the ground, and he hung his head. "I have a problem...my heart..." Red tinged his cheeks. "I'm not supposed to exert myself, or I get pain."

"We can play at my stoop, and I promise we won't hit the ball too hard."

Robert's eyes widened. "All right. I'll meet you out front."

Excited, Eddie clambered down the steps from the back porch, grabbed his ball, and raced around to the front. Robert appeared a moment later.

"You just moved in a few weeks ago, right?" Eddie had watched the furniture delivery.

"Yes. We lived in Greenpoint, but my mother liked this area better, plus my aunt lives a few blocks away."

Robert's dark hair ruffled in the breeze, and his blue eyes matched the summer sky.

Eddie had always known he liked boys, but kept it quiet. He didn't think it was something he should talk about, especially when he'd hear his friends whispering about the girls they liked. Nobody knew his secret.

"We've lived here forever. Do you have any brothers or sisters? I have a younger sister, Rachel. She's okay, even if she does tag along all the time."

"No. Only me. I would've liked a brother or a sister."

"I'll lend you Rachel."

They shared a laugh.

"Do you want to play?" He pointed to the steep front steps. "I'll let you start." He handed Robert the ball.

"I'm ready." Robert tossed the ball once, then smacked it against the front steps.

Eddie returned the ball, and they went back and forth until the sweat ran down their faces and the sun began to set, making it too hard to see. He missed the ball, and Robert let out a cheer. After retrieving it from the street, he and Robert sat on the steps of Eddie's house.

"Good game."

"Same," Robert agreed.

He caught Robert's shy stare before he dropped his gaze to the sidewalk.

The front door of Robert's house opened, and a woman peered out. "Robert? It's dinnertime. Please come inside."

Immediately, Robert got to his feet. "I have to go home. Thanks for the game."

"Sure. We can do it again tomorrow if you like."

A flicker brightened Robert's eyes, and they shared a smile.

"Yes. Yes I would."

He watched Robert walk away.

The scene in the mirror faded, and Charlie gazed at his reflection. Ian's face was white, blue eyes glittering. Charlie waited for the ghost to reappear, but she didn't.

Eddie...wasn't that the name of the person he'd seen on the battlefield?

"Who were those people?" Ian tugged at his hand, bringing Charlie back to the present.

Charlie searched his memory. "Edward Robinson. That was the name on the death certificate we found in the lockbox, remember? It must be the same person."

"Shit, yeah..." Ian breathed. "But who is she? Why was that lady here in your mirror? What in God's name is going on?"

"I don't know." Helpless, Charlie glanced down at their hands, fingers still laced together. "I told you weird stuff's been happening."

"Yeah. Really weird." Charlie felt the weight of Ian's stare on their entwined hands. Then suddenly Ian wasn't touching him any longer, and his world got a little bit colder.

"I haveta go. See you."

Ian hurried out, and Charlie made no attempt to go after him. He assumed Ian would now go the way of all the other men in his life.

Charlie no longer questioned the strange happenings around him. He'd read books on ghosts that inhabited old houses in New York City, had even taken a ghost tour once. He wasn't so much interested in the ghost, but rather what the story unfolding in front of him meant.

"I know you're trying to tell me something."

"*In due time, Charlie. Everything must happen for a reason.*" Only the voice this time—she didn't reappear.

He went downstairs to get the pizza boxes and ate the leftovers for his dinner. Afterward, Charlie couldn't help the surge of pride as he walked around the rooms, touching the walls and the furniture. He owned this. A piece of New York history. For someone who spent his childhood never knowing where he'd next lay his head, this was unbelievable. Incredible. Every room he entered felt like a warm embrace welcoming him home.

He finally had a place where he belonged.

Chapter Eight

Something strange was going on.

Since that incident with Charlie and the lady in the mirror, Ian had kept away from his neighbor, but it had nothing to do with the old lady. Hell, no. That would be understandable.

Ian couldn't stop thinking about Charlie the man. Those long-lashed green eyes that Ian knew held some terrible secrets. How gently Charlie touched him when removing the thorns from his skin. How good he smelled. How soft his lips looked and sweetly shy his smile was.

Since when did being with a guy turn him on?

Not any guy. Only Charlie.

Those were the thoughts on his mind at work as

he pulled the last load of wires through the northwest corner of the building and clipped them into place. The skyscraper rose over fifty stories, but Ian loved working on high-rises. The taller, the better. He always had a bit of a danger fetish, but he knew when to concentrate. He could lose his balance and fall, ending up with a bigger problem than being a guy who wanted to kiss another guy.

"Yo, Ian, break time," Dave, the foreman, yelled up to him, and Ian waved to show he'd heard, then made his way to the construction elevator.

On his way down to street level, Ian's thoughts returned to Charlie. He hadn't seen the guy all week, but he'd heard him leaving in the morning for work and saw the lights on in the house at night. Ian struggled, wanting to see Charlie yet not understanding why. He didn't have the same urgency to hang out with his friends.

Then again, he'd never wanted to kiss them either.

Maybe it was his fault—he'd come on too strong, too friendly. After all, Ian mused as he exited the elevator to join the other guys for lunch, Charlie said he was a foster kid and didn't have many friends growing up. Could he have inadvertently scared him? Ian vowed to be more chill.

None of it, however, explained that weird glow around Charlie. It should freak him out, but it didn't. And it should more than freak him out that when they were standing by the rose bushes, Ian had noticed how soft Charlie's lips looked. But it didn't. Ian had never felt so comfortable and at peace as he did when he was with Charlie. Like everything inside him settled into place. He shook his head. It made no sense.

Neither did having an old lady talk to him through his TV or Charlie's mirror, but that happened too. Although, thank God, not since that last time. His TV played what it was meant for: sports and food shows.

His usual lunch crew of four waited for him. Dave, Chester, Miguel, and Lenny were all in their mid-to-late forties, all already married and with kids. At twenty-eight, he was the baby of the crew, and they loved listening to his dating stories. Living the life vicariously, as Miguel put it with a hearty laugh.

"What's going on, Ian? Meet any cute girls lately?" The questions started as soon as he joined them.

Ian opened his sandwich bag. Imagining what would happen if he said, *"Nah, no girls, but there's this guy..."*

Before answering, Ian took a bite of his turkey wrap, chewed, and swallowed. "No. I think I'm gonna stay single for a while."

"Attaboy. You're young. Play the field. Why tie yourself down?"

"Yeah. I've been busy in my garden, and helping my neighbor with his house. He's got some personal shit going on in his life, so I'm trying to be a friend. The guy's all alone, so I feel bad for him." Wouldn't hurt to get the guys' opinions, Ian decided.

"That's nice. You can hang out together. Grab a beer or go to a club."

The thought of going out with Charlie brought a smile to Ian's face.

"What's so funny?" Dave asked.

"Oh, nothing. Just that he's gay, so I don't see that happening."

"Why not?" Chester asked. "You can be each other's wingmen. My cousin's gay and always goes out with his straight friends. Says they help him weed out the losers and vice versa." Chester finished his sandwich. "He can scope out some cute girls for you, and you can pick out his dates. Win-win."

"Maybe. I guess I could take him out with me."

"Yeah. Especially if he's by himself." Lenny set his sandwich down. "Lots of people feel alone these days and get depressed. You see the news. You know what happens."

Dave tossed out his sandwich wrapper and wiped his mouth with a napkin. The big, brawny ex-Marine had served two tours in the first Iraq War, and Ian looked up to him. "My neighbor's kid was bullied in school 'cause he's gay. Tried to kill himself, but thank God his parents found him and stood by him. Now he's in therapy and doin' okay. I say you do what you can for your neighbor. Be his friend. So he's gay. So what? You can't be his friend, go out for pizza and a beer? Why not? I've been with guys and girls. It shouldn't be no big deal who I sleep with to anyone but me."

Stunned by his foreman's words, Ian gaped at him. "What? You're gay? I thought you were married."

"First of all, I ain't gay. I like guys *and* girls. That makes me bisexual. Don't they teach you nothin' in school no more? Second of all, I *am* married, you idiot. You've met Jennifer. And our kids too."

"But, but…you were with guys? Really? I'd never think…" Ian couldn't imagine the foreman in the same vein as gentle, sweet Charlie. Proof once again that looks could be deceiving.

Dave's eyes twinkled. "Hey. Don't knock it till you try it. And yes, because I know you're gonna ask, yeah, Jenny knows. But just 'cause I'm married to a woman don't mean I ain't still bi. Sexuality ain't a water faucet. You don't turn on and off who you are inside. I happened to fall in love with a woman."

From the unruffled expressions of the others, Ian guessed they already knew. Or maybe they didn't care. It gave him something to think about for the rest of the afternoon as he was running wires and testing circuit boxes.

Was he wrong for leaving Charlie to himself? What if he was depressed, like the guys said? And maybe, Ian could admit to himself, he wanted to spend more time with Charlie. That prospect sent him racing out of the worksite at the end of the day in record time, darting into the subway car right as the doors closed. He made it back to Brooklyn in less than half an hour and let out a grunt of satisfaction when he walked inside his house. No bills greeted him as he riffled through the mail, and he considered that a good omen.

"Okay. Shower, get dressed, and then me and Charlie are gonna have a sit-down."

Standing under the hot water, Ian still found it hard to process that big Dave had once had sex with guys and found it easy to discuss. But, he mused, soaping himself, maybe he was the one who needed an attitude adjustment. Looked like he had a whole load of preconceptions about people that in reality didn't mean shit.

Dressed again in jeans and a T-shirt, Ian grabbed his keys and phone, stuffed them into his pocket, and with determined steps, marched over to Charlie's house, up the steps, and banged on the door. It took several minutes and some extra firm bangs until Ian finally heard footsteps shuffling, and then the door opened. The tips of Charlie's messy reddish-brown hair sparked golden threads of light, drawing Ian inside without even waiting for Charlie to invite him.

"Wait, what're you doing?" Charlie protested, but Ian brushed past him and sat down on the staircase.

"I'm being a good neighbor is what. What're you doing tonight?"

Wide-eyed and with a mutinous thrust of his jaw,

Charlie glared at him. "Why?"

Ian gave him the grin that used to get him out of turning in his homework on time at school, and dates with girls a few years older.

"Because once you get out of those pajamas"—he pointed to the plaid pants and the T-shirt that read: *Vintage boys do it old-school*—"you and I are going out."

Charlie's lips thinned. "I don't think so, but thanks." And he walked away toward the rear of the house and disappeared from view.

Dumbfounded, Ian sat for only a second before he scrambled to his feet and ran after him, calling, "Charlie, where'd you go?" Receiving no answer, Ian checked in the kitchen, but there was no sign of Charlie, and a quick glance out the window overlooking the yard showed it to be empty as well. Ian didn't stop to think and took the hidden staircase in the kitchen that led to the second floor. Coming face-to-face with Charlie's closed bedroom door, he knocked.

"Are you in there?"

The door was flung open on its hinges. "Are you kidding?" Charlie's usually smiling eyes were narrowed to glittering green chips. "Who said you could follow me up here?"

"Why're you so mad at me?"

"You? This has nothing to do with you." Whirling around, Charlie stormed away and flopped on his bed. Ian chose to remain at the door. "Not everything is about you, Ian, even though I'm sure it usually is."

Ian flinched. "Hey. What'd I ever do to you? I thought we were friends."

"Friends?" Charlie snorted. "I don't have friends." He crawled under the bedsheets. "Go away and leave me alone." Charlie gave Ian his stiff, unyielding back.

But Ian didn't accept a no, he couldn't, especially with Dave's words from the afternoon running through his head. Determined to get Charlie to talk to him, Ian circled around the bed and climbed in next to Charlie.

"Talk to me. C'mon. What happened?"

"What're you doing in my bed?"

"Trying to be a friend, you idiot. Now, what's wrong?"

Looking younger than his age, which Ian guessed to be around his own, Charlie wiggled away from him but sat up against the old wooden headboard. "I had a really rough week at work, okay?"

Ian's protective instinct kicked in, and for the first time he noticed that golden glow around Charlie had dimmed to a pale, sheer light.

"What happened?"

"Nothing," Charlie answered automatically, but Ian knew he was lying.

"Well, it was obviously something, since you're holed up here like a hermit. It's Friday night, man, c'mon. Come out with me." Ian bounced on the bed, and despite the scowl on Charlie's face, he didn't miss the brief upward tick of Charlie's lips.

"You're like an annoying puppy."

Ian grinned. "I've been called worse."

"I'll bet you have," Charlie muttered.

"Seriously, let's go. We can go anywhere you want. I'll let you pick the place," Ian appealed to Charlie.

An interested gleam lit Charlie's eyes. "Yeah? Anywhere?"

Ian nodded with vigor. "Yeah. Promise. Anywhere."

Nodding thoughtfully, Charlie gave him his first full-blown smile of the evening, and the shimmering golden glow reappeared. What did it say about Ian that he'd kind of missed it? It now seemed to be a part of Charlie. At least for him, since it didn't appear that anyone else could see it.

"Okay, then. I'll get showered and dressed. You can pick the food, but I get to pick the entertainment. Okay?"

"Deal." He bounced off the bed. "I'll meet you outside in an hour?"

"Yeah, sounds good." Charlie slanted a look at him through the thick fall of his hair. "Thanks. I know you have better things to do on a Friday night than hang out with me."

"Don't be stupid. I'm doing exactly what I want to do, and with whom. See you in an hour." He left the room, ran down the steps, and as he let himself out the front door, he realized how true that was. He was looking forward to spending time with Charlie and finding out more about his mysterious neighbor.

* * *

"Nothing like pizza and beer to get the night started." Ian drained his glass and poured another from the pitcher.

"Yeah. I can eat it four times a week and I never get tired of it." Charlie sipped his beer, still only half-finished. "I-I really want to thank you for kicking me in the ass to go out. It was a shit week, and I let it get to me more than I should've."

Not liking the sound of that, Ian set his beer down. The Italian restaurant he'd chosen was casual and predictably crowded for a Friday evening. Most of the tables were occupied by couples out on dates, and from the perky way the waitress greeted them as "boys" and seated them in the back at a corner table, Ian surmised she assumed he and Charlie were too. The thought didn't bother him.

"What happened?"

Charlie averted his gaze and lifted a shoulder. "It's nothing. Stupid stuff."

"Hey, come on. I don't judge."

A faint blush painted Charlie's cheeks. "Just... someone I thought was a friend, maybe more...I don't know." He shook his head, letting the hair hide his eyes, but Ian saw the fiery burn of his blush.

"A guy? Charlie, you know you can talk to me about it."

"Yeah?" He propped his chin in the palms of his hands, defiance sparking in his eyes. "You're okay with me talking about boyfriends, but that one time in the basement when you came a little too close to me, you told me you weren't 'gay or anything.' So write me another story."

Shame, an emotion Ian wasn't too familiar with, coursed through him, and a painful knot tightened in his chest. "I was an idiot, okay? It was a dumbass thing to say." Especially lately, with his emotions jumbled and all over the place. Ian didn't have many regrets in life, but those words were quickly turning out to be his biggest.

Charlie cocked his head, listening, but didn't respond, and Ian, desperate not to have the evening end before it even began, made a fist and rested his hand on top of the table.

"I'm sorry. I was wrong, and it just came out of my mouth. Sometimes I say stupid things without meaning to. I haven't seen you all week, and I figured maybe you needed a friend. I dunno what else to say."

Making rings with his glass on the scarred wooden tabletop, Charlie responded in a voice so low, Ian had to lean over to hear, and he caught a whiff of the man's shampoo and aftershave.

"I don't really know what that is. I've never had real friends."

"Well," Ian said, knocking his foot against Charlie's under the table, surprising him into meeting Ian's eyes. "You can talk to me. I'm your friend."

"Moving around every year or so made it hard, you know? Kids didn't want to make friends with the poor kid. I had no money to go to the movies or hang out after school. Parties would happen on the weekend, but I wouldn't get invited."

"That sucks. I know." Ian tried to offer him comfort.

Charlie met his gaze with a frankness that took Ian's breath away. "No, I don't think you do. I can see you had an amazing childhood, and I don't begrudge you that. But you don't know about loneliness. You have no idea what it's like to grab on to a stranger you think might really like you and want to be your friend, or more, only to find out it was—you were—a joke to them."

Sick to his stomach, Ian poured Charlie another beer and pushed it toward him. "Drink it. And you're right. I don't know. I'm one of the lucky ones, so I'm not going to sugarcoat it and lie to you. 'Cause friends don't lie." He jabbed his finger at Charlie's surprised face. "But you made it out, Charlie. I hear enough stories and see the news enough to know that many, if not most people, don't make it out with their head on straight. But you did. So you won, man."

"It doesn't feel like it." He sipped his beer and hung his head.

"I'm not sayin' it's been easy for you. Don't get me wrong. As for those guys who treated you badly, fuck them. They don't know what they're missing." He hated the thought of anyone hurting Charlie, and that included Ian himself. "I don't want you to think I'm like that."

"I don't. But also…it's not the same. The guys I got with are gay, so there were different expectations there. You're straight."

"Right. I am. Straight." So straight, he'd spent the past week wondering what it would be like to kiss another guy.

"We can change the subject, you know. I don't wanna spend the whole evening talking about my failed love life."

They each ate another slice, but Ian barely tasted his. "I never understood why people gotta be nasty when they break up. It's as easy to be kind about it as it is to be a tool, so why not be a nice person?"

Charlie snorted. "A knight in shining armor, aren't you?"

"No." He leaned forward, close enough that Charlie's golden glow enveloped them both. Charlie's green eyes widened, and Ian's breath caught, a rush of pleasure soaking through him, settling in his bones. "Just someone who doesn't like to see a person who doesn't deserve it get used. In other words, a friend. And friends always have each other's backs. No matter what. So get used to it, 'cause you're stuck with me. I'm here now."

Charlie blinked, and the cloud of uncertainty in his eyes vanished. "Yeah, I guess you are."

"Anything else? You feel okay? Last time I saw you, you said your chest hurt. Did you get it checked out?"

Charlie nodded and spoke around a mouthful of pizza. "I went to Urgent Care, and they said it was probably anxiety coupled with lack of sleep. I feel better now.

Thanks."

"Good."

They finished their pizza, and the three beers he'd drunk made Ian loose and happy. So much for giving up drinking, like he'd promised himself the weekend before. But with no more sightings of the lady in the television, Ian decided to give himself the night off to enjoy.

Charlie held the door open for him when they left the restaurant, and they waited for an Uber.

"Where're we going?"

"To a club I know in the city."

Ian eyed him. "A gay club?"

"Yeah. Are you all right with that?"

"Sure." What the hell could happen? This was a night for Charlie to hopefully find someone. Ian could be there for support even if his gut crawled with inexplicable tension over the thought of someone kissing Charlie. Maybe it was because he hadn't had sex in a while. "Lead the way."

The car pulled up, and they climbed inside. It took less than twenty minutes to get to Alphabet City, where the club, Bedlam, was located. Ian rarely came to the neighborhood since it'd turned trendy.

"You sure you're okay coming here?" Charlie asked

"Yeah, of course." They shuffled up in the line and finally reached the front. Ian was fascinated, though he tried not to stare. He'd never been to an all-male club.

"Helloo, gorgeous," the bouncer said with a wink as he took Ian's ID. "Where've you been hiding all my life?"

"Uh, Brooklyn?" Ian answered, flashing him a smile in return. "I'm here with my friend."

The bouncer peered at Charlie. "Hey, cutie. Haven't seen you in a while. You picked a good night, but I see you've got your evening covered."

"Nah, Bruce. Ian and I are just friends."

"Mmmhmm." Bruce handed Ian back his license. "Not the first time I've heard that. Go inside and have fun." Another wink, and the big, good-looking blond turned to the next group impatiently waiting.

Ian followed Charlie into the darkened club. The music boomed, and everywhere he looked there were men. Ian had never seen so many in such a crowded space. Some were dressed like him, in a T-shirt and jeans; others wore tank tops, displaying incredible tattoos. Then there were others who had leather straps buckled across their chests, or collars around their necks. The smell of cologne, sweat, and heat enveloped him.

Charlie wiggled his way up to the bar. "What do you want?"

"Anything on tap." Ian leaned over. "I'll get the next round."

A group of men surged up behind him, and not only had Ian found himself pressed against Charlie's ass, but his shoulders overlapped with the man beside him.

"Sorry." Ian gave him an apologetic smile and took the beer Charlie handed him.

"Don't be." The man, in his early forties with a tattoo of a snake wrapped around one muscular bicep, took his hand. "Let's go dance."

"Sorry, but I'm here with my friend."

"He won't mind. Will you, honey?"

Charlie's eyes danced with amusement. "It's okay if you want to, Ian."

Defiantly, Ian set the beer on the bar. "Sure. Why not?"

He followed Snake Arm to the dance floor, where they joined the writhing mass of people. Ian found himself pulled tight to his dance partner, the man's hand cupping his ass.

"You're fucking hot."

"Uh, thanks?" Ian put his hands on the guy's chest and gave him a slight push. "But I'm also straight. Like I said, I'm here with my friend."

"Oh, yeah? He's pretty cute too. I could do both of you. Ever been in a threesome?" The man's white smile gleamed in the flashing lights, but Ian didn't join in the laughter with him. At the thought of this crude man touching Charlie, disgust and anger welled up inside Ian, and he stopped swaying to the music.

"I think I'm done. Thanks for the dance."

"Hey, what'd I say?"

Too much, buddy.

"Nothing."

Ian walked back to Charlie, who'd been watching them as he drank his beer. "Here," he said, handing him the beer Ian had left. "Have fun?"

"Guy was a jerk."

"He hit on you? You're going to have to expect that, Ian. You're good-looking, and guys have never seen you here, so you're fresh meat to them."

He drank his beer down. "I didn't mind him trying to pick me up. It's just…I don't know. He was crude."

"Oh? What'd he say?"

Ian finished his beer and caught the bartender's eye, lifted his cup, and raised two fingers. "He said you were pretty cute and he wouldn't mind a threesome."

Charlie choked on his drink. "You're shitting me."

Ian quirked a brow. "Do I look like it?"

"N-no."

Ian handed the bartender his credit card. "Start a tab, please."

"Whatever you want."

Ian didn't think the club could get any more crowded, but a sudden swell of people filled the room. The bartender slid him over the two he'd ordered, and Ian handed Charlie one. This night was proving to be anything but normal, and as he drank the cold beer, Ian decided it wouldn't hurt to take a walk on the wild side.

"Have you ever?" The words popped out of his mouth before he knew what he was saying.

"Ever what?" Charlie's cheeks flamed, so Ian knew he understood what he'd asked.

"You know"—Ian nudged his shoulder—"been in a threesome."

"No." Looking everywhere but at him, Charlie drank his beer as if it were water. "I'm lucky if I get a twosome."

"Why? You're cute and have a great body. I bet any of these guys would want you."

"Thanks for the props, but it's been getting harder and harder to find someone."

"They're assholes, then. Don't know what they're missing."

Humor lit Charlie's face. "How do you know? You've never been with me."

At his words, something hot slid through Ian's veins, and a vision of Charlie under him appeared before him, so sharp and clear, Ian felt like he could reach out and touch it. He knew, without ever having kissed Charlie, what he would taste like. An uncomfortable ache rose inside him, and his dick swelled to a semi hard-on.

"*You want to kiss him, don't you?*"

He glanced around to see who spoke in his ear, but everyone had their backs to him, facing the stage, where a microphone stand was being set up.

"They're going to do the show now." Charlie craned his neck and pointed to a sign. "They usually have these special events on Friday nights."

"Oh? What kind?" He drank more beer.

"It's called the Hot as Hell contest. They'll take people from the audience, and we get to vote."

"You should enter." Ian couldn't believe the words came out of his mouth. It had to be the beer. But Charlie did look hot. He wore skinny pants and a shirt with a cute bow tie and a vest. On any other guy, the outfit would look stupid, but on Charlie it looked good. He looked like a sexy librarian or something.

"You're crazy. Look at those guys up there. They look like you, more than me."

Three guys stood onstage. One had a shock of wheat-blond hair and a rainbow of tattoos covering his muscular arms; the next was a body-builder type, his oiled, gleaming brown skin and huge biceps on full display in a tight, white sleeveless muscle tee; the third, a tall, lean guy, wore one of those leather get-ups and had piercings up and down his ears, a ring through his nose, and a line of pink running through his dark hair.

"I don't think I look like any of them."

Before he had a chance to answer, a bald man picked up the microphone. "Welcome to Bedlam. How's everyone tonight? I'm Marko, your host with the most."

The crowd clapped and cheered, and Ian joined in. The beers buzzed inside him, and he was swept up in the excitement of the crowd. He might be the only straight guy in the club, but he didn't feel uncomfortable or out of place. He put two fingers in his mouth and whistled.

The host continued. "Tonight we have our famous Hot as Hell contest. We need at least one more entry. Who's it gonna be, boys? Nominate your friend or a stranger. Come on."

"Why don't you try? The prize is a hundred dollars." Charlie poked him in the side. "You can win, I bet."

Ian gulped his beer and wiped his mouth on his hand. "Sure. Why not? I could use the money." He gave Charlie the beer and raised his hand. "I'll do it," he called out as he shouldered his way through the crowd. He ignored the indiscriminate grabs at his ass, the whistles and kisses blown his way, and climbed onstage. The crowd cheered.

"Well, hey, handsome. Never seen you before. " Marko ran his hand over Ian's arm. "What's your name?"

"Ian."

"Mmm, listen up, everyone," Marko purred into the mike. "Say hello to sexy Ian."

More wolf whistles and catcalls sounded from the crowd. His head spun, but Ian found Charlie leaning up against the bar and smiled at him.

"Who you smiling for, handsome?"

"My friend Charlie over there. We came together."

"Aww, he's a cutie. Bet you'll be coming together later tonight too." Marko nudged him.

Ian opened his mouth to correct the man but decided not to bother. Why should he? He was having more fun tonight than he could remember having with either his friends or Deena.

Whatever will be, will be.

Chapter Nine

Charlie was in trouble.

His week had been such a shit fest. After that failed threesome attempt, Bryan had come to the store, and in front of everyone—Mona *and* customers—called him a freak and a weirdo and told him not to ever come near him again. It transported him back to the days of foster care when none of the kids wanted to be his friend and called him names because he didn't have a real mother or father. Not that he'd ever stayed in one place long enough for it to matter, anyway. The only good thing that week had been the appointment with the doctor. At least nothing was physically wrong with him.

But then came Ian, busting into his life with his good-natured charm and smile, trying to be his friend, and it had become impossible to keep him at arm's length. Charlie never thought Ian would be willing to go to a club like Bedlam, but here they were, and Ian was hotter than ever.

A jolt pushed him forward, almost to the front of the room, moving him so fast, his feet skimmed the floor. Ian's eyes widened with shock as their gazes met.

What the fuck? Charlie stared into his cup, wondering if someone had slipped something into his drink.

Marko continued. "The contest is very simple. Each man will step up, take off his shirt, and strike a pose. You all clap, and the one who gets the most and loudest claps wins. Easy, right?"

The crowd roared.

"Yeah!"

"Get the show started!"

"Oh, and one more thing. Each contestant has to finish one of our famous Bedlam Bowls. It's a secret concoction, with a combination of ingredients only our gorgeous bartenders know." Marko paused before Ian and flung an arm around his neck, and Charlie felt a growl escape his lips.

"He shouldn't be touching Ian. No one should touch Ian but you, Charlie," a voice spoke in his ear, startling Charlie. He glanced around, but he was shoulder to shoulder with the rest of the crowd.

Marko asked Ian, "Do you think you'll have a problem finishing the Bedlam Bowl?"

"Not at all."

"Mmm, I bet you don't have a problem swallowing anything you put in your mouth."

The crowd roared again, and Charlie almost choked.

Marko walked the line, asking the other three

contestants the same question. None of them had an issue with drinking a Bedlam Bowl. "Okay, people, it's time to start the Hot as Hell contest. First up is Franco."

The tattooed blond pulled his shirt off, displaying a waxed chest with an eagle tattoo across it and nipple rings. He walked up and down the stage to whistles and applause and shouts. He swiveled his hips, thrust his pelvis, then returned to his spot, receiving nice applause and cheers.

"Thank you, Franco. Next up is Maurice. Give it up for gorgeous Mo."

Maurice obviously knew how to do the walk. He slowly drew his sleeveless shirt up over his broad chest and rubbed his ripped abdomen. The muscles clenched under all that smooth skin. It shone under the lights, and Maurice smiled.

"Oh, damn, he's so sexy," the man next to Charlie breathed. "Lookit them arms."

Maurice did have an amazing set of guns he flexed and showed off. The applause rose, and people screamed, and Charlie couldn't imagine anyone else getting a bigger reception.

"Whew. Thank you, Maurice. I need a moment." Marko fanned himself with his hand. "Now say hello to Tyler."

The tall guy in the leather harness undulated his hips, showing off the bulge in his skin-tight leggings, and flicked his nipples. The crowd yelled their pleasure, and Charlie's heart pounded. Ian was next, and he wondered what the man would do. Ian had studied each contestant, and Charlie knew he had something outrageous planned.

Tyler returned to his place, and Marko faced Ian. "Now we have the sexy Ian. Give it up for our newcomer. Ian's a virgin...at least to Bedlam."

Ian hooked his thumbs in his jeans and sauntered to the center of the stage. His hips swayed side to side, and he smoothed his hands over his abs and chest. In a deliberate, unhurried motion, he pulled the T-shirt up and over his head while pumping his hips.

"Damn." Charlie's neighbor exhaled a huge appreciative sigh, and Charlie had to agree.

Ian's pelvis began a rolling motion. To catcalls and whistles, he popped open the tab of his jeans, hesitated a second, then unzipped them halfway. That dark happy trail reached below the elastic of his briefs, and Ian brushed his fingers over the waistband, then teasingly dipped inside. Charlie could see the outline of Ian's dick. It was a big one.

"Oh my God," Charlie whimpered. His pants grew tight, and for once he was thankful for the dense crowd as he touched his crotch to discreetly adjust himself.

A lazy, wicked smile teased at Ian's lips, and his blue eyes glowed as he trailed his fingers around his chest, again flirting with the thin trail of dark hair. The jeans lowered to reveal the waistband of his briefs.

Thunderous applause shook the club, and people around Charlie were screaming themselves hoarse as Ian strolled back to his place, his jeans hanging dangerously low on his hips. A gorgeous bartender appeared with a tray of drinks in deep globe glasses. Ian took his; then the rest of the men followed until they all stood with glasses in hand.

Marko brought the mic to his lips and held up his drink. "Once everyone finishes their Bedlams, we'll have the final judging. Now be careful, boys. They go down sweet but pack a punch." He snickered. "Like you all do, I'm imagining."

"I'd like to go down sweet on that Ian," Charlie heard

the guy in front of him cackle to his neighbor. The crowd was now so jam-packed, it was impossible to not overhear everyone's conversations. "Look at him. He's hung like a fucking horse. I want a taste of that before I leave tonight."

Anger bubbled inside Charlie.

"*They all want him, but only you can have him,*" that reedy voice spoke in Charlie's ear again. "*Make sure you get him this time.*"

It took less than five minutes for the men to finish their drinks. Swaying a bit, Ian stood next to Marko, face flushed, one hip cocked. He'd zipped up his jeans but left the button popped. Glittering blue eyes met his, and Charlie thought he might be drunk himself as desire flooded him, lighting up every nerve ending under his skin. Even the brush of his shirt against his nipples sent tingles shooting like fireworks. All thoughts of keeping his distance floated away like feathers in the wind. Charlie could almost taste Ian and smell his skin. Struggling for self-control, Charlie clenched his hands into fists.

"Are we ready to vote?" Marko cried out. "Let's start with Franco."

Applause and hoots came from the audience.

"Thank you, everyone. Now for our delicious Maurice."

Loud cries and yelling hit Charlie's ears. Ian didn't seem concerned and continued to slouch with that half smile tilting his lips.

"How about Tyler?"

Cries and whistling rose around him.

"And last but definitely not least, our virgin, Ian."

At the bright flash of Ian's smile, the crowd went wild. Several men tossed their shirts up onstage, and rhythmic clapping began with the chant: "E-yan! E-yan!"

Clearly loving the spotlight, Ian bowed and almost fell forward, Marko catching him before he hit the ground. "Easy does it, honey."

"I'm good," he said.

"I'll bet you are. And you are the winner. You win the one-hundred-dollar prize from Bedlam. All right, everyone. Enjoy the night and say hello to your new Mister Hot as Hell."

The other contestants grouped around Ian and gave him hugs, kisses, and a few random squeezes. The crowd near the stage dissipated, but Charlie remained. Waiting.

Ian extracted himself from the other men and hopped off the stage to reach Charlie. "I won the money," he exclaimed, voice slightly slurred from the drink.

"I know."

People milled around them, slapping Ian on the back, congratulating him. Ian brushed them off, his gaze fixed firmly on Charlie. Those blue eyes glowed bright, and his lips were pink, soft-looking, and shiny from the sticky sweetness of the drink.

"Did you think I was hot as hell?"

It's the drink talking. He doesn't know what he's saying.

"You did a great job. Everyone loved you."

"Here you go, lover boy. Another one on the house. It'll keep the hair on your chest." Marko pressed another of those Bedlam drinks into Ian's hands, and Ian drank most of it before Charlie took it away.

"Whoa. Those are killer. Take it easy."

"Hey," he whined and licked his lips. "Gimme back."

Charlie opened his mouth to answer, but the man

who'd earlier expressed his desire to suck Ian's dick grabbed Ian around the neck.

"You're fucking hot. Gave me a hard-on just watchin' you."

Perhaps his reflexes were slowed by the drink, but Ian didn't pull away, and the man, obviously taking that as a positive sign, kissed him, shoving his tongue into Ian's mouth. Rage thundered through Charlie, and a red haze descended over his eyes as he watched the man ravage Ian.

No. Ian's mine. I want him. The cup he held flew out of his hand and dumped the dregs over the man's head, causing him to pull away from Ian and sputter with rage.

"Who the fuck did that?" He wiped his face, and his small eyes narrowed. "Never mind. Come on with me."

"Don't worry. Wait."

"God, you're so hot." The man grabbed hold of Ian and kissed him again, but this time he pulled away in disgust and spit on the floor. "Argh. You taste like puke. You throw up in your mouth? Get the fuck outta here." He spit again and grabbed a beer out of his friend's hand, taking a long swig before stomping away.

Ian stood swaying, seemingly unaware of what had occurred. Smiling, he touched his lips, and Charlie ached to feel them on his own.

"Ian, you okay?"

Looking cute and sexy as hell, Ian blinked and stared at him. "Mmm, yeah. I was good, right, Charlie?"

"Yeah, Ian. You were great. You heard the applause."

Ian's eyes lit up. "Yeah." Ian took a few shuffling steps toward the bar but stopped to lean against the wall. The music pounded around them, and though at least three men stopped by to congratulate and flirt with Ian, he only smiled at them. Charlie wondered if Ian felt uncomfortable and wanted to leave. Shoulder to shoulder, he stayed at his side, waiting for him to speak and tell Charlie what he wanted to do next.

"Lemme buy you a drink, now that I'm flush."

"No, it's okay. I'm good."

"I bet you are." Ian snickered and nudged him. "Why don't you have a boyfriend?"

He couldn't help his stupid heart jumping at Ian's words. "Why don't you have a girlfriend? You're gorgeous and funny and have tons of friends."

"I've had lots of girlfriends, but they don't do it for me," Ian murmured, closing his eyes. He swayed closer. Dangerously close. His head fell to meet Charlie's, and Charlie almost moaned at the smell of Ian, a combination of earthy cologne and tangy sweat.

All man.

Ian's stubbled cheek rubbed his, and all Charlie needed to do was move a fraction of an inch, and his lips would touch Ian's.

"They don't?" Charlie whispered.

Ian's cheek rested by his and Charlie froze, trying to be strong, but his entire body vibrated with need. The need to touch Ian. The need to kiss him.

"Charlie, I've been thinking about you all week." Ian breathed and kissed him, sending his world up in flames. Ian's strong body pinned him to the wall, and Charlie lost track of everything except the feel of Ian's T-shirt between his grasping fingers, the slick sweetness of Ian's tongue sweeping through his mouth to rub against Charlie's own, and the incredible heat pouring off him to soak into Charlie. Their bodies molded together, and what he felt wasn't wishful thinking on his part. The thick bulge of

Ian's erection thrust into his groin. Charlie whimpered and rocked his hips.

"Charlie...oh, damn. Oh, shit." Ian rolled his pelvis, thrusting his hips faster. His hands clamped down on Charlie's shoulders, and his eyes squeezed shut tight as they moved together. If Charlie didn't stop this, they'd be having sex right there in the club. Ian didn't want Charlie. He was drunk, and anyone there for the taking would have sufficed.

"Ian, stop. Ian." Charlie gave him a push, and Ian stumbled back, breathing hard and wild-eyed.

He blinked and stared incredulously at Charlie. "Oh shit, I'm sorry. I-I don't know what I was thinking. I'm sorry, Charlie." His gaze fell to the obvious outline of Charlie's dick in his thin linen pants, and his eyes widened. "Maybe...maybe we should go."

Charlie's cheeks burned as he tried to gather his composure. "It's okay. I know you're a little drunk."

Ian adjusted his crotch. "Yeah, but I don't want you to be mad at me."

Charlie couldn't help his lips twitching up in a smile. "I'm not." And it was true. He wasn't mad at Ian. People got caught up in the moment, and with all the alcohol in his system, Ian had let his libido take control. "I know you didn't mean it." He licked his lips, tasting the sweetness of the drink and Ian. His mouth felt bruised and sore and wonderfully alive.

Ian raked his hand through his hair, smoothing the inky strands. Blue eyes captured his, and his heart began to pound as Ian studied him before answering. The man was so delicious-looking with his full red lips and those strong arms Charlie wanted to sink into. This had been such a mistake. Ian, his straight friend, was front and center in his fantasies, blowing away every other man Charlie had been with.

Ian set his hand on the wall by Charlie's head, his strong arm caging him in. "I'm not so sure. What if I do?"

Stunned, Charlie blinked, his jaw hanging open. "Not sure about what? Do what? You're not making sense."

What he expected was Ian to blow it off with a laugh and a joke, blaming the strong drinks. Instead, Ian's gaze traveled up and down his body, and Charlie sprang to life.

"Not here," Ian said, a bit more confident in his speech. "Let's go to your house. We can talk better there."

"Take him home with you, Charlie. It's his home too," that same reedy voice whispered.

So Charlie allowed Ian to take him by the hand, and then he waited while Ian paid his tab, received his winnings from the contest, and got more congratulatory hugs and kisses, which Charlie knew were merely an excuse for the men to touch him. It got Charlie's back up when he saw the men cop a feel or try and slip their tongue into Ian's mouth. He vibrated with anger and wanted to scratch their eyes out. They had no right to touch Ian. To kiss him. Charlie couldn't understand the emotions battering him. He'd fought them until tonight, when he'd let the armor slip.

"That was fun," Ian said when they were finally in an Uber, going home. "I can't believe I won." He yawned and scratched his stomach, leaving his hand to rest on his bare skin. Charlie forced his gaze away from temptation.

"I can. You were the best."

Ian's head lolled against the backrest. "You're only saying that because you're my friend. Did you have a good time? That's why we came here, but I didn't see you talk to anyone."

Remaining silent, Charlie allowed the car to carry them

through the streets, only speaking when they approached the Brooklyn Bridge. "I didn't see anyone. And I had a good time watching you. Really."

Ian said nothing until the car let them out in front of Charlie's house. "Can I come in?"

Nodding, he walked up the stairs, Ian on his heels. His hand shook, and it took him a second to slide the key into the lock. Once inside, he turned on the hall light, and a soft, golden glow shone down on them. Charlie felt different once he stepped through the doorway, as if the house infused him with a superpowered charge of strength. He could hold off Ian. Really.

"Want some water? I think we've both had enough to drink." Charlie headed to the kitchen.

"I know I have," Ian mumbled and rubbed the back of his neck, following in his wake.

Charlie, about to hand Ian a glass filled with ice water from the refrigerator, set it on the counter. "Look. You don't have to say it. I know you were drunk and got carried away and that's the only reason you kissed me. It's okay. You don't have to worry that I'm gonna get all caught up in a crush on you or—*mmph*."

Ian slammed his mouth over Charlie's, and there was no denying that this second kiss was even more spectacular than the first.

Chapter Ten

Sweet. So damn sweet.

The man tasted like honey and sweet cherries. Ian held on to Charlie's trembling body and drank from his delicious mouth. It wasn't a fluke, he decided hazily as he sucked and licked Charlie's velvety-soft tongue. The cheek brushing his rasped rough with stubble, and Charlie's muscled chest pressed hard and firm, but though unaccustomed to either, Ian didn't care. *Finally*, a kiss that ignited a fire inside him. A kiss that unleashed a hunger in him to take and possess, not walk away and forget. No one could convince him that this fucking kiss wasn't exploding his brain.

This kiss was with a man, and Ian didn't give one flying fuck.

"Goddamn," he muttered into Charlie's silky hair. Breathing hard, Ian looked up in a daze to see them both now enveloped in the soft glowing light. Hesitantly, he reached out, and when his fingers touched the light, that same curious warmth as before soaked through him, as if he stood in a summer rain, with his face held up to the sky.

"Ian," Charlie spoke into his neck. "What's happening?"

"I don't know. But do you feel it?"

"Not sure what 'it' is, but I feel something."

"I'll bet you do." He chuckled. His dick was hard as a rock.

Charlie snorted. "Not that, idiot. The light. What does it mean?"

"Not a damn clue."

The urge to hold Charlie closer hit him, so he did, molding himself to the other man, their bodies fitting together, filling the yawning emptiness inside him. Before his brain could fit the puzzle pieces of the crazy night together, a silvery light brightened the room, and the hairs on Ian's arms and the back of his neck rose.

"What's that?" He pushed Charlie away, and the two of them stood watching as a shimmering curtain lowered from the ceiling to hover in front of them. Then by some means Ian couldn't figure out, an elderly lady appeared. Her hair was tucked under a Little Miss Muffet hat, and her old-fashioned gown looked like she belonged on the cover of one of those boring books he was forced to read in high school. Silver-rimmed glasses perched on the tip of her nose, and her unblinking gaze pierced right through him.

Shit. It was the woman from the television set and Charlie's mirror. God, he hoped he didn't pee in his pants.

Charlie clutched his arm, but Ian was just as freaked out.

"What the fuck is going on?" Ian hissed to Charlie.

"I don't know."

"*Charlie and Ian,*" the woman said. "*Sit down. It's time we talked.*"

"Who are you?" he asked, trying to bluster through his fear.

"*That'll come,*" she said. "*Now sit.*"

And before Ian could answer, he and Charlie pretty much flew across the room to the chairs at the kitchen table. Charlie's hand crept into his, and he squeezed it without taking his eyes off the shimmery figure.

"*Good. Now, my name is Rachel Warren.*"

"Okay…" Tilting his head with obvious confusion, Charlie said, "I don't know that name. What's going on?"

"*It doesn't matter.*" She dismissed his concern. "*I've been waiting for you, Charlie. All these years. Waiting for you to come home.*"

"W-waiting for wh-what?" Charlie asked. "What're you talking about?"

"*Why,*" she said with a smile, "*for you to meet your young man.*" She raised a ghostly arm and pointed to Ian.

Charlie's mouth fell open. "Ian? He's not my boyfriend. We aren't together."

"*From what I saw before, you certainly looked like you were.*" Her merry laughter rang out in the kitchen. "*What about that risqué nightclub you came home from?*" She looked down her nose and shook her finger at them. "*Very naughty boys.*"

"I don't believe this. I'm getting scolded by a ghost? A ghost? This shit is crazy." Ian jumped out of his chair. "I'm drunk, right? Either that, or I'm high. That's it, isn't it? I'm stoned and seeing things." He glanced around wildly, as if the kitchen cabinets held the secret instead of dishes.

He faced Charlie, who'd remained seated, those big green eyes fixed on the ghostly figure hovering above the ground.

"This isn't really happening. I'm dreaming."

"N-no, you're not," Charlie said quietly. "This is really happening."

"You're crazy. As crazy as everything else around here. I'm going home." Ian turned to leave but found himself unable to lift his feet from the floor.

"*Stop.*" Ghostly Grandma pointed at him, then moved her finger to the chair he'd vacated, and he flew into it and sat down with a *whoosh* of expelled breath. "*Now both of you listen to me. This is happening. Charlie isn't crazy, and neither are you.*"

"But there's no such thing as ghosts," Ian said.

She smiled. "*Oh, we like people to think that. If everyone could see us, we wouldn't be so special. But make no mistake. We're here all the time.*" Ian's cheeks burned at her insinuation.

"It's impossible," Ian said stubbornly. "I don't believe it. Any of it."

"*Why do you think Charlie has a golden glow around him only you can see?*" Her smile broadened. "*Didn't you wonder why that was?*"

Ian's eyes widened. "That's you?"

"*No, that's you.*"

Ian opened his mouth, then closed it with a *snap* and a shake of his head. "I don't understand." A quick glance at Charlie showed the golden glow always shimmering around him blazing with a brighter intensity. A strange, discomforting need to protect Charlie rose through Ian as if he were some Viking warrior. He wouldn't let Charlie be hurt. Not like those other guys before. Not ever again.

"*You will,*" she said mysteriously. "*You've both been listening to my stories. Together and separately.*"

Ian's head whirled. "You've seen stuff too? In the television?"

"N-no," Charlie whispered. "In the mirror. I've seen things in the mirror. Like that other night."

"*The story has only just begun, but by the end, you'll know what you have to do.*"

"What do you mean, what we have to do?" Charlie cried out. "What are you talking about?"

But of course she only smiled, and then began to rise up, until she hovered above them. "*Listen and learn from the stories that couldn't be told. We'll talk again.*"

Before either of them had a chance to speak, she was gone, enveloped by the shimmering silver light that vanished in the blink of an eye, leaving them sitting and staring at each other in the empty kitchen. Charlie blinked nervously.

"What the fuck was that, Charlie? You wanna tell me what the hell is going on here?" Cautiously, he tried to stand, and relieved he was able to move his legs, he shifted away from Charlie. It hurt him to see Charlie's mouth droop and his eyes turn shiny, but this whole situation was creeping him out, and he needed answers.

"I-I don't know." Charlie balled his hands into fists on top of his knees. "Something bizarre's been happening here since I moved in. Even before."

Despite himself, Ian couldn't help being curious. "What do you mean, even before?"

"At the lawyer's office, when I picked up the keys to this house, they, um…" His fingers laced and unlaced in his lap. "They glowed."

"Glowed?" Ian cocked his head. "I don't get it. Like one of those glow-in-the-dark key chains you see?"

Charlie nodded solemnly. "Kind of, but brighter. Like, they sat in the palm of his hand, and when I reached out to pick them up, they glowed. But the lawyer didn't see it happen or feel anything strange. I thought it was a trick of the light, but now with everything else that's been happening…"

Ghosts didn't exist. Except, apparently, they did to him and Charlie. In his television set and in Charlie's mirror.

"Other stuff, you said. Like what?"

Miserable, Charlie covered his face with his hands. "Remember I told you that the first time I came to the house, I was with this guy I used to hang out with? We started to fool around—"

Unbidden, a growl burst from his mouth. "I don't wanna hear this."

Red-cheeked, Charlie kept his gaze trained to the floor. "Okay. Well, we were together, and the chandelier began to swing and the mirror fell off the wall. But I also saw her. That ghost."

Ian stared at him. "You did? Are you sure?"

"Yeah. And then when I had the date with Morgan, the same thing. In fact, every time I've tried to be with someone, something crazy happened to keep us apart."

That caught him short. "Hmm." Ian thought back to Savannah, the girl in the club, who ran away from him, and the one in Trader Joe's, who wound up with fruit all over her. "What kind of crazy stuff?"

Charlie said, "As soon as we'd start kissing, doors would slam open and shut, the lights flash on and off, things like that. The guy ended up leaving before anything could happen."

"Good," Ian muttered. "Bastards better keep their hands to themselves."

Charlie stared at him. "Um, Ian?"

"What?" Ian responded, breathing heavily. The thought of these men touching and kissing Charlie set his blood boiling, enough to allow him to push aside the fact that he'd been talking to a ghost earlier. That, he could deal with later. But Charlie kissing someone else? *Fuck, no.*

"Your eyes…they turned all silvery again."

What the hell?

"I wanna see."

He remembered a large gilt mirror in the living room and raced to it. Skidding to a stop, he drew in a deep breath and gazed at his reflection.

"What the fuck?" Charlie was right. Normally bright blue, his eyes were pure silver.

"I told you," Charlie spoke at his side. "They were fine until I mentioned fooling around with Bryan and Morgan."

He grabbed Charlie by the shoulders. "I said I didn't want to hear about that."

"Why?" Charlie tipped his chin up and gazed steadily at him. "It's not like we're dating just because you kissed me. You only did it because you were drunk."

"Oh, yeah?" He ran his fingers down Charlie's jaw and heard the hitch in the man's breath. "Well, guess who's not drunk now?" He brushed his mouth over Charlie's, capturing the moan escaping Charlie's lips with his own.

Again, that sweet oblivion poured through Ian, spreading through his blood like wildfire.

"Oh, God." Ian sighed before again plunging his tongue into Charlie's velvety-smooth mouth. Their tongues swept against each other, licking and tasting, and their teeth clashed as Ian kissed him deeper, with more intensity. "You're so fucking sweet. I can't stop thinking about you. All week, every night."

His eyes shining, Charlie looped his arms around Ian. "Really? I-I thought about you too." He cast his gaze downward, and that adorable shyness made Ian want to pull him closer and kiss him harder.

Ian nuzzled into the curve of Charlie's neck, inhaling the scent of his hot skin. "God, you turn me on."

"I do?"

"You don't believe me? Look." Without taking his eyes from Charlie's, Ian took his hand and held it to his hard-on. Charlie's eyes grew wide. "That's from you. Nobody else. So don't be thinking you don't turn me on."

Ian hoped it would help Charlie's lack of self-confidence, but Charlie said nothing, merely nodded and walked away. Ian followed him back to the kitchen, where Charlie took a seat at the table, and avoiding his eyes, said, "I know you must be freaked out by all this. You can go home if you want."

As if Ian hadn't heard him, he took the seat he'd had before and stretched his legs out. "You know, this afternoon, I was talking to the guys I work with, and my foreman, a big guy, ex-Marine, told me he's bisexual. I gotta tell you, I was surprised. I never would've expected him to say that."

"Why?"

Ian shrugged. "I don't know. I guess I have a prejudice

that Marines, or big tough guys who look like they can break me in half, wouldn't be into getting dick."

"Maybe dick gets into them." Charlie snorted. "Not everyone's a top, you know."

"I don't even know what you're talking about." Ian scowled, hating that he was obviously missing some inside joke. "What I'm trying to say is, I never understood why people said sex was so incredible. It was nice and felt good, but nothing like fireworks. I went along with them because I didn't wanna look stupid. But now I do know what I was missing, 'cause kissing you turned me on like nothing ever has."

Charlie's eyes grew big, and the golden glow burned brighter than he'd ever seen before, almost like a comet shooting across the sky. "I-I don't know what to say to that."

"You don't haveta say anything. It's how I'm feeling. But Charlie, man. What the hell is this ghost shit? Is she trying to say we're like, supposed to be together? Like fate or something?"

"I dunno. I think it's all tied in with that lockbox we found with the death certificate and those pictures."

"I still don't know what any of it means. She keeps talking, but I'm more confused than ever. I don't understand what's going on."

"*You don't?*" Rachel's voice spoke at his ear before she floated past. She hovered in front of them, her eyes twinkling.

His heart slammed. "Shit. Give a guy some warning. Stop popping up like this. You're scaring the crap outta me."

"*Language, dear.*" She shook her finger at him. "*Would you like to see more?*"

"Now?" Charlie squinted at him, then at Rachel. "It's after midnight."

"*All the best stuff happens after the clock strikes twelve.*" She giggled. "*Aren't you curious?*"

Charlie nudged him. "What do you think?"

"Might as well ride the crazy train to the last stop. What do we have to lose?" Aside from his mind, that was, but Ian felt *that* train might have already left the station.

Chapter Eleven

His plain, ordinary life had turned upside down and read like he was living inside the pages of a fantasy novel. Instead of Charlie trying to write his own book, this story was unfolding in front of him. All he had to do was take that first step and turn the page.

"Okay, Rachel. Let's do it."

"*Upstairs to the bedroom. The mirror is bigger there, and you'll be more comfortable.*"

"Lead the way." Ian waited by the foot of the back staircase, and when Charlie passed by him, Ian grabbed his arm. "Listen, I don't want you to think I'm pushing you. I just figured with everything that's happened tonight, you might be interested in figuring out what she was talking about as soon as possible."

"You're not. Pushing me, I mean. I am interested. It's just…" He waved his hand in the air. "Everything else tonight…you and me…it's a lot to take in." Charlie glanced at Ian's hand on his arm. With a frown, Ian removed it, and Charlie hated the lost connection.

"We don't have to get into that." Ian paused, then added, "Not tonight, at least."

At the thought of a tomorrow with Ian, a thrill ran through Charlie. "Okay."

They trudged up the stairs and into Charlie's bedroom. Ian sat on the bed, and Charlie's lips tingled as he remembered the feel of Ian's mouth pressed to his.

To distract himself, he retrieved the lockbox. "There are pictures in here, along with the deed and the death certificate." He took out three pictures and put them on the bed. They showed two men in their late teens to early twenties. Charlie guessed the time period was somewhere between 1915 and 1919, as reflected by the clothing—and given the date on the death certificate. One bent-edged photo showed the two men together, arms around each other's shoulders, mugging for the camera. It was faded and cracked, reflecting how often it had been handled.

"They dress like you," Ian pointed out.

"Yeah…" Charlie continued to gaze at the pictures in his hand and the faces from so long ago. A chill came over him, and goose bumps rose on his skin.

Two other pictures had stood out to Charlie. In the first, one of the young men wore a sharply pressed uniform; in the second, the other man stood unsmiling, in a top hat and tux, a young woman by his side in a wedding dress, gazing up at him with adoration in her eyes.

"Can I look at them? It's like a puzzle—a mystery." Ian wiggled his fingers. "Lemme see."

Amused at Ian's interest, Charlie handed him the pictures. "Have at it." He kicked off his shoes, enjoying watching Ian. Because watching Ian was fast becoming one of his favorite things to do.

While Ian studied the three pictures, Charlie sat crossed-legged, surreptitiously watching him, fantasizing what it would feel like to have Ian's dick inside him. Unaware of the dirty thoughts in Charlie's head, Ian flashed him a grin.

"Okay, boys. Are you ready?" Rachel appeared in the mirror.

Ian jumped. "Jesus. I'm never going to get used to this." He moved closer to Charlie, who froze. It was one thing to sit across from Ian and fantasize about him, but now he'd kissed Ian and felt him, and God help him, nothing was more perfect in this world than feeling Ian's big dick thrust against him. Charlie's pulse hammered. God, he wanted him.

"We're ready," Charlie managed to croak out.

Rachel waved her hand, and a young man appeared in the mirror. He was bent over the desk in what Charlie recognized as his bedroom, only the furniture and curtains were different. The young man stared out the window as Charlie often did, and then he picked up a sheet of paper and began to write.

Robert,

I must say, I was surprised by what occurred last evening but not unhappy. Not at all. In fact, just the opposite. I'd long wished your feelings to equal mine, and now that we've spoken, I'm hoping we can continue to explore what it all means. If you are interested, please leave your answer where it all happened."

Yours,

Eddie

The scene faded, and Ian turned to face him. "What do you think it means? The language is pretty stiff. Sounds like one of those old-fashioned books."

"Back then—the early 1900s—people didn't speak as informally as we do. It's a product of the times."

"Okay. But what do you think they were they talking about?"

Something personal must've happened between Robert and Eddie, and if he had to guess, it was sexual.

"Maybe Robert and Eddie kissed? Or touched? Something obviously happened between them, and Eddie wanted to make sure they were on the same page."

"But what about the end? Leave your answer where it happened?"

That stumped him. "Hmm. I don't know." Ian was right. It was like a puzzle to discover. He climbed off the bed and walked to the mirror, which had returned to its normal state. "Rachel? Are you there? Did Robert respond?"

She reappeared. *"He did. Do you want to continue?"*

He peered over his shoulder at Ian, who'd moved to sit at the foot of the bed. "Do you?" He sat next to Ian, prepared to watch the next story.

"Hell, yeah. I wanna find out who these guys are and see what happened."

Charlie knew, even without learning anything further, that this was the story of a doomed love affair. Dim memories rolled through him—laughter and kisses, fear, pain and anger. But always underneath it all, love and longing.

"Whoa, Charlie. Are you okay?"

"What? What's wrong?" But he knew. He could see it in Ian's eyes. How they roamed over him hungrily. Like a wolf after its prey.

"You're all glowing. Like, even your eyes are lit up from the inside. Like emeralds."

Ian reached out and touched Charlie's chin, tracing a fingertip slowly up and down his jawline. "Your skin feels so hot and soft. I never thought another guy would feel like this."

Charlie's vision blurred until Ian's face turned hazy, and desire washed over him. His heartbeat kicked up, and his breath came in short, hard pants. Ian's hand dropped away from his face, and Charlie wanted to grasp it and hold on tight.

"We shouldn't…"

"Sorry. I don't know what happened. Your eyes glowed green, and I…" Ian blew out a harsh breath and shook his head.

"*Are you boys ready?*"

Charlie had forgotten Rachel was waiting, and he met Ian's eyes. "Are we?"

Wide-eyed, Ian chewed his bottom lip. "Yeah, I think so."

"*Very well.*" Once again, Rachel waved her hand in front of the mirror and disappeared.

Another man, in a different room, sat on his bed. He wrote in a notepad, stopping frequently to stare off into space.

Dear Eddie,

You can't imagine how full my heart is right now. But where do we go from here? Do we dare? If we are discovered, I can't imagine the consequences, so we must plan accordingly. See you tomorrow at half past the witching hour under the oak tree."

Always,

Robert

"I recognize that room. It was mine in my parents' house," Ian said, sounding bewildered.

"How sad for them," Charlie said. "Now do you see? They were in love, but because in those days homosexuality was a crime, they were afraid to show anything."

"So Robert lived next door? That means…Eddie lived here, and Robert in my house?" Ian's smooth brow furrowed in thought. "And the oak tree must be the one in my yard."

"I'm sure they left the notes for each other somewhere in that tree. I bet if we look, we'll find a clue."

"Damn." Ian yawned. "We should go look."

"Not tonight. We're both tired and need some sleep, and besides"—he grew more determined, watching an argument brew in Ian's eyes—"it's dark. We'll never be able to see anything. Let's wait until morning. Do you have time?"

The possibility of another day spent with Ian had Charlie on tenterhooks, waiting for his answer. Did he have a date? Was he sorry something had happened between them and now wanted to retreat? And what about Rachel's insinuation that the letters Eddie and Robert wrote to each other meant something to him and Ian? Was it simply because the men from the past had lived in his and Ian's houses?

Suppressing another yawn, Ian nodded. "Yeah, sure. I'm definitely in. You're right. It's been a hell of a night."

"No shit."

A slow smile tilted Ian's lips, and Charlie's heart slammed in hard, painful beats. He became aware of their position on the bed, and his nerves tingled as again, Ian's eyes turned that odd, arresting silver that drew him in like an iron to a magnet. His breathing quickened, and he almost swooned when Ian licked his lips and leaned forward. Charlie swore he could already feel the touch of Ian's lips on his, and his eyes shut in anticipation.

"Don't curse please."

They both jumped at the sound of Rachel's voice, and Ian rolled off the bed.

"Stop doing that," Charlie said irritably. "You're scaring us to death."

Her tinkling laughter surprised Charlie. *"Did I interrupt something? So sorry. Guess whatever was about to happen will have to wait another day."* She floated to the club chair in the corner and sat primly, straight-backed, on the edge.

Incredible. Cock-blocked by a ghost again.

"So what do you think?"

"It was interesting, but we're not really sure what any of it means," Charlie said.

"You will. You'll both figure it out. See you by the tree."

And like mist, she faded away in that silvery, shimmering light Charlie was getting used to, leaving them alone. Charlie rubbed his face as if he could scrub away all the doubt and questions running rampant through his brain. If he were alone, he'd swear all that happened tonight, starting from the club, was his imagination, but with Ian standing by him, blinking and staring at the empty space previously occupied by Rachel, it was reality. As much as talking to a ghost could be considered reality.

"I think I'd better get some sleep, and maybe this will

all make sense in the morning." Ian was out the door before Charlie could respond, and he trailed after the man down the steps to let him out. As eager as Ian had seemed earlier to figure out Robert and Eddie's story, he now couldn't wait to leave.

"Night. See you tomorrow."

"Yeah, sure, okay. Stop by when you're ready," Charlie called out after him, and Ian held his hand up in farewell. He shut the door behind him and leaned against it.

What the hell? Was Ian so freaked out, he'd had enough?

He shook his head and took himself upstairs to bed, with the conviction that he'd most likely be going forward in this quest alone.

* * *

Morning found Charlie drinking orange juice on the deck, with the sun already warm on his shoulders. It was impossible to remain in a bad mood while listening to the birds and knowing that no matter what, this house was his. The insanity of the prior evening had faded, and Charlie had woken up with a new, determined mindset.

Keep away from Ian.

He didn't blame his neighbor. Two of those Bedlam drinks in a short period of time, on top of several beers, could cause anyone to lose their inhibitions, especially a guy like Ian, who, despite what he said, must've had a full and healthy sex life. Enough mistakes with straight-but-curious guys in his past had taught Charlie not to put too much stock in a few hot kisses.

So he stood on the deck, listening to the birds chirping

in the trees, the breeze whispering on his face, and stole a look at the large oak tree in Ian's backyard. If Ian woke up and wasn't interested in finding out more about Robert and Edward's history, Charlie would move on by himself.

"Yo, Charlie."

The screen door banged, as did Charlie's stupid heart. Ian stepped out on his deck in nothing but a pair of boxers that hung so low on his hips, all Charlie's good intentions vanished at the sight of that mouthwatering deep V and the dark trail of hair disappearing beneath the elastic. Charlie raised his eyes to the sky, sending a silent prayer for strength, and tipped his head to his neighbor.

"Hi." *That's good. Light and casual.* He could pretend he was unaffected and not a ball of lust inside.

"I'm gonna take a shower, and after, you wanna go take a look at the tree?"

Was it stupid that his heart did a happy conga dance inside his chest? "Sure. Sounds good."

"Great. Meet you at my front door in fifteen?" Ian downed the cup of coffee in his hand, all his movements strong and authoritative.

"All right," Charlie called out and left the porch. He raced around his bedroom to get dressed, then washed his face and brushed his hair. He decided not to wear his usual vintage clothing, as they'd be grubbing around in the backyard and he didn't want to ruin good linen pants. Instead, he pulled on a pair of basketball shorts, slipped on a T-shirt, and shoved his feet into his battered Converse. With one final glance in the mirror, he picked up a straw skimmer and set it at a jaunty angle on his head, gave his reflection a smile, and walked outside.

Ian was waiting for him on his stoop, and as Charlie passed by, he inhaled Ian's rich scent. God, he wanted to bury himself in that smell of chocolate and coconut and man.

"Um, sleep well last night? Do you have a hangover?"

Ian flashed his now-familiar cocky grin. "Nah. It would take more than that to keep me down. Of course, I popped three extra-strength aspirin and drank a ton of water. Aside from peeing half the night, I feel good. How about you?"

"I'm fine."

Not so much. In truth, Charlie had woken up numerous times from his dreams. Dreams of the shadowy figures of Robert and Edward meeting under the very tree he and Ian approached, plus flashes of the two men sending longing looks at each other over lunchtime at school and dinners at each other's homes. Snapshots in time. It was difficult to fall back asleep with the pictures playing like a movie reel in his head when he closed his eyes.

But there was no time to dwell on the darkness of night when sunshine beamed down on them. Ian's blue eyes sparkled, and Charlie's heart surged, but he deliberately turned away from his neighbor's handsome, smiling face. A bevy of chickadees set up a chorus of cheeping, and with a shake of leaves, departed the tree branches in Charlie's yard, flying to the tall evergreen in Ian's while continuing to scold them. He and Ian stood underneath the spreading arms of the oak tree. The gnarled trunk's width was greater than either his or Ian's torso, with various bumps along its length.

"This is definitely the tree. It's over a hundred years old for sure." Charlie placed a hand on the trunk, as if he searched for a heartbeat.

"What do you think we're looking for?" Like him, Ian ran his hands over the tree trunk. "I played in this tree as a kid and used to climb near to the top." He laughed. "Used to drive my mother crazy. She used to scream that I was gonna fall and break my neck."

"I've never climbed a tree," Charlie confessed. "Only one or two of the foster families I was with had a backyard, and there were never any trees like this."

"Well, feel free to come on over and climb this baby anytime you want."

"Right now I'm more interested in seeing what we can find at ground level."

A large black crow winged down from the sky to perch on the edge of the deck, let out several loud caws, and flapped its wings. Then it cocked its head, flew into the oak tree, and began to caw again. Loudly.

Was the bird trying to tell them something?

Chapter Twelve

Ian had woken up early Saturday morning, not with a throbbing headache from too much to drink, but with a throbbing hard-on from not enough Charlie. Drinking enough water to irrigate the Sahara was bad enough, but dirty dreams of Charlie sucking him off made it doubly hard to relax and fall back asleep.

Staring into the darkness of his bedroom, Ian had rolled to one side, then the other, but he was too restless. He'd figured a tried-and-true jerk-off would settle him enough to fall asleep, so he touched himself. The moment his eyes closed, Charlie's wide, full-lipped mouth popped into his head, and his dick stiffened. He'd never been attracted to a man before, but Ian couldn't deny that it was Charlie he was thinking of when he finally gave in and jerked himself off. He came hard and fast, groaning out loud and seeing stars. He wiped his hand on his boxers and closed his eyes.

When he next awoke it was nine thirty, and feeling immeasurably better, he'd bounced out of bed, and started a wash. He ate breakfast, thinking about his middle-of-the-night jerk-off to Charlie giving him head. Maybe he'd use this time with Charlie to figure out what the hell was going on inside his brain, Ian wasn't used to being confused. In his everyday life he made decisions and took action without hesitating. Charlie made him stop, think, and question, and Ian wasn't too certain he liked it.

But it was Saturday and beautiful out. Ian didn't want to delve too deeply into what happened the previous night and make any quick decisions. Although he was considering buying a new television set.

"If I didn't know any better," Charlie now said, eyeing the crow, "I'd swear it was trying to tell us something."

"Well…" Ian gave the bird a hard stare. A month ago, if you'd told him he'd be standing almost nose to beak, playing come-at-me-bro with a bird, he'd have thought he was high. "Since I don't speak crow, I'll take my chances and look around myself." He got on his knees to start examining the base of the tree.

"What are you doing?"

"I have no idea," he confessed. "But the letter mentioned the tree, so I figured it might hold a clue, like in one of those *Nancy Drew* mysteries."

"Dude. You're kidding, right?" Charlie held his stomach and cackled with laughter.

"What?" Ian blinked. Between the bright sunlight and that golden glow around Charlie, Ian's eyes hurt.

"*Nancy Drew*? Really? You read that shit?"

"Hey, *Nancy Drew* was not shit. I have three sisters.

What do you think I had to read? Besides, don't knock them. They were cool. Nancy was a badass."

"This is the weirdest conversation." Charlie kneeled beside him.

"Really? This is your weirdest? Not the conversation last night with a ghost dressed like a grandma?"

Loud caws split the air.

"Now I got birds on top of me, squawking like it's a fucking Hitchcock movie. I swear if one poops on my head, I'm gonna be pissed." Ian passed his palm over his hair.

Again, laughter burbled out from Charlie as he fell onto the grass. "Oh, my God. You're killing me." He remained on the ground, shaking with hilarity.

Ian ran an assessing gaze over Charlie's long body lying in the green grass that matched his eyes, and with a start, he realized what was different.

"You're not wearing your other clothes."

Charlie propped himself up on his hands. Sunlight glinted off his reddish-brown waves and brightened the hairs on his forearms, adding to the glow that drew Ian in.

"My other cl…oh." He glanced down. "My vintage stuff, you mean. Yeah, well, I didn't want to get them all messed up."

"I didn't think you owned anything normal." As soon as Ian said the words, he wanted to grab them back at the hurt in Charlie's eyes. Ian rushed to apologize. "I'm sorry. I didn't mean—"

"Yeah, you did," Charlie said stiffly. "But it's not the first time I've heard it. It doesn't bother me. It's who I am. Like some guys wear makeup or are covered in tattoos. I like vintage clothes." Averting his eyes, Charlie stood and propped himself against the tree. His head hung low, gaze fixed on the grass at his feet. "Can we do what we came for, or would you rather not? You don't have to anymore if it's not your thing. I understand. You probably have better things to do with your Saturday."

Rarely had Ian regretted his words more than at that moment. "No, I can't forget. It was a stupid thing to say, and I'm owning up to it. I thought you only owned your funky kind of stuff. So I apologize." He held out his hand. "Forgive me?"

Charlie's gaze flickered upward, and at the darkness he saw, something painful twisted inside him.

"Okay," Charlie said. "Sorry if I'm touchy. I already told you I got made fun of a lot growing up. It wasn't only 'cause I was a foster kid, but I dressed like this in high school. Some kids were goth. I was vintage. So the popular kids would call me weirdo and all sorts of other names. I thought I'd put it behind me, but…" He shrugged. "Anyway, apology accepted."

Charlie grasped Ian's hand, and that same peculiar warmth seeped through Ian as when they'd touched before. He wanted to hold on, but Charlie let go and moved away.

"Let's start for real."

He allowed Charlie to take the lead, and together they circled the big tree, stepping over the exposed roots. Ian didn't expect to find anything. After all, the scenes Rachel played for them concerned events that occurred over one hundred years earlier. Still, you never knew.

That crow continued to squawk its ass off, and soon, another, slightly smaller one joined it on the tree branch. Ian wondered if it was its mate.

And that was how Ian knew he'd gone off the deep end, when on a beautiful Saturday morning he was feeling up a tree, thinking about two dead gay guys and crows rather than hanging out with his friends, watching the ball game. Yet, he mused, watching Charlie stop closer to the trunk to examine something, he had no desire to be anywhere else.

How fucked up in the head was he?

"Ian, c'mere. Look at this."

"Hmm? What?" Ian shook himself out of his headspace to see Charlie pointing.

"C'mere." Charlie's nose was almost pressed against the trunk, while his fingers traced something.

"What?" Standing at Charlie's shoulder, Ian peered at where his fingers rested. "I don't see anything."

"No? There are two sets of initials carved into the trunk. See?" His fingers traced along the edges.

"Really?" Ian squinted and reached out himself. "Lemme see." His fingers replaced Charlie's, and he trailed along the outline of ragged bark. "Hmm, yeah. I see what you mean. This feels like an *E*, and the one underneath is…" He moved down. "An *R*. So?" His gaze found Charlie's. "What do you think it means?"

"Don't you see?" Excitement rose in Charlie's voice. "The *E* is for Edward, and the *R* for Robert. They carved their initials in it. They couldn't show it to the outside world, and it might've been the only way they could immortalize being together."

"Yeah, maybe. That's kind of sad if it's true, you know?"

"If it's true?" Charlie rested against the tree. "Not like it's anything new. I mean, it still happens today even when it's legal, so imagine how they felt, knowing they could be arrested if they were caught. Or worse."

"I still can't believe they used to arrest people."

"Arrested them and worse. When it doesn't affect you personally, I guess it's easy to remain ignorant," Charlie answered softly, and the heat of embarrassment rose in Ian's face.

"Guess so, but it doesn't mean I'm not willing to learn." Ian rested his fingers on the carved initials, and something deep inside him shifted.

Loud cawing startled him, and he peered around the tree. The birds sat on the deck, but the backyard had darkened to almost nighttime.

"Holy shit. Charlie. What the fuck is happening?"

"I…I d-don't know."

Ian grasped his arm to hold him near, and he was kidding himself if he thought it was only to protect Charlie. He was pretty damned freaked out but couldn't stop watching.

Nighttime, and in the thick blackness, Robert stood beneath the sheltering tree. A shadow entered through the row of hedges separating his yard from the one next door. Heart pounding, Robert melted into the shadows and flattened himself against the tree.

"Robert." The whisper carried in the breeze. "It's me."

Eddie crossed the yard, and when he reached the tree, entered his embrace. Their lips met in a kiss.

A shiver ran through Ian's bones. He'd felt that kiss. Felt it in his mouth, on his tongue, in his blood.

"Ian?" Charlie peered into his face. "You okay?"

He blinked. All had gone back to normal. His backyard was once again sunny and bright. Relief poured through him. "I think so. Are you?"

"Yeah. They kept it a secret during the day, and this is

how they'd meet. I guess the fence between our properties was put in later."

Before Ian had a chance to answer, the crows let out screeches and flew away. He and Charlie watched until they became two black specks and disappeared into the sky.

"Do you want to come over and figure out what to do next? We can have something to eat too? If you don't have plans."

"Sure. I was hoping you'd say that. I'm starving."

They left the leafy coolness of the oak tree and trudged across his yard to Charlie's house. Ian wondered what else their search would bring, with the history they were delving into, plus the unfinished business simmering between him and Charlie.

Chapter Thirteen

Perhaps bringing Ian into his house again was a risk, but Charlie had woken up with a renewed sense of purpose. What was the importance of the two men to both him and Ian, and why was Rachel pushing them to figure out a hundred-year-old story? Why was she pushing them together in the first place? It puzzled Charlie, as he and Ian were strangers, and although he'd spent the better part of his morning wracking his brains, trying to figure out the connection, he'd come up blank.

Meanwhile, here Ian stood at his kitchen table, relaxed and smiling, looking like a snack he'd like to take a bite out of. Charlie opened the refrigerator and stared blindly at the shelves.

"What were you thinking?"

He jumped at the voice over his shoulder. "Um, I don't know." Truth, because he didn't have much food and didn't know how to cook anyway beyond boiling pasta or boxed mac-and-cheese.

"How about if I make us something?" Ian stuck his head into the fridge and began pulling out eggs and milk. "You have bread, right?"

"Yeah, sure."

"I make a mean French toast. Wait'll you taste it."

"Sure, but you don't have to."

"I know I don't, but I'm hungry." Ian opened the cabinet door and took out a bowl. "You have a frying pan?"

"Yeah, of course. It's on the stove."

"Okay. So while I'm making the food, you can figure out what comes next. I gotta go home and look at some stuff for my job—I'm starting a new project, and I have to learn the ropes—but we can at least begin to figure out what happened between Robert and Eddie."

Oh, Charlie had a pretty good idea what happened. "Where's your new job?"

"By the Barclays Center. A reno of a block of town homes."

"Yeah? I work right near there."

"You do?" Ian grinned. "Maybe I'll have to stop by."

"Yeah. Maybe you should. We could, uh, walk home together or something. Maybe pool resources for food shopping."

Charlie had never really had a friendship, so he wasn't sure he was doing this thing right. Did that sound weird? Or like he was flirting? They hadn't really talked about the kiss between them at the club or after, and Charlie wondered if it would be chalked up to Ian being drunk.

Leaving Ian to the cooking, he cleaned up a little and grabbed his laptop. Maybe they could google the two men and find out other information. Along with the pictures and death certificate, he set the computer on the dining-room table, then stopped at the entrance of the kitchen to sniff at the delicious aroma that hit him.

"Oh my God, what is that?"

Face alight with a smile, Ian turned to him with a dishcloth over his shoulder and a spatula in hand, in a scene so domestic, Charlie had to mentally kick himself from wishing it could be a possibility every day.

"I told you, French toast. My favorite meal. Breakfast for lunch."

"Dude, that is not like any French toast I've ever had."

"I make it sexy. Just you wait."

I'll bet you do.

Ian made every damn thing sexy. Charlie slid into his seat at the kitchen table and watched the show. The man wasn't kidding—he knew his way around a stove. Ian placed a pat of butter in the frying pan, and when it sizzled and spread out, he placed the egg-soaked bread on it. Charlie sniffed appreciatively.

"I smell cinnamon and something else."

"My secret ingredients." He waggled his dark brows, the bright blue of his eyes gleaming with laughter. Expertly, he flipped the piece in the pan, and when it was done, slid it on a plate, replacing it with another. Six slices later, the show was unfortunately over, and Ian placed a plate with three slices in front of Charlie and another in front of himself. Charlie's stomach growled.

"This looks and smells amazing."

"I'll get the syrup and OJ." Without waiting for Charlie

to tell him where the items were, Ian bounced over to the refrigerator and took them out.

Charlie doused his food with syrup and took a big bite. Bliss slid through him. "Oh God, that's so freaking good. *Mmm*. It's almost like cake."

"Yeah. My mom taught me how to do it."

Charlie plowed through his food, and when he finished, slid his finger through the crumbs and sticky syrup on his plate, wiping it clean. "Mmm…" He released a happy sigh of contentment. "That was *delicious*."

Ian's smile brightened the kitchen. "Thanks. I haven't cooked in a while. When it's just me, myself, and I, there's no need. I eat mostly sandwiches or cereal."

"Yeah, I'm addicted to the little blue box myself."

Ian wrinkled his nose. "Yuck. My mom wouldn't let us eat that. She made her own."

"Well, lucky you," Charlie said lightly and brought his plate to the dishwasher. "I didn't have that luxury. Sometimes I was lucky to get anything to eat." *Shit. Why did I say that?* The last thing he wanted to do was sound pitiful.

"Hey, I'm sorry." Ian rested a hand on his shoulder. "I didn't mean to bring back bad memories. Sometimes I speak without thinking."

"I can't help it. Those are the only memories I've got." He pressed his lips together, determined not to bring down the day with negativity. "Forget about it."

"Charlie—" Ian began, but Charlie would rather die than see the pity in Ian's eyes.

"I'm fine," he snapped, a bit sharper than intended, and instantly regretted it. The pain of his lonely childhood wasn't Ian's fault. "Really, I am." He smiled to soften the earlier words. "Let's go into the dining room."

Uncertainty clouded Ian's eyes, but he followed Charlie.

Charlie had spent little time in the overly formal room, with its long, shining table and glass-fronted hutch filled with delicate china and figurines. "I figured we could search online for information."

"Good idea."

Charlie picked up the one picture of the two men together. Mugging for the camera, their faces lively and bright with laughter, neither boy resembling the sad, strained-looking men in the later photographs. Charlie ran his fingers over the faded black-and-white photo, and a tingling ran up his arm.

"It's a nice picture of them, isn't it?"

A shimmering, silvery haze drifted down from the ceiling, and Rachel appeared.

"Jesus," Ian muttered. "Can we put bells on her so we can tell when she's coming?"

"*I heard that. You're lucky Charlie likes you.*" She glared at Ian and turned a sweet smile on Charlie. "*It's the only picture of the two of them. It was taken at a street festival the year before Eddie left for the army. Now turn around and watch.*" She waved her hands and pointed to the mirror on the wall.

A photographer stood a distance from them, waiting to take their picture as they talked among themselves. Waiting patrons shuffled in line behind them.

"*Are you sure? You think it'll be okay?*" Robert searched Eddie's face. "*I'm afraid.*"

"*Yes, I'm positive. It's not a big deal. We're just two guys. Friends.*" His eyes softened. "*We might never get another chance to do this, and I want to have something of the both of us."*

With that, Eddie slung an arm around Robert's neck and waved at the waiting photographer. "My pal and I are ready."

An overwhelming wave of foreboding suffocated Charlie, and he struggled to draw in a breath.

"Everything all right?" Ian watched him anxiously.

Charlie rubbed a hand over his face as if to wipe away what he'd seen, but he couldn't erase the haze of darkness hanging over Robert and Edward as they stood for their picture.

A portent of things to come?

"Yeah, of course. Everything's fine."

Ian already thought things were crazy—Charlie probably included. Maybe he should sell the house, take the money, and run. But then he recalled his great-great-aunt's will, the requirement that he live in the brownstone for the year or forfeit ownership, and he knew he'd never be able to leave. He couldn't afford to give up this house... his home.

"All right." Ian shot him a look of disbelief.

Charlie deliberately chose to ignore it and picked up the wedding picture of Robert with his bride. "This is not the face of a happy man."

"Would you be? Marrying someone you didn't really love because you couldn't marry the person you did?"

Charlie jerked his gaze from studying the photo to Ian, whose emotionless, blank face freaked him the hell out. Always expressive and alive with laughter, Ian stood frozen, almost as if he were asleep, eyes fixed on the opposite wall, open but unseeing.

"What are you talking about? Ian? Are you okay?"

"No, he's not, Charlie."

Rachel floated down, and Charlie jerked in fright, having forgotten she was there. She blinked behind her silver-rimmed glasses. How and why did a ghost wear glasses? Shouldn't she see perfectly? Charlie rubbed his face. Was there ghost protocol? He cast a fearful glance at Ian, who hadn't moved.

"What did you do to him?"

Her lips pursed. *"Me? I did nothing. I can't hurt you or cause harm. I'm here to help you see the way."*

The way to what? Charlie was about to ask, but Ian had come out of his funk and said, "I keep seeing them in my head, you know? Like the more we discover about their story, the more I see. I had a vision of the wedding again, and I could feel how unhappy Robert was."

Rachel floated nearer to them. *"Because he never should've married her. He didn't love her. But he wasn't a strong man. He let his parents make decisions for him."*

Before Charlie could gather his scattered wits, Rachel waved her hands again, and Ian's room appeared in the mirror. Robert sat at the desk, carefully using a pen and ink to write his letter. Occasionally he'd set the pen down and cover his face with his hands.

Dear Eddie,

I'm so sorry about last night. I tried to wiggle my way out of that dinner party at my aunt's house, but both she and my parents insisted. It seems there was a young lady they wanted me to meet. Her name is Charlotte, and her family lives nearby.

As I could have predicted, it was a long, boring affair, and Charlotte claimed to be almost as embarrassed as I by the obvious machinations of both my family and hers. She is a pretty girl and sweet. I'm sure she'll make someone a perfectly lovely wife.

But not me.

Can we meet? Say, tomorrow night? I must confess it's been hard not seeing you, but I understand your family needing you to work at the store. Send me a signal if you can make it, and I'll come at half past midnight.

Yours,

R

"Dammit, that's sad. The whole thing is." Ian picked up the picture.

"So Charlotte is the woman in the picture with Robert?" Charlie reached out, and Ian handed him the photo.

At the point of contact, when they both had their hands on the picture, that same tingling sensation ran up Charlie's arm, and his heart slammed against his breastbone. Ian didn't let go, and from the rapid cadence of his breath and his widened eyes, Charlie suspected something similar was occurring on his end.

"Ian?"

He blinked, and his cheeks flooded with color. "Huh? What?"

"Is that Charlotte in the picture with Robert? Do we know?"

Ian ran his fingers over the photo. "Robert and Charlotte Nolan were married on June 2, 1918."

Charlie sucked in his breath. "Ian…how did you know that? Did you look them up?"

He jerked his gaze to Charlie, his face a mix of confusion and shock. "I-I don't know. It just came out of my mouth." He swallowed hard, his throat moving convulsively. "Charlie…can I ask you something?"

"Yeah, sure."

Ian set the photo down as if he couldn't bear to look at it any longer. "What do you think is going on?"

"You mean this—Rachel and the pictures and stuff?"

Ian stared at the picture. "Yeah. Sometimes I have dreams where I can't tell if it's real life or I'm asleep. I'll wake up unsure about what happened or even where I am for a sec. But they were so, so…what's the word I'm looking for?"

"Vivid?" Charlie offered.

"Yeah." Ian pounced on his word, giving way to his more animated self. "And about a week ago…well, I wasn't gonna say anything, but now with everything happening with Rachel and the stuff she's showing us in the mirror…you're gonna think it's crazy, but she came to me in my television set."

"You think after everything we've seen lately, I'm going to think you're nuts?" Charlie's lips twitched.

Ian snickered. "You got a point." His grin faded. "But she, uh, showed me something."

"What?"

"She played me part of Robert's wedding night."

"Really?" Charlie breathed out.

"Yeah." Ian picked up the photo again. "They were in their bedroom, and Robert was still in his clothes. Charlotte came out in this sexy nightgown and took charge. She gave him a blowjob. Turned out it was the first time for both of them. She did everything she could to make it good for him, but all Robert could think about was Eddie."

"You could tell all that from watching them on a screen?"

"I told you, it was different. Almost like…"

"Like you were living it?"

Ian's gaze jerked up to meet Charlie's startled one. "Yeah. Exactly. Even when they had sex, he had to think of Eddie to get it up. It made me a little sick and depressed."

Ian studied the photo for a moment before handing it over. Charlie noticed his own hand trembling but ignored it, figuring the afternoon had already been weird enough. The sepia-toned photo showed off Robert's finely drawn cheekbones, a strong, clean-shaven jawline, as were most men of that era. "Damn, he was handsome." His fingertips traced Robert's face.

"And sad. He should've been happy on his wedding day. My sisters and their husbands couldn't stop smiling when they got married. Why do you think he married her if he wasn't in love with her?"

"I guess we'll have to see what else she has to show us." Charlie continued to gaze at the picture as if it could offer an answer to the hundred-year-old question.

Chapter Fourteen

Over a week passed since Rachel had given them more hints of Robert and Eddie's relationship, but neither he nor Charlie could figure out why she was so insistent on them discovering who they were or what Rachel had to do with any of it. Plus—and here was where he needed to talk to Dave—he was still having seriously erotic dreams about Charlie. Downright filthy, in fact, and it all weighed on him.

"Can I ask you something?" Ian had waited to ask his questions until everyone else but Dave had left to throw out their scraps from lunch.

"Yeah, kid, sure." The foreman crossed his muscled arms and leaned against the doorway. "What's the problem?"

"Why do you think there's a problem?"

Lines fanned out from Dave's eyes as he smiled. "Because I've known you long enough. You barely said a word during lunch, and I seen you staring off into space. So…what's wrong?"

The words he wanted to say stuck in his throat, and Ian wasn't even certain they were appropriate for what he was feeling. Probably because he didn't know what the hell to call the emotions swirling around inside him.

"How did you know you liked guys and girls? Like… did you have to, uh, be with both of them, or did you just know?" God, he sounded so lame. He stopped floundering and slumped in his seat.

"Is that what's bugging you? You think you might be bisexual?"

Ian shrugged.

"You can say the word. Ain't nothin' dirty about it." Dave pushed off the doorframe to sit opposite him. "C'mon. Lookit me."

Ian chewed his lip and met Dave's kindly eyes. "Okay, I'm looking at you."

"Tell me what's goin' on inside your head."

"If I knew that, I wouldn't be so confused."

"How about starting with, 'I met this guy…' " Dave said encouragingly.

Ian picked at his cuticles, then heaved out a sigh. He could only talk about Charlie so far, because there was no way he could mention the crazy ghost stuff happening, so Ian knew to choose his words. "Okay. I met this guy. My next-door neighbor—I mentioned him before. We kinda clicked."

"Clicked how?" Dave propped his chin on his hand.

"You been hanging out?"

"Yeah." Their French toast lunch was the most fun he'd had in a while, and he'd hated leaving Charlie to go home to his empty house.

"Goin' out together to bars and clubs?"

Recalling their night at Bedlam, Ian shifted in his seat. "Yeah. We, uh, we went to one club. A gay club he likes."

"You kiss him yet?"

Ian hesitated, and Dave's eyes narrowed. "Don't lie, kid. I don't tell tales outta school, and anything you say to me ain't gonna change my opinion about you unless you tell me you were mean to this guy." His voice gentled. "It's hard to admit something you're confused about. I've been there myself. So tell me: did you kiss him?"

Ian's lips tingled. "Yeah."

"And you liked it."

"Yeah, kinda."

"Kinda?" Dave's lips twitched. "You either did or you didn't. So you did. And now what? You weirded out and trying to forget it? Or you liked it and want to do it again?"

Ian pushed his hands through his hair. "I dunno. I mean, Charlie's funny and sweet and—"

"And you like him, and you're confused because you don't know what to do next."

"What're you, reading my mind?"

Dave arched a brow. "Well, dating a guy ain't no different than a girl. What would you do if Charlie was a Carla?"

Hmm. "Probably go out to dinner. Maybe a movie. Then back to my place and see what happens."

"So?"

"So what?"

Dave raised his gaze to the ceiling and shook his head. "Here I thought you were the smart one." He slapped his palms flat on the table, but his expression was kind. "Take it as it comes. If you want to see him, and it looks like you do, then go with your instincts. But if you're afraid of what people might say or think"—his gaze sharpened—"don't fuck with this guy and keep him like he's a dirty secret. That ain't fair to him."

Ian flinched at Dave's harsh words. "I wouldn't. That's why I don't know what I'm doing."

"Most of us don't, kid. We just throw it into the wind and hope it don't come back to smack us in the face. If something's meant to be, it'll happen."

* * *

Throughout the day, Ian wrestled with his conflicting emotions. He genuinely liked Charlie as a person, and what he'd revealed of the life he'd lived as a foster child broke Ian's heart. Having had the support of a large and loving family, Ian grew angry that someone as sweet and sensitive as Charlie hadn't and that he'd never found a real friend or lover. He'd always been the champion of the underdog and hated seeing people being taken advantage of. It made him want to protect Charlie and shield him from any future pain.

Ian was certain he wanted to be Charlie's friend. As for being his lover…a shiver ran through Ian. Well, maybe Dave was right, and they should take things as they came. Because one thing he couldn't deny was that Charlie turned him on like nobody ever had.

That was why when five thirty came around, Ian found

himself walking through the front door of the funky little shop where Charlie worked. Only he didn't see Charlie behind the desk, but rather a girl with pink hair, a nose ring, and curious, pale-gray eyes lined in black. She gave him a smile as bright as her hair.

"Oh, hi. We're going to be closing soon, but if there's something special you were looking for…" Her question trailed off as she raked her interested gaze over him.

"Actually, I was looking for Charlie. Did he leave yet?"

"Ian?" Charlie appeared to his left through the door marked STAFF ONLY, and Ian couldn't help but grin. An old-fashioned straw hat rested on his head. Ian had seen Charlie wear one like it, but it had a black band around it. This one had a purple band that matched the bow tie he wore with his short-sleeved, gray button-down shirt. Gray skinny jeans hugged his long muscular legs and thighs.

"Looking sharp there, Charlie."

"What're you doing here?"

The other salesperson unabashedly stared at them. "You know each other?"

"Yeah, this is my neighbor Ian."

"Hi, Neighbor Ian. I'm Mona, Charlie's friend and coworker."

"Hi." He could sense her interest, but it was Charlie he was after. "Charlie, I figured we could walk home together like you mentioned. Maybe stop off at Trader Joe's and pick up something, and I can cook you dinner. You've never seen my place."

"Dinner? Me?" Charlie's mouth hung open.

Like a ping-pong ball, Mona followed their conversation.

"No, not you for dinner. Maybe some chicken. What do you say?"

Charlie stared at him, and before he could answer, Mona grabbed him by the hand and yanked him aside, where they held a frantic, whispered conversation. Charlie returned and adjusted his hat.

"Okay, sure."

"Awesome. Ready to go?"

"Yeah."

They walked down Atlantic Avenue, window-shopping at all the funky stores and stopping to look at the menus of the little restaurants that had sprung up in the last few years.

"My mother used to love antiques-shopping, but most of the stores have closed." Ian pointed to the different cafés. "All these places were once shops where she'd drag my sisters and me on weekends when we didn't have something else to do." He pressed his nose against one of the windows. "It was one of the main reasons I took up soccer and softball."

"You didn't like it? Sounds like a perfect Saturday to me."

"What did you use to do on the weekends when you were growing up?"

Knowing how touchy Charlie was about his past, Ian tried to be careful with his questions, but he hoped his probing would lead to Charlie opening up a little more to him.

"Cleaning, mostly. I learned to be a whiz at scouring bathtubs and toilets," he said lightly, but Ian sensed a whole lot of pain in those words.

"Bet it's nice to have your own place now."

Charlie threw him a grateful look. "It's crazy how at home I feel in that house."

"I'm glad." They walked farther down the block, and Charlie had to hold on to his hat as a sudden breeze tilted it. "Did you always like the funky clothes? When did you start wearing them?"

They'd stopped before a men's store with hand-tailored suits and handwoven sweaters. Charlie touched the glass. "When I was nine, I had a foster mother who loved old movies. She's the one nice memory I have. We'd sit up late and watch black-and-white classics. The men all looked so clean and happy, their clothes new and elegant. I'd go to bed thinking that if I could only dress like them, I'd be clean and happy like they were, and nothing dirty could ever touch me."

So much hurt lived inside Charlie. Hurt he'd tried to hide, but now Ian was being given a hint of who Charlie really was. "How long did you stay with her?"

"She died of a heart attack after I was there a year."

Almost afraid to ask, Ian had to anyway. "And afterward?"

Charlie shook his head. "It doesn't matter. I survived."

It absolutely did matter, but Ian let it go. Standing on a busy street wasn't the right place to really have this conversation.

"Let's go food-shopping." He nudged Charlie. "And don't forget the dessert."

* * *

Two hours later, Ian pushed away the remnants of his chicken. "Was I right about the honey mustard? Made the chicken good, huh?"

Charlie licked his fingers. "Yeah. Everything was. Thanks again." He glanced around the kitchen. "Can I ask you something?"

Ian finished his beer. "Yeah, sure. Of course."

"How come you live in the basement apartment and not in the main part of the house?"

Before answering, Ian retrieved two more bottles of beer from the refrigerator and handed Charlie one. "Let's go hang out on the couch." They left the paper plates on the counter that doubled as his table and took a seat in the living room, Charlie on one end of the couch and him on the other. "Two reasons, really. First, I look after the place for my parents, but they sometimes want to come home from Florida, especially in the summer when it gets crazy hot down there or a hurricane might hit. My sisters and their families come to visit too, and I'd feel weird if I had a date stay over and they were all there too."

"Yeah." Charlie took a swig of beer. "I get it."

"Plus, I like having my own space."

"It's funny." Charlie fidgeted with his bottle. "I still wander around, touching things, not really sure it's all mine, but the minute I walked inside the house, I felt comfortable. Like I already belonged. Yet your house seems familiar to me too, and that's even weirder."

Ian wished Charlie could relax. Maybe it was time to watch a movie.

"Want to choose what to watch? Whatever you want. I'm not picky." He handed Charlie the remote.

"I'm probably not the best judge, since I really only watch those old movies." Charlie returned it to him.

"That's okay. I'm fine with it." Ian might've never

watched one, but he didn't care. He wanted Charlie to enjoy himself, so he tossed the remote over. "Pick whatever you want. I'm good with it."

Charlie shot him an unreadable look but flicked on the television and chose some black-and-white movie. Ian thought he'd be bored, but instead he was drawn into the story of a woman who fell in love with a man but then discovered she was losing her sight. By the end of the movie, as the credits rolled, he found himself moved enough that he had tears in his eyes.

Charlie shut off the television. "Did you like it?"

Blinking back the sting of tears, Ian needed a moment and could only nod.

Charlie broke out in a big smile. "Are you crying?" He nudged Ian's shoulder.

Ian drew in a shaky breath. "N-no." At Charlie's skeptical expression, he gave it up and shrugged. "Maybe, okay, yeah. But it was sad. I mean, she goes blind at the end. How fucking awful is that?"

"I never took you for a romantic."

All during the movie, Ian had been conscious of Charlie sitting next to him. The occasional brush of their fingers when they both grabbed for a handful of chips in the bowl, or the press of their thighs, tied his stomach in knots. He'd hidden behind his beer bottle, watching Charlie eat and drink, and the tension inside him built as he thought about what Dave had said that afternoon.

"I can be romantic. I'm not a Neanderthal."

Charlie snorted. "I never said you were. I don't know you well enough. But tell me this." He faced Ian, cross-legged. "You've dated tons of women. What's the most romantic thing you've ever done?"

Ian eyed Charlie, who sat waiting with a tiny smile on

his lips.

He'd liked kissing Charlie—more than liked it, in fact. His body had almost vaporized when their tongues played together, and he grew hard just thinking about doing it again. Dave's words from earlier in the afternoon sounded in his head. *"Go with your instinct, kid."*

"The most romantic thing?" he repeated, shifting closer, watching Charlie's big green eyes widen and his smile fade. "Maybe this."

Ian slid his palm around the nape of Charlie's neck and brushed his lips lightly over Charlie's once...twice. The third time he pressed them harder, covering Charlie's mouth with his, and groaned when Charlie, who'd turned stiff, softened beneath him and sighed.

Their tongues slid and rubbed together, and feeling bolder, Ian allowed the fire burning through him to take control. His fingers threaded through Charlie's silky waves, and he slanted his mouth over Charlie's, drinking in every drop of his sweetness and heat. Blood pounded in his head, and he closed his eyes. Their teeth clashed as Ian surged against Charlie, devouring his mouth.

"Ian, what the hell?" Charlie panted.

"You don't like it?" Ian rested his cheek next to Charlie's, surprised he enjoyed the rough scrape of his scruff. Back in control, he peppered smaller, lighter kisses along Charlie's jawline and inhaled deeply. Already hard, his dick stiffened to an almost painful fullness when Charlie trembled. "You don't want this?"

Charlie placed his hands on Ian's shoulders, their gazes locking, and Ian felt himself spin away, falling into the fathomless green pools of Charlie's eyes.

"What do you want, Ian? What's happening here?"

"I thought one of us knew what we were doing," Ian

joked, feeling shaky and light-headed.

"Come on," Charlie whispered. "Tell me the truth."

"I am." He cupped Charlie's face, skating his thumb over Charlie's slightly swollen lips. "I thought I was being romantic." Charlie's breath fanned warm over his skin.

"With me."

Ian peered over Charlie's shoulder. "Do you see anyone else here?"

"Please don't joke about this."

Ian trailed his fingers down Charlie's jaw to his throat, feeling the wildly beating pulse thrum under his hand. "I'm not. I'm really into you. I-I don't know how or why it happened, but it did."

Next thing Ian knew, he found himself on his back and breathless. His brain turned to mush when Charlie, unsmiling and intense, leaned over him, their noses almost touching. "So you want me?"

His heart slammed so hard, he thought he might faint, but he had the capacity to nod. "Y-yeah. I think so."

Charlie kissed him, licking and sucking his mouth with more purpose. Their movements grew more frantic, Charlie rubbing up against him, and he moaned, clutching at Charlie's shoulders.

"You think so?" Charlie murmured in his ear, the thrust of his erection poking into his belly.

"I know so, okay? Oh, God." The slow ache of pleasure rolled through him, and Ian hissed when Charlie's hand brushed along the waistband of his jeans. No woman, not even Heather O'Leary, the girl he'd lost his virginity to senior year of high school, had turned him on as much as Charlie. "Charlie, please."

"Please? What do you want?" But he didn't stop

the back and forth teasing along Ian's stomach. Charlie dipped his fingers below the waistband of his jeans, and Ian groaned.

Charlie stopped. "Do you want me to go further? I need to hear you say it."

"Yeah, yes. I do. I…I want it…want you."

Things moved in slow motion, as if he were viewing himself through a lens. When Charlie popped the buttons of his jeans, the release of pressure brought a rush of blood to his groin, and his dick stiffened even further to a hardness Ian had never imagined possible.

"Oh fuck, oh…oh…" Agonized moans broke free when Charlie pulled his jeans down and off. He wasn't uncomfortable to lie naked with his dick sticking out, waiting for a guy to touch or suck it. He wanted it. God, did he want it. And the more Charlie stared at his junk, the harder he grew and the more he needed the next step to happen.

"Commando?" Charlie's brow quirked. "I shouldn't be surprised, should I?"

He couldn't formulate words, not when Charlie's mouth hovered close to his dick. Ian's breath came in short, hard pants, and he wrapped his hand around his length. He waited, barely breathing. "Feels good."

Charlie licked his lips, and Ian's dick jerked. "I can make it feel even better."

"You can?" Ian could barely speak. He glided his hand up and down his erection, needing the friction, but it wasn't enough…God, not nearly enough.

Golden light shimmering around him, Charlie leaned closer, and Ian almost ceased breathing as he watched those full lips move nearer and nearer. Hot breath hit his stomach, followed by a fiery wetness sliding over the head of his dick, and he cried out.

"Oh, my God. Fucking hell."

His body took over, hips thrusting up higher and higher to get more of Charlie's magic mouth on him. Charlie's lips clung to his erection, hot, wet, and perfect, and then he did something with his tongue that fried the circuits of Ian's brain, nearly taking the top of his head off.

"Ah, fuck. Holy shit." Charlie did it again, flicking his tongue while sucking hard. "Charlie," Ian choked out, too far gone to send up a warning that he was about to have the most intense orgasm of his life.

"Mmhmm."

A humming vibrated against the sensitive skin of his dick, and his vision blurred. Ian came, groaning loud and long, his body twitching through his release. Charlie swallowed everything he'd let loose, and Ian lay blissed-out with his eyes half-closed, still caught up in the fire burning through him. He'd been turned upside down and inside out, revealing who he was finally meant to be.

Ian held out his hand to Charlie. "C'mere."

But when Charlie neither spoke nor moved, Ian forced his eyes open.

"What's wrong?" Ian shook free of the fog of pleasure in his brain to see Charlie sitting back on his heels, an almost frightened look on his face. When Charlie didn't answer, Ian struggled to an upright position and braced himself on his elbows. "Hey, what's going on?"

"Is it okay? Do you want me to leave?"

Confused, Ian brushed sweaty strands of hair out of his eyes. "Leave?" he repeated stupidly. "Why?"

Spots of pink bloomed on Charlie's cheeks. "Well, because…" His eyes darted side to side, and he pressed his lips together for a second before blurting out, "Because this happened." He waved his hand between them. "And it's not the first time I've been with a straight guy who suddenly forgot my name and couldn't wait to run away or get rid of me, and I just wanna know because—"

"Hey. Whoa. Slow down and take a breath." Ian sat up. "First of all"—he pointed to his naked lower half—"I'm gonna get dressed."

Charlie ducked his head. "Yeah, sure. Of course. Sorry."

Charlie shifted away, and Ian swung his legs off the couch and slid the soft, worn jeans up his legs but left the buttons undone. With his face in profile, Charlie remained motionless, staring blindly at the dark television screen.

"Okay," Ian said. "Now let's talk."

Chapter Fifteen

Charlie *so* did not want to talk. Mainly because he knew what would happen. Ian wasn't the first straight-but-curious guy Charlie had unwittingly fallen for. But how many times had he allowed himself to believe that *this time* would be different? Too many.

"Nah, man. I'm not gay. Just wanted to see what it was like."

"My girlfriend don't like to do it, so I figured why not? We're both getting off, so no harm, no foul, right?"

"I thought I could tell people, but I can't. Can I still come over, though? Nothing has to change."

Every time, Charlie vowed not to be so stupid again, yet here he sat with his heart in his eyes.

"I know sometimes you do things you think you might want, but afterward you regret what happened."

"So I regret what we just did, is what you're saying."

Charlie shrugged. "I don't know. I'm just saying I won't hold it against you if you do." When Ian didn't say anything, Charlie grew nervous, and when he grew nervous he tended to babble. "I'm sure you must be weirded out because, well, I mean, you've never had a guy—"

"Suck my dick," Ian broke in. "You're right. I never have. I never wanted one to either. Until you." A slow smile spread over his face.

Charlie's stomach tumbled, and once again, he watched Ian's blue eyes gleam and turn to that molten silver. "What're you saying?"

His steady gaze drew Charlie in until their foreheads touched. "Being honest? I'm not sure I'm ready to reciprocate. Not yet, but I don't want you to think I don't want this." Ian slid a palm over his jaw, and Charlie stifled a moan of pleasure at the featherlike touch of Ian's fingertips on his lips. "I'm not running away. And you're not going anywhere either."

"No?" Charlie whispered. Maybe this was another of those crazy dreams, but if so, sign him up. Charlie would gladly sleep all day to keep Ian's hands on him.

"Nope." Ian tipped his chin up. "Do you know how hot you are? All lit up, golden and bright. It's like looking into the sun."

A nervous laugh escaped him. "I thought you were never supposed to do that."

"I don't like people telling me not to do things. Makes me wanna do the opposite." Ian's face hovered dangerously close to his.

So close…almost there.

"You're a rebel, then?"

If he breathed, their lips would touch.

"I told you. I like living on the edge."

Charlie was on the edge. The edge of losing his self-control. It wouldn't take much with Ian's glittering eyes capturing his. An almost feral smile deepened his dimples, and Ian licked his lips, sending shivers through Charlie at the rising hunger in that intense gaze. The tip of Ian's tongue flicked against his lips, and Charlie's dick throbbed.

"Please," he whispered.

"Dammit," Ian ground out, and slammed his mouth over Charlie's. They fell back together on the couch, Charlie opening his mouth to grant entrance to the slick, hot slide of Ian's tongue. The velvet-soft sweetness of Ian's lips played over his, forcing pleasurable moans from him as the mounting pressure turned unbearable. Desperate to touch himself, Charlie pressed a hand to his dick, which so far had been woefully neglected and would no longer be denied.

"I have to…I need…" He fumbled with the button of his jeans and finally got it opened and unzipped himself.

"Do it," Ian urged. "I wanna see." He sank to his knees, gaze riveted. "C'mon."

Charlie shimmied his jeans and boxers off. His dick jutted out, and even Charlie could smell how much he wanted Ian. He wrapped his hand around himself.

"Oh shit," Ian breathed.

Charlie gazed down, shocked to see Ian, cheeks flushed, eyes wide, nostrils flaring. His cock jerked, and pearls of precome dripped from his crown.

"Fuck, that's the hottest thing I've ever seen."

Their gazes locked as Charlie began to jerk himself

off. Ian couldn't seem to take his eyes off him, and Charlie hissed, his hand stroking his shaft faster. Harder.

"Can I?" Ian reached out, and Charlie almost stopped breathing when Ian's large palm touched him.

"Oh…my God," he groaned. The friction of Ian's rough hand against the sensitive skin of his dick replaced whatever might've been at the top of Charlie's favorite-things list. Certainly any other man who'd ever touched him prior to this moment. Helpless now, Charlie thrust into Ian's grip, holding on to his shoulders. Colored spots danced before his eyes. "Oh fuck, oh fuck." Wave after wave of lust hit him hard, and he couldn't breathe.

He closed his eyes and was shocked to see two men hidden by darkness, arms around each other, frantically kissing behind the oak tree, their hands busy between them. But Charlie had no time to think about what it meant. He couldn't think at all once the familiar stirrings of his climax overtook him.

His toes curled, his balls tightened, and he found himself incapable of warning Ian before exploding into his hand. He felt raw and shaken from the inside out, and his vision whitened. He collapsed onto the sofa, the force of his orgasm leaving him barely able to move.

When he could see once again, Ian had left him to wash his hands in the kitchen. Embarrassed that he sat ass-naked on the couch, Charlie pulled on his jeans and boxers and zipped himself up. Uncertain as to what would happen next, he joined Ian, who dropped the paper towel on the counter.

"Does that answer your earlier question?"

"Kind of?" Charlie chewed his lip. "It's just that… what now? Is this something new between us, or are you testing the waters and I'm your first toe in?"

"Hell, no." Ian's vehement response startled him.

"Okay."

"Look, Charlie." Ian took him by the hand and led him back to the couch. "I'm not good with words and stuff, but I've never had this kinda feeling before. Ever since we met, I've had this...I don't know, call it a feeling about you. Us. Almost..." His gaze dropped. "You'll think I'm stupid."

"Ian, stop. Don't be embarrassed. I'm not making fun." Charlie had no idea where he'd gotten this bravery to be so open and honest with Ian. "Tell me."

Adorably flustered, Ian bit his lip. "I just kinda felt from the start like I knew you. Even though we'd never met. See? I knew it sounded stupid."

"No, it doesn't. I-I felt that way too, but I didn't wanna say anything."

"You did?"

"I told you when I walked in here, it felt familiar. Safe. Like I'd been here before even though I know that's stupid 'cause I haven't."

They sat silently for a few minutes, digesting their conversation. Charlie could see Ian struggling to figure it all out, and he was happy to be with a guy he'd had amazing sex with who didn't walk away from him after zipping up his pants or ask when he planned on going home.

"Something else is going on, that's pretty obvious."

"Something else?" Charlie repeated. "Oh, you mean because of Rachel the ghost?" Charlie wasn't sure if Ian was aware they still held hands, their fingers playing together, but they were. God, it felt so good.

"Yeah. And what she's showing us, she said it would

explain everything, including our connection."

Warmth suffused him, and he couldn't hold back a smile. "You think we have a connection?"

The smoldering fire in Ian's eyes left no doubt in Charlie's mind, and when Ian lifted their entwined hands and brought them to his lips, Charlie nearly swooned at the gesture.

"Do you need more persuading than what we did together just now?"

"N-no, I'm good."

So fucking good, if he could bottle this elation, he'd be a millionaire. Charlie forced himself to remember what brought them together in the first place. The chronicle of the life and, from what he'd parsed and what they'd been shown, the love affair between Robert and Eddie. "What do you want to do?"

"Well, my laptop's on the fritz, so let's go to your place and check them out. I'm curious to know more about what happened."

"Yeah, sure. Me too."

"Then let's do it." Ian bounced off the couch and stuck his feet into a pair of flip-flops while Charlie laced up his sneakers. Side by side, they walked outside.

"I wonder if we'll see that ghost again. She's only been to my place once, but she seems to pop up whenever and wherever at your house." Ian's brows shot up. "Shit. Do you think she's seen us...you know?"

"You worried she might give you some pointers?" Charlie cackled.

"Yo, Ian."

Two men approached from down the block, and Ian quickly stepped away from him. A sinking feeling hit the pit of Charlie's stomach, even though he wasn't surprised. After all, he'd traveled this road before. And because of that, he knew the part he had to play.

"What's up?" Ian called out as he closed the wrought-iron gate behind them.

"Was about to ask you the same thing." A tall, lanky redhead leaned against the tree in front of the house. "You been holding out on us?"

Ian stiffened. "What're you talking about?"

"Haven't heard from you. Figured you found a new woman and was too busy. Know what I mean?" The two men snickered, elbowing each other.

"Nah. Just hanging out with Charlie, helping him with his house." To Charlie's ears, the relief in Ian's voice was evident.

The two men gave him curious but not unfriendly looks.

"This is my neighbor, Charlie Muir. This doofus is Mickey." Ian pointed to the redhead. "We've known each other since third grade, and we met Patrick in junior high."

Patrick, a little shorter than Charlie and with bulging biceps that spoke of way too many painful hours at the gym, gestured to Charlie's house. "You live in old lady Muir's house?"

"Yeah," Charlie said, resigned to repeating the story. "She was my great-great-aunt, but I never knew her. I inherited the house since I'm her only living relative."

"Yeah, I don't remember seeing you next door when I'd come over to Ian's house. Cool for you." Patrick folded his arms. "We were coming over to see if you wanna go get a beer, Ian. You can come too, Charlie."

Ian shifted another step away from him. "We gotta

take a rain check. We just finished dinner, and I promised Charlie I'd help him fix some shit around his house."

"Oh."

Was Charlie imagining the curious looks from Mickey and Patrick?

"What about Friday night? My buddy at work got tickets for this club in the city from his brother who's a bartender." Patrick grinned. "Said it's a hot spot."

"Sounds cool," Ian said.

"You too, Charlie," Patrick said with a friendly smile. "Can you make it?"

He wondered if Mickey and Patrick would be so friendly if they knew he was gay. "Yeah. Thanks."

"What happened with Brianna and Andi?" Ian asked his friends. "You still seeing them?"

"Hell, yeah." Mickey's eyes lit up. "Brianna and I are going out Saturday to the museum and then to some place she likes in Park Slope. She's babysitting for her sister Friday night."

Ian doubled over with laughter. "You? A museum?"

"Yeah, what's so funny about that?" Mickey said, affronted. "I got culture. I'm no ignoramus."

Charlie bit back a smile.

"Andi has plans with her girlfriends, but I'm seeing her tomorrow night." Patrick gave Ian a sly smile. "You know, she said Savannah was still into you. You'd probably be able to get a date with her if you tried. I could get you her number." Patrick cackled. "You shoulda seen it, Charlie. Our boy Ian here was making out like a bandit before all this weird shit happened."

Savannah? Who the hell is named Savannah? And what weird stuff?

"Yeah? Tell me." Charlie eased himself against the fence and arched a brow at a distinctly uncomfortable Ian. "Making out like a bandit, huh? So she was hot?"

"She was okay," Ian mumbled. "Do you wanna get going?"

"Okay?" Mickey stared at him like he had two heads. "Don't listen to him, Charlie. Girlfriend was smokin'. Really filled out her dress, if you get my drift." He gave Charlie a conspiratorial wink.

"Oh, I do." Charlie directed a bright smile at Ian, who looked ready to murder Mickey with the nearest available weapon. "Sounds perfect for you, Ian."

"Shut up. I'm not interested."

But Mickey was on a roll. "They were making out on the dance floor, when all of a sudden Ian charged through the crowd like his pants were on fire. Had to gulp down a whole pitcher of ice water. Said her tongue tasted like hot sauce or some shit like that. Then, when we were all sitting together, they start goin' at it again." He snickered. "She starts screamin', and said his kisses felt like her mouth was being stung by bees." He shook his head. "Maybe she had too much to drink, 'cause we all know how our boy is. He's the master. All the girls love him."

"Fuck you twice, Mickey," Ian growled.

"Sounds like it was a fun night. And how terrible for you, Ian," Charlie commiserated, but he could barely contain his grin. And Ian, from the death glares he shot Charlie's way, saw right through him. "All that prime kissing gone to waste."

"I said I'm not interested. She was crazy. And Friday sounds good, although right now, hanging out with you assholes is the last thing I wanna do." He nudged Charlie's shoulder. "Are you ready to go fix that thing in your house?"

"I guess we'd better."

He was cute when riled up, Charlie had to admit. Cute and hot and perfect. *Shit*. He needed to rein it in around Ian's friends.

"Nice to meet you, Charlie. See you Friday."

The two men walked off, and Charlie called after them, "Same. Looking forward to it."

He mounted the steps to his house with Ian on his heels, breathing down his neck. The moment he turned the doorknob, Ian grabbed him, pushed him inside, and slammed the door behind them. His body covered Charlie's.

"Did you have fun out there?" Ian's growl reverberated through Charlie. His chest heaved, and Charlie could feel every hard-muscled dip and curve of Ian's body. Damn, he was fucking sexy. If this was how he acted when poked, Charlie was ready to find a nice big stick to keep close.

"Mmm. I did, kind of. Tell me more about this girl, Savannah? Was she a good kisser?" Charlie licked his lips and felt Ian's dick twitch and thicken. Ian's eyes widened, and Charlie did it again. Slower. Ian's breath grew short.

"Stop doing that."

Charlie wriggled underneath him, and Ian's grip on him tightened.

"I said stop that."

"No, you said to stop licking my lips. Make up your mind."

Ian's dick lengthened against him, and Charlie's insides clenched from all that beautiful, thick hardness. Ian's growl deepened, he grabbed Charlie by the back of the neck, and after an intense gaze, slowly brushed their lips together. He hadn't anticipated that.

The kisses were gentle. Sweet. So tender that Charlie didn't know how he managed to keep his footing and not melt into a puddle all over the floor. Their breaths mingled, and Charlie was ready to give Ian anything and everything he might want.

Oh, God.

Now he couldn't help the wriggling and rubbing up against Ian. Charlie's bones dissolved, and he looped his arms around Ian's neck. The world faded away as they stood frantically kissing and touching. Ian nuzzled his neck.

"Fuck what everyone else says. Hear me? I'm not into that girl. I'm into you."

The visual of that—Charlie on all fours while Ian rammed inside him with his big dick—nearly brought him to his knees.

Reeling from Ian's hot, wet mouth tickling his ear, Charlie was a second away from dragging Ian upstairs to his bedroom. He didn't care if it was too soon. He wanted Ian, and he spiraled out of control.

"Fuck, Ian…" he moaned. "Let's go—"

"Boys, please. Such language."

They both jumped at the silvery, reedy voice. Heart pounding, Charlie shook away the fog of lust in his head and witnessed Rachel floating toward them from the top of the stairs.

"What the hell?" Ian panted, flushed and wild-eyed. He looked ready to kill.

"Did I interrupt something? So sorry."

Was it possible for a ghost to pretend contrition? Because Rachel might've seemed apologetic, but her eyes brimmed with amusement.

"You could say that. Can't you knock or something?" Charlie rubbed his face, willing his body to calm the hell down.

"*Knock? I'm a ghost, not the postman. It's one of the perks.*" She giggled, and Ian made a sound of disgust.

"Just what we need. A ghost who thinks she's funny."

She glared at him. "*I'll have you know, Charlie Chaplin thought I was a hoot.*"

"I'll bet he did," Ian muttered. "He'd say anything to get you to be quiet."

"*Have you forgotten*"—she shot them a quelling look—"*that I see and hear everything?*"

He and Ian exchanged glances. *Uh-oh.* This could get sticky. "Everything?" Charlie asked with trepidation.

"*Well, I do have a little discretion, so when I see... private things...I leave you alone.*"

"Whew," Ian muttered. "Thank God for that."

"*Like before in your house, Ian.*" Her smile grew broader, reminding Charlie of the Cheshire cat. "*Weren't you the little eager beavers?*"

"Ah, shit," Ian muttered in disgust.

"*Again with the foul mouth. You need to clean up your language, young man.*" She shook her finger at him.

"You know, you're not my mother. I get grief from her about enough things. I don't need a ghost nagging me too."

"*That's the problem with children these days. No respect. You'd make a much better impression if you spoke without cursing.*"

Ian snorted. "You might think you know everything

'cause you're a ghost, but you've obviously never been to a construction site."

"Okay, can we break this up, please?" Charlie had grown tired of the back and forth and was more than a little annoyed that the promise of more sexy alone time with Ian had been cut short. "Rachel, is there something you wanted? Ian and I were busy."

"Mmhmm, so I noticed." She floated down the stairs, stopping by his side momentarily to whisper, *"He's a very good kisser, I'm guessing?"*

He refused to be baited by a ghost.

Rachel didn't seem to expect a response. *"Have you been talking about what I've shown you?"*

"Yes." Face burning, Charlie started walking toward the dining room and waved at Ian to follow. He'd left his laptop on the table. "We were going to look up Robert and Eddie on the Internet. See what we could find."

"Oh, you're going to use the Google?"

Charlie rolled his eyes. "Just Google, Rachel. And yes."

"Well, you won't find anything. I thought you might've tried that already, knowing how you young ones live on your electric machines. I guess that was before you got sidetracked. But who could blame you both? You've been waiting so long."

"What does that mean?"

Without answering, she sailed through the tall wooden chair and sat. Charlie's eyes popped out of his head.

"Jesus, I can't get used to this," Ian whispered to him.

"Now, boys, I'm a little disappointed you haven't figured it out yet."

He exchanged an uneasy glance with Ian. "Figured out

what?"

But it seemed Rachel would not be denied her moment. "*I should apologize now for spying on you, but I got worried when I saw you sneak out of the house late at night.*"

"Spying?" Charlie asked.

"Sneaking out?" Ian asked.

She clasped her hands together. "*It must be wonderful to be together and not have to hide.*"

Ian crossed his arms and raised his voice. "Will you tell us what the hell you're talking about?"

A bit gentler, Charlie held his hands out wide. "Rachel. Can you please tell us what's going on?"

Ignoring Ian's language, Rachel faced Charlie, with a warm, loving smile. "*You're Eddie, my brother come back to me. And you,*" she said to Ian, a bit less sweetly, "*if you haven't already guessed, are Robert. The man who broke my brother's heart.*"

Chapter Sixteen

"You're fucking kidding me."

At Rachel's frown, Charlie elbowed him in the ribs and hissed, "Don't curse. You know she doesn't like that."

"Dude. She's a ghost." Ian snorted. "She's not real."

The lights flickered, and a fire roared out of the empty fireplace. Ian jumped back, dragging Charlie with him. "What the hell? You could've burned us."

"Is that real enough for you?" Her lips pursed, and a cold chill ran through Ian as she fixed him with a look so steely, he shivered. God, he was so going to have nightmares from all this like he did when he was a little kid. He'd beg to stay up late and watch television with his sisters, and they'd always pick scary movies, knowing he

hated them. He shifted closer to Charlie. "*And don't worry. I wouldn't have hurt Charlie.*" She beamed at Charlie then directing a withering gaze, as only a ghost could, at him. "*I can't say the same about you.*"

"*Argh.*" Ian threw up his hands. "This is nuts. We're standing here talking to a ghost who told us we're dead boyfriends reincarnated from a hundred years ago, and we're just supposed to accept that?"

She shot him a furious look before smiling sweetly at Charlie. "*You understand, don't you, dear? You were the one with a heart.*"

"I have a heart," Ian yelled. "I'm a fu-I'm a really nice guy. I call my sisters and parents every week and feed stray cats."

Rachel sniffed. "*So you say. Now.*" Dismissing him, she spoke directly to Charlie. "*I'm going to show you something.*"

"Rachel, I don't understand anything you're saying."

She floated off the chair and pointed to the table. "*Sit down and watch the mirror.*" Her voice echoed in the room as she vanished in a silvery haze, leaving Ian and Charlie staring at each other.

"Well, that was weird." Charlie brushed his hair back, and—giving the chair Rachel vacated a wide berth—sat at the table. "Do you want to stay and see what she has to show us?"

Ian couldn't be sure. Seeing his friends had already freaked him out slightly, and he knew he had some serious thinking to do.

But then there was Charlie.

Charlie, with his head bent over the table, a shaft of light sparking that fascinating golden glow around him.

Charlie, with the sweetly crooked smile and heavy-lidded bedroom eyes, who made Ian's heart pound, his cock hard, and his breath grow short.

What happened to his happy-go-lucky, easy way of life?

"Ian?" Charlie's questioning green eyes met his. "Do you want to do this?"

What the hell was he going to do about Charlie?

Apparently, whatever Charlie wanted, because Ian couldn't figure out how to say no to him.

Nor did he want to. Ian might be confused about many things, but not about how it felt with Charlie. Different. Exciting. And so damn right.

"Sure."

He took the chair next to Charlie, and they gazed up at the mirror. They didn't have to wait long before it flickered to life.

Eddie sat in the yard, a book in his lap. A sheet of writing paper covered the pages, and he gripped the pencil in his hand. A cap shaded his head from the sun. Ian sensed uncertainty and foreboding around him as Eddie wrote his letter.

Robert,

I've missed you very much, and it might be selfish, but I was glad to hear you missed me too. That dinner sounded terrible, although I'm glad Charlotte wasn't too awful to be around. You have a knack for making people feel comfortable.

After we met last night, I lay awake, thinking about the future. Our future. I had a thought that we might leave New York and head out west, maybe start a new life where no one knows us. Somewhere we might be able to live freer, without the constraints our families and friends would put us under.

Don't say no outright. I know how scared you are of things coming to light. You're hesitant and probably thinking me insane, but please don't discount it. If it's the only way for us to be together, I'd rather live a full life with you, leaving everything behind, than a sad and lonely life without you, pretending to be who I'm not.

I've never been so serious in all my life.

You are the rainbow in my soul.

Yours,

Eddie

"Wow. Damn. That's a lot to handle." Ian rubbed his eyes, waves of pain pushing against him. They hit him hard in his chest as if he were Robert reading the letter. When Rachel's words echoed in his mind—*"You are Robert, the man who broke my brother's heart"*—Ian hung his head. "I don't get what's going on, but you don't really buy into this reincarnation shit, do you?"

The golden light around Charlie pulsed brightly. "I don't know," he answered softly. "It could be true." His finger trailed over the photo of the two men. "I mean, we *are* talking to a ghost. Anything's possible now, right?"

"Huh." Ian picked up the picture of the two men with their arms around each other's shoulders. "It's nuts," he said, ignoring how his heart picked up speed as he traced the men's faces. "The whole thing is." The longer he stared at the picture, the crazier the tricks his mind played, until a thought hit him, and he dropped the picture on the table. "Wait. What if she's the one making everything else happen?"

Holding the wedding picture, Charlie gazed at him, his smooth brow furrowed, green eyes confused. "Everything else? What are you talking about?"

"Like us. The stuff we did. What if she's making it happen?" Like a dousing of icy-cold water dumped over his head, the shock of his rapidly spinning thoughts hit him hard, and Ian couldn't control the words spilling from his mouth. "It makes sense if you think about it. It's not really us feeling this. It's Rachel making it happen. You're not really attracted to me, and I'm not really into you. She's the one doing it."

Twin spots of fire stood out on Charlie's otherwise pale face. "Is that what you think?"

Ian nodded eagerly. "Yeah. I mean, I've never been into guys before, so why now?"

"You think Rachel put some kind of spell on you, so you'd want me?"

Caught up in his head, Ian sprang up from the table. Everything became clear. Now that he figured it out, it all made sense. "Rachel's been manipulating us both. She wanted her brother with Robert, so she was going to make sure to put us together because she thinks we're them come back to life."

"Oh."

"Don't you see? It's not only me. It's you too."

"Me? How so?"

"You don't really want me like that either. Now that we know, it's better. We can just be friends and not let any of this other shit make a difference."

"Yeah. Just friends. That makes sense."

But even as Charlie spoke, Ian recalled the penetrating heat of Charlie's body and the sweet softness of his lips. Was that all made-up too?

Despite the words sounding wrong and tasting bitter,

Ian focused on the letter. "So what I gather is, Robert was the guy who wasn't sure about it, and Eddie was. Eddie wanted to get away."

He waited a moment for Charlie to respond, but when he didn't, Ian poked him.

Charlie jumped. "What? Oh, yeah. Sounds right to me."

"You okay? You look funny."

A bright grin stretched Charlie's lips wide. "Me? No, totally. I'm great. Just great."

Ian continued. "So I wonder what happened between them. Like why did Robert get married and Eddie go to the army?"

"Well, I'm sure Eddie had to go. In those days, there was the draft. You didn't have a choice. Robert's heart condition probably got him out of serving."

"Oh, yeah. I didn't think about that. You're right."

Charlie's shoulder drooped, and Ian wanted to put his arms around him but held off. It wasn't him. That was Rachel. He wasn't really attracted to Charlie, just like he wasn't attracted to other guys. And Charlie didn't really like him like that either. It was all some crazy spell Rachel had put over them.

"Well, I'm gonna get going. I'll see you Friday night, right?"

Charlie met his gaze with uncertainty, his face still pale. "I dunno. I'll see. I'm sure you and your friends don't need someone like me hanging around."

"Someone like you? What the hell does that mean?"

Charlie squared his shoulders. "Gay. Remember, Ian? That wasn't a spell Rachel put on me, if that's what you're thinking. I'm still gay. I still like dick."

A hot flash of Charlie's mouth on his cock sent a surge of lust rocketing through Ian, and he gritted his teeth. It took all his willpower to keep his hands away from Charlie.

"I know. I don't care, and I'm telling you, neither do they."

They faced off, and Charlie jerked a quick nod. "Okay. So I guess I'll come and see if that's true."

"Great. See you Friday night, then."

* * *

"Ian, you ready? C'mon. Stop looking at yourself in the mirror. You're pretty enough."

Mickey waited by the front door as Ian checked himself out one last time. "Shut up, dude. I'm ready. Where's Patrick?"

"He was talking to Andi, so he's waiting for us outside."

"He really likes her, huh?" His wallet went in his front pocket to deter pickpockets, and he grabbed his phone and keys. "Let's go."

"He does."

As he locked the front door, Mickey asked, "Is your friend still coming?"

"Charlie?"

"Yeah, him." Mickey glanced at the house next door. "What's his story? He's...you know..." Mickey waved his palm back and forth.

Irritated, Ian ground out, "What the fuck does that mean? You got something to say, say it."

"I meant, he's gay, right?"

"So? What's that got to do with anything?"

Patrick, finished with his call, joined them at the front stoop of his house. "What's wrong? Ian looks like he wants to murder you."

"He's pissed 'cause I asked him if his new friend was gay."

"No. I ain't pissed about that. It's that stupid thing you did with your hand." Ian made the back-and-forth motion again. "What does that even mean? So what if Charlie's gay? He's a nice guy. You guys got something against gay people?"

"Whoa, Ian, back it up." Laughing, Patrick put up his hands. "I'm sure Mickey was just asking, and of course not. My boss is gay, and he's a cool guy."

"Great." Ian simmered with annoyance. "I'm sure he's glad he's got your approval."

"Dude, chill."

Mickey leaned against the gate. "I didn't mean nothin' by it. I was just asking, is all."

"Okay, well, I feel bad for him 'cause he doesn't have many friends, and I think he's a little shy. So I'm glad he's coming out with us."

He sent Charlie a text that they were ready, and got a thumbs-up. A minute later Charlie walked out in a tight, black short-sleeved button-down with a black skinny tie and pair of gray skinny jeans that showed every bump and curve of his legs.

Ian's mouth went dry. "Are we ready to go?" he asked roughly. Now that he'd figured out it was all Rachel's doing, shouldn't he have stopped wanting Charlie? 'Cause if so, it hadn't happened yet.

This was going to be one long-ass night.

Two hours later, Mickey nudged him. "You sure you know your boy? He don't look so shy to me."

Goddamned if Mickey wasn't right. For the past twenty minutes, Charlie had been cozying up with a tattooed guy who, upon their entrance, had made a beeline for him. After buying him a drink, they hadn't left the dance floor, and now they were slow-dancing, the man's arms wrapped around Charlie in a close embrace.

"Whatever. He's an adult. He can do what he wants." Deliberately turning away from Charlie and his man, Ian smiled at a very pretty dark-haired woman at the bar, with whom he'd been making eye contact for the past fifteen minutes. He pointed to her drink. "Can I buy you another?"

"No thanks, but you can sit and talk to me while I drink mine." She took a sip.

Taken aback by her response, Ian found himself intrigued enough to sit next to her. "I'm Ian."

"Denise. Nice to meet you."

Ian wished he could turn around and see what Charlie was up to with Mr. Tattoo, but he couldn't without being rude.

"You too."

"I don't let guys I've never had a conversation with buy me drinks. Then they don't think I owe them anything, like a kiss or something."

"I never thought of that. You're right." He was so glad his sisters were all married and didn't have to put up with shit like that. It had been hard enough for him to back off while they were dating and saw their hearts get broken by boyfriends.

Denise sipped her fruity drink and licked her luscious

lips. He leaned closer and caught the scent of her musky perfume. "How about if you go out on a date with a guy? Do you let them buy you dinner?"

Her eyes sparkled. "I guess I'd have to see."

Ian was about to ask her out, when he heard a shout from the dance floor, and they both craned their necks to see what happened. Red-faced, Charlie stood a foot away from the guy he'd been dancing with. His dance partner's lip was curled in a sneer. Without a second thought, Ian left Denise's side for Charlie's.

"What's wrong?"

"None of your business," Tattoo Man spit at him, then reached for Charlie, who shrank away. "Come on."

"I said no." Jaw thrust out, Charlie crossed his arms. "Leave me alone and get out of my way."

"What the hell is happening?" Ian stepped between them. "Is he bothering you?"

The guy snarled at him. "I said it's not your business. Your little friend here is a cocktease."

"I am not," Charlie cried out. "Just 'cause you buy me a drink doesn't mean I gotta go with you." Equally furious, he glared at Ian. "Go back to your friends. I'm fine. I don't need you to fight my battles."

Charlie and the guy faced off against each other, while inside Ian a storm of emotions raged. How fucking dare this guy think he could put his hands on Charlie? And why was Charlie so angry with Ian?

"Whatever. You ain't worth it." The guy stomped away, but Ian saw Charlie flinch at his words.

"He's a fucking asshole. Don't pay attention to anything he says."

"I'm all right," Charlie said. "Leave me the hell

alone. I just wanna go home." He pushed his way past Ian. Mickey and Patrick had been standing there all along without Ian even realizing it, but he left them to run after Charlie, who'd reached the entrance.

"Yo, Charlie, hold up."

He didn't stop and pushed his way out of the bar. Ian didn't hesitate, following him out to the street. It might've been dark, but Charlie's golden light followed him everywhere.

"Charlie." Finally he waited, and Ian caught up with him. "C'mon, why're you leaving? You can hang out with us."

"No. It's fine. You're having a good time with that girl, and I wanna be alone. I'm gonna go. Talk to you soon."

Before Ian could gather his wits, Charlie loped away and took the stairs down to the subway entrance at the corner. Shaking his head, Ian returned to the bar and Denise, still sitting and waiting. Her eyes lit up when she saw him.

"You're back."

"Sorry I ran out on you."

Her glossy hair swished over smooth bare shoulders. "Don't be. I like a man who stands up for his friends. And that big guy with the tats was being creepy."

"Oh, yeah? What'd you see?" Ian signaled to the bartender. "I'll take a Brooklyn Lager, please."

"Well..." She sipped her drink, eyes narrowed in thought. "He was holding your friend really tight and tried to kiss him. Your friend shook his head, but the guy laughed and squeezed his ass, and that's when your friend pushed him away."

Cold rage poured through him. "That bastard."

"No one has a right to put their hands on someone else if they don't want it."

"Ian, dude, what happened to Charlie? Did he split?" Mickey asked as he and Patrick walked over to the bar. "And who is this beautiful lady?"

Rolling his eyes, Ian introduced Denise to his friends, and soon they were all laughing, but Ian couldn't stop the gnawing feeling that he should check on Charlie.

"Will you excuse me?" Denise stood and flashed him a smile. "I'll be right back." Ian admired the swing of her hips as she moved across the bar toward the ladies' room.

"Dude." Mickey shoved at his shoulder once Denise was out of earshot. "If you wanna score with her, you gotta stop frowning. You're bringing the vibe down."

"I can't help it," he muttered. "I feel bad for him."

"Who?" Patrick's brows knitted together.

"Charlie."

"Charlie? You've gotta be fuckin' kidding me." Mickey's eyes popped wide, his mouth hanging open. "Why the hell are you worried? He's a grown-ass man."

"Seemed okay far as I could tell," Patrick chimed in. "Told that dude off."

Ian glared at them. "That guy put his hands all over him. That's not right and you know it."

"And he handled his shit. Case closed." Mickey dismissed him and drained his beer. "What I do know is, you got a gorgeous babe right here, who you better not fuck up your chances with by yapping about some gay guy."

Mickey was right. Especially after finding out that Rachel had been pulling the strings and pushing them together, the right thing to do was to forget about Charlie and concentrate on the beautiful woman walking toward him with a body made for sin and a smile that drew the attention of all the other men in the bar.

He really should.

And yet he couldn't.

When Denise reached him, she cocked her head. "You're leaving."

Pretty *and* smart. Surprised at her insight, he wondered with trepidation how well he was able to hide his other emotions. "How did you know?"

"You didn't seem into it...or me, once you came back from talking to your friend." She held out her hand. "Take my number if you want, and maybe you can let me know how he's doing?"

"Definitely," he said and watched her enter her number in his phone.

"Text me so I'll have yours?" She gazed up at him through long, dark lashes.

"I will." He did so, then hesitated. "Can I kiss you good-bye?" He needed to prove to himself she could turn him on.

"I'd like that. And I'd rather it be a see-you-later kiss."

She wound her arms around his neck. Ian held her around her supple waist and pressed their lips together gently. Denise surprised him again by taking the lead. She ran her tongue along the seam of his lips and slid inside, touching her soft tongue to his. He pushed himself to respond, concerned that he wasn't feeling it. Feeling her.

He should want to push her up against the wall and taste all that sweetness she was offering him. He should love her full breasts and the perfume of her smooth, velvety skin. Instead Ian remained tangled up in the kisses from Charlie, wishing for the hot, hard scrape of a rough jaw on his.

"I'll call you," he said and kissed her cheek, then turned on his heel and left the bar, ignoring his buddies hollering after him. He clambered down the steps to the station, and hearing the train's screech of arrival, pulled out his MetroCard and zipped through the turnstile. Once inside the subway car, he held onto the pole, his heart and mind troubled.

Forty minutes later, ringing the bell to Charlie's house, Ian still had no clue. All he knew was this insistent, driving force inside him to make sure Charlie was all right. He pushed the lighted bell over and over again, hearing the chimes.

Charlie wrenched open the door. "Who is it?" Upon seeing Ian, his jaw tightened, and he crossed his arms and planted his feet wide. "What do you want?"

"To see if you're okay."

"I'm okay. Bye." He made to close the door, but Ian put his hand out to forestall it.

"Don't, please. Can I come in?"

Charlie glared at him. "Whatever." He shrugged and walked away into the gloom of the house, the golden light around him glittering.

Ian scrambled inside after him and closed the door. He thought Charlie might've brought him inside the house to sit and talk, maybe to go into the kitchen or the living room, but he stopped at the staircase with that same stubborn jaw.

"Hey, look. I'm really sorry that happened to you."

"You said that at the bar. You didn't need to come here and tell me again. I heard you the first time."

"Why didn't you stay and hang out with us anyway?"

"What're you doing here?" Ignoring his own question, Charlie leaned against the newel post of the stairway and said, "I thought you'd be chatting up that woman I saw you with."

Ian stood in front of Charlie, their surroundings melting into the darkness behind him, but with Charlie's unique golden glow, no lights were needed. Being with Charlie was like living in a perpetual sunrise, and like with sunrises, came anticipation.

"I did, but I couldn't concentrate." Ian's skin prickled, and goose bumps rose on his arms. Charlie's wide eyes burned with a fire that drew Ian in, even as his confusion grew. "I was concerned about you."

Charlie licked his lips, and Ian's dick stiffened. His heart accelerated, and he couldn't catch his breath.

This isn't real. It's all from the ghost.

He'd spent the past week telling himself that, convincing himself the attraction to Charlie wasn't real. It was all conjured up by Rachel, the same as those scenes from the past she revealed to them.

But this was no dream, and the reality was, Ian wanted Charlie more than ever. He couldn't walk away.

"I'm fine, as you can see. So I'm sorry you left that girl for nothing, but maybe you can go back and—*uhh.*"

Ian seized Charlie and held him tight. "I don't want her. I...I want you."

Chapter Seventeen

He'd tried to be strong. Especially after their last time together and Rachel's revelation, Charlie hadn't expected to hear from Ian again and had steeled himself to have their budding friendship reduced to waves over the backyard hedges and awkward conversations that would eventually fade to nothing. But when Ian texted him that they were still on for the night, Charlie's stupid heart leaped. He'd given himself a stern talking-to while getting dressed, and by the time they all met up, he was fully prepared to keep his distance.

But damn Ian for making it difficult as hell for him to keep that promise. Charlie tried everything to forget how gorgeous Ian looked with his smooth muscles flexing under all that golden, tanned skin. He ignored how Ian's tight black T-shirt clung to his broad shoulders and stretched across his chest.

He hardened his heart as he watched Ian flirt with the beautiful woman at the bar while he danced with the guy who'd approached him when they'd entered. Charlie thought if he could lose himself in someone else for the night, it would be the first step in forgetting his sexy neighbor.

With his thoughts so wrapped up in Ian, Charlie had missed his usual cues and warning signals, and when the guy—he hadn't even said his name—grabbed his ass, fear drowned him, and Charlie froze.

Then Ian rushed to his aid. He'd never had someone watching out for him before. He'd always been on his own. Alone. It would've been easy to be pulled into Ian's circle of friends and hang out at the bar, but he couldn't stand to see Ian flirt with the woman he'd been talking to. He wondered if Ian had kissed her.

The last thing he expected when he opened the door was to find a concerned Ian. It meant he'd left his friends and a woman he'd been interested in to come and check on Charlie's well-being and make sure he wasn't upset or hurt. Maybe he did want Charlie and wasn't interested in anyone else. Maybe Ian was wrong, and it wasn't Rachel the ghost's doing after all.

Maybe it was real, and in that case, Charlie needed a little more time to think.

But with Ian's lips moving firmly over his, Charlie's resolve went out the window, and he clung to Ian's broad shoulders while Ian took him apart kiss by kiss, breath by breath. Charlie pressed up against Ian, fitting their bodies together, practically purring at the thrust of Ian's huge erection into his stomach. Hell yeah, he wanted that. He had no shame in being a size queen.

"Oh God, oh God," Ian gasped. "Charlie, fuck. I can't…I want…"

And Charlie knew what Ian wanted and cupped his groin, tracing that big bulge. There was nothing more he wanted to do than yank Ian's pants down and swallow him whole. Charlie's body cried out for it, practically screamed to taste him, so when Ian popped the button and lowered his zipper, Charlie buried his face into the crook of Ian's neck.

And smelled perfume.

A woman's perfume.

Charlie had no idea where he got the inner strength to take a step back and push Ian away, but while the scent of the woman's musky fragrance remained like a fog between him and Ian, Charlie saw the situation crystal clear.

"No. You don't want me."

Wild-eyed and flushed, Ian gazed at him with a dumbfounded expression. "What the fuck? Of course I do." He almost whined. "Please." He reached for Charlie again.

Sidestepping Ian's outstretched hand, Charlie sat on the stairs. "Remember what you said? You stood right there"—he pointed—"and said you didn't really want me. That it was Rachel making you feel that way." He paused. "I know you kissed her. I smell her perfume on you."

"Kissed? Who? Oh, Denise?" Ian's chest heaved as if he were winded, and he burst out with a nervous laugh. "I…yeah, I did. I even thought about you when I was kissing her."

"So I'm the consolation prize because you know I want you and you think I'll give it up because of what we did before? Well, guess what?" He poked Ian. "I'm not the runner-up. I deserve to be number one."

"You do. And I didn't mean it that way." Ian adjusted himself, wincing as he pulled up his zipper and buttoned his fly. "After you left, yeah, I chatted up Denise. She's gorgeous and smart, and any other time I would've been really into her, but after that shit went down on the dance floor, I couldn't concentrate on anything other than you and your safety."

"Well, here I am. I'm safe. So you can go home or go back to her. I don't care."

"Charlie, look—"

"Do you still think what happened between us was because of Rachel?"

"Let me ex—"

"Just answer me."

Complacent Charlie had gone out the window when Ian had declared whatever had happened between them wasn't real. He hardened himself against wanting Ian so bad, he'd capitulate at the first sign of Ian wavering.

Ian chewed his lip. "I don't know anymore. I thought so, but...dammit, I should've stopped thinking about you like...like..." He pushed his fingers through his hair.

"Like what?" Charlie asked, almost unable to breathe at the naked desire on Ian's face.

"Like I can't be near you without touching you. I can't look at you without wanting to kiss you." Ian rubbed his face and gave him a wary smile. "There's a lot of shit I need to figure out, I know."

Charlie didn't know whether to laugh or cry at Ian's honesty. He'd never had anyone speak from their heart before.

"I think this is a good start."

Ian's face screwed up, his brow creased, blue eyes

anxious. "But we can still hang out, right? I mean, I dunno about all that reincarnation shit, but I still want to figure out what happened between Robert and Eddie."

"Why?"

Nonplussed, Ian blew out a breath and rubbed the back of his neck. "I dunno. Like I said, it's like a puzzle we started. I want to see what happens. Besides, I thought you and I were friends, aside from everything else between us."

That wasn't what Charlie had expected. "Oh." It hadn't occurred to him that Ian might want a simple friendship. The guys he knew, especially the straight, curious ones, usually wanted to get off, then disappear.

"Yeah, oh. I like hanging out with you. Before all that shit happened at the bar, we were having a good time. And my friends thought you were cool."

"Not anymore. They probably think I'm a fucking weirdo. That's what always happens." He shut his mouth quickly, but Ian jumped on it.

"I know you've been hurt before, and I'm sorry. But I'm not gonna be one of those people who walks into your life to take something from you and disappears once he gets it. I'm your friend. And when I'm your friend, you're stuck with me for good."

Words like that should make his heart happy, but Charlie remembered Ian's other words.

"It wasn't us. It was Rachel making us feel this way."

Not for him. But until Ian worked through whatever was swimming around in his brain, Charlie had to be strong. So he smiled at Ian and pretended to be okay. Something he'd been mastering all his life.

"I appreciate you checking up on me, but I'm fine. Really. I'm not mad at you. I'm mad at myself for slipping up with that asshole."

"Why don't we start with a clean slate? Friends and neighbors. Okay?"

Frowning, Charlie studied Ian's hopeful face.

"Okay. But this can't happen again. You can't get horny and come over, expecting to have sex. It's not fair."

"I promise." Ian bounced on his toes. "So, you wanna hang out tomorrow night? Those two have dates."

"I'm sure if you called up the woman you met tonight, you could go out with her."

"But I wanna watch the game and eat junk food and then go out."

And despite how hard Charlie tried, he couldn't hold back his smile. There was something about Ian that made him impossible to refuse.

"Okay, I guess."

"You can pick the place we go out." The cocky grin returned. "Maybe we'll both get lucky."

Lucky was having a guy like Ian wanting to be his friend, something Charlie didn't have much experience with.

"That didn't work out so great the last time. Remember?"

Shit. He shouldn't have said that. Ian's bright eyes darkened, and a flush rose over his cheeks. "Yeah. I'm sorry about that. But, uh, it'll be okay."

"If you're sure...we can go to this place I've been wanting to try."

"It's a deal. Ball game, barbecue, then the bar."

"Don't you wanna know where?"

"I don't care."

If Ian was okay with it, so was he.

"What should I bring for the barbecue?"

They walked to the front door. "Hmm, I have burgers and dogs." His eyes lit up. "Ice cream."

"What flavor?"

"Anything with chocolate." Ian rubbed his stomach, and Charlie had to fight the urge to stare at Ian's fingers stroking his firm abs. The man was built so fine, Charlie could see the ridges of muscle through the clinging, thin shirt.

They reached the entrance, and the streetlight hit the half-glass front door, illuminating Ian's bright, open face. How could Charlie stay mad at a man who grew excited over ice cream?

"Okay, I'm sure I'll find something." Visions of Ian licking a cone or spoon chased through his mind.

"How's two o'clock? Game starts at four, which means we can probably eat around seven thirty. If that's okay with you."

"Yeah. Sure."

He opened the door and watched Ian tramp down the stairs to his house. Maybe it would all work out eventually, and he could stop feeling like he wanted to hold on to Ian and not let go.

* * *

At 2:05 the next afternoon, Charlie rang the bell, and Ian pulled open the door. "Hey. I haveta go upstairs to the house. Come with me." Ian brushed past him, bounded up the steps, and unlocked the door to the main house. At a slower pace, Charlie followed after him, gazing around as they walked through. Ian closed the door behind him.

"You've never been here, right?"

"No, of course not." The house was smaller than his and much less formal. Family pictures covered the walls, and the furniture was well worn, with throws tossed over a comfortable-looking couch and knickknacks and more photos taking up space on mantels and tables. Charlie could almost see and hear Ian's family, which he pictured as happy and loudly boisterous. A lot like Ian. "This is nice."

Ian halted in midstep. "Yeah. We had fun here, although I didn't realize it until everyone left. They were some good times." His smile wavered. "I miss them. Then they come for a visit, and it's great for a few days until the questions start: When are you getting married, Ian? Why don't you have a girlfriend?" His eyes twinkled. "Then I'm ready to not see them for another six months. Wanna tour?"

"Sure." He had to admit he was curious to see where Ian grew up.

Like most town homes, the house was a side-hall, with the staircase running up one wall. A hallway led to the back of the house, with all the rooms facing the staircase. Even before he entered any of the rooms, the house wrapped its warmth around him like a gentle hug, welcoming him home.

"The front room was where we put the Christmas tree and where my mother used to have her book-club meetings." Ian pointed to the rectangular room with shining original plank floors. A window seat, complete with puffy, colorful cushions, fit beneath a large bay window which let in streams of light to warm the floors to a soft, honey-golden hue. One large, comfortable couch patterned in faded chintz faced the wall, with several smaller club chairs surrounding it. It was a room filled with love, and Charlie could picture the loving family memories.

"The family room is behind it, and then the dining room at the end of the house. I'll show you the kitchen when we go get the grill stuff. C'mon upstairs first." Talking and not waiting for an answer, Ian mounted the steep staircase.

Surprised Ian wanted him to go upstairs, Charlie took the steps slowly. As he ascended, a strange tingling began beneath his skin. Ian led him to the first door, but before he said a word, Charlie blurted out, "This is your room, right?"

Ian's hand closed around the knob. "Yeah, why?" His brows pulled together, and Charlie shifted under his bright blue gaze. "Oh, shit. Don't tell me..."

Charlie broke eye contact. "No, I mean, yeah, I have this weird feeling, but that's all."

Looking unconvinced, Ian pushed the door open. The room was about ten by twelve, with a queen bed, a wooden dresser, and a desk. A small table with a plain lamp stood next to the bed, which was pushed against the wall with a single, albeit large window for light.

Without waiting for an invitation, Charlie entered, headed for the bed, and sat. "I know you're thinking I'm crazy."

Ian, who'd remained by the doorway, walked into the room. "Why would I? Not like we both haven't seen the ghost and had weird shit happen." Yet despite his words, Charlie made a mental note that Ian remained a distance away.

The sensation of familiarity rose inside him with an almost choking intensity, and Charlie rose from the bed as if scorched. He moved to the window and placed his hand on the glass, watching a scene unfold in front of him.

At the sound of the front door opening, Robert sprang off Eddie and scrambled upright. His lips were red and swollen from kissing, blue eyes glazed. Eddie hadn't believed his luck—Robert had allowed him to rest his hand on the bulge of his crotch. Eddie, taking a chance, had run his hand down the steely length, then cupped the firm sac he could feel through Robert's thin linen trousers. He wanted so desperately to unbutton the front of his pants and see Robert naked, but now it seemed that wasn't meant to be.

"My parents. They're home early. I knew this wasn't a good idea."

"Robert, relax. We're just studying for an exam. Don't worry."

The fear vanished. "You're right. It's fine." He sent Eddie a yearning look. "I'm sorry."

"About what happened?" His heart fell. Eddie's lips still tingled, and his balls ached. Nothing had ever been as perfect as having Robert's mouth on his, first gently, then harder. Frantic and hot.

"No. No of course not." His smile was shy. "That was amazing. I meant about my parents coming back so early."

"There will be other days."

"Charlie? You okay?"

He gazed into Ian's concerned face and blinked. "Yeah. Sure."

"You had a funny look on your face. And that glow... it faded to almost nothing."

"What? You forget I don't see it, so I don't know what you're even talking about."

"It flared up again once we started talking."

"It did? I'm fine. Really."

Not really, but what could he say that wouldn't give Ian the wrong idea? Charlie was determined to keep it light and casual between them, like Ian wanted.

"Are you sure?" Doubt resonated in Ian's words and showed in the pucker of his brow.

"I said I am. Nice room."

"Yeah. I had some good times here. I liked being the first room at the top of the stairs. I could sneak in if I was late coming home, or sneak out after everyone else went to bed. Made it easier not to have to pass anyone else's doors, you know?"

No. He didn't know. A happy night for him was not having to share a bed with another kid, or having a bed to begin with, instead of a lumpy sofa.

"Show me the rest of the house."

After a quick glance inside his sisters' rooms and the larger master bedroom, they returned to the main floor, where Charlie could breathe easier.

"Come to the kitchen. I gotta get some stuff for the grill."

Charlie followed him into a large, old-fashioned, country-style kitchen and stopped short and stared. Red roosters marched in a line up and down on the white cotton curtains, the wallpaper pattern featured roosters scattered about, and all the dish towels and items like salt-and-pepper shakers, cooking utensil containers, and refrigerator magnets were all…roosters. Pictures of roosters hung on the wall, staring at them in all their beady-eyed, beaky splendor.

"Wow," Charlie said, surveying the room. "This is… something." His lips twitched, and he tried to hold it in, shaking silently.

"Don't say it." Ian put out a hand, doubled over with

laughter.

Charlie let out a *whoop* and covered his mouth. "Oh my God, this is priceless. I love it." Even the long wooden trestle table was covered with a tablecloth with a rooster pattern.

Ian waggled his brows. "You would. It's all about the cock."

Charlie's face heated, but he rolled his eyes. He could handle the teasing playfulness with Ian. It must be what friendship was all about.

"They keep the grill stuff in here. Hold on and I'll get it." Ian opened a door, and Charlie saw a small pantry with shelves up to the ceiling. "Just haveta get the charcoal."

"You don't use gas?" Surprised, Charlie picked up a saltshaker and stared at the red rooster with the yellow beak and shiny black eyes. He shook his head and set it down.

"Never got around to it. Don't know why." Ian hefted a bag, and Charlie had to tear his gaze away from Ian's straining biceps.

"We can go. I went to check my stash this morning and found an almost empty bag. Guess I forgot to buy last summer, but this'll last me. Grab the keys from my front pocket and open the security lock on the kitchen door, please? The grill is up here on the deck."

"Sure."

No big deal at all to feel around inside Ian's jeans for the keys. He found them, warm from Ian's body heat, and pulled them out. Yeah, no big deal at all.

Fake smile in place, Charlie unlocked the bar across the back door and held it open for Ian, who breezed past him. Why couldn't he be more like Ian, who, from the looks of it, had taken their talk to heart and had firmly friend-zoned him?

Charlie followed Ian outside to the deck and vowed to not only enjoy the day with a friend, but to meet someone later that night when they went out. He watched as Ian set up the grill.

"Getting it ready for when the game is finished. Let's go…unless…what the hell. We can just watch the game up here. More comfortable." His infectious grin set Charlie's heart slamming, but he managed to keep his smile casual.

"Whatever you want."

"I'll go and grab the food and stuff."

"Shit. I left the ice cream at home."

Ian groaned. "Ah, no, man. I had my heart set on some chocolate. Go get it and meet me here. I'll leave the front door open for you."

Charlie followed Ian outside and squinted in the sunlight. "I'll only be a few minutes."

"No worries." Ian checked his phone. "It's close to three, so they're doing pregame shit. I don't need to see that."

They separated, and Charlie flew up the stairs of his house and got the ice cream out of the freezer.

"You believe me, don't you, Charlie?"

"Wha—" He spun around to see Rachel hovering in the arch of the kitchen. "Oh, for God's sake." Heart pounding, he collapsed in a chair. "Stop *doing* that. You can give a guy a heart attack."

"Oh, dear. I thought you'd be used to me by now." She floated closer. She looked different. Lighter, more transparent. Was she sick?

Wait a minute. This was insane. She was a *ghost*. Charlie shook his head at his strange mindset these days.

"Seriously? You think it's easy to have someone appear in front of you out of the blue?"

"*I'm sorry, but...*" Here she turned anxious and started wringing her hands. "*It was so hard waiting for you to come here and find your home.*"

The stress of Ian telling him he only wanted to be friends and of suppressing his emotions got to Charlie, and he snapped. "What good are you? Why couldn't you have found me before, when they used to hurt me? Why couldn't you have let me know?"

"*Until you showed up here, I didn't know. I was trapped, waiting. I wasn't allowed to leave. But once you came, it set me free.*" She floated close, closer than Charlie had ever seen her, and as far as that was possible with a nearly invisible person, he saw the anguish in her eyes. "*But know this. That woman who used to hit you?*" Her eyes turned a bright, glowing red, and fear rippled through Charlie. "*I made sure she never hurt anyone ever again. Those boys who teased and bullied you? They understand now what it's like to be pushed to the limit.*"

When his teacher had seen the bruises he'd tried to hide with long sleeves, Charlie was taken out of Mr. and Mrs. Hunte's house, and off he went to another foster home. It might've seemed crazy to want to stay in a place where he'd get beaten for sitting in the wrong chair, but he'd gotten used to staying out of the way, and they never hurt him too badly once he learned all the rules. The devil you know, sometimes.

"You saw that?" For some reason he was embarrassed and ashamed, as if a dirty secret had been exposed.

"*Not when it happened. Once you arrived here, all your past became visible to me. Now.*" She pointed her finger at him. "*I don't want you to give up.*"

"Give up?"

"*With Ian.*"

Not going there. He put the ice cream in a bag. "There's nothing with Ian. He knows you manipulated us…him… to like me."

"*What do* you *think, dear?*" She tilted her head, a smile tipping her lips up. "*You don't believe that, do you?*"

"I think I don't want to have this conversation. Ian and I are friends, and that's how it's going to stay, no matter how you try and push us together. Telling us we were reincarnated from your brother and his lover didn't prove anything. Even if I did believe you, Ian doesn't. So that's that."

Her smile grew broader. "*Funny how you used to call me the annoying one who couldn't take a hint.*" She faded out, and Charlie rubbed his eyes.

Damn, even seeing it happen over and over, it wasn't ever going to get easier to watch that without thinking he was going nuts. Rachel might think she knew it all, but Charlie knew the truth.

Ian wasn't ever going to believe they'd be anything more than friends.

Chapter Eighteen

"Aw, man. The Mets suck ass this season." Disgusted, Ian turned off the game.

"Is that a bad thing in baseball?" Charlie asked. " 'Cause speaking as your gay friend, don't knock it till you try it."

Ian's jaw dropped. "Huh? What?"

Charlie gave him a sunny smile. "I'm just saying. Getting rimmed is fucking hot."

"Rim…okay, I have no idea what you're talking about, but it doesn't sound like I want to either. I'm starving. Lemme fire up the grill."

Charlie had sprawled on the sofa during the game, and Ian had to force himself to look at the Mets rather than

Charlie's muscular legs and the flashes of his taut, pale skin where his T-shirt had ridden up on his stomach.

Nothing to see there. It wasn't real. "Rachel and her spells," he mumbled under his breath as he got up from the sofa.

"I'm not a witch, you fool. I'm a ghost. Get it straight," that reedy voice whispered in his ear.

He whipped around, but there was no one there but Charlie and him. *Dammit.* He wished she'd stop doing that.

"Can I help?" Charlie finished his beer, and Ian watched his lips clinging to the bottle, remembering their softness against his mouth and how hot, wet, and tight they felt sliding down his dick.

"Nah. I got it. You can find something else to watch or get some more beers and snacks from the fridge. I think we finished the chips." Phone in hand, Ian walked out onto the deck and lit the coals. As the flames danced in front of him, he went online and searched "rimming" on Google. The images on his screen made his eyes pop out of his head and his breath catch. Was that guy sticking his tongue inside the other guy's...*fuck*. It shouldn't make his balls tingle and his dick stiffen. And yet it did.

He slipped the phone into his pocket and stared into the flames. That ghost had fucked with his head, but he couldn't stop wondering what it would feel like to have someone do that to him. Maybe he—

"Hey, Ian?" Charlie stood in the doorway, a quizzical look in his big green eyes.

Ian jerked his thoughts away from what he'd seen on his phone. "Yeah?" Did Charlie know what he'd been looking at? Did he suspect? Ian dared a glance but relaxed when he saw nothing out of the ordinary on Charlie's face.

"Are you sure you're not too close to the heat? Your face is awfully red."

He blinked and stepped away. "Oh, yeah. I was thinking about something."

Something like your tongue in my ass.

Okay. Calm the fuck down. He scanned the area to see if Grandma Ghost was floating around, but he came up empty. Ian squeezed his eyes shut. "Lemme go get the burgers out of the fridge. He pushed past Charlie to enter the kitchen, and opened the refrigerator, appreciating the cool air on his burning cheeks. Plate in one hand, Ian grabbed one of the beers Charlie had taken out with the other.

"This'll cool me off. I didn't realize how hot it was outside."

"Mmm."

He sent Charlie a sharp glance, but he was busy opening his beer.

"Hello, boys."

He dropped the bottle, and thank fuck his parents didn't have a tile floor. The beer ran over his feet. "Goddammit." He ran to the sink and grabbed some paper towels while Charlie snickered. "Will you stop doing this?"

"What do you want me to do? Ring a bell?"

He'd like to wring her neck, but she didn't really have one. "What do you want?"

"For you to see more of Robert and Eddie."

She pointed her finger at the dining-room table, and with a *whoosh*, he and Charlie were flung into the chairs. Like before, she waved her hands, and this time they were at the ocean. Ian could hear gulls crying and the sound of waves crashing against the rocks. The smell of salt filled the air. A lone young man sat staring at the water. His pants were rolled up above his ankles, and a straw hat rested on his head. He was barefoot with his feet in the sand.

Eddie,

I'm sorry we haven't been able to see each other. As you know, my parents and aunt and uncle always go away for the summer months to my aunt's home on Long Island. They don't like me to be in the city during the summer as the doctor said it's better by the sea for my heart. I used to look forward to these summers, but now I wish I was back in Brooklyn.

Tell me what I'm missing. Is Rachel still following you around? Is it unbearably hot and muggy still? It's cool here in the mornings, and I've seen some dolphins and even whales. I've gone for long walks on the beach, soaking in the sea air and sun.

I wish I could see what you proposed happening. I don't know how we could make that a reality. Your father plans for you to take over the store, and mine wants me to learn the insurance business and to help him. I don't know how to go against what they want for me.

This weekend my aunt is throwing a party. There are lots of people to meet, and some people from home. I was surprised to see Charlotte, but it was nice to know a familiar face.

Robert

This time Rachel faded away before they had a chance to say anything.

The painful reality of Robert and Eddie was coming through clearly to him now. As were the machinations of the families to push Charlotte and Robert together.

"That's so sad. It's obvious what was happening. Robert's and Charlotte's parents decided they wanted them to get married and were using every chance they could to make it happen. Damn," he said, shaking his head. "And I thought my family butted into my business too much. I can't believe Robert let himself be pushed around like that. He should've had the guts to stand up to them."

"How? He wasn't well, and back then, many men did follow in their fathers' footsteps for business. Plus, he couldn't really tell them he wanted to run away with another man."

"I still can't believe his parents wouldn't stand by him."

"Would yours?" Charlie challenged him.

"What do you mean?"

"If you told your parents you were gay, do you think they'd be okay with it?"

Ian scratched his chin, thinking. Would they? It wasn't anything they'd ever discussed, but Ian wanted to think his parents were accepting and loving people.

"I think they would be. They always taught us to be kind and loving to everyone, no matter what. Be good to people and treat them well. 'That's all that matters,' my father told us. 'Don't let anyone push you around. Stand up for yourself and people around you.' So yeah." Ian expelled a rush of breath. "I think my parents would be okay, as long as the person I was with made me happy."

"I hope that's the truth." Charlie looked him dead in the eye. "But it doesn't matter. You're going to end up with a woman."

He shifted uncomfortably at the golden light pulsing around Charlie. It coincided with the throbbing of his dick. That kiss they'd shared the previous night gave him more pleasure than the ones he'd received from Denise or any of his previous girlfriends. "I think the coals should be ready," he said loudly, more cheerfully than he actually felt. "How do you like your burger?"

"Medium."

"Me too. Let's get this party started." He rose from his seat and breezed past Charlie to the kitchen, picked up the plate of burgers, and headed outside. The sun beamed down warm and bright, not a cloud marring the deep blue of the sky. No wind rustled through the trees, and he could hear the chirping of the birds.

"Your garden is really pretty. Did you always take care of it?" Charlie joined him on the deck and leaned over the wooden railing.

"Yeah. Me and my mom. I always loved working with flowers and plants and stuff. Miss Muir used to let me take care of her bushes when she was alive. There's something about digging in the dirt and seeing something you put in yourself grow into a plant or a flower that's always been really cool to me. You know?"

Charlie propped his chin in his hands. "I never had a yard to play in, but I guess I know what you mean."

Ian couldn't resist. "I could tell. Man, you killed all my hard work. It's like a jungle."

"Hey. Anytime you wanna come over and work on it, be my guest. You have an open invitation. I told you that before."

Ian remembered more than the flowers he'd pruned and the ivy he cut. The gentle touch of Charlie's hands on his had sent his blood singing. He wanted Charlie to touch him everywhere.

Ian forced himself to think of Charlie's garden, not the freckles dusting his nose or how his muscles shifted underneath his T-shirt. "I wasn't sure you meant it, but I wouldn't mind. I'll make it look really good—cut the grass, clear the weeds and stuff. I don't believe in cutting flowers for decoration. They belong in their natural state, where everyone can see them."

"Sure. If you mean it. I wasn't looking for free yard work. I'll pay you."

"Shut up with that." Ian waved him off. "I don't take money from friends." He lifted the lid of the grill to check the burgers. "Almost ready. If you want," he said casually, "you could help me."

"Me? I don't know anything about gardening."

"I could teach you. Then you could take care of it yourself if I'm not around." He grinned at Charlie and received an answering, tentative smile in return.

"Okay. Yeah, sure."

"Okay. Now let's eat." Ian rubbed his stomach. "I'm starvin' like Marvin."

* * *

"This was good," Charlie said, finishing chowing down his second hot dog, and Ian sat and watched, bemused how someone with such a tight, fit body could pack away so much food.

"Really? I thought after the second burger you might not've liked it, but the second dog really clinched how much you really hated it."

"You're a riot. Has anyone ever told you how funny you are—not?" Charlie licked his fingers.

Averting his eyes, Ian tossed his napkin onto his paper plate. He didn't want to see Charlie's pink tongue wrapping around sticky knuckles and fingertips. It was torture being with Charlie and acting casual when all he wanted to do was grab the man and kiss him.

"Where are we going tonight?"

"I figured we'd go to a dance club I know, then see where the night takes us. If one or both of us hooks up." Charlie shrugged. "I guess we'll play it by ear."

"Is it one of the gay dance clubs you were talking about? Not much chance of me finding someone there. But I don't mind."

"Dude, are you nuts? Those places are filled with women. Half the tables are bachelorette parties."

"Huh. Never thought about it that way."

"Don't worry. You'll have fun."

"I'm not worried. We have fun when we hang out even if nothing happens. And if you meet someone, I can make my own fun."

Charlie's eyes twinkled. "That's the spirit."

"I'm gonna leave the grill to cool down and clean it tomorrow." Ian checked his phone, surprised to see it was already nine thirty and, from the quick glance out the kitchen window, dark outside. "How about we shower and meet in like forty-five minutes?"

"Sounds like a plan."

Charlie grabbed his paper plate and plastic utensils and tossed them into the trash. They put away all the condiments and cleaned the table. A strange sense of déjà vu hit Ian. He closed his eyes for a moment and was jolted back to the past.

"Here, take a bite." Eddie held out a sausage. "It's good."

Dubious, Robert examined it. "Really? I've never eaten one."

Eddie's eyes danced. "Why am I not surprised? I'm happy to be your first." His voice dropped. "In every way."

Robert's bright blue eyes grew round, and his face grew hot. "Don't say that."

Eddie bit his lip. "You're mine too. My only one."

Robert's heart pounded, and it wasn't only his face that burned. Robert's whole body throbbed, and he wished...he wanted. ....If only it could be night and he and Eddie could meet under the oak tree when everyone else was asleep. Then they could kiss and touch each other like they'd been doing.

Perhaps Eddie read his mind, because he offered Robert the sausage again, and when he wrapped his hand around Robert's, he whispered, "Tonight. I want to show you something special."

"Really?"

Eddie put his lips to Robert's ear. "I'm going to put my mouth on you."

"Ian?"

He blinked back to the present and Charlie's anxious face peering into his. "Everything okay? You had a funny look."

That sharp, green gaze pierced right through him, and Ian pulled away quickly, but not before he saw the flash of hurt in Charlie's eyes. *Dammit.* It wasn't what Charlie thought. He wasn't upset having Charlie near. Exactly the opposite, in fact. The more time he spent with Charlie, the more he wanted him.

"Nah, I'm fine." He forced a smile. "Ready to go?"

"Yeah, I definitely need a shower. I'm all sweaty from hanging over the barbecue."

They separated at the foot of the stairs, and once

inside his apartment, Ian stripped and showered, hoping the hot water would clear his mind. Instead, the opposite happened. Thinking about Charlie washing himself in the shower, Ian ran his soapy-slick hands over his chest, under his arms, and down to his groin. He'd stiffened to an almost painful hardness, and before he knew it, he was jerking off, imagining it was Charlie's hands on him... Charlie's mouth. Through narrowed eyes, he watched his dick swell and redden, the thick head peeking through the white suds. Ian rolled his hips and thrust hard over and over into his grasping hand.

"Oh fuck," he sighed, spilling streams of come through his fingers. Eyes closed, he leaned against the cool tile with the water beating on him, then rinsed himself clean. He reached behind him blindly to shut off the shower, left the stall, and wrapped a towel around his waist.

His reflection in the mirror showed nothing unusual: same dark hair and blue eyes, same angular jaw like his father's, and high cheekbones like his mother's. Since childhood, Ian had been told how handsome he was, how his good looks would help him get ahead in life. How much easier everything would be for him with only a smile.

Right now nothing seemed easy, and he didn't feel much like smiling. Everything was mixed up. "I don't understand anything anymore..." he muttered.

"Yes, you do. It's Charlie. You want to be with him."

By now he recognized, even expected Rachel's voice, but when he spun around to see her, it was only him.

"Where are you?"

"Everywhere. I told you already, I see you. Why can't you admit who you want?"

"Because it's not me. That was you. You made me want Charlie." But even as he said it, the words sounded wrong, and his chest hurt, as if someone were squeezing his heart.

"*Oh, Ian,*" the voice reprimanded. "*I thought you were smarter than that. Maybe you are just another pretty face.*"

"I am not. But I've never been attracted to guys before."

"*Charlie's not just a regular guy. He's special.*"

"You don't have to tell me. I know he is."

"*So what's the problem?*"

"I still can't be sure it's not you. I know what you said about Robert and Eddie, but all this talk of reincarnation…I just don't know."

"*You don't know what? Are you ashamed of your feelings for Charlie? Are you that much like Robert, who'd rather live his life as a lie than admit who he loved?*"

"It's not that." But the words, echoing in the small bathroom, sounded weak.

"*Then what?*"

A buzzing sounded in his ears, but he ignored it to listen to the almost hypnotic voice.

"*Why do you think you've never been satisfied with any relationship? Haven't you felt more comfortable with Charlie than with anyone else? It's time to admit who you are and who you want.*"

The buzzing grew louder, and realizing the sound was coming from the front door, Ian ran to answer it. When he flung the door open, Charlie was waiting outside.

"Shit. I'm sorry. I lost track of the time." *Thinking about you.*

A mix of relief and laughter filled Charlie's face. "Oh, okay. I thought maybe you'd fallen asleep or someone else

227

came by and you changed your mind."

"No, I wouldn't blow you off even if someone else did call. C'mon in while I get dressed." He closed the door behind Charlie.

If it were Mickey or Patrick, he would have dropped his towel and walked naked through the apartment to his bedroom to get dressed. But he'd never jerked off in the shower thinking about Mickey or Patrick, and neither one had ever sucked his cock like a fucking Tootsie Pop, looking for the special chewy center.

"I'll just be a sec." He raced into the bedroom while Charlie waited on the sofa. Standing in front of his dresser, he pulled out a pair of soft jeans and a bright-blue shirt. A quick brush to his hair and a slap of Acqua di Gio, and he was ready to go.

Toward what, he had no clue, but tonight he was determined to find out.

Chapter Nineteen

He knew people were giving them the once-over as a couple only because Ian was so hot. Even Charlie couldn't resist sneaking peeks at him as they sat at their table and waited for the show to start. The bright-blue shirt brought out the intensity in his eyes, and those well-worn jeans cupped a firm ass and were just tight enough across the front to showcase his hefty bulge.

"Dude, you were right. The place is teeming with women."

Charlie grimaced. "Yeah, and it sucks. Makes it hard for us gays to meet someone in our own space."

"I can see that." Ian grinned at a woman at the table next to them, who was pouring a drink from a pitcher of Bellinis. "Like you wanna put a sign out that says, 'Only cocks allowed.' "

Charlie snorted, and the cute waiter passing by stopped and put a hand on his hip while balancing a tray.

"You know it, honey." The waiter fluttered his lashes at Ian, then leaned over to whisper to Charlie, "And aren't you the lucky one. I can see that's one nice big cock he's got waiting for you. Yum, yum."

He should be so lucky. God, he missed sex. Having Ian next to him put Charlie in a state of perpetual arousal, and he occasionally had to adjust himself under the table. Thank God it was relatively dark. All the lights went down, and the spotlight shone onstage.

"Show's about to start."

Wide-eyed like a kid during Christmas, Ian nodded. "I see."

The music started booming, and lights flashed. Three men came onstage and began a set. They gyrated, swung around on poles, and did a few dance routines. Charlie wasn't that impressed and certainly not aroused. The women at the table next to them attracted the most interest, mainly because they were sloppy-drunk and waving bills at the guys.

Twenty minutes later they were done, and the house lights came up. Waiters began circulating to remove empties, take orders, and settle bills.

"So what did you think?" He finished his beer and thought about where to go next. He didn't want to waste his time at a place with mediocre dancing and watery drinks.

"I've never been to a male strip club, so I don't have anything to base it on. I thought it was okay."

During the performance, Charlie had observed Ian's reaction to the dancers, and he was surprised to find him watching and not bored out of his mind.

"They weren't the best, but they tried hard."

"Have to give them credit, then. Do you want to stay or find someplace else?"

"I wouldn't mind leaving. We can hit up Stonewall if you want."

"Oh, the big gay bar in the Village?" Ian drained his beer. "Yeah, sure. Why not?"

Why not indeed?

An hour later, he and Ian were squished in a corner of the landmark bar, drinking beers and listening to the blasting dance music.

"Have you ever been here before?" He doubted it but wanted to hear from the source.

"Nah, but I've heard about it, of course." Ian scanned the large room, where a combination of men and women were drinking, dancing, and playing pool. "It's a cool place. I didn't picture it like this."

"No?" Charlie tipped his head. "What'd you think it would be like?"

The Stonewall Inn, epicenter of the gay rights movement, was a small, unassuming building from the front, identifiable by the numerous rainbow flags on and around the windows and the surrounding streetlights, along with the landmark plaque on the face of the building. Inside, the ceilings were low, the floors and walls dark. The bar ran the length of the wall, hectic bartenders filling orders like machines. A pool table occupied the rear of the bar, and Charlie had spent many hours watching and playing. The music thumped, and people danced in place, standing or at their tables. It was noisy and crowded with people on all sides and the safest place Charlie had ever been to.

"I dunno. Not so woodsy and down-to-earth. I thought it would be one of those glitzy places with lots of lights and mirrors."

"You mean more gay?" Charlie watched the flush rise to Ian's cheeks and felt sorry for baiting him. "It's okay. Just getting on your case." He elbowed Ian.

"Idiot." Ian snorted, then grew somber. "But I guess you're right. I'm sorry. It's stupid of me, huh, to have all these stereotypes? I mean, what does '*more gay*' even mean?"

"Well, what do you think it means?" When Charlie suggested going to Stonewall, he didn't plan on having a discussion of the meaning of being gay. But Ian had something on his mind, and Charlie understood him enough by now to know the man enjoyed talking out his feelings instead of keeping them bottled up, so he gave him the time and space to allow him to verbally feel his way through the conversation.

Ian set his beer bottle down on the sticky ledge. "I dunno anymore. I mean…I don't care who anyone dates and sleeps with, but saying it the way I just did makes me cringe. What does looking gay mean? Or bisexual? I told you, the foreman I work with is a big, tough ex-Marine I always assumed was straight, but when he told me he was bi, I was floored. Like I didn't expect a guy like him, a buff dude whose muscles have muscles, to have been with guys. So that's a prejudice I need to work on."

"Not all gays are twinks, you know."

Ian screwed up his face. "I don't know what that means, but I've been doing a lot of thinking lately and learning stuff."

"I hope you haven't hurt your brain with all the overwork," Charlie teased.

Ian turned to him, those bright-blue eyes now the strange molten silver that made Charlie's heart beat faster and his mouth go dry with longing.

"No. I've been trying to figure out one good reason why I should stay away from you, and I keep coming up empty."

He's been drinking. He's high and doesn't know what he's saying.

"I thought we were just going to be friends. Nothing more. Remember? You think Rachel is manipulating you to have feelings for me. Please don't play with me because you're curious. I'm not an experiment." He didn't want to push Ian away, but it was for the best. His heart might yearn, but he was tired of it getting broken over and over again. Much safer to listen to his head. The one on his shoulders, this time, instead of the one between his legs.

"I'm not."

"Sure you are. I already told you I've been with enough straight guys who only wanted to have their dicks sucked, and then they'd walk, no, *run* away when I'd start thinking there might be something more. I can't—I *won't* go through that again."

Ian gave him a hard look. "I get it. And I'm sorry. I don't want to lead you on. I'm just confused."

"Confused? You're confused? Let me lay it out for you." Charlie began to tick off on his fingers. "First you have a girlfriend, then you break up. Then we fool around and have sex, and then you say you're not into guys, that it's really Rachel making you feel things. Then you come on to me again. Finally, we agree to be friends. And after all that"—he glared at Ian—"you claim you want me? All true, right?"

"Yeah, but—"

"Fuck it, Ian. You've flipped on me more than a fucking stack of pancakes at IHOP. Everything I laid out is all the more reason to put the brakes on whatever it is you're thinking. It's much safer for us both to be just friends."

Nothing had ever been more painful for Charlie than to keep Ian at arm's length, especially now. It would be easy to take him home, where he knew they'd have the most mind-blowing sex he'd ever had. But at what cost? He couldn't risk his heart, but even more than that, it was because Ian had become something Charlie had wanted but never expected to find. A true friend. And that was worth more to him than a sexual relationship he knew would eventually fade.

"Besides," he said, hating the words but forcing himself to speak because he knew it was for the best. "There are plenty of guys who'd be happy to experiment with you."

Ian's reply was swift and unexpectedly harsh. "That's dumb. That's not what I want."

Losing his patience, he snapped, "What do you fucking want? Do you even know? You wanna fuck me and get it out of your system? Is that it?" He challenged Ian, who'd paled at his angry words.

"That's not what—ah, fuck it. I gotta piss. I'll be right back." He lurched out of his stool and stomped over to the bathroom. Charlie figured with the crowd, he'd be there a while, which would give both of them time to cool off. He sipped his beer and stared at the floor.

"Don't be upset with him."

Charlie whipped around to see the entire inside of the bar frozen, and *man*, if his hair didn't stand on end at the sight of all those motionless people. He slipped off his stool, and the screech of his chair broke the dead silence. Rachel, lighter and more translucent than the last time he'd seen her, appeared before him, a silvery, glowing aura around her. She sat in the middle of the pool table with a smile on her face.

"He's trying to work things out in his head. It isn't easy for him."

"What're you doing here?" Charlie hissed. "And you shouldn't sit on that. The two guys are in the middle of a game, and I know them. They're very competitive." The two leather daddies came for a weekly game, and Charlie had seen how intense the competition between the strong-willed men could get. He would not want to be around if one thought the other was cheating.

"Oh, don't worry. They can't hear or see me. Only you can. They'll think it was all a dream, and from what I know, this isn't the strangest thing people have ever dreamed about." She shook her head and tsked. *"Some of the things I've seen...I never imagined..."*

"Rachel," Charlie interrupted her. "What's so important that you had to come here? I can't believe you followed us to Stonewall."

"Reminds me a little of the speakeasies during Prohibition." Her inquisitive gaze peered over and around people's heads. *"Although people certainly don't dress as nicely now. So messy and inelegant."* She huffed out her disappointment. *"What happened to wanting to be well clothed? In my day, ladies and gentlemen wouldn't be allowed into a speakeasy, looking like this."*

"Rachel," he prompted impatiently. "What do you want?"

Dragging her attention back to him, she pressed her lips together. *"I'm here because you should talk to Ian again."*

That was what she came to tell him? Frustrated, he attempted to brush her off. "Oh. We've already talked and decided we're better off as friends."

"Yes, yes. I'm aware of that, remember? But I think if you talk with him and speak from your heart, you might be surprised at what he has to say now."

"But he thinks you're—"

"You're not listening to me." Shooting him a look of pure frustration, she shook her finger at him. *"He's questioning who he is, and that's always a good thing. If Robert hadn't been so afraid to talk to Eddie, perhaps my brother might've known some happiness in his short life. Ian is having a second look at who he is. You can't expect a man who never thought he was interested in another man before to jump headfirst into a love affair without questioning things. Give him time, but give him something to hold on to."*

If Charlie thought it might be true, he'd be doing a happy dance. But he'd allowed himself to be fooled so many times by men who'd deceived him with pretty words, this time he was determined to guard his heart. He thought of that line in that song from The Who: "Don't get fooled again."

The emotions spinning through his head were splitting him in two: one half knowing the right thing to do was keep the friendship between him and Ian casual, the other having dirty thoughts of licking Ian up and down from head to toe.

"I can't risk it. I know you're making him feel this way, and I don't want that. I'd rather have him as only a friend." Charlie grew weary of the internal battle, and now wished he'd never come to this place.

Skirts swishing, Rachel flew across the table to point a finger in his face. *"I'm telling you, I cannot make someone feel love or hate toward another person."*

Charlie folded his arms and shot her a look of disbelief. "Are you serious? Do you remember my first time in the house? The shaking chandeliers and falling mirrors? Or what about my date with Morgan and the bowl of spaghetti over his head?" He glared at her. "And don't tell me you weren't behind the pepperoni missiles and the out-of-control pizza when I was with TJ and Bryan."

"*You were making foolish choices. They weren't the right people for you.*" Rachel shrugged, a decidedly unghostlike gesture, but the way her lips twitched and her eyes danced, Charlie could see she wasn't truly sorry.

"So you made them leave."

"*Let's just say I put up obstacles. They chose to run. Ian isn't going to.*"

He gnawed on a fingernail. "I just don't want to get my hopes up like always. I've been too stupid over too many guys because I ignored warning signs. With Ian they're right in my face. Choosing to overlook them would be foolish."

"*But there's one big difference.*"

"What?"

Her smile lit up the room to daylight brightness. "*If those other men had truly cared for you, they would've come back. Nothing can stand in the way of love. That's what I've been trying to tell you—why I'm here in the first place.*"

"What?"

"*Ian is here. He knows it all—Robert and Eddie and me. The pieces you've given away of yourself. And he didn't walk away. He came back again and again and is standing with you. Just give him the chance for his head to catch up with his heart.*"

Maybe it made sense to a ghost, but all Charlie could

see was himself giving another straight guy the key to his heart. "Sure. I will. I promise." Anything to get her off his back.

She hovered over the center of the pool table and pointed at him. "*Don't make promises you don't intend on keeping.*"

Damn. A ghost *and* a mind reader. Rachel sailed around the bar, and Charlie thought she'd disappear, but then he watched in dismay as she stopped over the pool table again, took the balls, and moved them around.

"Why're you doing that?" he yelled out. "Don't mess up their game."

"*Oh, pishposh. It's not a big deal. What's the worst that could happen?*"

And with those words, she faded away. The bar sprang into action as if nothing had happened, and Charlie sipped his beer, nervous over Rachel messing with the leather daddies' game. His fears proved correct as one of the men slammed his cue on the table.

"What the fuck is my ball doing over there? Why'd you move it?"

The other man's eyes spit fire. "I didn't touch shit. You're crazy."

Nose to nose, they stood screaming, and Charlie backed away. He searched for Ian and saw him approaching, oblivious to the admiring looks he was getting from both men and women.

"What's going on?"

"Let's get out of here." Charlie set his bottle down. "Ready?"

"Yeah, sure, but what happened?"

"I'll tell you when we leave."

The two big men had moved away from the table and were busy slinging insults, each accusing the other of cheating. The argument grew heated, and their voices grew louder. Their faces were an inch apart, and Charlie wondered if they would end up fighting or fucking. He'd recognized a familiar gleam in their eyes.

They walked out onto Christopher Street and across Seventh Avenue to the Downtown subway. Once inside the station, the sign said it would be eleven minutes until the next train, so Charlie sat on the wooden bench with Ian next to him.

"So? What happened?"

Should he tell Ian that Rachel showed up and they talked? Or should he simply speak from the heart and once again take the risk of having it broken?

Ian nudged his shoulder. "Are you mad at me 'cause I said I was thinking things out again even though we talked already?"

"I'm not mad." He didn't want to look at Ian. It was too easy to capitulate, and Charlie knew where that would end—with him giving in and ultimately getting hurt. Despite what Rachel said, Charlie remained unconvinced that Ian's bouncing ball of emotions had landed in the spot marked "Ready to admit I'm bisexual."

"C'mon. You don't even want to look me in the eye." A rat scuttled across the platform toward the garbage pails. "You'd rather see that?" He pointed to the scavenging rodent.

"Ian, please." He didn't know what to say. "It's not that simple, and I don't want to get into it here."

"Dammit. You didn't want to talk in the bar. Now you don't want to talk here. Where *do* you want to tell me what's going on?"

"I promise, when we get back home, I'll talk to you." Finally he met Ian's eyes and saw the obvious frustration, but also fear and pain. The wind picked up, foretelling the train's imminent arrival. "Please. It's not going to be easy, and I think we need privacy."

"Okay. But I have things to say too, and you're going to listen."

He had to smile. "I have no doubt."

The train ride, even with the need to change lines, took less than fifteen minutes, and by unspoken agreement, they ended up at Ian's house. Ian kicked off his sneakers and sat heavily on the couch.

"Okay. Let's hear it."

Charlie took the recliner chair, not trusting himself to sit too close to Ian. "Rachel showed up at Stonewall tonight." Ian's eyes bugged out, and Charlie nodded in response. "Yeah. Exactly. You probably don't realize it, but she froze everyone at the bar, and we talked."

"Oh?"

"Yeah. She said you were questioning things and that I should let you. She also said that she can't make anyone feel love or hate. That what's happening between us…" Here the words were harder to voice. "Might be real."

Ian glowed. "And? What do you say?"

"I told her the truth." He lifted his chin, deciding to lay his heart out in the open. "I don't want to be someone's experiment again. Every guy I've ever been with has used me. I'm tired of it. I know I'm nothing special. I never had anyone to lean on and listen to but myself. And all I'm hearing are the same warning bells and signs I've gotten from every other straight guy. So yeah, I'm not going to deny that I want you. I think that's pretty obvious. But unless I can be sure that you won't walk away in the morning, telling me, '*Sorry, but I'm not really into it anymore*,' I don't see how this can go any further."

"Can I talk now?" Ian scooted to the edge of the sofa, hands clasped over his knees. " 'Cause the first thing I need to say is you're absolutely right."

Charlie's heart sank. "Oh. Okay, then. I'm glad we talked."

"You know, you got a bad habit of interrupting me." His eyes danced. "You gonna let me talk now or what?"

His heart pounded, and he nodded. "Yeah, sure." But he couldn't imagine anything Ian could say that would change the course.

Chapter Twenty

When he left the house that evening with Charlie, Ian had made up his mind to let the night unfold and see what happened. He saw the admiring looks people gave Charlie, even if the man didn't notice them himself. Someone had beaten down Charlie's self-confidence, and if he didn't realize how desirable he was, Ian intended to show him.

And yet, how could he tell Charlie who *he* was when Ian hadn't yet figured himself out?

But maybe…maybe he did. How long could he go on fooling himself that his attraction to Charlie was supernatural, when everything he felt about Charlie was as natural to him as breathing?

Like the brightness surrounding Charlie, a light switched on in Ian's head. Charlie turned him on like no one else had. But it was more than sexual. There was no one else he wanted to spend time with. Talk to. Share the parts of himself he'd never told anyone else about. Ian knew Charlie would understand his insecurity that no one would like him other than for his good looks.

He'd done such a damn good job of convincing Charlie their attraction was manipulated by Rachel, now he had to reverse course and use all his powers of persuasion to prove to Charlie his emotions were, in fact, real.

Ian asked, "Did Rachel tell you that she talked to me?"

Those big green eyes gazed at him unblinking, and Ian felt the pull of their glowing depths.

"Yeah. She said some things that made me assume you two had talked." Charlie frowned. "But I'm not sure how anything has changed from last night."

"Look." He rubbed his face. "You already know I've never been with a guy before, never thought about it. But why does that matter? Why can't it be the same as if I saw some girl walking down the street and her smile or her face made me go *whoa*, and I needed to get to know her better and want to be with her?"

"Because I'm not her. I'm not a woman, and no matter how much you might want it to be the same, it's not. Heterosexuality…it's the norm. What's expected. And when you said Rachel manipulated you to be with me, it hurt. Bad. So hell yeah, I'm going to take it slow. I'm going to be a goddamn snail if I have to. 'Cause you said it yourself: you've always been straight; it's not your normal to be attracted to guys."

This was getting him nowhere, and growing frustrated, Ian threw his hands in the air. "I'm not attracted to guys, Charlie. I'm attracted to you. Period. Only you. I see *you*, and it's like everything inside me goes on alert. I can't be near you without wanting to touch you."

"You're a guy who likes sex, and I made it easy for you, like I always do." Charlie's lower lip trembled, and Ian wanted to hunt down every person who'd ever disappointed Charlie and hurt them. First in line being himself.

"No. Sex wasn't ever anything special until you. Nothing felt right until you." Ian stood over Charlie, who paled. "For fuck's sake. Listen to what I'm saying, please. I don't want anyone else, man or woman. I want you." He put his face in front of Charlie's so their noses almost touched. "Only you. Ghost or no ghost, Charlie, I felt it the first time I saw you. Before we found out about Rachel."

"You did?" Charlie blinked rapidly. "But the sex? You don't have to lie…"

"Hell no, I'm not lying. Nothing compared to the other night. Nothing. Ever."

Charlie's proximity drugged Ian's senses, and he felt reckless enough to initiate a kiss. Their lips touched, and as always when he kissed Charlie, a wildness rose inside him. He needed to hold Charlie tight and never let him go. He tugged Charlie up to standing.

"I'm not only here for the sex. In a way, that's the easy part. I think the reason I couldn't get you out of my head is that it's the place you're supposed to be. The place you always were even before I knew you."

"So you believe what Rachel said about us being Eddie and Robert?"

"Oh, no." He smiled against Charlie's cheek, inhaling his soapy-clean scent. "When I kiss you, it's with regret from the past but the hope of a future. I don't want us to relive their story. I want to make our own."

"I'm afraid."

"Of what, me?"

"No." Charlie tipped his head up, and Ian knew courage when he saw it there, in Charlie's eyes. "Myself. Settling for half when I know I should have it all."

"I already told you, I don't do things by halves." Ian rested his hands of Charlie's shoulders, hoping. "And I'm ready to give it all to you. Everything. But I want it all from you. Your body and your heart."

"Feel me." Charlie picked up Ian's hand and placed it on his face. Ian trailed his fingers over the high cheekbones, then his neck until he rested them on Charlie's chest and felt the pounding of his heart. "Feel me," Charlie whispered and placed his hand over Ian's.

Together they stood listening to Charlie's heart, so damaged and broken in the past, beating strong and powerful with renewed vigor.

With Charlie unresisting, Ian pressed his mouth to Charlie's, drinking in his scent, his heat. The rough stubble scraping his chin enflamed him, and Ian pushed his tongue past those lips he couldn't stop kissing. They played and tangled, and Ian held Charlie closer, as if afraid he was a dream that might disappear.

Should it matter that the body he held close was hard and muscled, not curvy and smelling sweet like perfume? Ian slid his leg between Charlie's and felt the ridge of his stiffening dick. No, it didn't matter. The lick and slide of Charlie's slick tongue was a wonder wheel of sensation, spinning him around until he didn't know up from down and in from out.

All he knew was Charlie. And being with Charlie was so damn right.

He slanted his mouth over Charlie's and swallowed his sighs of pleasure. The hard prod of Charlie's erection pushed against his thigh, and Ian groaned, rocking his pelvis, desperate to get the friction he craved for his aching dick.

"I want you." He smoothed his hands across the broad planes of Charlie's back and cupped his ass, kneading the muscled roundness. Charlie's breathing grew heavier, and he let out those sexy whimpers that set Ian's blood boiling. "God, Charlie, please?"

Charlie tipped his head up to capture his gaze. "I want you too. But I need to trust you."

"You can. I promise. I won't run away." He cupped Charlie's cheek. "I won't ever hide you and pretend you're not mine."

The air shifted, and Ian waited, on the edge of something he'd never imagined possible, yet now couldn't live without. Inside Charlie's eyes, he watched the walls come down from a lifetime of hurt to the possibility of hope.

"Please, Charlie. What can I do to make you understand it isn't only about the sex? I'm not saying what you want to hear to get what I want from you." He recalled Patrick staying the night with his girlfriend without having sex. "If you just wanna go to bed and cuddle, we can do that too. No sex."

Charlie quirked a brow. "Are you serious? You'd be satisfied with that?"

"I'm satisfied with what you choose. For once you get to make the decision, start to finish."

"Are you sure? I know you say you wanna fuck me." Charlie didn't wait for him to respond and took off his jeans, boxers, and shirt so he stood completely naked in front of Ian. "Here I am. Do you want to be in bed with me? Feel me up against you—my dick, my balls? The hair on my chest? You want me kissing you? You like my tongue in your mouth, right? It's a man's tongue. Sometimes I like to take it from behind. Are you gonna want it that way?"

Aside from gym showers, Ian had never been alone with another naked guy. Yet it seemed natural to him to undress until he was as naked as Charlie. The wild expression in Charlie's eyes as Ian disrobed fueled his desire, made it burn brighter, but he also wanted to feast his eyes on Charlie. Surprisingly broad shoulders tapered to a narrow waist, slim hips, and a tight, muscled ass. A smattering of reddish-brown hair dived from a tight six-pack to his groin. Ian's gaze zeroed in on Charlie's cock. Under his fascinated gaze, Charlie's erection stiffened further until it stood straight out, and Ian, instead of being hesitant, wanted to feel that hot, velvety skin. He moved closer but wouldn't reach for Charlie unless he allowed it.

"Can I touch you?"

The head of Charlie's dick bumped his stomach, leaving a wet, sticky spot, and Ian's dick jerked when Charlie nodded. "If you want."

"I want." Ian let his fingers roam over Charlie's rigid length. It wasn't as long or thick as his. Ian knew he was bigger than many, and he wondered how he would ever fit inside Charlie. The thought of piercing through Charlie's little pink hole hit like a lightning strike to his cock. Goddamn, he was so hard, it hurt.

The sight and sounds of Charlie sighing out his pleasure fired Ian's desire. He was the one giving Charlie that brighter glow. It was his hand on Charlie's dick that had Charlie thrusting into his fist. Charlie wanted him.

"Harder," Charlie grunted. "Faster and harder."

Ian clenched his jaw and watched in fascination as Charlie's whole body flushed. Charlie's ass clenched tight and pistoned back and forth, and a long, drawn-out groan escaped his lips. Hot, sticky come spurted into Ian's hand, and he jumped in surprise.

Fuck, that was hot as hell.

Breathing heavily, Charlie pushed the sweaty strands of hair off his face, and Ian, curious what his come tasted like, hesitantly licked one of his fingers. Surprisingly bitter and a little salty, which he didn't mind. With Charlie's shocked eyes on his, Ian licked another finger.

"Next time…maybe…maybe I wanna try sucking you."

Charlie's eyes widened. "You do?"

"Yeah. Why should you get all the fun?" He reached down and wiped his sticky hand on his briefs, then cupped Charlie's cheek. "And I'm ready to have more fun. What about you? You want me inside you?"

"Fuck, yeah." Charlie sighed. "So bad."

At Charlie's lust-filled eyes, Ian felt his erection swell further until it rose up almost flat on his belly. God, he was so turned-on, he might come before he had the chance to do this. Wouldn't that be a fucking embarrassment?

"Come on, then."

They walked into the bedroom, where Ian grabbed Charlie around the waist and tipped them onto the bed. Their lips met in frantic, deep kisses, tongues licking and teeth biting. Ian didn't only want to fuck Charlie. He wanted to possess him. Own him. Claim him as his own. He'd never been so out of control and out of his mind for someone else, and he didn't care. All his life he'd waited for this moment. To discover what he'd been missing. He was on fire with passion. Need. Desire.

"Hold on a sec." He scrambled across the bed to his night table, where he got the lube and condoms.

Charlie lay on his back, legs spread wide. One hand stroked his cock, while the fingers of his other played with the cleft of his ass, and Ian groaned out his hunger.

"Fuck, that's so hot." His fingers twitched. "Can I try?"

"God, yeah. Put some lube on your fingers and play with my rim."

His fingers trembled as he followed Charlie's directions and touched the soft pucker of skin. Charlie shivered and moaned, and Ian, figuring it was what he wanted, pressed into the hole and nudged his finger deeper, past the tight little ring. His breath grew short, imagining his dick piercing through, surrounded by all that heat. It couldn't be comfortable, but Charlie didn't seem to have any problem with Ian pushing up inside him.

"More. Stick another one in me." Charlie rocked his pelvis, and Ian added a second finger, growing more confident at the pleasure rippling through Charlie. At Charlie's urging, he slid a third digit inside, knowing he'd have to stretch his tiny hole. From his whimpers and rising cries, Charlie seemed to love it, and Ian couldn't get enough of seeing his fingers enter and disappear inside Charlie's body. He kept them buried in Charlie's ass for a moment, then decided to wiggle them, and Charlie bucked. He dragged them in and out of Charlie, who writhed and rolled his hips.

"You like that?" He bit his lip and crooked his fingers up and down, stroking along Charlie's passage. "How about that?"

"Fuck me, Ian, come on," Charlie gritted out, green eyes blazing, and the golden glow around him pulsed bright as fireworks. "I want your dick inside me."

Ian's normally steady fingers shook while opening the condom wrapper, and it took several tries before he sheathed himself. Making sure he was well lubricated, Ian rubbed the wide head of his dick against Charlie's hole, catching it on the rim.

"Oh, yeah. That's it." Fascinated with Charlie's responsiveness, he continued to play with the edge of Charlie's hole. "Fuck, Ian, push it in. All the way." Charlie flailed and grabbed his arm, tugging him closer. "I need it. Please, Ian. Please."

Those broken words pushed Ian to the brink. Fueled by the surge of lust jolting through him, and needing to finally know what it would be like to be inside Charlie, Ian thrust the head of his dick past the ring of muscle. Charlie let out a shout and wrapped his legs around Ian's waist, and Ian lost himself in the viselike grip Charlie's snug ass held him in. Mindful of his size, he started with shallow thrusts, allowing Charlie to become accustomed to him, but Charlie wasn't having that. He held Ian tighter and pumped himself hard on his cock.

"Jesus," Ian muttered, watching Charlie shake under him. His breath came in short, hard pants, and sweat drenched his body. Charlie was beautiful falling apart.

"*Ahh*, oh my God." Charlie trembled and wailed, and Ian let go. Having Charlie rocking and rolling under him, spearing himself up and down on Ian's cock, was a sight he wanted to last forever.

"Fuck me, oh God." Charlie grasped his cock and jerked only twice before his lithe body bowed up and he came again. Limbs quivering, Charlie lay gasping for air.

Ian grabbed Charlie's biceps and hammered into him, hips punching hard, driving his dick to the hilt. Finally having Charlie beneath him blew the little restraint Ian had to shreds, and the fire of his orgasm swept through him like a spark to dry tinder. Ian got sucked into Charlie, fused together as if the two had become one.

"Holy hell, oh shit, oh…" He exploded, slamming into Charlie so hard, the bed smashed against the wall. Electricity shot up his spine, traveling straight to his dick.

"Goddamn," he gritted out, unloading into the condom. Attempting to breathe seemed futile. His heart thundered in his ears, and he fell facedown onto the bed, yet still gently holding on to Charlie, afraid he might disappear and take away all this joy and passion Ian had never known.

Several minutes passed until he could catch his breath, but moving his arms and legs was still not an option.

Charlie smiled on the curve of his shoulder. "Are you alive?"

"Are you?"

"I think so." A soft kiss touched his neck. "That was… I'm not sure what to say. Amazing doesn't seem to capture it."

Ian smiled to himself, then carefully tried to pull out of Charlie, who hissed and tensed. Immediately Ian stopped. "Am I hurting you?"

"It's okay. The perils of being a size queen. I love it, but it hurts like a bitch afterward."

Jealousy tore through Ian at the thought of Charlie with other men, but he knew he was being irrational. He certainly wasn't Charlie's first. "I don't like the thought of hurting you."

Charlie inched away and lay on the pillow. "It's easier to heal from damage to the body than the heart."

Unsure how to respond, Ian got rid of the condom and lay next to Charlie. "Are you gonna explain that to me? You're the writer. I'm no good with words."

"Aspiring writer. Never mind me for the moment. How do you feel?"

Ian pillowed his head on his arms and stared at the ceiling. "It's funny. You'd think I'd be freaking because it was so different. I should be analyzing it to death and thinking on my feelings because it's my first time with a guy, but the truth?" He rolled over to face Charlie and ran a finger down the muscle of Charlie's thigh, feeling the wiry brush of hair. A shiver ran through him, and his dick twitched. "It felt right. Like I was finally where I was supposed to be." At Charlie's expression of surprise and fear mixed with hope and longing, Ian slid his palm over Charlie's stubbled jaw and threaded his fingers through the wavy hair at his nape. "And who I was supposed to be with. You. I've never, ever had anything close to this happen to me when I was with anyone else. Don't ever think you're coming in second place, because you've already won the race before you left the starting gate."

Green eyes shining, Charlie nibbled on his bottom lip, and even though his body was exhausted, desire pulsed through Ian, and he wanted Charlie again.

"You mean it? I don't want you saying it just to make me feel good."

His dick stirred and began to thicken, and Ian drew Charlie's free hand down so he could feel him. At Charlie's wide eyes and indrawn breath, his lips tilted up in a lazy grin. "You do this to me. Only you." Charlie rubbed the smooth head of his dick, and he stiffened even more. The now-familiar ache of need rolled through his chest to his heart, spreading through him like a web of fire, melting his insides to warm honey.

"I love how big you are," Charlie whispered shyly. "When you were inside me, I didn't feel empty anymore. I felt good."

"I want to make us both feel good. I'm going to make you feel so good all fucking night long if you'll let me." He meant to only brush their lips together but, as he was beginning to learn, there was nothing gentle about the passion that sparked between him and Charlie. It ignited like fireworks and burned bright, and soon they were grinding against one another.

"Too soon," Charlie gasped. "I can't."

"But I can," Ian panted, and he came again, the gentleness of his orgasm wringing out the last bit of energy from him. "You're staying right here tonight. With me." A statement, not a question. He had no plans to let Charlie go.

" 'K." Charlie sighed, and drained as he was, Ian still managed to cuddle close to him.

Chapter Twenty-One

Charlie opened his eyes to the sight of an unfamiliar room and needed a moment to figure out where he was.

Ian.

A smile settled on his lips, and he winced at their soreness as he snuggled under the comforter. God, he could still feel his mouth tingling. He licked his lips and tasted Ian, so he licked them again. His ass ached, but he didn't care. Careful not to disturb his still-sleeping bed partner, Charlie slid from under the covers and went to use the bathroom. On his way back to bed, he checked the time on the stove and saw it was only six twenty. Obscenely early to be up on a Sunday morning, which meant more bed time with Ian. He lowered next to him and sighed.

A heavy arm draped over him and pulled him close. So

close, in fact, he could feel the thick ridge of a very erect dick between his ass cheeks.

"I woke up and you weren't here." Ian nuzzled into his neck, right behind his ear, and Charlie's dick zinged to attention. "I didn't like that."

"Had to use the bathroom." Charlie sighed and wiggled his butt into Ian, who growled into his ear and slipped his hand over Charlie's hip to grasp his dick.

"Fuck, you're gonna make me come if you don't stop wiggling."

"Mmm. That's the point." Charlie snickered and kept up his rocking motion.

"Uh-huh." Ian loomed over him, his muscular arms planted on the bed on either side. His heavy dick rested on Charlie's stomach, and Charlie couldn't help eyeing it.

"I like when you look at me like that."

At Ian's words, Charlie licked his lips, loving the response of Ian's cock jerking against his stomach. "I like what you look like. What's wrong with that?" The penetrating stare from Ian unnerved him. "What's the matter?" he blurted out, afraid it was all a dream he'd be waking up from.

Ian bent over and kissed him hard, but then his lips turned soft and seeking. Charlie melted under Ian's mouth as their tongues played together.

"Why do you think something has to be wrong?" Ian asked when they separated.

"I don't know. When you were staring at me, it was like you were figuring out a way to get me out of bed and say good-bye."

Ian ran his hand up Charlie's torso and tweaked his nipple, drawing a hiss. He did it again, licking each pointy tip until they were sore and aching.

"Does this feel like good-bye?"

Charlie shook his head, and Ian trailed a finger from his jaw to his throat and all the way to his chest, where he circled a reddened nipple.

"I'm ready to stay in bed all day. With you. I didn't know that this would feel good." Again he licked Charlie's nipples, then bit them lightly, sending Charlie into a paroxysm of whimpers and moans beneath him.

"Good, oh my God, so good."

Ian continued exploring his body, gaining confidence with every kiss and lick. Ian nibbled at his neck, sucked at the jut of his collarbone, and licked a path down the side of his torso. Charlie remained very still, supremely aware that his very erect dick rested only inches from Ian's face. He imagined what Ian's lips would feel like sliding over him. Charlie rarely got head from people, though he loved it.

His breathing turned shallow as Ian moved closer, so close that his rough cheek rubbed against Charlie's shaft, and he couldn't help the hiss of pleasure that escaped him.

"You like that?" Ian ran a finger along his length, and Charlie's eyes opened wide. "You like when I touch you here?"

He nodded and bit his lip when Ian hesitated only for a moment before grasping him.

"Is this too hard?"

"No," he whispered. "I like it hard."

That cocky grin of Ian's ticked up his lips. "I know you do." A bit more confident, Ian squeezed him and began to jerk him off with one hand, while fondling his balls with the other. "Is this good?"

"Oh, yeah." He sighed and thrust into Ian's strong grip. "Oh, oh yeah."

"How about this?"

He had no chance to answer, because Ian kissed the tip of his dick. Then Charlie forgot how to breathe as Ian used the flat of his tongue to slowly lick across the swollen head. His fingers curled into the sheets, and his heels dug into the bed. He wished Ian would suck him down to the root and swallow every bit of him because he knew if he did, it would be the most mind-blowing orgasm he'd ever had.

He understood Ian was still learning about all this, so he wasn't too disappointed when Ian gripped him and continued to lick the head but didn't go any further. Charlie was okay with that. For his first time tasting a man's dick, it was better than he'd expected. But when Ian opened wide and took the whole crown of Charlie's dick between his lips, Charlie cried out. The hot, silky wetness of Ian's mouth and tongue over his sensitive flesh shredded him, and though he struggled to hold on, he knew he only had seconds before he exploded.

"Ian, I can't stop, gonna come."

Ian let him go. "It's okay. Wanna see it happen." Ian rubbed his cheek over Charlie's throbbing erection and played with his sac. He brushed lightly over Charlie's taint, and that was the breaking point.

"*Ahhh*, oh God, oh my God." Charlie shook, his dick pulsing out streams of come over Ian's hands.

"Fuck, that was hot," Ian said, and when Charlie had finished, he took his own cock in hand.

Charlie reached out. "Don't you dare beat off when I want to suck you so hard."

Ian's eyes turned to silver, pulling Charlie into their

molten depths. "Do it. Come on." He stretched out and began long, lazy glides up and down his rigid length. Charlie's vision blurred with lust, and the earlier soreness forgotten, he worked his mouth over Ian's thick shaft. His tongue pushed on the pulsing vein, and he lost himself in the rhythm of Ian's hips pumping in time to his sucking.

"Ah, fuck, suck it, yeah. Dammit. Can you take me?"

"Yeah, all of it. Give it all to me. Hard."

Ian grunted and lightly held Charlie's head while he pushed into his mouth. Charlie's breath grew short, but he'd never felt more alive than when Ian exploded, his come spraying the inside of Charlie's throat. Charlie swallowed all he could, yet some drops still escaped his lips. Panting, he flopped down next to Ian, who rolled onto his side.

"God, you look hot. Your lips are wet and sticky, and your face is all red."

"That's 'cause your dick is a monster." He worked his aching jaw as pleasure buzzed through him.

Ian's hand touched him gently. "I didn't hurt you, did I?" Genuine concern radiated from his eyes, and Charlie rushed to reassure him.

"Hell, no. I loved it. You're perfect."

Ian grinned. "Oh, yeah?" He lazed back but kept a possessive hand on Charlie's thigh, running his fingertips up and down his leg, then gave him a squeeze. "Tell me more."

"Brat. Now you're just fishing for compliments." Charlie loved having Ian's hands all over him. This easy joking and friendship with a sexual partner was foreign to him. Usually he'd find a partner, they'd fuck, and that would be it. He was almost afraid to believe there could be something more.

"Okay, if you don't want to go first, I'll start." Ian crossed his arms and pillowed them under his head. "Like I said last night, I never imagined it would be like this. Obviously, I've had sex, but something always seemed to be missing. A spark or something that would make it worth all the talk and hype."

"Wait, what?" Charlie sat up. "What're you saying?" Barely breathing, Charlie waited. Avoiding his gaze, Ian concentrated on the ceiling, his cheeks tinted pink. God, he was adorable, and Charlie's heart soaked up the joy around him and unfurled from its shriveled bud.

"Between last night and this morning, it all makes sense why I've never been satisfied. When we fucked, it was electric. Even right now, when I'm so damn exhausted, I can barely move, I want you again."

"That's because it's new. It'll wear off."

In his head, Charlie knew to take a step away and not let the rush of being with Ian overtake common sense. More than anything, he wanted to let go of the mistrust and wariness to give himself a chance to explore every little thing with the man, but he couldn't be sure, despite all they'd said to each other the previous evening, that this would last beyond the thrill of sex. For Ian, at least.

"You think?" Ian ran a hand up his leg, and Charlie couldn't help the full-body shiver rolling through him at the touch. "I dunno." He let out a huge yawn.

"Maybe we should go back to sleep for a while?" Charlie suggested. "We can talk later."

"Mmm." Ian rolled over to grab pillows and lie down again. "Good idea. C'mon. Too early to talk."

He patted the place next to him, and Charlie happily settled in. A contented sigh huffed from Ian when he wrapped a sleep-heavy arm around him and pulled him close. Charlie's eyes fluttered closed.

When he next woke, he found himself alone in bed. Sunlight streamed in through the window, and he heard Ian banging around in the kitchen. Smiling to himself, he hopped out of bed and gathered his clothes from where they lay scattered on the floor. In his jeans and button-down but remaining barefoot, he went into the bathroom and ran his finger over his teeth with some toothpaste, then finger-combed his unruly waves. Salivating at the enticing aroma of something cooking, he left the bedroom, following his nose. When he entered the kitchen, the source of what caused his stomach to growl lay sizzling in a pan on the stove.

"Mmm. Is that the same French toast you made the other day?" He drew a barstool up to the wraparound counter Ian used as a table.

"Kind of." Ian turned around with a spatula in his hand. He wore a T-shirt and a pair of workout shorts that hung on his hips, giving Charlie a tantalizing peek of that deep, perfect V of muscle. One day Charlie hoped to get the opportunity to spend time exploring every dip and curve of Ian's perfect body with his lips and tongue. "I added some bananas too." The same shy, endearing smile from earlier reappeared. "I hope you like it."

Charlie would eat cheese gone moldy with the green parts cut off if it meant Ian would keep smiling at him like that.

"I'm sure I will. But what does a guy have to do to get a cup of coffee around here?" He gave Ian a smile, and Ian snorted.

"You're lucky you're cute. Otherwise I'd make you get it yourself."

His face warmed. "Just milk, please."

Contentment settled in his chest as he watched Ian pour his coffee. When he was a kid and used to see groups of kids leaving school on Friday, talking about whose house they were going to hang out at for the weekend and parties he wasn't invited to, Charlie would go to whatever foster home he'd been sent to and dream up the perfect boyfriend.

He'd be strong and caring and would pay attention to what Charlie had to say. His boyfriend wouldn't let people make fun of Charlie having no parents and wouldn't care that Charlie never had cool clothes or the newest phone. The perfect boyfriend wouldn't care if Charlie couldn't afford to go to the movies. He'd rather stay home together and make popcorn and watch old movies. Charlie's perfect boyfriend didn't spend hours playing video games blowing up people and buildings. He'd like kissing, especially kissing Charlie.

Ian slid a plate with three fluffy pieces of bread that smelled like cinnamon, maple syrup, and heaven. Slices of banana were stacked high on top of the steaming, fragrant bread. Strips of crispy bacon filled the rest of the plate, and Charlie couldn't resist picking a piece up and crunching his way through it in three bites.

"Oh," he whimpered in delight, "this is so good."

"It's the maple syrup from the French toast. I heated it in the pan, then cooked the bacon in it."

Charlie didn't bother answering. He was too busy stuffing his mouth and didn't speak until he'd polished off more than half the plate. Ian, meanwhile, only chewed on a few pieces of bacon, staring at Charlie until he couldn't take it any longer.

"What's wrong? Why're you looking at me like that?"

"Just thinking how crazy it all is. You 'n me, I mean."

"Yeah," Charlie said. "I knew what you meant." Suddenly the food no longer tasted as delicious as it had only moments ago. "What are you thinking?" He was afraid to ask if part of how crazy it all was meant Ian was having second thoughts.

"I wanna know what happened with Robert and Eddie and why Rachel said Robert broke Eddie's heart."

Oh, Charlie had a pretty good idea what the reason was, but knew that Ian, not attuned to the issues of hiding one's sexuality and living on the down low, probably wouldn't.

"I guess we'll have to wait for Rachel to tell us."

The sparkling silver light signaling Rachel's appearance shone from the ceiling. It wasn't Charlie's imagination. Rachel was definitely more transparent and harder to see.

"Oh, look at you both." She clapped her hands. *"I'm so happy."*

Charlie, not wanting to push, remained practical and steered her to what they wanted. "We were hoping you'd show us more of Robert and Eddie."

"Yeah, we really want to know." Ian chewed a piece of bacon.

"I'm happy to. But it's not going to have a happy ending. Not like you two." Her eyes glistened, and Charlie felt sorry for her. But surprisingly, it was Ian who stepped in to soothe Rachel.

"We know, Rachel. And we're really sorry. Robert couldn't admit who he was, and I can see by Eddie's words how much he loved Robert. If only they were born in a different time, things might've been different for them."

Surprised by Ian's insight, Charlie kissed his cheek. "You do understand."

"I promise that if I don't, I'll always try."

For the first time, Rachel directed a soft smile at him. *"I'm hoping you two can find that peace they couldn't with each other."* She waved her hands over the television, and Charlie sat next to Ian on the sofa and watched. Rachel disappeared, but Charlie barely paid her attention.

Eddie lay stretched out on his bed with a glass of iced water next to him. He chewed the end of his pencil and started writing.

Robert,

Of course I'm not angry with you for accompanying Charlotte to that party. You know each other, and it would've been rude to say no. I daresay impossible, truth be told. I hope you know I've been lonely without you. The city is hot and steamy, and I'll confess sometimes I go to your backyard late at night and sit under the tree and think. You can imagine what I think about, can't you? Surely you must.

I look forward to your coming home, when we can meet again.

Yours,

Eddie

"I think I'm beginning to see what happened," Ian murmured to him, and Charlie took his hand. Was it foolish to grieve for the doomed relationship of two men who'd been dead for a century?

"It's so sad."

Robert sat in his backyard with his back to the oak tree. He gazed up at the sky, then wrote furiously.

Eddie,

It was so good to see you last night. Good. *What a silly, ineffective word. Incredible, amazing...still doesn't describe how I feel.*

What happened last night was beyond anything I could have ever imagined. I never dreamed I could feel that way. And yes, I want to do that to you. Soon.

For the time being, I can't see a way out of our problem except to continue as we have been these past years. Never doubt that I miss you.

Yours,

Robert

He folded the paper and slipped it into a little hole in the tree trunk.

Ian sat still, his face hard and unreadable. "Eddie introduced Robert to sex, and the double life he was living was too much for Robert. He dated Charlotte and knew he needed to show her affection, when all the time he wanted Eddie. His parents' expectations of him, plus his own fear of someone finding out he liked men, drove him crazy. He loved Eddie, but at the same time he wanted to be accepted, since he was always coddled as a child because of his heart issue. He was too fearful of his parents' reaction."

Listening to Ian talk, Charlie wondered if he was in one of those states where the past and the present melded. "I can't imagine his struggle, or how hard it must have been for Eddie to see him with Charlotte and have to keep hidden how he felt."

Silvery eyes met his, and Charlie sucked in a breath at the fire burning in their depths. "It was like being caught in the pit of hell for Robert to know he'd never be free no matter what. He knew how much he hurt Eddie by being with Charlotte, but he also knew a life for them was an impossible dream. No matter how much Robert cared for him, they could never be together like they wanted." Ian reached out to touch his cheek, and Charlie swayed toward him. "I'll never hurt you."

"We can't help hurting each other. But we have to have trust. I have to try and believe you when you say you want me."

"I do. I'm not playing with you. I'm not lying. I know I gotta prove it to you, but you'll see."

It was embedded in Charlie's DNA to be mistrustful of people and to prepare himself to be hurt. After all, he grew up on a diet of disappointment and dreams. It began when his mother gave him up at two years old and never thought of him again. He'd had his fill of disappointments, and at this point, with Ian's earnest gaze on him, Charlie was ready for the dreams.

"How do you know all that stuff about Robert and Eddie?" Charlie finished his coffee.

Ian squinted and shook his head. "I don't know. It came out of my mouth like I had no control over it." A frightened expression settled in his eyes. "It's like I can see them but not really. They're sort of in a house of mirrors where you think it's real, but they're out of reach."

They finished their coffees, and Charlie grimaced. "I need to shower and change. This underwear is gross." He rose from the couch and pulled the stiffened fabric away from his legs.

Ian chucked. "Yeah, I'm pretty sticky myself." His eyes warmed and turned that smoky silver. "Let's go shower together. Save water and the planet and all that."

"You're such an environmentalist." Charlie snickered and left Ian sitting on the couch.

"Hey, wait for me." Ian caught up with him by the shower stall and pushed him under the water, where Charlie's laughs turned to moans of pleasure.

Chapter Twenty-Two

Nothing like a lazy Sunday to put Ian in a good mood. He and Charlie had fooled around in the shower, then gone back to bed and taken another nap. He woke up first and decided to leave Charlie sleeping and go watch the ball game. Plenty of times the guys would drop by, but since they were now with their girlfriends, Ian figured Sundays could be his and Charlie's. He liked that. But he liked everything about his times with Charlie. Whether it was watching one of his corny old movies or hanging out in the backyard together, Ian had never felt more comfortable and himself than when he was with Charlie.

Smiling, beer in hand, he flipped on the ball game and saw the Mets were ahead, 3-0 in the sixth inning. "Plenty of time for them to screw that up," he muttered darkly. He grabbed a six-pack and a big bag of chips and flopped onto the sofa.

His mind drifted to the previous evening. Sex with Charlie had been wild and off the charts and blew apart any preconceived ideas he'd had about sex with a man. It was exciting, rough and hard, and even now his dick stirred at the memory of the velvet heat of Charlie's ass. Earlier, Charlie had gone on his knees in the shower, and the sight of him drenched to the bone, lips clinging to Ian's erection as he bobbed up and down, was a picture Ian would never forget.

"Damned if I'll ever be able to shower again without getting a hard-on." He adjusted himself and took another hit of beer. What would it be like to take Charlie fully in his mouth? Maybe later he'd surprise Charlie and do it to him. He had a feeling the guys Charlie was with before didn't do it for him, and Ian wanted to be better than that. He'd always been a considerate lover.

Charlie was all the buzz he needed.

Now he understood why people loved sex and couldn't stop thinking about it. He'd been hard since last night, and instead of concentrating on the game, his mind strayed to the man sleeping in his bedroom. What would the rest of the day and night bring? Anticipation building, he was ready to say to hell with the game and jump back into bed and into Charlie. He set his beer down.

The doorbell rang, jerking him out of his dirty daydreams.

"Who the hell is that?" He heaved himself off the sofa to answer the incessant ringing. "Jesus, enough already," he grumbled. Yanking open the door, he came face-to-face with Patrick and Mickey. "What're you two doing here?"

"Hello to you too." Mickey breezed past him into the living room. "Oh, good. We were hoping you'd be watching the game." He plopped himself on the sofa and popped open the tab on a can of beer.

Patrick followed Mickey to the sofa and dug into the bag of chips. "Whassup? What'd you do last night?"

Ian stood in his boxers and T-shirt, staring at his friends making themselves at home in his apartment. It wasn't anything different than countless other Sundays they'd spent together, hanging out to watch the game, drink beer, and eat junk food. Problem was, he'd planned on doing that, only with Charlie.

Bigger problem—Charlie naked and sleeping in his bed.

"I went out with Charlie. We hit up a few bars."

Mickey finished his beer. "Oh, yeah? Where'd you go?"

Not wanting to have to face his friends, Ian hurried into the kitchen and got another six-pack out of the refrigerator. "I dunno. A few places. Don't remember their names."

"So what you're trying to say is you struck out." Mickey snorted. "Happens to the best of us. Even you, my man. Gotta get right back in the saddle, so to speak."

"Shut up. What about you? How were your dates?" He put a can to his lips, not because he wanted another beer, but to hide his expression.

Mickey went first. "Me 'n Brianna had a great time. After the museum, we walked around the zoo, then over to Park Slope. She likes this Mexican place on Fifth Avenue, so we had some nachos and a pitcher of sangria before going to my place. She wanted me to watch some show she's into on Netflix."

The Mickey he knew would never walk around a zoo or drink sangria at some bougie-ass place in Park Slope. But, he mused, the Ian they knew wouldn't be having sex with a guy.

Looked like he'd won that Get the Fuck Out of Here contest by a mile.

"What about you, Patrick?" He sat in the chair opposite the guys and stretched out his legs. And froze. One of Charlie's black Converse stuck out, partially hidden under the couch. He'd been sitting in the room all afternoon and hadn't noticed, but of course now it was as if there were a giant blinking arrow pointing to it. He forced himself to look at Patrick and not allow his eyes to stray to the floor and that damn sneaker.

"Oh, Andi and I went for pizza at Juliana's and then took a walk in Brooklyn Bridge Park to see the sunset."

"Nice. So are you seeing them again? Sounds like it." Ian might've drunk his beer down a little too quickly to calm his nerves. He shouldn't be anxious. He'd done nothing wrong. Charlie had given him the best night of his life.

He was...bisexual.

It sounded great in his head. Now he just had to figure out how and when to say it out loud.

"Yeah," Patrick said, checking his watch. "I told her I was coming here for the game, but we're meeting around six." His smile told Ian he'd fallen hard. Ian might know that feeling. "She's cooking me dinner."

"That sounds good." He kicked Mickey's foot. "What about you? Seeing Brianna again?"

"Yeah, we're gonna go to the movies at the Alamo Drafthouse, and then I wanna take her to the One for drinks."

"Damn, that's some bucks. Who knew you were such a romantic?" Mickey blushed, stunning Ian. "Jesus. You're really into her."

Face as red as his hair, Mickey shrugged. "Yeah, I like her. A lot. She's different. Sexy in a quiet way. She pays attention to me when I talk and isn't busy looking around at anyone else. She never had a boyfriend, and I like that I'm her first." He quickly drank down his beer.

From the way Mickey couldn't meet his eyes, Ian suspected it was more than like. Looked like his best friend had fallen in love at first sight, something he thought only happened in one of his mother's romance books.

"That's cool, man. Happy for you."

They sat around for a while, and when it became apparent that the Mets were blowing out the Phillies, Patrick and Mickey made noises to leave and Ian had no desire to keep them longer. He wondered how long Charlie was going to sleep.

"Don't worry if you gotta go. I know it takes a long time to make you guys pretty for your dates."

"Shut up, asshole." Mickey slid his phone into the pocket of his shorts. "What're you doing tonight?"

Ian turned off the set and used the excuse of the game being over to stand and place himself in front of Charlie's sneaker.

"Nothing. Gonna figure out dinner, then hang out in the backyard."

"Want me to ask Andi if she's got any friends—not Savannah," Patrick added hastily. "That was some weird shit. But I'm sure she could hook you up with one of her girlfriends."

"No thanks. I'm cool. Taking a break." He should tell them about Charlie, but he couldn't figure out the right way to say it. Both guys were hurrying out to make their dates, so Ian figured to wait for another, less rushed time. They walked to the door, and he opened it for them.

"Talk to you later."

From the back of the house came the sound of a flushing toilet. Mouths open, Mickey and Patrick stared at him, and then Mickey broke out into laughter. Ian tensed and waited.

"You dog. You had someone in there all along and didn't say? Who're you hiding?" Mickey clapped his hands and shook his head.

Heart beating madly, Ian forced out a weak smile. "Not hiding anyone. They're, uh, just sleeping. You know how it goes."

Mickey elbowed him. "Wore her out, huh? Ian, you're an animal. Why didn't you say anything? We would've left sooner."

"It's fine. Forget about it."

Patrick hadn't joined in with Mickey's laughter and was gazing at Ian quizzically. Ian's heart slammed.

"You guys better go. Don't wanna be late for your ladies."

"Yeah," Patrick said quietly. "Talk to you tomorrow. Let's go, Mickey."

With a slap on the back and still laughing, Mickey walked out with Patrick behind him. The tightness in Ian's chest loosened, and he shut the door, but not before he saw Patrick shoot him a troubled glance over his shoulder. Ian chewed on his lip.

"Are they gone?"

Lost in his head, Ian jumped. "What?" He spun around to see Charlie fully dressed, big green eyes wary.

"Yeah." He walked into the living room and sank onto the couch. "They watched the game for a while, then had to leave. They both have dates."

"I heard. I'm sorry, I tried to hold out, but I had to go to the bathroom."

How sad was it that Charlie felt he had to apologize for taking a piss?

"Don't be. It's fine." But it wasn't. Not really.

"Ian."

At Charlie's voice, he lifted his head. "Yeah?"

"I'm not going to force you to come out to your friends, if that's what you're worried about. That would make me the worst kind of person. You take the time you need." Charlie pointed to the floor. "I was looking for my sneakers."

Ian reached down and pulled them out from under the couch. "Yeah. Here you go. Are you leaving?"

Charlie slipped his feet inside the Converse. "I need to go home and change my clothes. Figure out what's for dinner."

Relief swept through Ian. As long as Charlie wasn't mad at him for not telling his friends that they were together right then and there.

"Wanna order a pizza? I figure we could eat, and then I can show you my garden. I've got some nice tomato plants and zucchini I can give you if you want."

Charlie's smile lit up his face. "Yeah. That would be great."

With things settled between them, Ian felt brave enough to put his arms around Charlie and kiss his neck. "I really had a great time with you." ——

"Me too," Charlie whispered. He initiated a kiss, and for several minutes they got lost in each other, lips seeking and searching. Charlie's mouth tasted sweet on his, and what Ian liked was that it wasn't a prelude to sex. It was simply a kiss. And that wasn't simple at all.

"I'll walk you outside."

They left his apartment, and Ian breathed deeply of the fresh, late-afternoon air. He opened the gate and let Charlie out, and they stood together on the sidewalk. At this point, if Charlie were a girl, he knew he'd kiss her good-bye and no one would think twice. But Charlie was a guy. And the fact that he hesitated and Charlie gazed at him, knowing his internal struggle, made his chest hurt and his throat swell with sadness.

Charlie nudged his shoulder. "It's okay. I'll see you later? Like an hour?"

He nodded and watched Charlie as he walked away, mounted the steps to his house, and went inside. Huffing out a frustrated breath, he returned to his apartment.

* * *

The next day at lunch, he found himself alone with Dave. Miguel was out sick, and Lenny and Chester had finished lunch early and went to buy the weekly lottery tickets they all chipped in for.

Dave crushed his can of soda and tossed it into the recycling bin. "So, how's it going, kid?"

He finished chewing his sandwich. "Okay, I guess."

But Dave was no fool. "Uh-huh. That tells me a whole lotta nothin'. You see that guy again you were talking to me about?"

Ian's fingers curled into his palms. "Yeah. Well, he's my neighbor, so I see him every day."

Dave's chair screeched as he hitched it closer. "That's

not what I mean, and you know it. Did you go on any more dates with him?"

Despite his effort to remain cool, Ian could feel his face heat. "Yeah. We got together this weekend."

Dave's brows flew up. "No shit. Like you had a date or you had sex?"

Fuck, he wanted to crawl into a hole and die. "*Shh*, Jesus." Why was it so hard to talk about him and Charlie? If it had been a woman, he'd have no problem talking about it—bragging, more likely. How pathetic did that make him?

He and Dave sat in a small public gathering area on a bench, but the nearest person wasn't even within earshot. Dave made a show of glancing around. "Ain't no one listening. Not like I'm talking into a microphone or taking out a billboard ad."

He hung his head. "Well...yeah. We did. He stayed over Saturday night until Sunday."

"And? How'd it go?"

He'd been trying to put into words how he felt even to himself but kept coming up short. Every word seemed inadequate to explain his emotions.

"It was good. Really, really good. We're seeing each other tonight too. Gonna have dinner together."

"Oh, yeah?" Eyes alight with interest, Dave rubbed his chin. "Well, that's good, but be careful. 'Cause if it don't work out, it's not like you can just move away easily." They both stared ahead, watching the people walking by. "Have you told anyone besides me?"

"No. And I feel bad about that. My friends came over yesterday, and I was afraid they might find out he was there. Not because I'm ashamed of what we did, but it didn't seem like the right way to tell them."

"What is?"

He met Dave's piercing dark eyes. "What do you mean?"

"Well, what do you think is a good way to tell people?"

"I dunno. I haven't thought about it."

"But you know what the wrong way is."

Frustration bubbled over. "I'm trying to figure it out, okay?" He raised his hands in the air. "It's all new to me, you know? I don't want Charlie to think he's someone I'm ashamed of, 'cause I'm not. But I also don't think it's something casual. Like, *Do you want pepperoni on your pizza, and by the way, I'm bisexual now.* Because I don't know what I am, really."

"What're you talking about, '*what you are, really*'?"

He had no clue, but Dave was the only person he could be totally honest with about what he was feeling. Besides Charlie.

"I'm not attracted to any other guys. Just Charlie. It's not like I've always had these feelings and kept them under wraps. It's him. And I don't know how to handle it all. I don't wanna hurt him."

People streamed by, and Ian watched them walking and talking to each other, wondering if any of them were as confused as he was or had secrets so deep. Silence rose between them until Dave turned on the bench to face him.

"Why do you think you're gonna hurt him?"

Moodily, Ian stared at his work boots. The weekend with Charlie had turned out better than he could've imagined. Better than any he'd spent with Deena. After pizza, they'd hung out in the backyard, where he'd shown Charlie the rosebushes, and the tomatoes beginning to ripen. Under the cover of darkness and the old oak tree, they felt brave enough, without the fear of prying eyes, to kiss and touch each other. Ian wanted to get naked with Charlie under the stars. He imagined Robert and Eddie doing the same.

Charlie wasn't a dirty secret, but Ian wasn't ready to share his sex life yet with his friends when he was still working things out in his head.

"He's not like me. He never had a family and grew up in foster care. He doesn't have any friends he can count on. He's always been alone."

"Yeah…with someone like that, you need to be careful."

"I already said I am. We've talked about it." Annoyed, he worked his jaw. "I've talked more with Charlie than with anyone I've ever been with. You know, it's not so simple for me either. All of a sudden I've gone from being only with women to only wanting this guy." Not to mention the added complication of Rachel and Robert and Eddie, but Ian was deliberately leaving out that information. He couldn't reveal that to Dave or anyone else. Ian expelled a *whoosh* of breath and gazed up at the blue sky before continuing. "You don't know Charlie. He's sweet and kind and trusting. He's never had a real relationship, and he's special."

Dave favored him with a penetrating stare that sent him squirming. Ian couldn't help feeling sorry for the people under Dave's command in the Marines. "Listen, kid. Did you ever think maybe it's more?"

"More?" He licked his dry lips but couldn't meet Dave's eyes. "I-I dunno what you mean."

"Sure you do." Dave gentled his voice. "Know what I think?"

"No, but you're gonna tell me."

"Smartass." Dave knocked him on the shoulder. "I think you got real feelings for this guy, and it might not only be the first time you're with another man, but the first time you might really have this kind of deep emotion for anyone. Maybe even love."

His stomach bottomed out, and a nervous laugh escaped him. "What? You're crazy. I'm not in love."

"Would you know if you were?"

"I-I'm not in love. That's crazy. I really like Charlie, and we had a great time together, but…no."

The attraction between him and Charlie was real, but he wasn't in love.

Chapter Twenty-Three

"Wake up."

Mona poked him in the side, and Charlie jumped, letting out a surprised yelp. He'd zoned out, thinking about the weekend with Ian. A weekend that for him had been nothing short of magical. But not too magical, because Rachel swore she didn't have anything to do with Ian's feelings for him.

"Sorry." He rubbed his eyes and focused on her. "I'm up. What's the matter?"

That all too knowing gaze assessed him steadily. "That's what I'm trying to find out. You've got the strangest look on your face." Her pale eyes gleamed. "Whatever happened with that gorgeous Ian?"

"We've been hanging out. That's all."

Skeptical, Mona folded her arms and arched her brow. "Define hanging out."

Without answering, Charlie left her side and crossed the store to start rearranging the racks of men's clothing. Undeterred, Mona traced his steps, continuing to fire questions at him.

"Why're you being so secretive all of a sudden? You and Bryan used to flirt all the time in front of me, and I always knew when you'd hook up. I tell you when I meet people. For the last couple of months, ever since you moved into that house, you haven't been the same."

Charlie's fingers tightened on the hanger he was holding. "I haven't changed. I'm the same person."

"Are you two dating?" She leaned against the counter, big eyes pinning him down. "Is it serious?"

What were they, really? Dating? Friends with benefits? Charlie's mind returned to their Saturday night. Ian's face painted a story of wonder and desire, his eyes aflame with a passion impossible to fake. And Charlie had never felt so alive. So desired.

And yet, still, he held back part of himself, unwilling to let go in case it all turned sour.

"We're figuring it out. That's all I know."

"What's there to figure out? He's into you, you're into him."

Maybe he could tell her something. He couldn't keep it all bottled up; he was ready to explode. And, he rationalized, she didn't know Ian.

"Well, see...he's never been interested in guys before. I'm his first. So he's a little confused."

She chewed on a rainbow-painted nail. "You've had

sex, though, right?"

His face grew hot, but he remained silent, his gaze fixed on the scratched wooden floor.

"Charlie. Do you think that's the smartest thing?"

When he first came to A Vintage Affair, he and Mona had clicked, and they'd shared their dating disasters. She was well aware of his penchant for guys who kept him in the shadows, the straight-but-curious guys always making him their dirty secret, so he knew Mona's concern came from friendship.

"I don't know. It wasn't planned. I never thought we'd end up together that night."

Eyes narrowed, she placed her hands on her hips. "Were you drunk? Was he?"

"No. Of course not. We'd had some beers, but trust me, we knew what we were doing." He had a flashback of Ian's mouth on his and how sweetly he'd kissed Charlie good-bye Sunday night. "Ian wanted it as much as I did."

"So what now?"

The million-dollar question. "I have no idea. We're friends and enjoying each other. Right now that's enough for me."

"I'm worried you're going to fall for another jerk who's only going to use you for sex."

"Ian isn't like that. He's a good guy. He knows what I feel and respects that."

"Oh?" Her lips thinned. "Have you met his friends and family?"

"Yeah, I have, as a matter of fact. Not his family because they don't live here, but I met his friends and even went out with them last Friday."

"Hmm." A plucked brow arched. "Do they know

you're together?"

"No, but give us a minute. It just happened. I'd never push Ian to come out to his friends or family. That would make me as bad as the men who hid me away. Opposite sides of the same coin." After Mickey and Patrick showed up on Sunday, Charlie spent the better part of a sleepless night wondering if Ian would have second thoughts.

The door opened, and Charlie blinked in shock. A thrill rolled through him when Ian sauntered in with a smile that reached across the room and pulled him into the pools of those impossibly blue eyes.

"Hi. What're you doing here?" Drinking in the sight of Ian in his work clothes, Charlie almost couldn't believe this gorgeous man wanted him...had been inside him and kissed him until he almost passed out from pleasure.

"I thought maybe we'd go home together again. Pick up something for dinner on the way."

Home together. Dinner. As if they already shared their lives.

Blue fire burned bright in Ian's eyes, and a smile curved his generous mouth. The deep dimples beneath his cheekbones winked at him, and Charlie had to hold on to the rack of clothes to keep upright. Ian made him weak in the knees and in his heart. Heat simmered in waves between them.

"Damn, Charlie, I'd forgotten how hot he is. And hot for you," Mona murmured to him. "I'm going to go into the back and give you guys a minute to yourselves." She slipped away, and Charlie promised himself never to get annoyed with her again.

He waited until she disappeared in the stockroom, then made tracks to where Ian stood. "Hi, again."

Ian's breathing hitched, and Charlie liked seeing how

affected he was merely by their close proximity. Because they were alone, Charlie took Ian's hand in his and laced their fingers together. Ian licked his lips.

"Where'd she go?"

"She wanted to give us some time alone."

"Oh?" Ian's eyes widened, and his breathing sped up. Charlie moved close enough that their chests touched. Ian's slight shyness was such a turn-on, and for the first time Charlie felt like he was in control.

"Yeah. She thought maybe I wanted to greet you properly."

Ian blinked and zeroed in on Charlie's mouth. "L-like how?"

Charlie brushed their lips together and bit Ian's lower lip, sucking its full poutiness into his mouth. Ian sighed and grabbed Charlie around the waist, pulling him close. Charlie hummed with pleasure as their kiss deepened, and feeling the thick ridge of Ian's dick pushing into his stomach, his ass clenched, wanting to feel all that power inside him. God, he was so far gone for Ian, but he closed off his brain to anything but physical desire.

Ian's tongue slid tentatively inside his mouth, and Charlie grew light-headed, sucking on it with a whimper. An answering growl rumbled against his lips, and Charlie almost purred with delight at the possessive tone.

"We'd better stop."

Another grumble, then Ian, after giving him several long, deep, openmouthed kisses, finally let him go. "You done for the day?"

He was about to answer that he had another half hour to go, when Mona called out from the back of the store, "Yeah. He can go. Get out of here and go have fun."

Ian grinned and yelled, "Thanks. I love you." Then he whispered to Charlie. "I forgot her name."

"That's Mona."

"Thanks, Mona," he yelled out. "I owe you." Eyes glittering, he focused on Charlie. "Are you ready?"

"Not as ready as you are, it seems?" Charlie stared pointedly at Ian's obvious erection. "Keep it in your pants." He licked his lips. "For now."

Ian expelled a harsh breath. "You're fucking enjoying this, aren't you? Let's go."

Charlie waved good-bye to Mona, who'd stuck her head out from the stockroom, and then they walked down Atlantic Avenue toward their neighborhood.

"Do you really want to stop for food?" he asked as they passed by a pizza place, already crowded with diners sitting outside under the umbrellas.

"Hell, no. That's what DoorDash is for." Ian waggled his brows. "I'm hungry for something else right now." He lowered his voice. "Or someone. You."

"God, you're corny."

"What I am is horny. For you." Ian nudged his shoulder. "Corny and horny. Admit it. You love it."

I love you popped unbidden into his head. Frightened that he'd spoken out loud, Charlie sneaked a look at Ian, who walked with a smile and the sunshine on his face. He'd never say the words to him, but he could hold them inside and say them at night, out loud, when he lay alone in bed. After all, like a tree falling in the forest when no one was around to hear it, didn't words whispered when no one could hear them remain unspoken?

Didn't they?

They reached their block, and Ian pulled out his keys.

"How about another barbecue? I still have stuff left over from the weekend to make one."

"Sure. Lemme change, and I'll meet you on your front steps."

"Okay, but you know I like you in these cute clothes." Ian tugged the newsboy cap Charlie wore over his face. "See you in a few."

"I'll get you for that," he sputtered, pulling it up, his heart squeezing with joy.

Please let this be for real.

Ian winked. "I'm counting on it."

They separated, and Charlie picked up his junk mail and raced upstairs, where he wrangled himself out of his clothing and took a quick shower. He stepped into a pair of gym shorts and had pulled a T-shirt out of the dresser drawer when he sensed he was being watched.

"Hello, Charlie."

He jumped and almost knocked his head on one of the bedposts. Heart pounding, Charlie yanked the shirt over his head. "Rachel, what the hell."

The ghost hovered in the doorway to his room, less visible than the last time he saw her. He could only see the outline of her features. *"What's wrong?"*

Charlie collapsed onto the bed. "Give a guy some warning before you pop in. I swear you're gonna give me a heart attack."

"I'm always here. I just take myself away to someplace else." Her smile broadened, and Charlie wondered if she'd seen what happened between him and Ian the past weekend.

"Uh-huh."

"No need to ask if you had a good weekend."

Well, there was the answer to that.

Averting his eyes from her hovering figure, he scrambled off the bed, anxious to leave. "What is it?" He stuck his feet into flip-flops. "I'm meeting Ian for dinner."

"*Given the, ahem, change in circumstances of your relationship with Ian, you know I only have your best interests at heart.*"

She flew after him as he walked down the stairs and wound up facing him.

"Everything's fine. We're friends."

She quirked a brow. "*Are you trying to fool me? Friends don't kiss friends like that.*"

His face grew hot. "You shouldn't be spying on us. Didn't you see enough when you used to sneak after Eddie?"

Her face tightened, and fire flared up behind her. "*I did it because I loved him.*"

"So you watched him and Robert together?"

"*No.*" She stamped her foot. "*I never did that. I only waited to see where Eddie was going in the evening. And after he left...*" The fire died out, her face fell, and shame rose through Charlie that he'd upset her. She might be dead, but she still had feelings.

Wait. Did that even make sense? Did any of this?

"What happened after he left?"

"*The night before he left for the war, I saw him put a letter in a little niche in the oak tree where they used to meet. I wasn't sure if Robert would go back there once Eddie had already said good-bye, so I went and took the letter.*"

"Oh no, Rachel, that wasn't right."

"I didn't read it. I took the letter and handed it to Robert, saying I knew everything and that Eddie had left this for him. To this day, I still don't know what it said."

Fascinated now, Charlie didn't care if Ian was waiting. He needed to know. "But he took it, right? Robert read the letter?"

"Oh, yes. He turned white, but he merely thanked me and put the paper in his pocket." Her eyes drooped. *"I know everything else they wrote to each other, the ones you and Ian watched, but I couldn't read that one, knowing it was their last."*

Was it odd for him to feel sorry for a ghost? For one hundred years, she'd been hanging about, caught in her own prison, and Charlie couldn't help it—if he could've hugged her, he would've.

"Well, Ian and I are having dinner. I don't know what's happening, but I'm grateful he doesn't seem to want to hide. He came to my job today, and we walked home together."

"Do you know when he's planning to talk to his friends and family?"

"No, and I'm not pushing him. We'll take each day as it comes. Together." Charlie would love to know the answer to that as well, but they'd only been together for a couple of days.

"I just don't want you hurt," Rachel said and faded away.

Charlie refused to dwell on what Rachel said and hurried outside. Ian wasn't waiting for him yet; either that, or he'd already gone inside. Charlie rang the bell, but after several pushes and hearing the chimes but no answering footsteps, he sat down on the top step and pulled out his phone. Checking his messages, he saw Ian had sent him a text.

My mom called. There's a hurricane heading to Florida, and I'm making sure they're securing the condo right. Be a few minutes late.

His fingers flew across the phone.

K. Sitting out on your stoop, catching some rays.

With the message sent, Charlie tipped his head up to feel the heat of the late-afternoon sun on his face. He loved this time of summer when the days were long. He heard footsteps and opened his eyes to see Ian's friends, Mickey and Patrick, standing at the foot of the stairs.

"Hey, what's up?"

When they didn't answer, Charlie grew nervous and decided it would be strange to keep sitting at the top of the stairs while having a conversation with them waiting on the street. He met them down on the sidewalk and leaned against the gate that opened to Ian's apartment.

Mickey planted himself in front of Charlie. "Where's Ian?" Unlike the last time when he saw Mickey at the bar, where he was friendly and joking, his belligerent tone hung heavy in the air like the threat of a thunderstorm.

"H-he's on the phone with his mother."

Patrick's gaze flickered over him, and he sat on the second step of Ian's parents' house. "You guys got plans. Together?"

Danger, danger. *Oh, hell.* Charlie knew the signs all too well and hesitated, attempting to herd his scattered thoughts together. "Uh, yeah, we were just gonna grill stuff for dinner. No big deal. Wanna join us?"

"I dunno. You sure you want us to?" Mickey crossed his arms. "Maybe you and Ian wanna be alone."

Dread crept up his belly, and he tasted raw fear in his

mouth. "Wh-what's that supposed to mean?" His whole body tensed, and he curled into himself. He'd been in this position before, and he prepared for the blows from Mickey and Patrick, either verbal or physical. Or both.

"Yeah." Ian stepped up behind him, and Charlie nearly fainted with relief when he heard his voice. "What do you wanna know? Spit it out. Stop beating around the bush."

"From the looks of it, you've been beating Charlie's bush." Mickey sneered. "Or maybe he's been beating yours." Mickey's blue eyes narrowed.

Charlie's heart almost stopped, and behind him, Ian stiffened and growled. "What the fuck're you talkin' about?" Ian's dangerous tone would've been enough of a warning to Charlie, but his friend didn't seem to care.

"You really wanna have this conversation out here? Where everyone on the block can hear us?" Patrick had risen from the steps and stood shoulder to shoulder with Mickey.

Charlie remained quiet, but his heart thundered. Pulling air into his lungs proved next to impossible. Ian hadn't even looked at or said a word to him.

"We can go inside if you want."

Charlie's stomach tumbled as he followed Ian inside his apartment. The four of them sat—Charlie and Ian on the sofa, Mickey and Patrick on the chairs facing them.

"Okay." Ian kept his hands loose in his lap, and Charlie wondered how he could remain so calm. His whole world was exploding, and he wasn't even the one facing down two best friends sniffing around his private life. "Say what you came here to say."

Patrick looked to Mickey, who gestured impatiently. "Go on, man. Tell him."

Patrick braced his head in his hands and spoke in a

monotone, his gaze firmly affixed to the floor. "When we came over on Sunday, it felt kinda off, like you were hiding something from us. I wasn't gonna say nothin', not even to Mickey, especially when we heard the noise in the bedroom. I figured you had a girl in there and didn't want to embarrass her." He chewed his lip for a second. "But when we were leaving, I saw a sneaker under your couch that I knew wasn't yours. I also knew I'd seen Charlie wearing one like it when we all went out that night. So when me 'n Mickey left, I told him. And he said I was crazy."

Mickey interrupted him. "Yeah. Ain't that funny? I said, 'Don't be a fucking idiot. Ian's a ladies' man. He loves chicks in high heels and short skirts. He's a boob man.' "

A muscle ticked in Ian's jaw, but he said nothing.

"I mean, c'mon, man," Patrick appealed to Ian. "You're the guy who never leaves a club without at least three numbers. You've been scoring with chicks since you were fifteen. You ain't never been into guys."

For Charlie, the worst thing was how he sat there, with everyone talking in circles around him, accusing him without saying the words, yet completely ignoring him.

Mickey snorted, and Charlie's stomach cramped further. "I told Patrick he was being a dick, so we decided to wait around."

"You spied on me. That's what you're sayin', right?" Ian asked in a furious voice. "You fucking waited outside to see who'd leave my apartment. Where? Across the street? In the damn bushes?"

"No. We hung out in front, and saw you two in the window. Kissing. We saw you kissing him," Mickey said, pointing to Charlie, his voice filled with disgust. "And you looked like you were loving it."

"You bastards. You sick fucking bastards," Ian hissed, and his hands curled into fists. "Fuck you. Fuck you both."

"I knew he was into you, and I had a feeling he would do this. What happened? You get drunk and he kissed you and pretended to be the woman? That's what happened, right?" Mickey jabbed his finger a Charlie. "He came on to you?"

Mickey kept spewing his bullshit, but all Charlie heard was white noise through the buzzing in his ears.

"Shut up, Mickey."

"He suck your dick? That's what they all want, you know. I ever tell you about the time some dude came up to me in the bathroom at a club and said he'd do me for a twenty?" His jaw tightened. "I told him to get the fuck away from me. I didn't whip it out."

Charlie hated himself for the teardrops trembling on his eyelids. He ached from holding back the sobs that threatened to rip from his throat, but he'd die before he'd let that happen. All he wanted was to go home and curl up in the fetal position.

"Shut the fuck up." Ian jumped up and jabbed his finger in Mickey's white face. "Get the fuck outta my house, you asshole."

"Why? You admitting it? You liked it? Maybe I should see if he'll suck me off too." Mickey stood, and all hell broke loose.

"You keep the fuck away from him." Ian lunged at Mickey just as Mickey swung at him.

"Stop it. Leave him alone." An angry cry ripped from Charlie, and only then did Mickey turn to him.

"C'mon, pretty boy," he snarled and reached out to pull Charlie into the fray.

A cold wind swept through the room, freezing Mickey and Patrick in place. Breathing heavily, Charlie and Ian looked to each other, then around the room. A silvery light descended from the ceiling.

"What in Great-uncle Godfrey's ghost is going on here?" Rachel hovered above them. Her gaze swept over the two frozen men: Mickey with his hands clenched into fists, Patrick with his mouth open, eyes wide. Ian wiped at his nose.

"Did he hurt you?" Charlie grabbed hold of Ian, who shook his head, and to his surprise, grinned.

"Nah. Mickey never could throw a punch to save his life." Ian cupped Charlie's cheek. "I'm sorry you had to hear that…that…shit."

"It's nothing I haven't heard before. Worse even." Dejected, he slumped onto the sofa. "I knew this would happen."

Ian worked his jaw. "They can't make stupid comments like that. Not about anyone."

"It seems they already did," Rachel said. *"The question is, what are you going to do about it?"*

Chapter Twenty-Four

It was creepy as hell to see Mickey and Patrick standing stiff and unblinking, like those wax statues he'd once seen at Madame Tussauds. But Ian had bigger things on his mind, the most important being Charlie.

"You okay?" Ignoring Rachel, Ian sat next to Charlie, who'd huddled in the corner of the sofa, shaking as if he'd already been beaten down. "I'm sorry. I can't believe they said those things."

"I can," Charlie said, his voice tight and thin. "I'm gonna go home."

"What? Why?" He reached out to touch Charlie, but he shrank back, and Ian put his hands up. "Whoa, okay. What's going on? Talk to me."

"No. I don't wanna talk. I wanna go home. You should work it out with your friends." Charlie uncoiled his lean body from the couch and stood, keeping a careful distance away, deliberately out of reach of Ian's touch.

His jaw tightened. "Why're you leaving? You think I'm gonna let them talk to you like that? I never heard none of that shit come outta their mouths before. I swear. They're gonna have to apologize and—"

"Ian, stop it," Charlie yelled. "You've known me barely two months. You've known them almost all your life. You're not going to throw away lifelong friendships for me."

"Lemme talk to them. They'll be okay. You'll see. Just sit tight."

Rachel huffed and glowered at him, but Ian ignored her. His focus remained on Charlie. "It's gonna be fine."

Charlie glared. "Are you serious? You must be crazy if you think it's all gonna turn out okay. What planet do you come from? Don't you understand what I've been saying all along?" Charlie asked, so heartbreakingly sad, Ian's world tilted as if his feet were kicked out from under him. Then Charlie ran from him, wrenched open the door and left, the echo of his voice remaining in the room.

Helpless, Ian glanced around. "What'd I say?"

Rachel floated in front of him. "*You think it's going to be as easy as you think?*" She pointed to his frozen friends. "*They said some terrible things, you know. Charlie's a sensitive soul. He's never had anyone in his corner. Are you going to stand up to them?*" Again she gestured to Mickey and Patrick.

And Ian understood that once the first step was taken, the journey was underway.

"Rachel, I need to do this alone. I know that sounds

stupid because you can see whatever you want, but can you give me five minutes before you bring them back?" Ian appealed.

Something touched him, a sensation rivaling extreme cold, but at the same time, searing like fire. Rachel hovered. "*I shall. You'll make the right decision. I've been very proud of you.*"

And like previous times, the shimmering light took her away, and Ian was left alone to wrestle with his thoughts. He walked around Mickey and Patrick, and it saddened him to see their angry faces. Why? Because he'd stepped off the pedestal they'd put him on?

He stopped in front of Mickey, remembering how they'd play hooky in junior high, buying sandwiches at the bodega off Atlantic, then hanging out at the dilapidated piers on the river. The night of their high school senior prom, Patrick sneaked a fifth of vodka into his gym locker, and they'd all gotten drunk and walked down the Promenade at two in the morning, singing "I Can't Get No Satisfaction."

Good times. The best of times. All times they'd sworn they'd always be best friends forever and never let anything come between them. How had it turned into this?

"I'm not breaking our promise. You're the ones with the problem. I never asked to be your role model. I don't have to live my life any way that matters to anyone except me."

The men began to move, and he waited for them to waken, or come out of whatever it was that Rachel did to them. Mickey blinked first, then Patrick. Both of them came to, and while Patrick rubbed his eyes, Mickey's gaze roved around the apartment.

"Where'd he go?"

"Who, Charlie?" Mickey nodded, and Ian crossed his arms. "He went home. Wanna know why?" Glaring, he poked his finger into Mickey's chest. " 'Cause he didn't feel safe. How fucking pathetic is that, huh? My friend not feeling safe because you acted like some goddamn fucking homophobe." He clenched his jaw for a moment as Mickey's eyes narrowed. "Don't. Don't you dare tell me you're not when I heard you make those comments."

"Ian, what the fuck, man?" Patrick broke into his staring contest with Mickey. "You're telling us you're really into guys? Like you've, uh…" Here he paused, and Ian bit the inside of his cheek, waiting to hear what would come out of Patrick's mouth. "You fucked him? Sucked his dick?"

He took a step back to get both guys in his field of vision and sat on the couch, needing to remove himself from striking distance and their angry faces. "Lemme ask you something. You fuck these new girls you've been taking out? Go down on them?" Inside he cringed at his crudeness, but he was making a point. "They blow you?"

"Shut the fuck up." Mickey took a step forward, but the coffee table was in his way. Ian couldn't be certain if Mickey wouldn't take another swing at him. "Don't ask stuff like that about Brianna. Have some fucking respect. That's none of your fuckin' business."

"Exactly." Ian's lips thinned, and he slapped his thigh. "It isn't any of my goddamn business what you got going on in your bedroom. Just like it's none of yours what happens in mine. Or with whom."

"But it's a guy…" Mickey shook his head and collapsed into his chair. "I can't…you…how the hell did it happen? You've never been into guys." He licked his lips. "Have you? You never made moves on me."

Ian winced at the thought. "Get the fuck out of here.

I'm not attracted to you. Or Patrick. Or any other guy." Ian ran his hand through his hair. "Me 'n Charlie…it's different with him." He snapped his mouth shut. "And that's all I plan on saying, because it's none of your business. If I wanna be with a guy or a girl, that's *my* choice. Not yours. I don't owe you nothin'. You're my friends—my best friends—but if this is how it's going to be, then the door is there." He pointed. "Walk yourselves out."

His two friends gaped at him, but he didn't blink. Mickey shifted in his chair. "I can't understand it. You really don't like girls no more?"

"I do. I'm…I'm bi. Bisexual."

"What's that?" Mickey asked.

"It means he likes guys and girls, you idiot. That's what he was trying to say," Patrick huffed impatiently.

"Yeah." Ian sighed, relieved that someone understood him. "I still like women. And before I met Charlie, I wasn't ever into any guys"—he pointed at them—"including you two idiots, and I'm still not, so you don't gotta worry. It's just Charlie."

Mickey looked unconvinced. "But why him?"

"Why're you so into Brianna when she's way different from any of the girls you've ever gone out with?" Ian challenged Mickey, who didn't answer. "See? Not so easy, is it? I dunno, man," he said, trying to work out his feelings as he spoke, partly because it was all so new and fresh in his mind too. "It just is what it is, and if you want us to stay friends, you're gonna have to accept it. Me. And Charlie."

Neither Mickey nor Patrick said anything, and his heart sank. But he wouldn't back down. He'd told them, but their opinions were irrelevant compared to Charlie's feelings. That was where his allegiance lay now. And his heart. Charlie shouldn't be alone, and Ian itched to go to him.

"I think maybe you guys should go."

"Yeah," Mickey said. "I think you're right." He rose, but Patrick remained seated. "You coming?"

"I will in a sec."

"Fine. I'll wait outside." Mickey strode out of the apartment without saying good-bye to Ian. Without even looking his way. The emptiness built inside Ian, creeping like a dark tide. He and Mickey had been a part of each other's lives forever, the two of them side by side since childhood. Without Mickey in his life, a piece of him went missing, but the ache remained, like the phantom pain from an amputated limb. But Mickey didn't seem to suffer the same, as he'd left without a care in the world.

Patrick remained, still sitting down, incessantly jiggling his leg.

"Listen," Ian said. "If you're gonna lay some bullshit on me like Mickey, you can leave right now too."

Patrick hung his head before blurting out, "I'm sorry for spying on you. It was wrong, and I should've said something to you instead of sneaking around behind your back." He sounded contrite, and Ian, who rarely held a grudge, was willing to accept the apology. To a point.

"Yeah, you shoulda, but thanks," Ian said and extended his hand. Patrick hesitated. "You know, every hand you touch has probably held a dick at some point. I remember you said you spent a year jerking off every night after Maryann broke up with you. So I don't think you should worry you're gonna catch something from me."

Patrick's gaze jerked up to meet his, and Ian quirked a brow. Patrick's lips twitched. "You're such an asshole. You're never gonna let me forget that."

Inwardly he sighed with relief. It might take a little

time, but he and Patrick would be okay. "I don't let anyone but my friends call me that. Is that still true? Are we still friends? Or do I have to threaten to beat your ass?"

"As if."

He and Patrick mastered a staring contest and as always, Patrick broke first and continued. "Yeah. Not gonna lie, I'm still in shock, but like you said, it's none of my business who you've got in your bedroom. I bet plenty of people lie about it, and you shouldn't have to. It's not the old days."

He walked out, and Ian remained rooted to his spot on the floor. Half the battle won, and Mickey would be a harder sell. But right now, repairing his friendship with Mickey wasn't the most important thing to him.

Charlie.

He ran out of his apartment and up the stairs of Charlie's house. He rang the doorbell and stood dancing on his toes, waiting for Charlie to answer. When no one came, he rang again and again, even resorted to banging his fist on the glass. Still nothing. Frustrated, he raced down the steps and stood for a minute before deciding to try the door to the kitchen. He reached the gate, and finding it locked, shook it.

"Dammit, Charlie. Let me in."

He wouldn't give up; he couldn't. He knew if he left Charlie alone with his thoughts, he might never be able to convince him that what he felt was real. And it was. He gazed up at the sky.

"Rachel, come on, help a guy out."

His plea remained unanswered.

"Dammit. Where's a nosy ghost when you need one?" He eyed the fence. It had been years since he'd scaled one, but desperate times and all that. He rubbed his hands together and put the toe of his sneaker in an opening. It took him several heaves to push himself up and over, and when he reached the top, he caught the pocket of his jeans on a piece of metal sticking out, but he gave one final push and landed on the ground on the other side.

"Done!" He brushed his hands together, then gazed over his shoulder and winced, seeing the whole pocket of his jeans ripped open along with a big piece of his pants, his briefs showing through. "Well, whatever. I'm not here for a fashion contest." He reached the deck and took the stairs two at a time. This time, when he tried the door, it turned and opened. Ian didn't know whether to be happy to have a way inside or angry that Charlie had left it open.

After peering into each room on the first level and finding them empty, he mounted the back staircase to the second floor and faced a hallway of closed doors. He went to Charlie's room and entered. Charlie lay in bed, huddled under the covers. Ian stepped into the room and closed the door behind him.

Charlie raised his head from the pillow. "What're you doing here?" he asked in a tight, hurt voice. The light around him burned brighter than ever, and his green eyes glowed. "How'd you get inside? The door was locked."

"You're trying to keep me away?" Two long strides took him to Charlie's bed, and he sat down, pretending not to notice how Charlie stiffened. "Not gonna happen."

"I thought you'd be with your friends. Talking to them."

"We talked. Or, I talked, and they listened."

Charlie blinked. "You don't have to tell me. I heard enough."

"No, you didn't. I said I talked to them."

"So what? You think 'cause you said something

they're gonna change their minds? News flash, Ian, I've been gay all my life, and you're naïve as fuck to think what happened with Mickey and Patrick is the first time this has ever happened. It's why I told myself not to get involved with another straight guy. I never should've. I knew it was stupid."

Ian kicked off his sneakers, pulled off his socks, and got into bed with Charlie.

"What the fuck are you doing?" Charlie sputtered.

"I told them it wasn't any of their business who I want in my bed, and it shouldn't have any effect on our friendship." Despite Charlie's chilly reception, Ian slid his arm around Charlie's waist and fitted their bodies together. Perfectly. "I told them I'm bisexual and that I want to be with you." He pressed a kiss to Charlie's nape and let his warm scent sink into his bones.

"What? You did what?" Charlie flipped over, and when their eyes met, Ian smiled and couldn't resist pressing a kiss to his half-open, astonished mouth. Sexy didn't begin to describe Charlie with his tousled bedhead and sinful, sweet lips. But it was more than sex for Ian. He wanted to know what made this man so cautious and who had hurt him so bad. Anger bubbled in Ian's gut as he thought about the men who'd earned Charlie's trust only to throw away something so precious.

He propped himself on his elbow. "I said I wanted you, and that I was going to be with you. And if they couldn't deal with it, they could walk out the door."

"You're kidding me." Charlie sat up, and Ian couldn't help eyeing his naked torso. "You said that? Really?"

"Yeah. I wasn't gonna put up with their shit."

Charlie's gaze fell to the bed, and he twisted the sheet in his hands. "So what happened then?"

Ian rested his fingers under Charlie's chin and tipped it up so their eyes met. "Mickey left, but Patrick and I talked. And here I am."

Grim-faced, Charlie pulled away from him. "You're going to tell me you're letting go of a lifelong friendship for me, a stranger? Someone you've only known a couple of months?"

"Maybe we're not really strangers. Maybe we've been inside each other all our lives." Ian ran a hand down Charlie's arm, and hearing Charlie's breath hitch, knew that this wasn't a mistake or a fluke. "Waiting to find the other half."

"What're you talking about?"

Ian had never been good at speaking his feelings, but now the words fell easily from his lips. "Our past is watching us through the eyes of the present."

"You're going to need to make me understand what you're saying."

"Charlie, why're you fighting this? We can be together now." Ian swooped in for a kiss. "It's all good."

"Just like that."

Charlie's flat tone and the skeptical tilt of his brow weren't encouraging, but Ian had never let that stop him when he wanted something badly.

"I never said it would be easy. But you need to help me out here a little. I answered every question you've ever asked me, and yet anytime I want to find out something about you, you give me a few details, then say you don't want to talk about it."

Moving out of reach, Charlie shifted to the center of the bed. From the steely set of his jaw and rigid posture, Charlie had once again slammed the gates he'd slowly begun to swing open.

"What do you want to know? That I was lonely and had no friends? That no one, starting with my mother, wanted me enough to keep me forever?" For the first time since they'd met, Charlie didn't try to hold back his tears, and Ian was glad. If anyone needed to let the pain bleed out, it was Charlie.

"I think talking about it might help."

"Why?" Charlie demanded. "How does talking about something that hurt so much help me?"

"Lemme ask you something," Ian said, choosing his words carefully. "Have I been like any of those other guys? Even before anything happened between us?"

"No, of course not," Charlie said irritably. "But that's the way it always starts. It's no different if it's a guy or a girl you wanna hook up with. You'll say anything to get in their pants." He looked down his nose at Ian. "And I'm sure, for someone like you, merely saying hello would be enough."

Ian's cheeks burned. "That's not fair. I never treated you like that."

"No, you're right. I'm sorry." Charlie's face fell, and he hung his head. A moment passed, and then he whispered, "What do you want from me?"

Ian hated how sad and defeatist Charlie sounded.

"All of you. Everything."

A lock of reddish-brown hair fell over Charlie's eyes, and Ian wanted to brush it off his brow but sensed Charlie would bolt at his touch. He was like one of those fantastical cakes on the cooking shows his mother used to watch. Beautiful, but so fragile and delicate, one touch would shatter and destroy him. Then he began to speak, and it was Ian who had to struggle not to fall apart.

"The first guy I was ever with was the son of one of my

foster families. Derrick was gorgeous and popular, and I, of course, was just plain me. I tried to hide my huge crush on him, but he knew. He was seventeen, and I was fifteen, and even though he had a girlfriend, she came from a very religious family, so they didn't have sex. Derrick told me it wasn't a big thing for us to fool around, and if I really liked him as much as I said I did, I'd make him feel good. He needed to let it out or he'd feel sick."

"Fucker."

Charlie shrugged, and the deadened monotone of his voice chilled Ian. "He said he liked me, and I didn't care. I just wanted someone to call me his, even if it was only between us. He said I was his real lover and Caroline was for show."

"What happened?"

The struggle it took for Charlie to speak revealed that it didn't matter how many years had passed, the hurt lingered. "His mother caught us. Instead of telling her the truth, Derrick said I came on to him. He went from fucking me to beating me up while his mother watched. Then she kicked me out that night. She was supposed to be my foster mother, but she didn't care. I didn't even have a place to go or my clothes or anything. I ended up in a shelter."

"Bastards. People like that should never be allowed to have kids."

"They found me a family the next day, and eventually I got my stuff. But it was two years until I felt safe enough to be with someone else. Toby and I were both seventeen, and we'd go to his place after school and fool around. He said he couldn't tell his parents, but once he went away to college, I'd come visit him and we could be together." Charlie's voice caught. "He said we'd be together and that he loved me. A month after he left for school, I saw online that he joined a fraternity and met a girl. He never answered any of my emails, and I gave up."

The more Ian learned about Charlie's heartbreak, the more strength it took to control his temper. "The least the bastard could've done was tell you."

"Wouldn't have made a difference," Charlie said fatalistically. "And isn't that how you usually do it? I'm assuming you're the one who does the breaking up."

That stung. "Please don't lump me in with these bastards. I've had my heart broken a few times too."

"But there was always a next one along pretty quickly, I'm betting. And you got to do the choosing." Charlie pressed his lips together. "Trust me, I get it. I know my place in relationships. There's always one who loves more than the other. I'm under no illusion—I know I'll always be that someone. The one who tries harder, loves more… it is what it is."

Wisely, Ian kept his mouth shut and changed the topic. "You mentioned some guy in a dance club?" he prodded Charlie to continue.

But Charlie wasn't so willing to move on. "It's easier to forget when you're the one who gets to do the choosing most of the time."

"It doesn't make it any less painful when it happens. Maybe I've been lucky, but I try to be a nice guy. And I try never to lie to or hurt the women I've been with. And I wouldn't fucking promise someone I'd be with them if I didn't intend to keep my word."

Challenging Ian, Charlie held his gaze until Ian blinked and looked away. Maybe he had hurt girls he'd dated in the past. He'd thought he'd been the good guy, but perhaps he was too quick to praise himself.

"After Toby, I only had one long-term relationship, if

you can count six months as long-term, with a client from the dance club, who told me even though he was straight, he loved me. It turned out what he loved was me sucking his dick. And each time he left, he made sure to tell me he wasn't gay." Color high on his cheeks, Charlie leveled a direct gaze at Ian's face. " 'Cause we all know, straight guys don't like having their dicks sucked by another guy."

He debated whether to punch the wall, but all that would do was take the edge off his anger. His entire life, Charlie had been used by people he'd trusted, and the last thing Ian wanted to do was add to that list and cause him more pain. If Charlie gave him the chance, Ian would never allow anyone to hurt him again.

"You're right. But that's what I've been trying to tell you. I'm not straight; I'm bisexual."

Charlie faced him with that same direct, unblinking stare. "And you're telling me you're willing to live your life like that? It's like tossing a pebble into the water: the ripple effect might end, the surface might appear smooth and unbroken, but that pebble will always be there underfoot to remind you."

"I told my best friends." Ian wondered if Mickey and Patrick talked about him after he kicked them out. He couldn't be sure he'd ever see them again. The way he and Patrick had left it gave him hope they could work it out, but Mickey remained a sore point. Grief overwhelmed him over the potential loss. The three of them had been like brothers; from the first they'd clicked, and it was a neighborhood joke that you didn't see one of them without the other two. Losing such an intrinsic part of him would be like losing part of who he was, but he wasn't willing to hide or change. Nothing worth having came easy, including friendship or love.

"And that's a good start, but you only told them

because you were pushed."

Irritated, Ian countered, "Can't you give me a break? I'm trying, at least."

"There's no break when it comes to sexuality. It's with me every day and night, every breath I take. It's the second skin I live in."

"You know, you're like that Eddie in the letters. He kept pushing Robert to make a decision and be with him, but the truth was, Robert couldn't find it in him to fight for what and who he wanted and gave up." He grabbed hold of Charlie's arm. "But I'm not Robert, and I don't have to answer to anyone but myself. I'm not giving up—I'm not giving you up. Not without a fight, even if it means fighting you. We don't have to live like Eddie and Robert, so why not give us a chance?"

Wondering green eyes met his. "You really mean it." It wasn't a question, but Ian jumped to respond. Disappointed badly all his life by people who should've cared and known better, Charlie needed that reassurance, and Ian was ready, willing, and more than able to give it to him.

"I really mean it."

"I'm sorry." Charlie twisted the bedsheets. "I've been projecting my hurt on you, as if you were the cause of all my past problems. It's not fair, when you're being so open and honest with me." Charlie leaned over and gave him a brief kiss, resting his cheek next to Ian's. "Thank you for standing up for me."

"For us," Ian said. "Me plus you equals us."

"I failed high-school algebra, but even I can understand that equation." Charlie's next kiss lingered a little more sweetly on his lips. "Thank you for coming here and being with me."

"There's no other place I want to be." And Ian meant

it. He was all in, pedal to the metal, ready to embrace a life filled with uncertainty at the moment, except for one thing. How much he needed this man to make him feel alive.

He picked up his phone. "Even though Mickey walked out on me, I'm going to send a text to him and Patrick and tell them that I'm still the same person I was a month ago, a year ago, and when we first met. I haven't changed. If they wanna come talk and apologize for the shit they said, they will. Then I'll know. If they don't show, then they weren't the friends I always thought."

Without waiting for Charlie's opinion, Ian sent the text, but he wasn't sure he'd be getting a response, and if he did, what the answer might be.

Chapter Twenty-Five

In the middle of the night, Charlie woke up with Ian curled next to him. They'd gone to bed late, and Charlie knew Ian hoped to hear from Mickey and Patrick, but his phone remained silent. Now, at two in the morning, Charlie couldn't sleep. Trying his utmost not to disturb Ian, Charlie slid out of bed and padded down the steps to the dining room.

First he made a pit stop in the kitchen and scooped out a bowl of ice cream, hoping the sugar would make him feel better. Then he sat at the dining-room table and stuck a spoon into the mound but didn't put any in his mouth.

"What's going on?"

His gaze flew up to meet Ian's. Sleepy bedroom eyes peered from under his messy bedhead, and Charlie's lips twitched at his grumpy tone. Every fiber in his body yearned for Ian, but still he couldn't give all of himself to enjoy being with this bright, affectionate man.

"I wasn't sure…" But that excuse sounded weak and lame, and Charlie knew it. Even worse, Ian did as well. He pulled out a chair and straddled it.

"I don't know what's worse. You sneaking off and leaving me sleeping so you can sit and brood, or you sneaking off and leaving me sleeping so you can eat a big-ass bowl of ice cream alone and not waking me up to have any."

His blue eyes twinkled, and Charlie couldn't help his heartbeat kicking up a drumbeat in his chest. He pushed the bowl toward Ian. "Go ahead. Take it."

"Nuh-uh. We'll share." Before he could answer, Ian bounced out of his seat and ran to the kitchen, returning in a moment with a spoon of his own. "Okay. So tell me what's wrong." He spooned a hefty amount of chocolate espresso ice cream into his mouth. "Mmm. This is good."

"What if Mickey and Patrick don't answer you?"

Ian's sparkling eyes dimmed. "That's their choice."

"I don't want you to lose your friends because of me."

"I think it would be because of their choice, don't you? I'm here." He spooned more ice cream into his mouth.

Charlie watched Ian, his movements so sure and strong, even in the dead of night he lit up the room with his own unique brand of energy and life. The man had not only scaled his walls, he'd knocked them down and used the pieces to build a new foundation where Charlie might believe a future existed for a guy like him.

Ian grinned around his spoon, and Charlie's heart flip-flopped. This time, he couldn't suppress his smile.

If this was happiness, bring it on.

A tinkling sound in the distance grew louder, and Rachel floated to them in her silvery light. *"Is that better, boys? Now you'll hear me coming."*

Ian gave his spoon a final lick. "How's it shakin', Rachel?"

Charlie shook his head. Now Ian was treating the century-old ghost like one of his bros, and from the smile on her face, she was eating it up.

"I'm fine, dear. So proud of how you stood up for Charlie. If only my brother had someone like you..." She sniffled into a handkerchief that appeared in her hand and dabbed at her eyes.

"I'm sorry," Charlie said. "Can you tell us more about them, or is it too painful?"

"I can try. But not too much. Their story is coming to an end, again, and it makes me so emotional, I can't summon the energy to show you more."

"We understand."

She waved her hand in front of the mirror, and Charlie watched as her figure faded. Was she disappearing as Robert and Eddie's story unfolded? Much as she crashed into his life at the most inopportune times, he'd grown used to her, and with a start he realized he might miss her when she was gone.

The scene in front of them was the front parlor of his house. Charlie recognized Eddie and a young girl he realized was Rachel. He opened his mind and listened.

Robert,

Please tell me it isn't true. This afternoon I was sitting in our front parlor when my mother came in from her weekly shopping, all smiles. She told us that a wedding was going to take place next year. Rachel, naturally, was excited even before I asked who the bride and groom were.

Imagine my shock, my dismay, when she revealed the bride was Charlotte Emerson and the groom none other than our neighbor's son, Robert Nolan. My face must've given my surprise away, as my mother laughed and said to me, "Oh, Eddie, don't pretend you didn't know. You and Robert are thick as thieves, like brothers. You most certainly know how to keep a secret."

I do know how to keep a secret, but obviously not as well as you.

Meet me tonight.

Eddie

Their story might've been a hundred years old and all the people involved might've long since passed away, but the heartbreak in those words was as fresh as morning dew. Eddie's pain resonated with Charlie most of all.

"Poor Eddie. He must've felt so betrayed. I'm so sad for him. To be in love and get blindsided like that must've devastated him. I can't believe Robert didn't tell him."

Frowning, Ian pointed at the mirror. "Look. Let's see if Robert had an explanation."

But for Charlie, no explanation could erase Robert's betrayal.

Once again, Robert was in his bedroom, but this time he paced the room. When he sat, it wasn't at the desk but at the window, where he pillowed his face in his hands. His shoulders shook. Ian heaved out a sigh beside Charlie.

Eddie,

I wish you might understand. You know my true feelings, but I never made a secret of the fact that my family expected certain things from me. There's no way out for me, Eddie. I can't go against them. I thought I could fight, but I couldn't come up with one good reason not to marry Charlotte, especially when her parents will be helping us buy a home near here. I must give in to my parents' wishes. My father isn't well and suffers from an odd shortness of breath. He's getting on in years and expects me to take over the business sooner rather than later. I'm their only child, and I must stay here, in case he grows too sick.

What else can I do? I'm a selfish bastard and held on to you...to us...because I can't conceive of not having you in my life. I don't want to let you go. I know you'll read this and hate me, and you have every right, but I'd rather be a memory in your eyes than a nobody to your soul.

Maybe we were supposed to find each other and have to let go, to know that if we can survive this pain, we can survive anything. Can we meet one last time?

Robert

Eyes wet, Charlie sniffled. "This is so sad."

Ian peered around the room. "Rachel's gone."

He nodded and wiped his face. "Yeah. I have a feeling playing out these scenes is wearing her down. Maybe she was sent to us to show us Eddie and Robert's story, and once it's played out, she's done her job."

Charlie yawned. "Well, I have to go to sleep, and so do you. We have work in the morning." He finished the ice cream. "And you don't have to stay and babysit me. I appreciate everything you said, but I'm still over here, not sure what's going to happen."

"So?" Ian thrust out his jaw. "Who is?"

"What're you talking about?"

"Look." Always voluble, even at three in the morning, Ian waved his hands while he spoke. "I know what happened in my apartment was traumatic for you, but it was for me too. You might not think so because this is who you are and always have been, but I'm kinda feeling a little lost myself." Charlie watched as Ian heaved himself up from the table. "But you're right. I should leave and go home and find myself." He remained where he was.

Don't go, Charlie wanted to cry out, and hold Ian, but he couldn't form the words. He watched Ian's face fall, then turn stony.

"Okay, then. See you."

And then he was gone. And Charlie didn't know what else to do but wash the dishes and go to bed.

* * *

When Charlie awoke and checked his phone, it was after nine, and though he'd hoped to find a message from Ian, his inbox remained disappointingly empty. If he didn't want to be late for work, he'd have to hustle. He decided to forget about shaving and brushed his teeth in the shower. He grabbed a yogurt from the fridge, and keys in hand, hustled out the door…to run smack into Ian, who sat waiting for him on the stoop. He stumbled, and Ian caught him as he rose.

"H-hi." His heart slammed. "What're you doing here?"

"Waiting for you." Already warm, the early morning sun beat down on their faces, but even squinting, Charlie could see the longing in Ian's pure blue eyes. "I figured if we can walk home together, we can walk to work the same."

Careful not to let his true emotions show, because inside Charlie was doing a Snoopy dance of happiness, he nodded. "Sure. If you want."

"I like the scruff." Ian's fingers left a trail of fire along his jawline. "You look hot." Charlie's heart pounded, but he merely ducked his head without answering.

They retraced their steps from the previous day, picking up coffee, which Ian insisted on paying for, at the Dunkin' Donuts off Atlantic Avenue on Flatbush Avenue. At the corner, Ian stopped and put his hand on Charlie's arm.

"I gotta cross the street. My work is over there." He gestured across Flatbush, past the Barclays Center. "Can we talk tonight?"

To Charlie, it was all a mass of condos and commercial buildings rising to dizzying heights, and he wondered how Ian felt about working so high in the sky.

"Do you really go up to the top of the buildings?" He tipped his head to the sky. "Aren't you scared?"

"Hell no," Ian responded with a cheeky grin. "I told you once before, I like living on the edge. Frankly, waiting to hear if you want to talk this out between us is more nerve-wracking than standing on a girder twenty-five stories up in the air."

"You're really serious."

Before he had a chance to say more, Ian grabbed him by the shoulders and crushed their lips together for the briefest second, leaving Charlie breathless when they finished.

"I'm really serious."

Then Ian sprinted across the street, ignoring the blare of horns from the trucks and cars as the light changed from yellow to red. Living on the edge? Ian wasn't kidding, Charlie mused as he walked down Flatbush to his store on Bergen Street. Of course the moment he entered, Mona pounced on him.

"So? What happened last night?"

"Good morning to you too." He set his coffee on the counter and removed his straw skimmer to stand under the AC vent, welcoming the blast of cold air. It might be over eighty degrees outside, but Charlie knew to wear layers, which was why he wore a linen button-down with a pinstriped waistcoat over it. He could roll up the sleeves outside, and his pants, also linen, hung from his hips, baggy and cool.

"Yeah, yeah, whatever." She leaned on the counter, cutting off his escape. Her bright-pink hair swung over her shoulders. "Tell me."

He gnawed on his lower lip before answering. "It was a shit show. Ian and I were supposed to have a barbecue. Instead, his two best friends came over and confronted him…both of us. They spewed all this hateful stuff, said I came on to him and made it easy for him to get sex."

"*What?*" she screeched. "Please tell me he set them straight and told them off. I hope he punched their stupid faces in."

Pain swept through Charlie as he relived that humiliation. "I dunno. I left and went home."

"No. Why? You should've stayed and stood up for yourself."

"Are you kidding?" He heard himself yelling but didn't care. "Two straight guys yelling at the gay guy for coming on to their friend is the story line for half the gay movies I've watched, and guess what? The gay guy always dies in the end."

"So that's it? Ian seemed so into you. I can't believe he just left it like that."

Mona was the closest thing he had to a friend. Someone to confide in who was on his side. "He did come over later.

To talk."

"Yeah?" Eyes shining, she motioned with her hand. "Tell me. Come on. You've been working here for over five years now, and I've never seen you like this." She touched his arm and gave him a gentle squeeze. "It's time you learn to trust the people who truly care about you."

"What if you don't know how because you've never had anyone in your life who has?"

"Well, I care." She flung her arms around him.

He hugged her tight. "Thank you. I know I'm moody and shit, but you're the only person I can talk to about this."

"Friends are friends no matter what. Good and bad. Thick and thin."

"What about gay or straight?" Charlie asked bitterly.

Mona's gaze turned soft. "What happened with Ian's friends? Please tell me he didn't let them get away with what they said."

"No. He said they basically forced him to admit he's bi. It was terrible, and I felt really bad for him. That's never the right way. It's not fair to Ian, and if it were anyone weaker, he might not have been able to stand up to them."

"But he did?" Mona asked.

The bells over the door jingled, and several customers walked in. Mona cursed under her breath and threw them a salesperson smile, while under the counter her leg jiggled.

"Feel free to browse, and if you need help, let us know." She rolled her eyes when facing him again, and Charlie bit his lip.

"I know you want the gossip, but we can't lose our jobs. And Ian and I haven't finished our talk."

"Miss?" Holding up several items of clothing, a

customer called to her from the racks. "Is there a dressing room?"

"Better go help her." He smirked and picked up the pricing gun. "I have to deal with the new stock that came in."

"Coming," she called to the waiting customer and hopped off her chair. "You're going to leave me hanging, huh?"

Charlie shrugged, not really knowing the answer himself.

* * *

When six o'clock rolled around and Ian didn't show up at the store, Charlie's spirits plummeted to match the weather, which had turned dark with low-hanging storm clouds. He'd thought after their night together and that morning, Ian might've wanted to have dinner together and finish the talk they'd started.

The air held a metallic smell, and Charlie speed-walked home, although he wasn't at all looking forward to sitting in that big house alone. He stopped at Sahadi's, the big Middle Eastern market, and picked up spinach pies, feta cheese, and hummus, along with homemade pita bread. Dinner now sorted, Charlie hurried down the final couple of blocks, anxious to beat the encroaching rain. He opened the front door…and stopped short.

Roses.

Everywhere he looked, over every surface, sat vases of roses. Pink, yellow, and white, their fragrance filled the air with sweet perfume. There must've been at least ten bouquets. Charlie blinked and rubbed his eyes.

"Aren't they beautiful?"

At the sound of Rachel's voice, Charlie dropped the bag and tipped his head to see Rachel hovering at the top of the steep staircase, a wide smile beaming from her face.

"Did you do this to cheer me up? It's really pretty, but—"

"Silly boy, of course not." Her smile brightened, and in a tinkling silver cloud, she vanished.

A noise behind him caught his attention. He spun around and stood openmouthed. He couldn't speak or move.

A bouquet of red roses in hand, Ian stood at the door. "Hi."

Somehow he found his voice again. "Uh…h-hi. Wh-what is this? How did you do this?"

"Through the back door. You better start locking it." Ian stepped inside, and when he reached the foot of the stairs, where Charlie remained rooted to the floor, he said, "These are for you. From my garden."

The lush, velvety petals of the roses stunned the senses with their vibrant red color. Hesitantly, Charlie reached out and brushed one of the blooms with a fingertip. "They're gorgeous. But I thought you didn't believe in cutting them. You said they belonged on the rosebush, where nature intended them to be."

"I was wrong. Things that are beautiful are worth showing off. They deserve to be seen and appreciated." Ian moved closer and set the roses on the stairs. "Like us."

He began to shake. "What're you talking about?"

Strong hands rested on his shoulders, and Ian gazed into his eyes. "Come with me? I have something to show you."

Chapter Twenty-Six

Usually, when Ian asked a girl out, he was already pretty sure she'd accept. He'd have been chatting her up in a bar, or they'd already had sex and he wanted to keep seeing her. But not with Charlie. He was so skittish and had such deep trust issues—rightfully so—that Ian held his breath until Charlie gave a quick jerk of his head and said, "Okay, I guess."

Ian's breath expelled in a *whoosh* of air, and he gathered up the roses in one hand and took Charlie's in his other. "Good thing I dethorned these."

Only a faint smile from Charlie, but he'd take it. Ian intended on making Charlie smile for always. Charlie locked his door, and when they entered Ian's house, he led Charlie directly to the backyard.

"Do you like it?"

He'd left work early to prepare. Dave had given him the go-ahead and even some advice.

"Go slow, kid. You don't wanna overwhelm him. If he's got trust issues, you'll wanna let him set the pace."

Charlie left his side and walked around the deck. More bouquets of flowers had been placed around the perimeter, and on the grass he'd set a table for two and had the barbecue at the ready. Taking Charlie's hand in his, they walked down the steps to the yard.

"What's going on?" Charlie stopped by a chair. "What're you doing?"

"Trying to make you see this isn't a one-off for me. I wanna be with you, Charlie. Not just for the nights. I want us to learn more about each other, every day. I don't know what will be going forward, but I'm not playing at this. It wasn't a joke, and I didn't do it to get sex."

He put his arms around Charlie's shoulders, pulling him close so their chests pressed together. Close enough to hear the frantic kick of Charlie's heart. "From the first time I saw you, I haven't seen anyone else. I don't want to. It's only you." He kissed Charlie's sun-warmed hair. "You're all I need or want."

"But what about your friends?" A pucker of worry wrinkled Charlie's brow.

"You're my friend, aren't you?"

"Yeah, but…"

"Stop putting up obstacles. Sometimes it's easier to walk around the mountain than climb it and come up with the same result. I want to be with you and no one else. Is that enough for you?"

"You're kidding, right?" Charlie joked. "Are you

enough for me? It's the other way around."

"No. I'm not kidding. I'm confused. Things are changing, and I don't know what the future might bring. Maybe you'll get bored with me and want someone with more experience." An unexpected waved of shyness rolled through him. "I know I don't know much about the sex stuff." He cupped Charlie's cheek. "I just want to be with you."

Seeing the struggle inside Charlie, Ian didn't want to wait any longer. He meant the kiss to be gentle, but as always when their lips touched, a sweet wildness overtook him. Their mouths crushed together, lips seeking, sucking, teeth clashing and tongues licking any and all available exposed skin.

"God, you taste so good." Ian kissed down the strong length of Charlie's throat, pressing his lips to the rapid pulse beating in his neck. He unbuttoned Charlie's shirt and continued his exploration, still noting the differences in the rough hair on his chest, the hard planes of his muscles. Ian slipped Charlie's shirt off.

"Ian, what're yo—"

"If you're going to ask me what I'm doing, I must not be doing it right. So lemme figure it out." He licked the buds of Charlie's nipples.

"Oh shit, Ian." Charlie wiggled away, wild-eyed and breathing heavily. His golden glow, beaming bright even in the sunlight, lit up the yard.

"Come back here." Ian grabbed Charlie, and they stumbled under the oak tree. Charlie's mouth softened beneath his, and their tongues played and slid together. Ian sucked Charlie's until the man moaned and clung to his shoulders. He cupped Charlie's ass and pressed their hips together, the ache of pleasure rising inside him as the rigid length of Charlie's dick thrust against his.

"I wanna…I…please?" He touched Charlie's bare stomach, then dipped his fingers beneath the waistband of the baggy linen pants, feeling the springy hair of Charlie's groin. A shot of lust blasted through him. "Can I?"

"Yes," Charlie whispered. "Yes."

He undid the buttons, and the loose pants slid to Charlie's ankles.

Maybe the cool air on his bare skin woke Charlie up. "Wait, the neighbors—"

"Can't see a thing," Ian replied smoothly. "Benefit of extra-tall hedges." It was true. No one could see them. "We're all alone." He trailed a finger over Charlie's bare stomach, then touched his erection, tenting out from his boxers. "I wanna taste you."

"Ian…*ohhhhh*." Charlie bit off whatever he planned on saying when Ian peeled the boxers off, revealing his cock. Ian sank to his knees and ran his fingers along the thick length. "Yes, yes."

"Okay." He wet his lips and licked the vein from the root to the tip, inhaling the musky scent. It tasted like Charlie's skin, and with the sun beating warm on his neck, Ian bathed Charlie's shaft with his tongue, growing more confident. So confident, in fact, that he decided to go for it and gently slid his mouth over the smooth head and the shaft, finally taking the length of Charlie's dick into his mouth. "Mmm," he hummed and began to move slowly up and down, swirling his tongue around. When he reached the top, he licked the precome trickling from the slit. "Tastes so good. God, Charlie…" He began sucking more vigorously and a bit harder, hearing Charlie's breathing speed up and feeling Charlie's hands tangle in his hair.

"Ian, oh God, right there, please," Charlie choked out.

Ian sucked hard at the head and took Charlie's balls in

his hand, gently squeezing them.

"Ian, oh, ooh." Charlie's hips began to drive his cock into Ian's mouth, and he loved it. His lips clung to Charlie's rigid cock, and instinctively, he ran his fingers through the cleft of Charlie's ass. "Fuck," Charlie shouted and unloaded in his mouth.

Ian choked a little, managing to swallow some but not all of Charlie's come. He held on to Charlie's muscular thighs, feeling him shake. As Charlie softened, Ian continued to lick at his cock and balls. He finally sat back on his heels and wiped his face with his hand. Charlie sank to the ground next to him.

"I'm sorry," he said, and Ian's smile faded.

"Why? I know I'm not experienced, but I thought…I tried to do what I thought would make you feel good."

"No, I mean yes, it was amazing. I…I loved it."

With his eyes hazy and face still flushed, Charlie was adorable and more desirable than ever, and Ian wanted him more than anyone he'd ever wanted before.

"Then what? What're you sorry for?"

"I should've warned you I was about to come so you didn't have to swallow."

Touched by his concern, Ian trailed his fingers over Charlie's jaw and leaned in to kiss him, sighing when their tongues touched. Charlie sucked his tongue, and Ian felt himself burning from the inside out. Charlie tugged at the waistband of his shorts.

"Wanna suck you."

"Nuh." Hard as it was to get his mouth to form words when Charlie cupped his dick and was rubbing him with a slow up-and-down stroke, Ian didn't want that. "W-wait," he gasped out and shifted away. "How hungry are you for dinner right now?"

A slow smile tipped up the corners of Charlie's lips. "Not very. You have a different plan in mind?"

Ian swooped in for another kiss. "I wanna make love to you. Please?" At Charlie's nod, his heart leaped. That one time wasn't enough. "Come on. I made it ready for us." He hopped to his feet and held out his hand.

Chuckling, Charlie took it and let Ian pull him up. "Pretty sure of yourself, huh?"

"No." Ian took Charlie's face between the palms of his hands. "I've never been more uncertain as to what to do, but I'm the most certain as to how I feel. You and me. It's right; we're right, together." He kissed him hard, and Charlie melted into his chest.

"No one's ever said such nice things to me. I don't think I've ever been made love to."

"I'm ready to be your first. Like you're mine."

They left the garden and reentered the house. Ian tugged Charlie toward the stairs. "This way. Up here."

"Not your apartment?"

He'd never brought anyone to the main house before, but he wanted it to be different with Charlie.

"No. I thought we'd stay up here tonight. Since we're having dinner later. It'll be easier." He led Charlie up the steps and stood outside the door to his old bedroom. Thank God his parents had bought every bedroom a new mattress when they moved their furniture out.

Whenever his sisters would come to visit and bring their husbands with them, they needed a place to stay, and Ian wondered what they'd think of this development in his life.

He pushed thoughts of his family out of his mind for

now. He closed the door behind them and quickly flung off his clothes as he watched Charlie remove his. Naked, Charlie was gorgeous, and again Ian was drawn to him and couldn't stop running his hands over Charlie's shoulders, chest, and back. As if he'd been kissing a man for years, he nuzzled against the scruff of Charlie's neck, drawing in his hot scent and licking his throat. He sucked at the tiny points of Charlie's nipples and traced the definition of muscles across his pecs.

Charlie reached between them, and their dicks slid together. Ian rotated his hips, trapping Charlie's hand between their bodies.

"God, that feels so good." He sighed when Charlie's fingers danced up and down his shaft, then cupped his balls and squeezed them.

"Ian, want you in me so bad."

Ian's hands roamed over Charlie's hot, naked body. He smoothed over the firm globes of Charlie's ass and ran a finger into the cleft, stopping briefly to rub around the tiny hole. Wetness spread across his stomach as Charlie's dick pulsed out precome.

"*Ahh*, yes, please." Charlie widened his stance to give Ian better access. "Touch me, get inside me."

"Let's get to the bed," Ian whispered, and they tumbled together, their arms and legs tangled in each other. To his surprise, Charlie raised himself above him. "Can I...I wanna rim you. Is that okay?"

Ian's dick zoomed to attention. "Hell, yeah." He lay back and let Charlie spread his legs wide. At the sight of Charlie licking his lips and diving in, Ian had to squeeze the base of his rock-hard dick to keep from shooting his load. A soft wetness touched him, and Ian jumped and cried out. "Holy fuck."

Charlie snickered and returned to licking around the rim of his hole, dipping his tongue in and out. Nerve endings Ian didn't know existed exploded, and he groaned, pushing his ass into Charlie's face, wanting that wet, flickering tongue inside him. Harder, deeper.

"Jesus, Charlie, fuck," he gasped as he flailed, banging the bed. His dick leaked all over his hand, and he knew if he didn't get inside Charlie soon, he'd implode. "Stop, stop."

Charlie sat up. "What's wrong?"

He gripped his erection. "What's wrong is if I don't get this inside you, I'm gonna come all over the sheets, and that would be a waste, don't you think?"

Charlie's eyes widened at the sight of him grasping his dick. It was painful for Ian to move, but he kept his eyes on the prize. Meaning Charlie.

"*Ohhh*. Damn. Yeah." Charlie lay down and spread his legs, touching himself. "Come and get it."

"Can I touch you first?" His hungry gaze roved over Charlie, his chest, taut abs, stiff, reddened dick, always coming back to the pink opening between his legs.

Color high on his cheeks, mouth open, wet and panting, Charlie nodded. "Please," he whispered, and Ian's heart soared. His greatest pleasure would be pleasuring Charlie.

Ian grabbed the lube and slicked his fingers. He rubbed the outside of Charlie's hole and watched with fascination as his finger sank into the snug passage. Ian couldn't imagine ever getting tired of watching that. "It feels like you're sucking me in."

"More, please." Charlie wiggled under his finger. "I need more."

" 'K, baby." Ian slid in another finger and then a third, always making sure Charlie was ready for him. It was hard as hell to keep himself from flying apart with Charlie sighing and writhing beneath him. Knowing how sensitive Charlie's nipples were, Ian reached up and tweaked them while continually fucking Charlie with his hand.

"Want you inside me, Ian, now." Charlie moaned and thrashed on the bed. "Now please."

Ian withdrew his fingers and sheathed his aching dick while Charlie watched him with avid eyes. At the hungry, naked lust on Charlie's face, Ian's heart pounded.

"Damn, you look like you want to eat me alive."

"I offered, but you wanted to fuck."

"This isn't fucking, baby." Ian pushed the head of his dick into Charlie, giving him time to adjust to his size. "This is making love." He heard Charlie hiss as he sank to the hilt. "Are you okay?" Ian asked. Buried to the fullest, Ian sure as hell was. Charlie fit him like a glove.

"I am now."

Like the first time, Ian lost himself in the silky inferno clutching his length and had to restrain himself from pinning Charlie to the bed and slamming into him hard. Instead, he pulsed short, shallow thrusts until Charlie grabbed his arms, his eyes alight with a fierce, primal hunger.

"Stop holding back. Give it to me hard. As hard as you can. I want it…want you. All of you."

Who could resist that? He gave Charlie what he'd been missing from a lover. He touched his lips to Charlie's, kissing him with gentle presses of his lips. Their tongues met and teased, and Ian murmured into Charlie's quivering neck, "I'll always be here for you. Good or bad. When everything around you looks dark, I promise to hold your hand and help you find your way."

"You're my way now."

Ian slid in deeper, and Charlie clutched him tighter. He practically folded Charlie in half and buried himself in Charlie's heat, pumping hard.

"Oh God, Charlie, Charlie."

The ever-present golden glow enveloped the entire room as Ian continued to hammer into him. Shouting out his pleasure, Charlie clawed Ian's shoulders and back as he came again, his release spurting between their sweating bodies. His passage clamped ruthlessly onto Ian's dick, leaving Ian breathless. He couldn't see or hear anything but his thundering heart. Charlie's heat radiated through him, and he smelled the scent of their bodies. Charlie had invaded Ian from the inside out, and he felt like their skin, bones, and blood melded together. He rocked his hips, grinding them into Charlie's as electricity shot from the base of his spine upward and he exploded, groaning through his orgasm. His cock throbbed, and he searched for Charlie's mouth.

"Baby. Oh, God. You're incredible."

They kissed, lips clinging, tongues sweeping and tangling, until Ian collapsed on top of Charlie, their harsh breathing the only sound in the room. Several minutes passed before it slowed and Ian could lift his head.

Charlie lay beneath him, red marks scattered over the golden skin of his neck and chest, which Ian recognized as coming from his mouth and teeth.

"Did I hurt you?" Gently, he ran fingertips over the tender skin. "I'm sorry."

Charlie blinked his eyes open, and that gorgeous smile filled his face with light. "You didn't hurt me. For the first time I know what it feels like to really feel alive, to feel wanted." His lashes swept down to fan against his cheeks, and Ian's heart squeezed at how much he'd come to care for this man.

"I hope you don't doubt it again. Ever."

Ian shifted to move off Charlie, but he grabbed Ian's arm. "No. Don't. I-I like it when you're on top of me. Inside me." Pink spots colored his cheeks, and Charlie bit that full lower lip. Ian's cock, miraculously still semihard, twitched. "I like it when you call me baby."

Ian smoothed his hand over Charlie's face. "I'm glad. It just slipped out. I don't want you to think it was like that stupid thing Mickey said, that you were the woman. I know you're a man." He kissed Charlie's half-open mouth. "You're all man and who I want to be with."

"Even if it means they don't want to be friends with you anymore?"

He couldn't have imagined his life without his two friends, yet it was easier than thinking about life without Charlie. That was unimaginable now.

"That's their choice, not mine. And I'm not so sure, even if they come back, that I want to be their friend if that's who they are." This time when he lifted off Charlie and slipped out, Charlie didn't protest, and Ian took off the condom and disposed of it. "Wanna take a shower and then have dinner? I have steaks for the barbecue."

Charlie lay with a dreamy smile on his lips, and Ian wondered if he'd ever be able to look at Charlie and not want to drag him off to bed. Or kiss him. He grinned to himself, thinking there could be worse problems.

"Sure. I didn't eat much today."

Ian frowned. "Why?"

Dropping his gaze, Charlie fingered the comforter. "I guess I was afraid I'd never see you again."

"Because of what happened last night with the guys? I told you I didn't care what they said." Ignoring their messy state, Ian sat next to Charlie on the bed. "I make up my own mind."

Charlie lifted himself up on his elbows. "Okay. I'm learning to believe, in you and myself."

Ian put out his hand. "Come on." Without further words between them, they walked into the bathroom, and Ian turned on the shower.

They stood under the spray, and Ian picked up the shower gel and poured a generous dollop into his palm. He swirled it over Charlie. Ian's cock thickened, and Charlie smiled.

"You gave me a pounding. Give me a chance to rest, and I'll be ready for you again."

"Hey. It's more than that. Being around you, I'm naturally going to be turned-on. It's just what you do to me." Ian tipped Charlie's chin up and met his gaze. "The sex, while amazing, isn't the main reason I want to be with you. I hope you know that."

Guileless, wide green eyes gazed at him from beneath sleek, wet hair. "I've had so many people promise me things. I spent my time holding on to hope and listening to false promises. I've given up holding anyone to their words."

"Then hold on to me now. I'm not letting you go." Ian braced his arms on either side of Charlie, peace settling into his bones from the close connection to this special man. "I want you to stay." Ian slipped his arms around Charlie's waist, and their wet bodies nestled against each other. "Right here, with me. It's time to forget about everyone else you've ever known."

It would take more than a few sentences in a shower to wash away the walls of mistrust Charlie had erected. Ian knew he would prove himself through actions, not words.

His stomach growled, breaking the mood, and Charlie

swept away the dripping hair from his eyes and grinned.

"Glad it was you and not me. I'm starving."

Ian cackled. "We worked up an appetite, I think. Let's go eat."

Dried off and dressed again, Ian put his arm around Charlie's shoulders as they walked down the stairs. On the way out, he grabbed a six-pack of the IPA he had chilling in the refrigerator.

Once out on the deck, he fired up the grill, and they sat in the chairs, waiting for the coals to get hot. He ran his bare foot over Charlie's, receiving only a half smile in return.

"What's wrong?"

The sun had begun its downward trajectory, but even in the half shadows of early twilight he could see Charlie's mood had turned somber.

"You're so comfortable with this. How? You've never been with a guy, and yet we've had sex, and you're so free about it, and even now, all these little gestures...I'm so confused."

Ian hitched his chair closer to Charlie. "You're confused because you think I should be?" At Charlie's nod, Ian said, "As I told you, I like living on the edge, and that's the way I look at life. When I jump, it's always the highest I can go for. When I'm in, I'm all in. These feelings I'm having for you, I've never had them, not with anyone."

"I don't want to just be a thrill ride for you," Charlie blurted out.

Ian grabbed Charlie's hand. "You're my greatest thrill. Being with you has not only opened my eyes, I'm seeing everything in a whole new light. When I'm with you, everything's new and exciting and...fuck it, Charlie.

I think I'm in love with you."

The words tumbled out, but he had no regrets. Even the frightened expression in Charlie's eyes didn't scare him off and make him want a retraction. Charlie's cold hand in his trembled, and Ian, knowing Charlie as he did, sensed his withdrawal but held on tight.

"Wh-what're you talking about? You can't...you don't..." As if afraid to say the words, Charlie shook his head. "Ian, that's ridiculous. You're just saying that."

"Why would I have to? To make you feel better?" In one swift move, Ian grabbed Charlie around the nape and kissed him deeply, devouring him, sucking his tongue, leaving no part of his lips and mouth untouched. "I know how to make you feel better without saying that. So try again."

Charlie touched his swollen lips. "But why...how? We haven't known each other that long."

A warm breeze blew over them, and Charlie's golden light shimmered in the early lavender twilight. "I think maybe I've known you forever. And yeah, you're my friend, but now I look at you and suddenly you're more than that."

Like tiny diamonds, tears glistened on Charlie's lashes. "I can't believe you're saying this. To me. You."

Ian brushed their lips together. "I already told you. You. Me. Us. Together." Their kiss deepened, and despite how hungry he was for dinner, he was hungrier for Charlie.

The loud cawing of two crows winging through the backyard broke them apart, and Charlie's eyes danced. "Don't you wonder if those crows are something else?"

"I'm not thinking about anyone but you."

He took Charlie's chin between his thumb and forefinger and kissed him hard, then put the food on the grill. Forty minutes later the dinner was demolished, along with two beers each, and Ian, sleepy and sated, held out his hand.

"Let's leave this and take a nap. We'll clean up later." He glanced at his phone. "It's almost nine. An hour power nap, and we'll be raring to go." He grinned.

"Aren't you always," Charlie said dryly, but let Ian take his hand and pull him to standing.

Ian gave him a hard kiss. "For you, yeah. Cleaning a dirty grill, not so much."

They dumped their paper plates into the kitchen garbage and headed upstairs, where they stripped to their underwear and climbed into bed. Ian wrapped his arms around Charlie, and with his face pressed into the sweet spot of Charlie's neck, closed his eyes.

* * *

Ian awoke to the bedroom light being switched on, momentarily blinding him.

"Hey." He blinked, rubbed his eyes, and stared. "Oh, shit."

"Surprise, honey. You *are* in the house. I told Daddy you must be. You wouldn't leave a dirty grill or a full wastebasket. He's in his bedroom," his mother called out. She dropped her purse on the floor and came at him with outstretched arms, then stopped halfway to the bed. "Oh, I'm sorry." She backed away. "I didn't know you'd be up here with someone."

"Uh, after the barbecue I figured it was easier…" He pulled the comforter over Charlie, but instead of snuggling under, Charlie rolled over and rubbed his eyes.

"What's going on?" he asked, sitting up.

"Oh. *Oh*," his mother said and turned away. "I-I'll leave you to get dressed." And without another word, she picked up her purse and ran out of the room.

"Crap. My parents came home unexpectedly." Ian jumped up and pulled on his shorts and T-shirt. "Come on."

"I'll leave, don't worry." Charlie shuffled around and pulled on his clothes, frantically smoothing his hair.

"Leave? Who's asking you to do that? I want you to meet them."

Giving Charlie no time to protest, Ian took him by the hand and pulled him downstairs toward the voices coming from the kitchen. His parents were sitting at the table, talking quietly. When his father saw him, he stood and smiled.

"Ian, you're looking great."

"Hi, Dad." They hugged, and Ian smelled the familiar Drakkar Noir and felt the same strength in his arms. "I can see you've been playing golf." Playfully, Ian squeezed his father's bicep. "Nice muscle."

"I can't complain. We came home because of the hurricane. Michelle is coming tomorrow." His father peered over his shoulder. "Care to introduce us?"

An incredibly uncomfortable Charlie had remained at the entrance to the kitchen, shifting from foot to foot. Ian waved to him to join them. "Yeah. Remember I told you Miss Muir's great-great-nephew had moved in? This is Charlie Muir." Charlie didn't move, so Ian walked over and tugged him closer. "Charlie, this is my dad, Andrew, and my mother, Cherie."

"Nice to meet you, Charlie," his mom said.

To his father's credit, he didn't blink an eye meeting and greeting Charlie, even though Ian had no doubt his mother had filled him in on what she'd seen upstairs.

"S-same to you. I hope you had a good flight."

Smiling as though it wasn't a shock to discover her son in bed with another man, his mother put her hand on Charlie's arm. "Typical delays, but we're here, and that's all that counts. Now, why don't we all sit down and have a drink, and Ian, you can tell us what's been going on." Her eyes twinkled. "I have a feeling it's going to be a long night."

"We might need more than one." Ian took the chair opposite his parents with Charlie reluctantly sitting next to him. "I think the best way to start is to be open and honest. I broke up with Deena because I never felt satisfied in our relationship. I never have with anyone I've been with."

He paused, and his parents gave him an encouraging smile. And like the golden glow surrounding Charlie, the warmth of their acceptance reached out to him. From his earliest memories, Ian had known only love. It was why he didn't hesitate to take Charlie's cold hand in his, and after giving it an encouraging squeeze, placed their laced fingers on top of the table.

"Charlie and I are together. From the first time I saw him, we had a special connection, and after a while it changed from friendship to something more."

His father rose from his chair, and Charlie jerked away and cowered. Startled, Ian put a hand on Charlie's knee. "What's the matter?"

"Please don't hurt me. I promise I'll go away and leave Ian alone." Charlie trembled, his eyes wide and glazed with fear.

"What?" His father stood, astonished. "I was only

going to get you both a beer from the refrigerator."

"Oh, no." His mother rushed to Charlie's side. "Oh, honey, what did you think, that Andy was going to hit you? Never."

Shaking and pale, Charlie pushed his hair off his face. "I didn't know. It wouldn't be the first time it's happened."

His mother's red lips tightened. "Well, you don't ever have to worry. We don't believe in fists. We talk things out."

"To death," Ian muttered. "Don't say I didn't warn you."

"Don't be fresh." His mother smacked his shoulder lightly. "You're not too big to spank."

And when Charlie's lips twitched, Ian knew it would be all right.

Chapter Twenty-Seven

Charlie walked into Ian's apartment and collapsed on the sofa. He'd never felt more drained in his entire life. Meeting Ian's parents should've been the scariest thing in the world, and yet it wasn't. They were kind, supportive, and willing to listen. The kind of parents he'd always dreamed of finding but never believed existed.

"What're you thinking?" Ian sat next to him and handed him a bottle of water. "I can practically see the thoughts running circles in your brain."

"I'm thinking that this should've been the scariest day of my life, and yet"—he cast his gaze to the floor—"it turned out to be the most wonderful."

At the gentle touch of Ian's fingers to his chin, he raised his eyes to meet Ian's. "I thought so too."

"Did you mean it? What you said earlier?"

"That I think I love you? Yes. I've never been in love before, but I know I wake up wanting to see you, and go to sleep wishing you were with me. You turn me on and light me up like a stick of fucking dynamite. One kiss and I'm ready to explode. I don't want anyone else near you. Just the thought of anyone but me touching you makes me insane. Even guys you used to be with." He ran a hand down Charlie's arm, leaving goose bumps in its wake. "I don't want you to be with anyone else. Only me."

Ian's mouth crushed his, kissing him so deeply, it took his breath away, and Charlie nearly swooned. He held on to Ian's shoulders and opened under the push of Ian's demanding tongue. He sucked on it hard, eliciting a groan from Ian.

"I don't want to be. It's only you for me too."

"God, you're incredible. No one's ever made me feel like this."

How could he say no to this man, and why would he want to? Ian had busted into his life with an open heart and joy for living, making it impossible not to love him.

He hugged Ian tight, speaking into the strong cords of his neck. "I grew up looking for someone to love me but never expecting to find him. Love wasn't meant for a guy like me, someone who didn't even know where he came from or where he was going. I was so lost, even if a light shined bright to show me the way, I wouldn't have seen it. But then I found you. And when that happened, I found myself. I found us, and I don't ever want to let you go."

Ian's arms tightened around him, and that painful ache in his chest disappeared, replaced with joy. Charlie knew he wanted forever with Ian. "You don't have to."

Ian's sure fingers reached for the buttons of his shirt,

when the doorbell rang. He growled and drew in a deep breath. "Dammit. I bet it's my parents wanting to talk some more."

Charlie snickered and rose from the couch. His linen pants were an absolute mess of wrinkles, he observed. "Can I borrow a pair of gym shorts? I have to send these to the cleaners."

"Yeah, sure. In the bottom right-hand drawer of the dresser."

He left Ian to deal with his parents and escaped to the bedroom. He quickly undressed, found the shorts, and decided to borrow a T-shirt as well. He pulled on the first one he found and returned to the living room, reassured that he was dressed properly to meet Ian's parents.

Ian's parents weren't there, but Mickey and Patrick were. Ian stood scowling, and Charlie's heart twisted. A bitter taste rose in his throat when Patrick noticed him and elbowed Mickey.

"Charlie, hey," Patrick said.

Ian rushed to his side, and Charlie, while grateful to have him there, approached the other two men warily.

With Ian hovering a step behind him, Charlie faced Ian's friends, who shifted on their feet as he drew near. Ian's lips touched his ear. "They said they had something to say to you. I told them if they were gonna insult you, to get the fuck out."

Patrick was the first to speak. "Uh, well, I wanna say I'm sorry for the things I said to you. It was really shitty, and being surprised isn't an excuse for, uh…"

"Acting like a dick?" Ian offered up.

Charlie pressed his lips together, even if it really wasn't a laughing matter.

"Yeah." Patrick dragged his gaze from examining the floor to meet his eyes. "I was wrong and outta line. None of that shit shoulda ever been said. Maybe we can start fresh?"

As apologies went, it wasn't a bad one, and Charlie heard Patrick's sincerity. "I'll accept your apology, but it's really Ian you haveta speak to 'cause you're friends. And you hurt him badly. Friends are supposed to have each other's backs no matter what. You don't know how lucky you are to have him as a friend. He told me how close you've all been since you were kids. When I was young, all I wanted was to have one or two people to count on and hang out with like you have each other. Do you know how much I envy you guys?"

To his credit, Patrick listened. Charlie didn't dare break eye contact with him to gauge Mickey's response. The rage he'd displayed along with the horrible things he said the other day still scared Charlie.

Ian put his hand on Charlie's shoulder. "Me 'n Charlie are together, and we're gonna stay that way. So if you've got a problem with that, like I said before, the door is that way. Walk on through. If not, then we can try and be friends again. '*Try*' being the operative word, because I can't just get over the shit you said. But lemme just say this. Being bisexual doesn't mean I wanna bang every guy and girl I see. You're not attracted to every woman, right? Well, same for me. I'm not attracted to every man or woman. Charlie's the guy. Period."

"I'm sorry I said those things." Those first words from Mickey startled Charlie, and he waited to hear what Ian would say.

"That's a fucking cop-out." Easygoing Ian wasn't making it so easy for Mickey. "You said some fucking shitty things to me and to Charlie. Don't ever assume

340

because someone is gay or bi that they aren't a real man. You know what makes a real man? Someone who can stand up and be himself, knowing that there are dumbass, ignorant people who hate them without knowing who they are."

"I was wrong, okay?" Mickey cried out. "I just couldn't believe you were with a guy."

"That's the problem. It's not about you." Ian threw his hands in the air. "You think I owe you an explanation for who I am and who I wanna be with, but I don't. Just be fucking happy that I'm happy."

Damn, Ian was hot when he got riled up—blue eyes flashing, chest heaving—and Charlie wanted nothing more than to kiss him.

Mickey met his eyes, and Charlie held his breath. "I talked to Brianna about it. I didn't mention your name or Ian or nothing 'cause I know it's not my place to tell nobody your business, but she got really mad at me and said the same stuff you did. That my only job is to be a friend and support you. And that it shouldn't matter who you go out with, and why did I think my opinion should matter."

"Damn, she's a smart girl. What's she doing with you?" Ian snickered.

"Shut up," Mickey retorted with a smile, but then grew serious. "I'm really sorry, bro. I shot my mouth off without thinking and was out of line. I can't lie that I ain't shocked, but if this is what you want, I'm happy for you."

Charlie watched them shake hands and hug it out. Mickey faced him, and though he knew nothing bad would happen to him physically, he still couldn't help taking a step back…right into Ian, whose hands settled on Charlie's shoulders, giving him strength. Someone was finally in his corner.

"It's gonna be okay, right, Mick?" Ian's tone was nothing less than challenging.

Mickey's eyes widened. "Whoa, yeah, dude. I don't know you, but I'm really sorry for saying those things about you. It was ignorant. I'd never touch you, though. Is that what you thought?"

"You took a swing at Ian, who's bigger than me. You also wanted to drag me into your fight, saying maybe I wanted to be your bitch. What should I think?"

Nose to nose, he faced off with Mickey, and it was as if Charlie were making up for lost time, confronting everyone who'd ever wronged him. No more hiding or faking it.

Under his freckles, Mickey grew pale. "I-I didn't mean it. I never would've hurt you."

"Yeah? And I should know that how? You say you've never acted like this before. But I don't know who you are."

Shame flushed his face red, but to his credit, Mickey faced him squarely. "Who I am was wrong. So if you'll accept my apology, like Patrick said, can we start over?" He stuck out his hand.

Charlie reached out, and they shook. Things might take some time to settle, but Charlie, with the newfound optimism of Ian's love, was willing to try.

Now that they'd cleared the air, Patrick grew talkative. "I talked to Andi about it too. She said, just like it's none of Ian's business what we do in the bedroom, it's none of our business what Ian does in his. Or with who."

"You guys are really that serious with these women? You've only known them a couple of weeks."

"Sometimes it only takes one look to fall in love," Charlie chimed in, then realizing what he said, and at the smile on Ian's face, bit his lip and wanted to crawl under a rock.

"You guys finished begging for our forgiveness?" Ian folded his arms. " 'Cause it's getting late, and I gotta be at the site early tomorrow."

Charlie stole a glance at Ian, who gave him a swift wink. He ducked his head, cheeks on fire.

"Oh, yeah, shit. I'm sorry. I told Brianna I'd stop by and tell her what happened."

"And I've been staying at Andi's." Patrick grinned. "We're planning to go away together next weekend, upstate, to her parents' cabin near Saranac Lake."

"Cool."

"So we're good now, right?" Patrick asked.

"Yeah, yeah," Ian grumbled, and Charlie knew he wanted them gone. "We'll talk tomorrow or something." He walked to the front door and held it open as Mickey and Patrick filed past him. The door slammed, and Charlie fell onto the sofa, laughing.

"Oh, my God. Could you have made it any more obvious how much you wanted them gone?"

Ian pounced on him, his eyes pure silver and so tender, he stole Charlie's breath and his heart simultaneously. Charlie didn't think twice; he'd gladly hand his heart to Ian.

"Yeah? Well, you're smarter than they are. I thought I'd have to spell it out for them." Ian's mouth descended on his, and Charlie sighed, wrapping his arms around Ian.

"Ready to go to bed? I know you have an early start." He cackled, and Ian, who'd begun to kiss his neck, nipped him.

"You know how they say, 'early to bed, early to rise'?

Well…" Ian placed Charlie's hand over his thick bulge. "I'm already risen." Desire pooled in Charlie's belly, and his ass clenched tight.

"Don't have to tell me twice. Race you to the bed."

* * *

Whereas every hour in the day once seemed interminable, now that he and Ian were together, they went by in a blink, and it hardly seemed possible they'd parted seven hours earlier. On their way home, Ian picked up a pizza from Table 87, and by mutual agreement, they decided to eat at Charlie's house.

"I figured," Charlie said, handing him a cold beer, "maybe Rachel can tell us the last part of Robert and Eddie's story."

"Yeah. I'm really dying to know what happened." Ian slid a slice of pizza across the table and took a bite of his own.

"Do you really not know? You haven't figured it out?" Charlie had a while ago. It seemed obvious to him.

"Well," Ian said as he chewed, "we know Eddie went to war and Robert got married. But I wanna know how it all ended. And then there's that last letter Rachel said she never read. I wanna see that too."

Charlie ate his slice. "It's sad, you know? Eddie had his life cut short in the war, and Robert lived a life married to someone who could never make him happy. A hundred years later, there are still plenty of people who hide who they are because they're afraid of what people might think or do."

"You were surprised last night, weren't you? I could

tell," Ian said, his pizza forgotten. "You didn't think I'd tell my parents everything so quickly."

"Well, yeah," Charlie admitted. "I mean, growing up, I spent more time hiding who I was than living my true self. Because as you saw, it's not always pretty being me."

"And now?"

Charlie thought for a moment. "Sometimes I still think this isn't happening. I wonder if I'll wake up and find out this is all a dream and I'll be back in my grungy apartment with the mice and the roaches."

"But it's not a dream. You know that, right? Me, Rachel…all this is real, as crazy as it might seem. And my parents?" Ian shrugged. "They just want me to be happy." Ian grimaced, and Charlie latched on to that.

"But you're not? I saw that look."

"Well, now that they know, they can't stop asking questions." Ian rolled his eyes, and then a slow smile tipped his lips up. "And I thought after this morning, I proved how happy I was."

Charlie snickered, and pleasure suffused him, remembering how Ian moaned when Charlie sucked him off. "Aside from the sex. We already know that's incredible between us."

"That's a pretty weak word to describe it."

"Do you have a better one?" Charlie asked.

Ian rubbed his foot up Charlie's leg, and he shivered despite the heat that had settled in the kitchen. He didn't use the air-conditioning anywhere except his bedroom. Too expensive.

"I don't think words have been invented that can describe how you make me feel."

Jesus. Charlie looked down, expecting to see himself

in a melty pile of goo on the floor from those sweet words.

Along the same serious vein, Ian reached out his hand. "I'm so damn happy, I can't stop smiling. Even at work, they kept asking me what's going on, but I've only told my foreman. There is one problem, though."

"Oh?"

Ian grimaced. "My sisters. You'll meet Michelle when she gets here later, and the other two have been texting me all day." The pained expression grew, and Charlie pressed his lips together to keep from laughing out loud. "They wanna have a video phone call with us as soon as possible. I can tell them no. You shouldn't have to be subjected to their interrogation."

"I don't mind," Charlie said softly. "It would be nice to have some kind of family, actually. People who cared about me."

"You got that now. But don't say I didn't warn you."

Charlie laughed. "I'll take my chances if it means being with you."

It didn't take long to finish the pizza, and Ian cleared up the table. They sat on the deck, staring out into the night sky. Ian's hand rested on Charlie's leg, slowly stroking his thigh. A sigh of contentment escaped Charlie.

"You like it when I touch you?" Ian kissed the top of his head.

"Yeah." Charlie loved Ian's hands on him. It made him feel secure and wanted. "So much."

The birds had settled down, and the only sound was the rustle of the trees, broken occasionally by a car horn or a siren.

"Do you think we can call Rachel? Ask her to come and tell us the rest of the story?"

The tinkling sound they were now familiar with filled the air, and Rachel appeared in her silvery glow. Charlie noted with sadness how much more transparent she appeared, as if all the memories she'd held inside her peeled away her layers.

"Are you ready for this? It isn't pretty."

"We know. But we've come so far."

"Very well." She swept her hand in front of them, and an army barrack replaced the night sky.

Eddie lay on a cot, his head bent over the paper he wrote on.

Dear Robert,

It's so different here. I'm not used to such a strict regimen. I keep my distance and listen to my drill sergeant. I'm not used to this food either and miss the street carts.

I miss home and the blue skies. Everything seems gray and dark now.

I miss my parents.

I even miss Rachel.

I miss you.

Am I allowed to say that, now that you're engaged?

I wish I could've seen you one more time, however briefly, before I left, but it was chaotic, and my parents invited all these relatives who stayed well into the night, and I couldn't get away.

Until I come home,

Eddie

Ian sniffed. "So sad. I feel so bad for Eddie. He must've been so scared there, all alone, wishing for something that could never happen."

Stealing a glance at Ian, Charlie watched him wipe his

eyes, and his heart almost burst with love. To know Ian had such a sensitive soul made the words easy for Charlie to say. He leaned over, kissed Ian on the cheek, and received a slightly sheepish grin.

"I—"

"Don't even think of apologizing for showing me how much you care. It's one of the main things I love about you."

Eyes shining pure silver, Ian touched his cheek. "You love me?"

Hesitantly, Charlie nodded. "I didn't have the nerve to say it before because I thought maybe it was too soon, but I'm feeling a bit reckless."

"I like being reckless with you," Ian whispered and brushed their lips together. "Reckless and shameless."

That dull ache that had languished inside him had vanished, replaced by something so foreign until now, Charlie needed a moment to name it.

Happiness.

"You've accomplished both, I think, these past few days."

"I'm glad it turned out okay with Mickey and Patrick, but you know, even if they hadn't come to apologize, it wouldn't have made a difference." Pensive now, Ian shifted his gaze downward. "Only you've managed to make me feel this way."

Still insecure, Charlie prodded him. "How's that? Tell me?"

"Like I'm the only man in the world."

Charlie put his hand over Ian's. "To me, you are."

The pure desire in Ian's eyes left Charlie breathless.

Ian squeezed his hand. "Look." He pointed to the sky. "It's my backyard. The tree."

Robert sat against the tree, stopping occasionally to brush at his eyes as he wrote.

Dear Eddie,

I hope this finds you safe.

Charlotte is in a frenzy of wedding preparations with her mother and best friend. I've been learning the insurance business at my father's shoulder, and it's not so bad. The wedding is scheduled for the first Saturday in June. Of course, because of the war, there will be no honeymoon. Charlotte is disappointed, but all these plans don't matter to me.

None of it does.

I'm sorry. I'm sorry about so many things, but not for our friendship.

Never that.

I wish things could have turned out differently, but you have to know I think of you often, and worry constantly.

Your sister gave me a letter from you, said you left it in the tree. I'm not planning on reading it until you come back. I'll wait for you to tell me in person what it says. You have to come back.

Until I see you again,

Robert

Ian scratched his chin. "They keep dancing around the subject. Why didn't they just come out and say how they feel?"

Charlie stared at him. "Because they couldn't. Ian, remember what I said? They couldn't acknowledge who they were here. It was a crime. And in the army? Eddie would get arrested, put in prison, maybe even killed. Hell, no." He shook his head. "No way could they say anything. I'm honestly surprised how much they *are* saying in these letters. Those got censored."

A dark, silent field appeared before them. No picture of Eddie, only the voice of a young, frightened man.

Robert,

I'm overseas now but can't say where. I've seen things I never imagined. So many people have died, many in front of me. I'm scared all the time.

Don't be sorry for things that can't be changed. You told me all along, but I thought...well, it doesn't matter any longer.

I hope I get the chance to wish you congratulations.

If you see Rachel, tell her I say hi.

Yours,

Eddie

To Charlie, it was almost as if these men were alive again, their story unfolding in front of them toward the inevitable sad ending.

"Rachel, is there more?" Ian's face was all hard angles and sharp lines, those blue eyes somber and reflective. Charlie's heart pounded as if he were running a race. Or escaping demons.

"*I'm trying. There's little left now. Hard for me...*" Bells tinkled faintly in the breeze.

The scene now was of an unfamiliar house. Charlie's hand crept into Ian's, and they held on to each other.

Eddie,

The deed is done, and I'm a married man. I wish...you know what I wish, but I'm bound and determined to be a good husband to Charlotte. She's talking about a house full of children, and I don't have an answer for that.

I hear the stories of the battles and see the newspapers, and I'm so afraid for you. I wish I could give you a promise to hold on to, but I have nothing to offer. I must hold to my vows. Charlotte deserves that, at the very least, but nothing's changed for me.

We're off for a weekend at my aunt's house on Long Island. Please take care of yourself and come back to us.

All the best,

Robert

An overwhelming haze of grief descended upon Charlie, and he found it hard to catch his breath. The metallic smell of blood filled the air, and smoke burned his eyes. "Eddie lost all hope after that letter. He was only twenty years old and felt his life was over. Robert was his one true love, and he gave up." His body felt curiously warm and light.

Ian backed away from him. "Whoa, Charlie. What's going on? You're glowing red and gold like you're on fire."

"Hold me. Please?" Without hesitation, Ian put his arms around him. The acrid scent faded, and Charlie could draw a breath.

"Better now?"

"Yeah," he whispered. "It was as if I were there with Eddie. A few weeks ago, I had a vision about his death, but I didn't feel as connected to him as I do now. It hurts."

"Like my dream about Robert's wedding night. Utter hopelessness. Like he knew his life was over."

Charlie closed his eyes, and Eddie and Robert appeared, sitting on the staircase, kissing. Charlie watched Eddie unbutton Robert's shirt, kiss his neck, and take him by the hand to lead him upstairs. A shudder rippled through him.

"You okay?" Ian tipped his chin up and kissed him, softly at first, then harder until Charlie's head whirled.

"If I wasn't, I am now." Charlie smiled against Ian's mouth. "I was wondering if Eddie and Robert ever slept with each other, and just now in my mind, I saw them kissing, then Eddie bringing Robert upstairs."

"They really loved each other."

"Remember finding Eddie's death certificate in the lockbox, before everything began? Seems like it happened so long ago to different people."

"Didn't it?" Ian brushed his lips over Charlie's. "I'm not the same man I was then...I never will be that man again. And I wouldn't change a thing. The past was theirs. But the future is ours."

By mutual agreement, they left the deck and entered the house, taking their seats at the kitchen table. Charlie said, "It's almost anticlimactic. We know everything that happened to them up until Robert got married, but what about afterward? What happened to Robert?"

A silver cloud appeared, and Rachel hovered over them. She was almost completely invisible now, except for a faint outline with occasional sparkles brightening when she spoke, and Charlie waited to hear the resolution.

"Now you know their story. My poor brother died in the war. He never stopped loving Robert."

"And Robert? Did he and Charlotte have their house full of children?"

Rachel shimmered and faded further. Only a faint sparkle indicated she remained. *"Charlotte died a year after they were married, from the Spanish flu. Robert passed away at the age of forty-five from the heart ailment that plagued him."*

Stunned, Charlie could've wept. "That's so sad."

Ian took his hand and squeezed it. "He never remarried, I assume?"

"No." Rachel sighed. *"His parents wanted him to, of course, but he remained firm and said no. They assumed it was because he was so devastated over Charlotte's death, but we know it's that he didn't want to ruin another poor girl's life. He mourned Eddie until he died."*

"How come they couldn't get together as ghosts until now?"

"I don't know. There was still work to be done." Her voice faded in and out. *"I don't make the rules. I was told what to do."*

It made as much sense as anything could make sense talking to a ghost about two men who died a century earlier.

"We've been waiting for you to fall in love, and once that happened, Eddie and Robert could finally find peace on the other side of the rainbow." Her voice brimmed with satisfaction.

His cheeks heated, and a swift glance at Ian found him smiling. Charlie answered her. "Yes. We talked everything out, but we both want to know what happened to that letter you gave to Robert? We don't know what it says."

A large satchel appeared on the table, startling Charlie. He didn't think he'd ever get used to people and objects popping up out of nowhere.

"Shit," Ian exclaimed, then mumbled, "Sorry," and inwardly, Charlie laughed that Ian had learned to watch his mouth around a ghost.

"It took a while to retrieve the letters the two of them

sent back and forth, especially Robert's. He kept his in a strongbox, which he'd hidden in a hole under one of the protruding roots of the oak tree, and after he died, I was able to sneak in and take them without anyone realizing. Of course, Eddie's letters were in his room. Our parents saved them and the pictures, and I took them before they sold the house and moved away."

"Do you think Charlotte knew about Robert and Eddie?"

"I hope not. Maybe she had a suspicion, but if so, she never told me. And then she got sick and died, so I'll never know."

"Who told you all this stuff?" Ian scratched his head. "I still don't understand."

"I don't know, dear. I lived a long and happy life, and when I died, I was told my brother and Robert's story had reached powers beyond that which I was allowed to understand, and once you two were together, I'd be able to see Eddie again and he and Robert would finally be reunited."

"You were the one who led us to find the death certificate and the pictures?" Charlie asked. "That first time, right? All the banging noises."

"I thought it was a good plan," she said. *"It worked."*

And even though she was no longer visible to them, Charlie could imagine her twinkling eyes and bright smile.

"But the last letter?" Charlie prodded. "The one you said you never read?"

"Yes. I have it here. I didn't want to read it when I gave it to Robert, and now only you two can. Reach inside the bag and take it."

The bells tinkled, and the silver light dimmed.

"Rachel, wait. Don't you want to know?" Frantic, Charlie searched the room for any sign of her, but there was nothing left.

"*I can't stay,*" she called out, and he rose to his feet.

"No. I want you to hear."

"*I'll know. I'll finally get to see my brother again.*"

And then she was gone, and Charlie felt lost. Alone. As if a piece of him had gone missing. Rachel had been with him along every step of this journey, and Charlie knew he'd miss her forever.

Strong arms came around him. "You okay, baby?" Ian whispered in his ear. And that was when Charlie knew he'd never be alone again.

"Yeah. I am now."

Ian kissed his neck. "You want to read it?"

"Yeah." Charlie's heart squeezed tight, and he took Ian by the hand. "But let's read it where it would mean the most to Eddie and Robert."

Ian nodded.

Together they walked out of Charlie's house, then through Ian's parents' house, to the backyard. As nice as they were, Charlie was glad Ian's parents were visiting friends, so they could proceed undeterred. It was close to eight thirty, the blue sky deepening to violet as sunset approached.

Under the spreading leaves of the giant oak tree, Ian opened the letter and took his hand.

Dear Robert,

If you're reading this, I didn't come home, but you must know my last thoughts were of you. Please don't worry. I'll always be with you. You'll hear my whispers in the wind, and my love will warm you in the heat of the sun. Stand under our oak tree and gaze up at the stars, knowing I'm there, waiting for you. One day we'll see each other again, at the end of the rainbow. I'll meet you on the other side, whenever that day comes.

Eddie

Unashamedly crying, Charlie leaned against the tree. "I can't help thinking about both of them. Loving each other so much, yet knowing they could never be together."

Raindrops pattered on the leaves, and Ian held him close as they remained in the shelter of the tree. "We're the lucky ones in that we can. And I intend to make sure you know, every day and night, forever, how much I need you. I'm not Robert, and I'm never going to be afraid to tell people I love you."

As suddenly as the rain started, it stopped, and the skies cleared. Charlie's breath caught in his throat. "Ian." He pointed up. "Look."

High above them, a rainbow arched in the sky, reaching up to the clouds.

I hope you enjoyed reading Charlie and Ian's story and consider leaving a review. Reviews make it easier for readers to discover new books to read, and more books is always a good thing! For an author, reviews are like potato chips. One is never enough.

About Felice Stevens

Felice Stevens has always been a romantic at heart. She believes that while life is tough, there is always a happy ending just around the corner. Her characters have to work for it, however. Like life in NYC, nothing comes easy, and that includes love.

She lives in New York City and has way too much black in her wardrobe yet can't stop buying "just one more pair" of black pants. Felice is a happily addicted Bravo and Say Yes to the Dress addict and proud of it. And let's not get started on House Hunters. Her dream day starts out with iced coffee and ends with Prosecco, because...why shouldn't it?

You can find me procrastinating on FB in my reader group:
FELICE'S BREAKFAST CLUB
https://www.facebook.com/groups/FelicesBreakfastClub/

You can find all my books—listed by series—at:
https://felicestevens.com/

To keep up to date on my latest releases and works in process, you can **SUBSCRIBE TO MY NEWSLETTER**
http://bit.ly/2JkIIu7

You can connect with me through social media here:
BOOKBUB
https://www.bookbub.com/profile/felice-stevens
INSTAGRAM
https://www.instagram.com/felicestevens
FACEBOOK
https://www.facebook.com/felice.stevens.1
TWITTER
https://twitter.com/FeliceStevens1
GOODREADS
https://www.goodreads.com/author/show/8432880.Felice_
Stevens